J.T. DOSSETT

8/10/15

To my good friends,
Auminta & Bill:
Long may you Run!

JT Dossett

Finding Bobby Ray

outskirtspress
DENVER, COLORADO

Finding Bobby Ray

v2.0

Cover illustration by Sam Chapman

Outskirts Press, Inc.
http://www.outskirtspress.com

ISBN: 978-1-4787-2008-9

PRINTED IN THE UNITED STATES OF AMERICA

“Since I was five, I’ve known that I was adopted, which is a politically correct term for being clueless about one’s own origins.”

—Jodi Picoult, “Handle With Care”

To Brenda, Nola June, Mary, Haley, and Lucy Ann.

INTRODUCTION

The idea for this story began crystalizing in my head many years ago, after my adoptive mother and father had passed. I was disappointed to think that I would never know my biological origins. My wife and I sought my adoption records without much hope of finding them; but in collaboration with fate and after months of searching, a dialogue was established with officials in Nashville, and my records became available. It was an incredibly exciting and poignant time for me as I discovered that I am of Scotch-Irish descent, much like many of the residents of East Tennessee, where I was born and lived for a while when I was a child. The records also revealed some facts about my biological parents, facts that I was unprepared to hear. We were shocked to learn that my father had been a criminal who was known all over East Tennessee, having escaped from jails and prisons in Tennessee, Georgia, Louisiana, and perhaps other states. He was once incarcerated in Alcatraz because authorities couldn't keep him locked up anywhere else for his numerous offenses. Newspapers from that era chronicled his escapades and escapes. Please note that some of the stories are born of my imagination, and details may not be entirely correct. One thing that is known for sure is that my biological father was a charming cult hero among the folk in East Tennessee, particularly Knoxville, where he was raised and where he did a lot of "business": burglary, robbery, mostly crimes where nobody got physically hurt. He drove local law enforcement agencies loopy with his daring escapades, and at the same time, politicians went on record saying, "He's a good boy; give him a break." He was given a break and was paroled, possibly in the late '60s or early '70s. He was killed in the process of a robbery in Louisiana not long after he was granted his freedom.

As far as I know, my mother disappeared at some juncture in their relationship. And I can honestly say that I am unsure if she had anything to do with some of his escapes. Although she is pictured as viciously unstable in this story; I have a strong feeling that she may have been a good person in reality, perhaps a prisoner of love, suffering the machinations of her clever husband.

The characters from Campbell County, Tennessee, are purely fictional, based upon an amalgam of people I've met and have worked with over the past fifteen years. I hope my acquaintances in Campbell County will not take offense that I've attempted to write some of the dialogue in the vernacular of the area and time period, and realize that many of the words and phrases ridiculed by strangers originated in a bygone time and culture—a culture overflowing with adventurers of Scotch-Irish and Anglo-Irish descent, who settled the Southeast and these mountains centuries ago. The remoteness of their destination served as a forge to strengthen their resilience and bravery, and the fact that they have preserved some of those expressions in their language, even as it is today. Perhaps the best description of many people in Campbell County, and throughout Appalachia, is in this poem by Leonard Tate *The Gentle Poet from Grundy County:* "We are the mountain people. We are a boorish set, they tell us, hard-bitten, coarse of feature and speech; shallow and brawling as the mountain streams, with morale friable as our sandstone. All my life I have wanted to tell them that we are the mountain people, that mountain streams have pools of deep quietness, and that beneath the sandstone of our hills, there is granite."

This book is dedicated to "The Mountain People" and especially to all women who personify the goodness and spirit of selflessness possessed by some of the characters in this novel.

JTD

CONTENTS

Part VI—RITES OF PASSAGE

Part VII—AIRBORNE

Part VIII—HOMEFRONT

Part IX—HEROES AND SAINTS

Part X—MADNESS DESCENDS

Part I

THE GOOD, THE BAD, THE BABY

Chapter 1

RENDEZVOUS AT BOB AND LIBBY'S

Five-year-old Elmer Kelly was soaked to the bone, but nobody cared, not even his older sister, Treva, who observed the tyke disinterestedly from the kitchen window.

"Don't ye hurt that dog, Elmer," she yelled as her brother plopped a broken-eared pup roughly into the bed of a rust-blanketed Radio Flyer.

The boy answered with a hoarse cough, then proceeded to tow the animal through the muddy ruts in the front yard, weaving and bumping in and out of piles of trash, junked appliances, automobiles, and other detritus.

"Little shit don't have sense enough to git in out of the rain," said 13-year-old Treva as she shuffled lazily across the sticky kitchen floor, gathered up dirty dishes from the table, and tossed them into the sink. She stood on tiptoe and reached to the top of the groaning, old Cold Spot refrigerator, found the pack of Pall Mall, and popped one into her mouth. She'd picked up the smoking habit from her mother, who'd taken off with a coal truck driver from Kentucky about two years ago. Her daddy, drunk most of the time, didn't seem fazed by her mother's departure or the fact that she'd left him with three kids.

He didn't care because the children had a roof, albeit a leaky one, over their heads, and neighbors and church folk pretty much kept them in clothing and food. Plus he had money to buy "shine", dip, and chew from doing odd jobs and plugging tires at the Pure Oil station.

Since he didn't buy cigarettes for her, Treva depended on the generosity of neighbors and had become practiced at her craft. "Mr. Marlow, ye wouldn't mind if I borried a cigarette, would ye? Oh, thank ye. I kin keep the pack? I appreciate ye," she would say, holding the cigarette daintily, touching his hand lightly (as she'd seen Bette Davis do in a movie). And as the gentleman lit the tip with his lighter flame, she riveted her sleepy blue eyes on his as she exhaled a stream of smoke through her cupid bow lips. She took pleasure in the fact that his hand was shaking when he clicked the lighter top shut.

When the rattling refrigerator completed a cycle, Treva could hear the radio playing in the living room and her father's mumbling. He'd been hitting the jug most of the day. "Quit it, Daddy!" came her sister Wanda's voice. Treva snuffed out her cigarette angrily on the counter.

"He's at it again," she said as she stormed into the living room. Thurmond Kelly had ten-year-old Wanda pinned in the corner of the rump-sprung couch. "C'mon, baby, give yore daddy a kiss; all I want is a little kiss," he slurred. "Git off her, Daddy! Ye know that's not right!" shouted Treva. Surprised, Thurmond released his grip on the youngster, and Wanda fell over the arm of the couch, scooting away, crab-like, to escape his clutches. "What the hell is wrong with ye?" yelled Thurmond, arranging the strap on his undershirt. "Ye know what's wrong, Daddy; ye tried to do it to me," screamed Treva. Indeed, Thurmond had tried to snuggle up to her soon after her mother took off, but a swift kick to the crotch denied his advances and any further attempts at molestation. That painful moment reasserted itself through the slush of Thurmond's moonshine-soaked brain, and he became irate. "Ye little whore, yore jest like yore momma, nothin' but a whore!" sputtered Thurmond, leaping off the couch and backhanding Treva across the face.

Something broke in Treva, but she didn't cry out. She picked herself up from the floor and walked quickly out of the room "Thass right! Git the hell outta here, ye whore. Jest like yore momma, a stinkin' whore!" screeched Thurmond, as he knelt down to retrieve his jug from under the couch, as Treva returned to the living room.

He didn't stand straight again for a long time.

Treva was still swinging for the fences when Wanda brought Mr. Marlow to the rescue.

After wresting the bat from the crazed girl, Mr. Marlow knelt beside the broken form of Thurmond Kelly. "Oh Lord, he's dead!" he yelled, as he rushed out of the house to call authorities.

Treva stared in amazement at the body and felt odd satisfaction at her handiwork.

"She's crazier than a shithouse rat," mumbled Thurmond as the constable and ambulance driver loaded him into the ambulance for the ride to the hospital.

Suffering excruciating discomfort from numerous contusions and fractures, including broken ribs and a broken collarbone, Thurmond later told officials that his daughter "snuck up on him" and beat him severely about the head and shoulders with a Louisville Slugger because he wouldn't let her go to a birthday party. While her battered father was en route to the hospital, Treva thanked Mr. Marlow politely as he lit her cigarette. And she didn't even mind when he gave her a kindly pat on the backside. During Thurmond's lengthy recuperation, members of Big Creek Church of the Living Word parceled Wanda and Elmer off to relatives in a nearby community. Treva was sent to live with her mother's older sister in Knoxville.

Mr. Marlow missed her company.

Treva's Aunt Ollie worked nights at the Levi's factory. She was morally straight but not the sharpest knife in the drawer. The savvy youngster outwitted her at every turn over the next four years. Unbeknownst to her clueless guardian, Treva quit high school by the time she was seventeen, hanging out at lunch counters and pool halls during the days, and frequenting honkytonks in the evenings, while Aunt Ollie sat on the assembly line, attaching red tabs to the rear pockets of Levi's. One of Treva's favorite hangouts was Bob and Libby's, a sprawling cinderblock dance hall out on the Asheville Highway. As far as honkytonks went, it was a fairly decent place during the week where couples gathered to dance, drink, and listen to the music from the jukebox, which contained the best selection of tunes around. The weekends were a different story.

"How 'bout another Schlitz, Roy?" said Libby Bowman, but her remarks were drowned out by the booming jukebox and the drone of conversation in the bar. Aggravated, Libby leaned into Roy's ear and shouted, "You want another beer or not, Roy? I ain't got all night!" "How much I drunk so far?" yelled Roy, clutching his beer glass as if it were a trophy. Libby checked a piece of paper by the cash register. There were lots of names and pencil marks on the paper and four marks next to Roy's name. "Three," she shouted his way. He fumbled in his pocket and pulled out a couple of wadded-up bills. "Yeah, give me one. I got enough here for three more, so you be sure and stop me, OK, Libby?" "All right, honey, but if you go over, I'll spot you." Libby slid back the cooler top, yanked a cold bottle out of the ice, popped the top with the opener nailed beneath the counter, and slid the bottle deftly down the bar, where it stopped obediently between Roy and the young man who had filled the space at the bar next to him. "What'll you have, good-lookin'?" said Libby. Lonnie Cavanaugh knew she meant the compliment and grinned a pearly grin that conjured possibilities of romance in Libby's mind, although deep down she knew she didn't have a Chinaman's chance with this boy. Actually Lonnie would have given Libby a whirl if she wanted a whirl, and he didn't fear that Bob would take a slapjack to his head. He loved women. He was always falling in love. It was a mutual thing; women were always falling in love with him too—pretty little Knoxville girls, single, married, someone else's woman; they were at once smitten with his boyish good looks and his incredibly charming way with words.

One person who wasn't impressed with Lonnie Cavanaugh was his father, Baxter, a mean-spirited malcontent who abused Lonnie, his brother, and their mother at every turn in the road.

When Lonnie grew into lanky, strong, young manhood, the old man wisely backed off of him but continued to beat his wife and youngest son when Lonnie was absent. Late one Saturday night, Lonnie came home and found his mother lying on the couch. Figuring she and the old man had had it out and she had opted to sleep in the living room, he bent to kiss her and to his horror found that her face, a swollen mass of bruises and abrasions, was hardly recognizable. "Mamma, Mamma! You all right?" he said in a pained voice, cradling her head, taking her hand into his own. "Don't do anything, son; it was my fault," she whispered through battered lips. Lonnie found his father at the kitchen table, drunk and peeling an apple. "She sassed me," said Baxter insolently, waving the paring knife threateningly in front of him. Lonnie neatly relieved the old man of the knife, grabbed the apple, and shoved it in his mouth. "Sassed you, huh? Sassed you?" screamed Lonnie as he repeatedly slammed the palm of his hand on the apple, stuffing the whole piece of fruit into his father's mouth. Baxter bounced off the kitchen counters and appliances like a pinball, trying to dislodge the apple, his windpipe deprived of oxygen. "Here, let me help you get that apple down," said Lonnie as he calmly stabbed Baxter in the throat with the paring knife.

Baxter lost a few teeth and spoke with a gravelly rasp for the rest of his life.

Lonnie was sent away. He served a year, and he learned his lessons well during that time.

When he was released, he plied his newfound skills and was arrested for larceny of auto and check forgery. After another stint at the State Vocational and Technical School, he honed his skills further. After his release he kept his nose clean for a while. But now he was hard at it, running with a trio he'd befriended at "school"—plundering homes and businesses throughout Knoxville and vicinity, acquiring substantial amounts of cash, jewelry, and whatnot. He had planned to meet his associates at Bob and Libby's tonight to discuss what to do with their latest haul: eleven cigarette lighters, sixty-four cartons of cigarettes, and a stamp machine burgled from a drugstore in downtown Knoxville. As fate would have it, his companions failed to show up.

"Hey, Bob, need some more ice down here!" barked Libby as she wiped down the bar top for about the thousandth time this evening. "Yeah, yeah, and people in hell need ice water," said Bob, beefy and bald, sporting a tattoo of a naked woman riding an anchor on his massive forearm. Bob was renowned for his scowl and bad temperament. But like Libby, if you treated him right, he'd give you the shirt off his back—but not in front of anybody.

Bob surveyed the Friday night crowd warily as he filled the bucket. Friday was payday, and patrons piled in, clamoring for beers, eager to rid themselves of the pressures and indignities, imagined or not, they'd suffered during the workweek. After a few brews, many achieved the euphoria they were seeking. Others were dangerously unpredictable: at one moment, a warm and carefree friend; in the next, a dark and spiteful stranger with a wicked agenda. Such was the piece of work commanding attention at the end of the bar, "Treva" something or another. She'd started making her appearance at the club about three weeks ago, and since that time she played the boys well, seeming to enjoy the palpable tension that permeated the atmosphere as they challenged each another for her charms. "She'll start some shit before the night is over, you can bet on that," muttered Bob as he slogged the bucket of ice to the cooler.

The boys were always telling Treva she could be a movie star. And she never had to spend a red penny on a beer or a ride home from her nightly forays into the seamy world of juke joints. Tonight was one of those nights—a hot, vaporous, August night—and Lonnie Cavanaugh spied her the moment he came through the doors of Bob and Libby's. She was leaning against the bar, surrounded by a gaggle of admiring suitors, laughing at their absurd comments between short sips from her beer bottle. Her thick shock of honey-blonde hair was not done up in the fashion of the day but was pleasing to men, a tousled "I just got out of bed" look. Her eyes, periwinkle blue and protected by thick, dark lashes, were sleepy looking; and when she laughed, which was often, she showed even rows of white teeth. Lonnie observed at once that, by her attire, she wasn't moneyed. She wore a simple, sleeveless, checkered blouse; well-worn loafers; and jeans (provided by Aunt Ollie), a bit frayed on the hip pockets but well-fitted, housing a tight, round little bottom that just screamed to be patted.

Unfortunately, one of her admirers could not control himself and did just that.

The sickening "thunk" of the beer bottle against his skull echoed above the din of the bar.

"Keep your fuckin' hands to yourself!" screamed the femme fatale as the offender toppled off the barstool, hitting the floor with a resounding thump. Merle Travis sang "So Round, So Firm, So Fully Packed" on the jukebox as a mob of knightly brawlers, eager to get in Treva 's good graces and possibly her pants, came to the aid of the damsel and the fallen offender. As Libby dialed the sheriff, and Bob fumbled for the sawed-off shotgun under the bar, Lonnie circled the squirming crush like a referee, searching for a glimpse of Treva at the core of the human whirlwind.

He threw up a protective forearm as someone tapped him on

the shoulder. “You lookin’ for me?” said Treva, leaning nonchalantly against the corner of the bar. “C’mon, let’s get out of here,” said Lonnie, grabbing her roughly by the shoulder and dragging her across the dance floor.

She fought against him for only a second, time enough to snatch a freshly served bottle of beer off a table. “The owner wouldn’t mind,” she thought; he was busy getting his ass kicked.

“Where we goin’?” said Treva, pseudo-innocently, as they skipped and ran out the door.

“Head toward that blue Ford over there,” said Lonnie, pushing her in the direction of the car. She grinned as she ran. She’d planned on leaving with Lonnie Cavanaugh the minute she saw him step across the threshold of the joint.

Treva loved drive-in theaters, and this was kind of like a drive-in theater, as she and Lonnie watched the fight spill out of the bar into the parking lot. “Go ahead, shoot that thang,” she giggled as Bob stood threateningly in the doorway, his shotgun at the ready. She laughed out loud too as heads were cracked against fenders, eyes were gouged, and teeth were loosened.

When the first police car careened into the parking lot, Lonnie started the Ford.

“Don’t leave yet; let’s watch them coppers wail on ’em,” said Treva, flushed with alcohol, excitement over the violence, and the touch of his hand on her thigh.

“You’d better watch where you’re putting that hand, honey,” she warned but made no attempt to move it. “You’re not going to hit me with that beer bottle, are you?” said Lonnie.

She laughed shrilly as they eased out of the parking lot. Lonnie gunned the engine, and they raced down the highway.

He took her to another beer joint way off the main roads. There, cuddled in a dimly lit booth almost hidden in a blue haze of cigarette smoke, they got to know one another. He told her all that she needed to hear: that she was gorgeous. She talked a lot about herself, her aspirations to be an actress. "I had the lead in *Arsenic and Old Lace* in high school," she lied. Lonnie knew it was a lie because lying was close to his heart. They would have stayed until closing time had Treva not tried to pick a fight with a woman at the bar who was ogling her newfound beau.

"What are you starin' at, you hag?" yelled Treva as Lonnie shoved her toward the door.

"Where do you live? I'll take you home."

"I'm not gonna tell you," giggled Treva as she poured herself into the Ford. "OK then, I'll take you to my place," Lonnie lied, maneuvering the car carefully around broken beer bottles and potholes in the parking lot and onto the rain-slicked highway. Treva dove across the seat onto his shoulder, causing him to swerve into the oncoming lane. "Then take me to your place, Lonnie, 'cause you're my boy," she slurred, sticking her wet tongue in his ear. They didn't make it to his place, which was good because his place was the apartment he shared with his wife. Instead they ended up at the Pilgrim's Rest Motel. "You don't really live here, do you?" said Treva, hugging Lonnie's back as he unlocked the door. "Nope, I've just had too much to drink. I don't want to get stopped by the cops," he said, locking the door behind them and tossing the car keys on the scarred dresser.

"I've gotta pee; don't leave," she ordered, wiggling a threatening finger at him as she staggered in the general direction of the bathroom. Lonnie sat on the edge of the saggy bed, listening to the tinkling in the other room and devising alibis. Eventually Treva flung open the bathroom door. "Well, whaddaya think?" she said proudly. Naked as the day she was born, she sashayed showgirl-like over to the bed.

Lonnie swallowed hard. He'd known a lot of women, but this girl had the finest body he'd ever seen: perky breasts; a flat tummy; long, smooth, sinewy legs; and a firm backside that maintained its shape even after her form-fitting jeans were peeled off. "I said whaddaya think?" she whispered seductively, and he could feel her moist heat through his trousers as she straddled his leg. "You're beautiful; you could be a movie star," said Lonnie as he cupped her perfect derriere in his shaky hands. "So could you," she answered huskily, biting his earlobe and stroking his throbbing crotch. "You got protection?" she said as he rolled on top of her. "It's too late for that," said Lonnie, smothering her perfumed neck with kisses and not believing his luck. They worked together like they'd been rehearsing for a long time. Thus was the start of a catastrophic relationship and the beginning of Bobby Ray.

Chapter 2

TAKING OLLIE'S DODGE

"Shaddup and hold still, you little bastard, and I do mean bastard!" Ollie Kitts bitched through clenched teeth as she changed the dirty diaper, a diaper that should have been changed about four hours ago. The baby, a blonde, blue-eyed boy about thirteen months old, balled his hands into tiny fists and squalled defiantly back at her as she roughly clamped his ankles together with one hand, lifting his backside off the oil cloth-covered kitchen table.

With her free hand, she expertly wadded up the soiled rag and tossed it in the corner. The baby's screams intensified as she quickly swiped his raw, chafed bottom with a coarse, threadbare washcloth. The child clutched Ollie desperately as she whisked him off the table and headed for the kitchen sink. She pried his arms off her neck disgustedly, then plopped him unceremoniously, like a chicken to be cleaned, in the sink filled with tepid water.

She grabbed a small pan from beneath the sink, dipped it in the water, and doused him well. He whimpered instinctively, closing his eyes as the water cascaded over his downy head and bony shoulders. "Oh, shut up, you big sissy," she griped, rubbing his scalp, soaping and rinsing his tiny body too vigorously with her rough, work-hardened fingers. "Got to git you clean," she smirked bitterly. "Your momma's comin' to pick you up today, and you know what I say? I say good riddance, you little cry baby!"

Ollie was tired and abnormally cranky. She was supposed to be sleeping now, but caring for Treva's baby was denying her the luxury. "She was s'posed to have been here two hours ago; but you know her, she ain't reliable," said Ollie to Bobby Ray, as if he could understand every word. Treva had run roughshod over Ollie despite all that she tried to do for her. She'd quit school, gone out honky-tonking, ran with a wild crowd. Now it had come to this, having a baby out of wedlock with a convict to boot. "Well, I can't wait all day for her to come take care of you. I got to get some sleep so I can make a livin', so I can feed you and that worthless momma of yourn," said Ollie, lifting Bobby Ray out of the sink and drying him off with a clean diaper.

She slapped the damp diaper on the child and carted him upstairs to Treva's room, where a crib stood in a darkened corner. "Now keep quiet. Aunt Ollie has to get some sleep," she said as the boy peeked tentatively through the railings at her. Amazingly the baby remained quiet, even after she shut the door to Treva's room. Ollie crept down the stairs to her room on the first floor. It was 1 p.m.; perhaps she could grab a few hours of sleep before it was time to go to her third-shift job at the Levi's plant. She had barely closed her eyes when the kid started crying again.

Exasperated, Ollie slammed her fist on the wall and screamed, "Shaddup!" After a short while, Bobby Ray quieted down. He knelt in the small confines of his baby bed/prison cell, grasping the bars, peering anxiously at the door.

Ollie's nap was short-lived when Bobby Ray started crying again thirty minutes later, and Treva slammed the kitchen door. "Where in the hell have you been?" said Ollie as she wandered into the kitchen in her worn chenille house robe. "With friends," said Treva curtly, as she scoured the pantry for a jar of peanut butter. Treva ignored Bobby Ray's muffled cries as she rummaged through the silverware drawer for a spoon. "Can you hear that? Can you hear it? I've been dealin' with that all morning while you were out with friends, whoever they are," said Ollie, her voice escalating, quivering with exasperation. "I'll tell you what," Treva muttered through a mouthful of peanut butter. "Let me get a quick bath, and if I can borrow your car keys, I'll take him out for a couple of hours while you grab forty winks," she said, tossing the spoon into the sink. "That would be nice," said Ollie as she lifted the keys off the hook behind the pantry door. "Make sure you have the car back by 8:30. I got to go to work, you know, to feed you two," said Ollie, tossing the car keys on the kitchen table. Later Ollie was awakened briefly when she heard the car start and back out of the driveway. "You'd better bring that car back by 8:30," she yelled. Lulled by the silent house, she fell into a deep sleep. Years later, before she succumbed to liver cancer, Ollie still ranted about the whereabouts of the car, Treva, and the baby.

Treva almost ran over the man in the curve, who jumped into a ditch to avoid her car. She could barely see anything through her veil of tears and convulsive waves of sobbing. Later she pulled the car over to the side of the road and sat idling for a while, in hopes of regaining her composure.

When she left Knoxville, she had every intention of bringing Bobby Ray along for the entire ride—the journey that would eventually take them to California, Hollywood maybe, where she might be discovered, you know, in a drugstore like Lana Turner. She'd make a lot of money. Lonnie wouldn't have to rob or steal. And Bobby Ray would grow up tanned and beautiful in the land of milk and honey. Then she thought of Lonnie's stern admonition: "Don't bring the kid! He'll only weigh us down, and we'll never get to California," he whispered to her during her last visit to Brushy. That's where he was supposed to spend the next three years at Tennessee's oldest prison up in Petros, punishment for six cases of home- breaking and larceny. She'd panicked, thinking that Lonnie would dump the kid *and* her if she didn't adhere to his warning. For Treva, life without Lonnie or California would be unbearable. In her state of mind, those were good enough reasons to do what she was about to do. "It's Saturday night; someone will find him early tomorrow morning before church services," thought Treva as she wrapped the sleeping boy in an old blanket, placed him in Ollie's laundry basket, and left them in the doorway of Mount Pisgah Primitive Baptist Church.

"He'll be all right, he'll be all right" was her mantra as she cautiously urged Aunt Ollie's Dodge through the switchbacks. Although it was a warm August evening, she had the windows up, fearful of bats, insects, and God-knows-what manner of winged creatures flapped and fluttered in this high mountain gloom. As she rounded the curves, her headlights occasionally reflected off beady red eyes, and she conjured visions of their owners, lurking, slinking through the thick, primeval stands of hemlock and pines bordering the road. She shuddered to think that Lonnie, at this moment, was wandering among them. Stepping on the gas, she slid dangerously around the next curve, speeding to the rendezvous point.

She was eager to greet her lover. He'd escaped once, about a year before, two months after the baby was born. But his freedom was fleeting. They caught him two days later, wandering in the pristine Frozen Head wilderness area. Exhausted from clambering over deadfall and negotiating dense undergrowth, cut and bleeding from the briars and thorn-bearing locust trees, and feasted on by ravenous insects, he gave up easily. He told her that he'd learned two valuable lessons during his ordeal: that it was a long and gruesome walk out of ole Brushy and attempted escape was a serious infraction. Disciplinary action included seventeen lashes, from head to foot, with a four-foot-long, four-inch-wide leather strap. Then he was thrown into the hole for thirty days. There, with no bed or lighting, he was fed bread twice a day. He was also given a "good" water bucket containing fresh water and a "bad" water bucket in which he urinated blood, a condition resulting from his corporal punishment. When the hole time was over, another inmate was assigned to lead him around until his eyes adjusted to the light. Treva was allowed to see him in January, but her visit was curtailed by winter storms. February was the same: sleet- and ice-coated roads that were treacherous to navigate even in fair weather. Finally in March they were reunited. They visited for a while in the public visitation room, and Treva was pretty sure he wasn't lying when he told her his divorce from the other woman was final. They talked about the baby but not too much. Then she was astounded when he asked her to marry him.

"I was thinking California, maybe sometime soon," he grinned mischievously, that grin that reduced her to jelly. She listened, engrossed, as he whispered his plan. She visited him three more times before he finally divulged the time, date, and the location of the rendezvous.

She'd followed his instructions precisely, and now here she was, driving on a lonely mountain road cut precariously into a hillside just below Rosedale and the community of Devonia.

As she crept down the road, she noticed an abandoned tipple teetering on a kudzu-infested ledge. There were no lights anywhere, no sign of habitation. When she shut the engine down and switched off the lights, she was horrified as suffocating blackness engulfed her world. As a demonic howl rose from the ravine below, she shrieked and dove to the floor of the Dodge.

Head count was a way of life at Brushy. Each member of the second-shift crew was counted as he marched from the main perimeter of the prison to the "man way," a portal, actually a wooden chute, through which the inmates were herded to the tram. Then, like sheep to the slaughter, they were counted again as they boarded a "man car," a rickety, plodding trolley that transported them the final yards to the mine entrance. Upon disembarking at the No. 7 mine at Frozen Head peak, they were counted again and then were set to work digging coal out of the earth for the next ten hours. But Lonnie Cavanaugh decided to leave work early that day. He walked out of the mine, already filthy with coal dust, after just thirty minutes labor. Granted permission to use the john, his shirt front quivered with each wild heartbeat as he strode swiftly past the two-holer at the edge of the camp fearing, with each step, the harsh shouts, the roar of the Remington 12-gauge, the vicious bite of pellets tearing into his back. Now he was running, falling, flailing through the dense underbrush.

After about twenty minutes of flat-out sprinting, he paused to catch his breath and listen for the shrill whistle blasts—one long, one short—announcing his departure, bringing a pack of baying hounds and the entire population of Petros down on his back. He strained to hear over his ragged breathing. All he heard was the distant clank-clink of mining machinery. He ran a few more yards and staggered to a halt, bending over with his hands on his knees. As he attempted to rid himself of the side stitch, he hoped against incredible odds that the guard assumed he'd returned to work, and he wouldn't be missed till later when the cons were rounded up and counted again at suppertime. The stitch still plagued him, but fueled by fear and whopping rushes of adrenaline, the fugitive continued his flight on what he hoped was the way to Devonia.

Lonnie crashed out of the deep underbrush and tumbled headlong into the red clay culvert bordering the road. As he scrambled out of the gully, he began his agonizingly slow climb up winding Route 116. He was close to his destination when he saw the lights of a car reflecting off the trees. Unwillingly he ducked back into the woods. Now, as he waded through the shallows of Stockstill Creek, he heard the eerie squall of a wildcat.

Treva squinted at her watch in the melancholy darkness; it was nearly ten o'clock. Per his instructions, she was to leave if he wasn't

there by ten-thirty. She squirmed uncomfortably. It was hotter than Hades in the car, but she wasn't about to roll down the windows, not after hearing that howl. Ten more minutes passed. Tears welled up in her eyes when she thought of coming all this way, of giving up Bobby Ray for nothing. She slipped a cigarette from the open pack wedged between the headliner and the visor. Fumbling in her purse, she found the Zippo he'd given her with the Marine insignia emblazoned on the front. Shakily she lit the cigarette, then yelped in terror as Lonnie rapped hard on the window.

Chapter 3

BRUSHY MOUNTAIN FOUNDLING

The deep hollows were already bathed in a blue-mauve haze, but the late summer sun still burned brilliantly on the slopes of Little Brushy Mountain, glinting brightly off the evergreen laurels, the holly shrubs, and the whitish belly of the Red Tailed Hawk.

A gang of crows harried the magnificent raptor, but he paid them no heed.

The bandits backed off as the hawk soared higher, surfing majestically on the updrafts from the mountainside. Its broad brown quills and rusty tail widely outstretched, the hawk circled round, ascending wraithlike into the cobalt-blue sky without the benefit of a single wingbeat.

The black man, alerted by the hawk's "kree-ee-ee" call, marveled at its aerobatics. "When I die, hallelujah by and by, I'll fly away," he sang under his breath, envious of the bird's freedom.

He watched intently from the roadside as the hawk folded its wings close to its sides and swooped earthward, toward some ill-fated varmint and supper. The traveler was hungry too and quickened his pace as he headed homeward. His name was Dwane "Benny" Baird, and he wasn't a black man at all, not from the inside out anyway. His ancestors migrated to this place from Scotland over a century ago. And like most of them, he was a coal miner, hence his blackened appearance, his sooty mantle of gritty coal dust. Benny's grandfather, Pierce, fought the state militia during the Coal Creek war back in 1891-1892, along with thousands of other miners who opposed leased convict labor and being swindled in general by the Tennessee Coal Company.

In 1902 his grandfather was killed in the Fraterville explosion along with 183 other men and boys. He left behind eight children, including Benny's father, who began working in the mines as a trap operator at age thirteen. "Pap," as he was later addressed by his kin, died at the age of fifty-two, wheezing and gasping, consumed by the dreaded "miner's asthma," later known as "black lung." Born in 1926, the sixth of nine children, Benny began working at the prison-run Brushy Mountain Mine along with his father in 1940. His first assignment at the mine led him deep into the earth where, on his hands and knees, shivering in the mud and cold, he scraped at a seam with pick and shovel. He was skinny as a rail and extremely bow-legged from a bout with rickets suffered in early childhood. But otherwise he was strong and weathered the ordeal admirably. Off and on he worked a succession of jobs at the Brushy Mine, sometimes alongside inmates, many of them products of cultures far alien from his own. The prisoners were treated poorly by the guards and punished severely for not making their tonnage quotas and other infractions. He winced as he remembered the plight of a prisoner caught weighing his coal bucket down with muck. The guards stripped the offender of his shirt, then strapped the man facedown on the back of a mule. The mule was led up and down a narrow mine corridor no more than seven feet in height. The prisoner's screams repeated pathetically off the blackened walls as his back was ripped to shreds by jagged rocks and coal protruding from the low ceiling.

The man begged for mercy, but the guards insisted he serve the sentence imposed—twenty laps. As Benny helped remove the unconscious, bloodied form from the back of the mule, he prayed for the broken man, a comrade with whom he shared a sentence of life at hard labor, a sentence imposed by circumstance and "King Coal."

It was purple dusk, and the frogs were doing their utmost to outshout the cicadas when Benny finally reached flat land. He was late getting home tonight, and as he rounded the curve, he beheld the façade of Brushy Mountain Prison, crouching beast-like in the shadows of a tapered valley. The foreboding structure, reminiscent of a fortress with battlements at the top, was originally constructed in 1896 for the purpose of using inmates to run state-owned coal mines. "The State," as locals called it, was rebuilt in 1935 and considered the lifeblood of Petros' folk because it was the primary "industry" for the area. Still Benny shivered to think of the horrible things that might take place within its walls.

The amphibian and insect chorus roared now as Benny neared his home. It was dark already, and he lit his carbide lamp, sweeping the light before him, searching warily for the rattlers or copperheads that sometimes lay stretched across the road, absorbing the waning warmth of the sun. He heard the crunch of wheels on gravel before he saw the car careening around the curve, and he leaped nimbly into a ditch to keep from getting run over. "God almighty, ye tryin' to kill me?" he shouted at the taillights fading in the twilight. He was climbing out of the ditch and reproaching himself for using the Lord's name in vain when he heard the scream.

Benny froze in his tracks as the scream, shrill and unearthly, withered to a whimper.

His hands trembled as he searched the hillside with his lantern for the source of the clamor, hoping that his headlamp would not fall on a panther or, worse yet, a haint that he'd been told as a boy, slithered out of the dark woods on occasion in search of human souls.

The whimpering continued, and the critter glee club ceased to chirp and chatter. Benny forced his rubbery legs through the weeds in the direction of the sound, which seemed to be emanating from tiny

Mt. Pisgah Primitive Baptist Church, nestled comfortably in a bend in the road. "I know ye ain't no screech owl, and I'm hopin' ye ain't no haint or a painter. If yore a human, tell me so, and I'll hep ye," said Benny as he cautiously approached the steps of the church, lantern in one hand, an opened buck knife in the other. The steps creaked mightily as Benny took them one at a time. He noticed erratic movement on the corner of the porch and shined his lamp in that direction. He almost let loose in his britches when the thing lurched toward him, howling like a ghoul.

She wore a flour sack shift. Her house was a tumbledown, tarpapered, two- room shotgun shack, and she was resigned to a hardscrabble existence that would offer few, if any, fineries in life. But sweet little Margaret was satisfied with her lot and what God gave her: her mountains, her family, and Dwane Benny Baird. She glided barefoot across the worn linoleum-covered floor, a ragged ballerina flitting from stove to cupboard to table, fixing Benny's supper. She knew he was on his way and hoped the enticing aroma of frying fatback and cornbread would tug at his nostrils, and he would hasten his step as he trudged homeward. She and Benny met over in Campbell County, where most of her people still lived. The occasion was the Mountain Assembly picnic, where Benny paid the princely sum of twenty-five cents for her entry in the cakewalk: a simple yellow cake with chocolate frosting. He courted her steadily for the next six months, and although her daddy said he was so bowlegged he couldn't stop a hog in a ditch, Margaret thought he was beautiful inside and out. They were married two days after her sixteenth birthday and three years later had not started a family. "Thar will be one of these days, God willin'," she said, unknowing that her prophecy would be fulfilled when her husband came stomping excitedly into the kitchen a few moments later.

"Look what I brung ye!" shouted Benny, a wide, white grin splitting his coal-blackened face.

Supper was forgotten for the couple. The fatback cooled in the skillet as the pair fawned over Benny's find: a scrawny baby boy they guessed to be a little over a year old, a baby that Margaret immediately labeled "a gift from God." "He's jest like Moses in the bulrushes," gushed Margaret as she spoon-fed the boy a concoction of crumbled cornbread in buttermilk. The cranky child was famished, reaching for the spoon as Margaret dipped it back into the bowl. "He like to skeered me to death," said Benny, wiping a crumb of cornbread off the youngster's soft, pouty lower lip. He was unable to keep his hands off the boy, rubbing his fuzzy head, stroking his thin shoulder blades and chest as Margaret cared for the waif.

Benny was delighted when, as Margaret finally handed the child over, the boy reached for him.

"Lookee, Marg, he likes me," said Benny, hugging the child close, not minding the aroma of the soiled diaper. "I kin tell by the look of him that little'un is starvin' fer love; he'd retch fer anybody," said Margaret as she put a kettle of water on the stove to heat.

Later the exhausted infant fell sound asleep while she was bathing him in a wash pan. At first Margaret thought there was a spot of blood on the back of his left shoulder and was alarmed until she determined its identity. "What is that thang? Did he git bit?" said Benny, pointing at the strawberry-shaped image. "It's jest a birthmark, honey. Why don't ye fetch one of yore undershirts fer me," said Margaret as she gently patted the limp body off with a clean dish towel.

Benny did her bidding, returning with the worn garment, part of his meager wardrobe.

"Pore little thang, he's tuckered," whispered Margaret as she swaddled the babe in the shirt and placed him on her lap. Benny stood and tugged at the string attached to the naked light bulb that hung over the kitchen table. They talked softly in the dark as the baby slept.

"What do ye thank we should do? Should we report this to the sherf?" said Benny as Margaret hummed a lullaby handed down from generations of mothers in her family. "It'll wait," whispered Margaret as the boy clutched her forefinger in his tiny fist.

The whistle blew at exactly ten forty-five, about the time Lonnie and his bride-to-be were fleeing down the slope of the mountain toward Briceville and freedom. One long blast, one short blast echoed down the mountainside, alerting the Petros community of the escape. Margaret failed to awaken, snoring softly in the crook of Benny's stringy arm. Dog tired, the babe stirred slightly, burrowing his peach-fuzzy head in the warmth of her bosom, breathing deep sighs in rhythm with her heartbeats. But Benny heard the warning as it reverberated through the mountains and the hollows. Margaret moaned as he gingerly slid his arm from beneath her curly head and slipped out to the front porch. As he stood there in his drawer tail, relieving himself in her hydrangeas, he laughed at the prospect of Brushy losing one of its houseguests. Then he thanked God for his life, his wife, and the gift of the boy.

He tiptoed back in and settled himself as quietly as he could in their creaky bed. Soon he was lost in deep slumber, dreaming that he was a Red Tailed Hawk and sweet Margaret and the boy rode his feathery back. Margaret laughed childlike, her flour sack dress fluttering in the breeze, and the fair babe sweetly cooed his approval as they soared high above the hardships on Brushy Mountain.

Chapter 4

THIS LITTLE PIGGY

Conjugal visits were not included as part of visitation at Brushy. And that fueled the situation, as somewhere in South Georgia a headboard banged with the ferocity of a jackhammer, denting the faded peony design in the mottled motel wallpaper. Treva exhorted Lonnie to do his best, and he did so with passion. This was a scenario repeated dutifully as Lonnie and Treva, alternately coupling and scrapping like a pair of cats in heat, fled southward toward whatever it was that Lonnie had in mind. She would admit that she wasn't the brightest, but she was immediately aware that they weren't remotely headed in the direction of California. At first she protested loudly and then pouted with a masterful fierceness. But Lonnie soothed her with promises. He told her that he had some business to settle in Florida, where he had relatives, and there he could score the cash they needed to fund their trek to California. She didn't ask about the nature of the business. She knew that he was a born crook and would naturally lean toward the seamy side in order to meet his needs, and hopefully hers. They only talked about Bobby Ray once. "Where's the boy?" he asked the night of the escape. "I left him with Ollie." "Good!" he said as they rumbled down the mountainside. His approval and happiness made things right for her, and she silently rejoiced in the midst of her fast-fading grief.

"How much money we got left?" said Lonnie, attempting to light a cigarette in the weak breeze created by the wall-mounted fan. Treva rolled out of the other side of the bed. He admired her body as she stood hip cocked and naked at the dresser, which was piled high with pocket debris. "Hang on, I'm countin'," she said, picking through the change, smoothing out the crinkled bills. This small mound of bills and change was all that was left of the money she had squirreled away over the past eleven months—money she had stolen from Ollie's purse, money she'd bummed from barfly admirers, money she'd received from the sale of various and sundry items from her spinster aunt's attic, including precious dreams from Ollie's hope chest that tragically would never serve its purpose. Thirty-five dollars of their stash was spent on a new sport coat, slacks, a couple shirts, underwear, and a pair of wing tips for Lonnie, who was donning his new duds at the moment. "Give me the money, baby, and toss me the car keys while you're at it," said Lonnie, tucking his shirt neatly into his pleated trousers." "Where you goin'?" glowered Treva, the infamous pout appearing like a sudden storm. "Don't you worry your pretty self about where I'm goin'," laughed Lonnie as he walked across the room and encircled her waist with one arm. "I'll be back in a little bit, and I'll have a few surprises for you," he said, snatching the money and keys off the dresser and sliding all but a five-dollar bill into his pants pocket. "Take this money and buy yourself something to eat; there's a diner up the road, and don't go flirtin' with folks just to get even with me," he said sternly, placing the five-spot in her hand. "But where you goin'?" whined Treva, the pout teetering on the ragged edge of fury. "I'm going to get us some money; that's all you need to know," said Lonnie, beating a hasty retreat to the door. "I'll bring some beer back," he said, closing the door quickly, half expecting a shoe to come sailing past his head. Treva heaved, not a shoe, but a sigh as she headed for the bathroom. As she ran her bath water, her anxiety lessened with the prospect of a little beer drinking.

Leeotis Calhoun was dreaming about Betty Grable when he was awakened by the familiar crunch of tires in the gravel lot. His chair groaned as the grossly fat man struggled upright and swung his short legs off the desk. "Damn!" he said, glancing at his watch and noting that it was almost quitting time at Piggy's Used Car Palace. Groggy from his nap, he struggled to his feet, bent to adjust his left pant leg, which had crept up over the top of his cowboy boot, and nearly fell on his face. Not that it would hurt his appearance much if he did fall on his face. Leeotis was cursed with a porcine façade: deep-set, vacuous eyes and a bulbous, upturned, snoutlike nose; hence the cruel nickname bestowed upon him at an early age by the townsfolk. On the outside "Piggy" Calhoun seemed to weather the derisive comments about his appearance admirably, his dead eyes never revealing the pain he suffered each time some smart-ass referred to his swinelike exterior. "Hey Piggy, how's the used car business? You bringin' home the bacon? Ha ha ha ha ha." Actually business at the Palace wasn't too bad. Piggy prospered, parlaying his fierce inner pain into a vengeful quest, becoming a maven in the art of ruthless transactions, bursting into fits of squeally laughter as trusting farmers, and sometimes even those who had insulted him, drove one of his junk heaps off the lot.

The trailer floor creaked loudly as Piggy lumbered over to the window and peeped through the blinds at his potential victim. The man had exited a nice-looking Dodge and was walking about the lot, checking out the modest inventory. Piggy couldn't make out the license plate on the Dodge, but he knew from the look of the driver that he wasn't from around here. He was wearing nice trousers instead of overalls and shiny black wing tips instead of red clay-caked boots. As the stranger turned to face the trailer, Piggy noticed that he was handsome: tall, heavy brow, square jaw. "Purty boy," muttered Piggy, as he adjusted his bolo tie and plodded to the door.

Lonnie leaned on the fender of a beat-up Studebaker, waiting for the "peeper" to present himself. He hadn't really known what he was going to do to get the money he'd promised Treva, but he was confidently creative, and a plan began to form in his mind the minute he saw Piggy Calhoun's humongous form pour out of the trailer. "Name's Leeotis Calhoun; what can I do you fer?" said Piggy, who'd already broken a sweat under the late afternoon sun. Lonnie cringed, fighting the urge to wipe his hand on his pant leg after shaking Piggy's slimy paw. Lonnie quickly went through his mental list of aka's. "I'm Phil Russell, nice to meet you," said Lonnie, as Piggy produced a tablecloth-sized hanky from his hip pocket and dabbed at his monstrous forehead as he sized up the Dodge. "Man, it's hot, ain't it, Phil? S'posed to rain later. You from Tennessee, huh?" babbled Piggy. Sensing the fat man's manic eagerness to wrap up a quick deal, Lonnie played the game. "Yep, we're on our way to Florida; just got married last night," he said, flashing a wedding band. "Well, congratulations," said Piggy with the sincerity of a hangman. "Where's the little lady?" said the wheeler-dealer, glancing at his wristwatch. "Back at the motel packing up; we like to travel at night," said Lonnie, restraining his desire to mimic the fat slob's rapid-fire delivery.

Piggy pointed a sausage-shaped index finger across the road in the direction of an enormous weeping willow tree that dwarfed the adjacent, non-descript, clapboard-covered farmhouse. In the yard was Piggy's prized Hudson Hornet, a gift from his recently deceased mother-in-law, who in life would not have given him the time of day. "My little lady, Roberta, and me live over there; comes in pretty handy when I feel like gittin' a little. Know what I mean?" snorted Piggy, and Lonnie flinched at the mental image of the act. He was saved from responding as Piggy changed gears. "So what can I do you fer?" quizzed Piggy, reusing the line that he thought was hilarious and a good opener that disarmed suspicious customers. "Well, we're traveling in two cars, and we'd like to ride together, so I thought I'd get rid of her car. Besides, we need the money," said Lonnie. Piggy's demeanor changed in an instant, brow furrowing, stupid grin morphing into a comical pucker. "Sorry, buddy, I'm mostly in to trading," said Piggy as he turned back to the trailer. "Fuckin' purty boy, wastin' my precious time," thought Piggy as he waddled toward the trailer. But he halted in his tracks as Lonnie spoke.

"How about $300?" said Lonnie, setting the abacus to clicking in Piggy's devious brain.

Piggy did a quick about face. "Well then, let's take her around the block, buddy. Mind if I drive, Phil?" said Piggy, moronic grin reappearing, tiny lips and teeth barely discernable in a sea of flesh.

Heat lightning skittered across the leaden sky, periodically illuminating Piggy's car lot across the road. Piggy sat on the stoop, simmering in the oppressive heat, struggling to endure the closeness of the steamy Georgia night. "By God, I'm goin' to have me one of them air conditioners next year," he spoke to himself. Piggy, who had been swigging from a jug of celebratory beer he'd bought over in the next county, was drunk as a skunk.

He giggled crazily as he remembered the visage of "purty boy" headed down the road, happy as a clam, with $300 measly dollars in the pocket of his purty pleated trousers.

That was the sum he paid the sucker for the Dodge, which was clean as a whistle and in his estimation worth about four times what he paid for it. "What a dumbass!" laughed Piggy as he tilted the almost empty jug to his lips. As Piggy partied on the front porch, he thought of his equally corpulent wife, Roberta, inside the home, taking a cool soak in the tub. He hoped like the dickens she didn't have romance on her mind. It was just too damned hot for that kind of thing; especially when he had to do all of the work.

Piggy figured Roberta must have finished her bath and gone to bed for the house was dark now, with the exception of the warm amber glow from the Philco radio in the parlor. "The White Cliffs of

Dover" wafted through an open bedroom window. Framing the window were lace curtains that fluttered like injured birds in the thick, sickly breeze generated by an oscillating floor fan (another gift from Roberta's late mother). A sweet voice called to Piggy. "You comin' to bed, honey?" "I'll be right there, sugar," he answered resignedly. He sighed heavily, then drained the last drop from the jug and struggled to his feet. The screen door squawked as Piggy reluctantly entered the furnace-hot house. He shuffled into the bedroom, dreading the stifling, sleep-robbing heat and the strong probability of a sweaty encounter with the ever-affectionate Roberta.

Lonnie stood beneath the drooping branches of the enormous weeping willow, nervously fingering a loose cigarette in his shirt pocket, deciding against lighting up lest he betray his shadowy vantage point. He stepped forward, peering anxiously through the willow's stringy tendrils. The light from the Philco was still glowing, and he could barely hear the music over the cacophonous chirping of frogs and buzz of insects. He listened intently to the fading strains of "White Cliffs of Dover," and now he silently hummed along with "Don't Sit under the Apple Tree." Fidgety, he squatted and leaned against the base of the tree, where he'd neatly folded his sport coat.

He fumbled in his pocket for a stick of Juicy Fruit, noticing that his hands were trembling slightly as he unwrapped the gum. Everybody said he was good with his hands. He could disassemble any mechanical thing and put it back together again without leaving any extra parts. Once he'd successfully hot-wired his daddy's Packard just to see if he could get away with it. But that was in broad daylight and under decidedly different circumstances. Popping the gum in his mouth, he chewed vigorously, rehearsing the hot-wire procedure in his head. In the midst of his mental preparation, he suddenly realized that the music had ceased playing. He leaped lightly to his feet, peering once more at the house in the distance. The light from the Philco glowed no more.

A trickle of perspiration crawled uncertainly from the nape of his neck, and he squirmed uncomfortably as it picked up speed, navigating his spine, coming to a halt as it pooled at his waist. After thirty more agonizing minutes of waiting in the suffocating heat, the back of his shirt was soaked, and there was a sizeable half-moon-shaped wet spot forming on the back of his new trousers at the apex of his butt crack. His heart thudded in his chest as he deftly parted the leafy curtain and stepped warily into the yard. The night critters seemed to increase their volume, applauding his entrance to this grassy stage. Thunder growled grumpily in the distance, and a welcoming hint of a breeze gently stirred the willow branches. Lonnie donned his coat, and as he made his way stealthily to the Hudson, he was delighted to discover that Piggy had left the keys in the ignition.

The storm grumbled for a long while in its approach and now, as if to say, "I've given you fair warning," unleashed its fury on South Georgia. Ozone permeated the air as perpendicular lightning divided trees with the precision of a wood-splitting maul. Exploding thunder sent little ones scurrying to Mommy and Daddy's bed. Bucketfuls of rain were driven obliquely by fierce winds, filling creek beds to the brim and carving deep, ankle-breaking gullies in the Georgia clay.

The wind and lightning took intermission after a while, but an intense downpour continued. Treva shivered as she stood beneath the eaves, listening to the burbling, overflowing gutters outside the motel room. She took a long drag of her cigarette and shivered again, not because of the temperature drop that rode the back of the storm, but because of her rage against Lonnie Cavanaugh. He said he'd be back soon, but he'd been gone for seven hours, leaving her with five dollars to her name! She replayed her suspicions in her mind for the hundredth time; he'd probably scored some cash, found himself a honky-tonk, and spent most of the money on some sleazy piece of trash who took him home for a roll in the hay. She took another heavy drag of the Pall Mall and blew a stream of smoke that was quickly obliterated by the curtains of rain.

"When that bastard comes back, I'll make him pay," she murmured, as she tried without success to banish the troublesome thought that he might not come back at all. She jumped as an automobile suddenly swung into the flooded motel parking lot. Slowly she slid her hand into her jacket pocket and anxiously fingered the steak knife she'd stolen earlier from the diner.

In the lot Lonnie sat in the Hudson listening to the rain tap-dance on the roof. It seemed to him that the torrent was slackening and the storm was abating; the thunder booms became fainter, and strobes of lightning illuminated distant skies as the gale crawled northward. Still an occasional bolt of straggling, jagged-blue lightning ripped the sky, accompanied by a thunderous aftershock.

Lonnie opened the door to the Hudson, unaware that another dangerous tempest was forming ominously at The Georgia Peach.

Chapter 5

THE GEORGIA PEACH

The Lucky Strike radio show was in full swing when the lights went out, and Frank Sinatra went silent, right in the middle of "I've Got a Crush on You." "Dadgummit!" grumbled O.P. Caldwell as the windows rattled in the front office outside the tiny room he called home. This evening O.P. was celebrating his twenty-ninth year with The Georgia Peach Motel, alternately tilting at a bottle of RC Cola and munching on popcorn that he'd popped on his hotplate, while listening to his favorite radio program. He shared the moldering, twenty-eight-room facility with only two guests: a hot-to-trot-looking couple that checked in early that afternoon. He assigned them a room at the far end of the building away from the office. "Let 'em howl all they want to; they won't bother me," chuckled O.P. as earlier he watched the pair unload their luggage from the trunk of the Dodge.

When the lights went out, O.P. bumped and fumbled in the sudden darkness, searching for a flashlight or a candle. As he knocked about, rummaging through drawers and cabinets, he heard other whumps and thumps in the distance, perhaps announcements of a coming storm. O.P. hoped it wasn't a tornado.

"Pack your bags, baby; we've got to hit the road," said Lonnie as he ducked under the eaves out of the rain. Treva didn't respond verbally to his comment. Instead she glided forward till she was within inches of him. Lonnie opened his arms to embrace her, but instead of snuggling into his chest as he had expected, she leaned in and sniffed his neck. "What're you doin'? You're actin' like a hound in heat," laughed

Lonnie, reaching for her. "You've been with some hussy, ain't you?" sneered Treva, brushing away his advances. "Now who in the hell would I be with? We don't know anybody here! Besides, we just got married last night!" said Lonnie. "That don't make no difference with you though, does it?" sneered Treva, her pretty white teeth showing like fangs in a mocking grin. Agitated, Lonnie said, "I can't win for losin'," as he turned and twisted the door handle to the room. But his words were reduced to nothing by a colossal clap of thunder.

When Lonnie stepped into the pitch-black room, he barely heard the low growl spill from Treva's throat as she leaped on his back. "What the Sam Hill?" he cried, as they pitched forward onto the floor, which was littered with unidentifiable debris. The impact of the fall separated the couple briefly. As Lonnie raised himself on one elbow, attempting to make sense of the chaos, she came at him again. As they tumbled and rolled in the darkness and clutter, Lonnie felt honest pain as Treva squirmed and scratched like a feral cat against him. A white-hot twinge accompanied one of her jabs, and Lonnie howled as it wormed through his shoulder. Infuriated, he grabbed her by the throat, and as he staggered partially upright, slammed her against the wall.

"What the hell is the matter with you?" he gasped. "You son of a bitch!" she gurgled beneath his grasp, and as his hands loosened around her neck, she dug bloody furrows in them with her long nails. Driven by pain, anger, and mostly fear, Lonnie hefted the thrashing hellion beneath her arms and threw her across the room, where she hit something solid with a resounding thud.

The silence was deafening as Lonnie leaned against the dresser, panting for breath, bracing for the next terrifying assault from his maniac companion. When his breathing returned to almost normal, he rationed that the best thing he could do was to get the hell out of there. Stuff crunched beneath his feet as he made his way tentatively for the door, and the lights came on, compliments of Georgia Utilities.

Startled, he cried out as he beheld the damage she had wrought during his absence. The bathroom door was open, and he could see the towel rack and shower curtain lying on the linoleum floor. But the main room looked as if it had been hit by a saturation bomb.

The dresser and the bed were the only items left intact; everything else was either splintered or shredded, including the King James Bible that was once in the drawer of the wrecked nightstand. The painting of the little girl with fairy wings above their bed was now impaled on the shadeless pole lamp, and even the sheets on the bed had been sliced to ribbons with a sharp object. In the midst of it all lay Treva, eyes wide, ghostly white; leaning crookedly against the far wall, feet and head askew, like a rag doll.

Fearing the worst, Lonnie made his way slowly to her eerily still form, debris crackling beneath his shoes. Something bumped against his collarbone, and he was suddenly aware that a steak knife was hanging loosely from the thick shoulder pad that lined his new sport coat.

"Shit!" he said, yanking the knife from the shoulder pad and kneeling beside his catatonic assailant. "Treva, Treva? You all right?" said Lonnie, concerned but vigilant, ready to spring out of the way should the wildcat gather the strength to strike again. He flinched as she reached for him, not with animosity, but tenderness. "I was so worried!" she sobbed, burying her head in his chest, clutching him with desperate hands, hands that earlier would have ripped his heart out if possible. As Lonnie held his pitiful lover, his shoulder began to burn. Against his better judgment, he gently lifted her to her feet. She seemed heavier than she had a few moments earlier. "C'mon, let's pack what we've got left and get out of here," he said as he released her.

"I will, but first let me take a look at your shoulder," she said, choking on the words, a single tear flowing down her cheek. The tears continued to flow as she cleaned the steak knife wound in his shoulder with soap and water. She kissed his chest and shoulders as she bound the wound with strips of mutilated bed sheets. Once the bags were packed, he grabbed them and walked out into the lightly falling rain. Treva followed like an obedient child, and when she opened the door to their new automobile, her mood changed dramatically as she spied the package on the front seat. “Hey, you bought beer!” she said, almost excitedly.

“Open up a couple of bottles,” he said. “There’s a church key in the glove box.” The beer tasted good as they drove away from The Georgia Peach. After consuming a few more brews, they laughed about the messes O.P. and Piggy would face the following morning.

Part II

A NEW LIFE

Chapter 6

LEAVING PETROS

Benny and Margaret were abysmally poor liars. Early on the couple made a pact to tell inquisitive neighbors the blue-eyed baby boy was her sick sister's child, and they were taking care of little Harley until she got better. This was a viable excuse, for in those days families often took in the offspring of other family members and neighbors when times were tough. But Benny and Margaret's inherent goodness sullied the plan, and soon they found themselves telling some real whoppers. Benny was the worst. "Yep, Marg's sister has the croup, and it jest seems to be gettin' worse," Benny told some folks gathered in the churchyard one Sunday morning.

When one of the group inquired about the sister's health after the following Wednesday evening services, Benny explained, "I heared her leg is healin', but the doctor don't thank it's set right." Being honorable people, it bothered Benny and Margaret to no end to tell lies.

But the most bothersome thing was the niggling prospect that, someday, someone would appear on their doorstep and demand the return of the child. Margaret's recurring nightmare featured a woman with piercing blue eyes, pounding on their screen door with the handle of a long-bladed butcher's knife. "If you don't give me my baby back, I'll kill you," shouted the wild-eyed, wild-haired woman, who spouted profanities that Margaret wouldn't dare verbalize.

At least once a week, Benny would awaken to the sound of Margaret's sniffling, mingled with the creak of the old rocking chair in the corner. "Marg, ye all right?" "Shhh, ye'll wake the baby," Margaret reprimanded in a whisper. As the rocking chair continued to creak and the gray light of morning filtered into the room, Benny made a critical decision.

Benny's kin were mostly dead or no-account, so it didn't bother him one bit to move on.

"I didn't like workin' at Brushy no way," he said to himself as he exited the truck for which he'd traded twenty dollars and Margaret's old wringer washer. "Who ye talkin' to?" said Margaret as she strode out on the porch, the ever-present baby straddling her thin hip.

"Nobody, jest me," answered Benny pleasantly, as he chucked a rock under the wheel of the vehicle to keep it from rolling off the hill. "Well, why don't ye git up here and talk this old rockin' chair into the back of that truck," laughed Margaret, who laughed harder when the baby giggled along with her. "Ye laughin' at momma, Harley? Ain't ye a funny boy?" she said, peppering the child's head and dirty face with wet kisses. Benny smiled too as he loaded the rocker in the back of the truck. It was one of few possessions they had to their name.

Later, after locking up the house, Benny hopped in the truck where Margaret and the baby were waiting. "Well, ye ready to git?" said Benny as he attempted to start the truck, without success.

"Ready as I'll ever be," answered Margaret as she wedged the baby safely between them.

"If air luck holds out, we should be moved in afore dark. Hang on, Harley. Marg, will ye git that rock that I chucked under air tar?" said Benny as he prepared to start the truck again. The warped passenger door creaked and popped as she slipped out and ran to the back of the truck to retrieve the rock that helped hold the vehicle in place on the hillside. "I'm agoin' to keep this old rock as a reminder of us afixin' to start out on this journey and a new life," said Margaret breathlessly, as she got back into the truck and slammed the complaining door. "Whar ye gonna put it?" said Benny. "I'll probably put it in air garden, or maybe we'll use it as a doorstop," said Margaret, placing the rock carefully on the seat between her and Harley, who caressed the sandstone with curious fingers. "Well, why don't ye put it to work right now and put it over that hole in the floorboard; it'll keep Harley from fallin' through," said Benny. Margaret followed his advice. Benny stomped on the clutch, and as the truck rolled backwards, he released it, jump-starting the vehicle to life. Later, as the old truck rumbled through the hollows and switchbacks, Margaret sat little Harley on her lap and sang to him. "Cumberland Gap is a mighty fine place, three kinds of water to worsh yore face," crooned Margaret as Benny joined in.

"Me and my wife and my wife's Pap, we're all goin' down to Cumberland Gap," sang Benny lustily and way out of tune. Margaret grabbed the baby's tiny hands in hers and clapped in time with the tempo. Later the baby clapped his hands by himself and giggled along as Benny and Margaret sang the chorus. "Cumberland Gap, Cumberland Gap. Hey! Way down yonder in Cumberland Gap." Their journey would end, not in fabled Cumberland Gap, but on nearby Cumberland Mountain in Campbell County, Tennessee.

Chapter 7

PAPPY SCRAP

Some historians say that Melungeons are the descendants of Portuguese, Moorish Arabs, Turks, and Berbers who were left behind when the Spanish abandoned their colonies in America in the 1500s. (The most northwestern garrison of Spanish Florida was near what is now Knoxville, Tennessee.) The castaways intermingled with Native Americans, other people of color, and later, settlers who settled in the Southeast, especially in the Appalachians.

According to some scholars, the term Melungeon is pronounced similarly to the Turkish word "melun can" and the Arabic word, "malun jinn." Both terms translate to "cursed soul."

Scrap Hopkins was a Melungeon, but he didn't know it. Many of his neighbors were also of Melungeon descent but, like Scrap, unaware of their lineage. All they knew was that most of their kin had lived on the rugged, northeastern Cumberland Plateau since time out of memory. Scrap's given name was "Homer," which he detested. He was unsure how he came to be called Scrap; maybe the moniker came from his penchant for fighting when he was a young man or for his huge appetite. "That boy would not leave a scrap of food on his plate nor anyone's; he'd clean 'em up like a buzzard at a dead thang," bragged Scrap's momma, who had gone to her reward years earlier. Through the years Scrap's enormous appetite begat his equally enormous belly. Mass quantities of beer and moonshine also added to his bulk, which was immense. The barrel-chested behemoth stood at least six foot four with shoulders that would fill the doorway to a church, if he attended. He would probably tip the scale at about three hundred fifty beefy pounds.

He was an imposing figure with coal black hair, swarthy skin, and heavy-lidded green eyes.

"Hep me git this mattress through the door, Melvin," ordered Scrap to his neighbor, Melvin Cross, who had been content just to observe as the big man attempted to squeeze the bedding through the cabin's narrow entrance. Melvin hopped to, lending a skinny shoulder to the effort.

Finally, after much tugging, cussing, and shoving, the mattress popped through the portal.

"I figger it's time to take a breather," said Scrap, plopping his humongous frame down on the stoop. Melvin joined the mightily sweating giant as he squatted on the top step.

"When they supposed to git here?" said Melvin as he stuffed a wad of tobacco in his jaw.

"I figger in 'bout an air," said Scrap, mopping his prominent brow with a faded red bandana.

"I 'member when ye and Haley June moved into this place," said Melvin, spitting a coffee-colored stream of tobacco juice across the weathered floorboards.

"Dadgummit, Melvin, why ye got to spit bakker juice all over the porch?" said Scrap, feigning anger in an effort to mask the fierce emptiness that filled his being every time the subject of his wife was broached.

Indeed Scrap had carried his wisp of a bride across the threshold of the cabin over thirty-two years ago. Over the next twenty-eight years, she had borne him four children: Rhonda, Ruby, Joyce Ann, and Margaret. She brought up the children mostly by herself, tolerating his drinking, fighting, womanizing, and occasional brushes with the law.

In his ignorant way, he loved her dearly. He built her a nice home on the ridge above the cabin and turned most of his pay over to her every Friday night or Saturday morning.

He never raised a hand to her, and she was the only one he would allow to call him "Homer", his given name. When she died four years ago of a sickness that was never diagnosed, he was devastated. And the grief their children suffered over the loss of their sainted mother turned to rage, as they remembered their father's misgivings and how Haley June quietly endured his lowlife escapades.

After the funeral, he reached out to his sobbing daughters, but three of them turned their backs to him. The only unmarried girl, the one most like her mother, Margaret, went back to the house with him. The big man took to his bed, burying his head in Haley June's pillow, hoping to find a trace of her scent.

In the months following her passing, he spent his days in a rocker on the front porch, gazing forlornly at the little cabin in the swale below. His nights were hellish as he replayed every wrongdoing he'd committed, and each time sweet Haley June had forgiven him. Through it all Margaret tended to his every need, helping him to regain his feet and his sanity.

His heart broke again when, a year later, she married bow-legged Benny and moved over to Morgan County with him. Now she and her husband were coming back, and they were bringing a young'un with them, his sixth grandchild. He'd spent weeks fixing up the cabin up for them, and now they were only hours away from the reunion. "Melvin, wipe up that spit, and let's git the bed set up," said Scrap as he struggled to his feet.

"I got to git to the house; Cora's probably got supper on the table," said Melvin as Scrap smoothed the quilt over the bed and turned the night-light on beside it.

Consumed with making the place presentable, Scrap paid no attention to Melvin's remark. "How's it look, Melvin?" asked Scrap, as he and Melvin walked through the tiny kitchen, outfitted with a rattling Amana refrigerator, a wood-fed Warm Morning stove, a Formica-topped table with chipped edges, and two ladder-backed chairs with raggedy woven seats. "Passable, it's clean at least," said Melvin as they strode through the living room, just big enough for a saggy couch decorated with doilies lovingly crocheted by Haley June. A bare bulb, screwed into a socket in the ceiling, illuminated the one-windowed room. A picture of Jesus knocking on a door was the only artwork to grace the water-stained and faded wallpaper.

Darkness was descending on the low-lying house. Waning rays of the setting sun still illuminated Scrap's place up on the hill as the two men clumped across the porch boards.

"I appreciate ye," said Scrap, slapping Melvin on the back, sending him flying into the yard.

"Durn yore hide, Scrap; ye 'bout knocked the wind out of me," coughed Melvin as he stumbled to his truck. "Hey, afore ye go, ain't ye got somethin' fer me?" said Scrap, reaching into his overall breast pocket and producing some wrinkly dollar bills. "Almost fergot," said Melvin, reaching through the open driver's side window for a brown paper sack. "I'll probably need another 'un next week," said Scrap as he attempted to trade the ones for the sack.

Melvin waved away Scrap's offer. "Fergit it. Ye helped me make this batch," said Melvin as he started the truck and rocked slowly down the deeply rutted path. Scrap pulled the jar, filled with a crystal clear liquid, out of the bag, unscrewed the top, and took a deep whiff of the contents. "Whew, Lord!" he exclaimed, scrunching up his jowls at the heady aroma of moonshine. He took several more gulps of the homemade elixir and was feeling the effects as he entered the little cabin for one more tour of inspection. As he walked through the doorway, the once cursed soul that was Scrap Hopkins was filled, not with sadness, but with hope for blessed redemption.

By the time Margaret, Benny, and the boy arrived, Scrap had polished off the jar of shine.

Obnoxiously happy, he heaved himself off the stoop as their truck bumped into the yard.

"Whar ye been? Whar's that young'un ye fount?" he growled as he lumbered across the yard.

Little Harley's eyes widened as he beheld the silhouette of the bearlike figure materializing in the lavender mountain dusk. The child attempted to climb into Margaret as the creature came near. "Lookee at that little yallar-headed thang," said Scrap, Dutch-rubbing Harley's head with a walnut-sized knuckle. Margaret stepped back defensively, and Harley whimpered, which seemed to fuel Scrap's ill-aimed enthusiasm. "What's a matter, little sissy feller? Ye afeared of yore pappy?" rumbled Scrap, poking the child in his thin ribs with a thick finger. "Stop it, Daddy! Yore a skeerin him!" said Margaret, shrinking further away from her father. "Ye ain't askeered of yore Pappy Scrap, are ye?" boomed Scrap, wrenching the terrified child from Margaret's grasp, dangling him high in the air like a sack of flour. Harley wailed and so did Margaret as the besotted giant threw him in the air and caught him clumsily on the way down.

"Whoo," howled Scrap as he prepared to fling the screaming infant into the air again.

But he was halted mid-hurl by a thin, yet stern voice. "Give me the boy, Scrap," said Benny, white with rage, sinewy arms outstretched, jaw muscles working furiously. Scrap turned to Margaret with an incredulous look that spoke, "Can you believe what that fool just said?" And as Benny scooped the petrified child from his grasp, the grin escaped Scrap's dark face, and his green eyes glowed with murderous intensity. "Ain't nobody goin' to talk to me like that, kin or no kin," said Scrap, advancing menacingly toward the slight man. But Benny stood his ground.

"Ain't nobody goin' to skeer my boy like that," said Benny, fists clenched and voice cracking.

"Stop it ! This ain't no way to git started," shouted Margaret, stepping between David and Goliath. There was a pregnant silence, punctuated by whimpers from the baby, who had developed a bad case of trauma-induced hiccups. Scrap studied his bold son-in-law spitefully. Then he turned to Margaret, ignoring Benny, who was actually kind of amusing as, shakily, he maintained his flimsy rendition of a defiant posture.

"The cabin's all fixed up for ye. It's got clean sheets on the bed and plenty of food in the 'frigerator: bacon, sausage, aigs, baloney, samwich spread, a crock of butter. Cora Cross sent over some maters and taters and canned pickles. I helped myself to some. Thar's some bread on the counter, and you'uns got salt and sugar too," said Scrap as he turned to leave.

"I got to git to the house. Give the boy a spoonful of that sugar; it'll cure his hiccups."

As he wobbled up the hill in the darkness, he soaked himself with a rain of heavy curses.

"Why won't ye ever learn?" he said as he staggered toward his home.

Scrap usually slept soundly, drunk or not; but tonight he tossed and turned, working the threadbare sheet on his bed into a wadded-up ball. His dreams usually featured himself hunting deer and turkey up on the mountain, pitching horseshoes and drinking with his friends down in LaFollette, or running from a falling tree in the logging woods. However, his best dreams featured Haley June. She would appear always as the young, beautiful girl he had courted with vigor. This night she presented herself, wasted and wizened, as she had been at the last moments of her life. She stood at his bedside and shook her finger in his face. "Thar all ye got, Homer. Thar all ye got," she said, her voice crackling like a wetwood fire. "But ye still got time, honey. Now git out of that bed and come to breakfast," said Haley June as she floated out of the room. In the next frame of the dream, the aroma of bacon wafted into the bedroom. He loved bacon, could devour a whole slab of it at one sitting. He awakened when his cheek touched a blob of cool drool on his mattress cover.

He shook the apparition out of his head as he tumbled out of bed and slipped into his overalls and boots. But the smell of his beloved bacon still hung heavily in the air. His stomach, devoid of sustenance except for Cora Cross's pickles and a quart of Melvin's moonshine, rumbled like a rolling oil drum, so loud that it almost drowned out the knock on the door.

"Durn it," said Scrap, dreading the tongue-lashing he expected from Margaret. He was relieved to behold Benny at the door, holding the baby in his arms. "Margaret's cookin' breakfast and says fer ye to come on down and join us," said Benny shyly, eyes cast downward.

"Well, that'd be nice, honey," said Scrap kindly. The baby seemed intrigued by the softer version of Scrap and reached out to his hungover pappy. "Hey, Scrap, I thank Harley wants to git to know ye," laughed Benny.

Scrap's vision blurred for a moment as he gently gathered the child in his massive arms.

"Boy, that shine really got a holt on me the other night," he said, clearing his throat.

"Could happen to anybody," said Benny. "Cap," said Harley. And he playfully tugged on the big man's ear as the trio followed the bacon trail down the hill.

Of all her sisters, Margaret was her mother's best student, especially when it came to matters of the hearth. The kitchen was her theater, and like many poor mountain folks, she managed to produce marvelous, creative meals with the meager ingredients at hand. She had rolled out of bed at four this morning in order to fetch water from the well, fire up the woodstove, and produce the repast spread out on the stovetop and counter: a skillet of fried potatoes, a platter of bacon and sausage, eggs, biscuits, and gravy.

At the table Scrap performed an admirable balancing act, shoveling in huge amounts of food with one hand and cradling the baby in his opposite arm. Harley was obviously delighted in the biscuit crumbs and spoons of gravy fed him by his pappy. "Here, little feller, ye want some of my coffee?" said Scrap as Margaret leaped across the table to prevent the act.

"Don't do that, Daddy. He's too young to drank coffee!" scolded Margaret. The baby laughed, knowing that his mother's anger was not real. So did Benny, his thin shoulders shaking so hard that he sloshed coffee on the table. "You'uns ain't funny," said Margaret, a smile playing on her face as she fetched a rag to wipe up the mess.

"Daddy, ye goin' to church with us this mornin'?" she said as she poured him another cup of coffee. "Uh...honey, I ain't been to church since afore yore momma died. I'm afeared that the roof would cave in if'n I walked through the door," said Scrap unapologetically. Actually after a night of drinking and carousing, Scrap had once promised Haley June that he would go the straight and narrow, and that he would even get baptized at the ceremony after church services the following Sunday. He kept his promise, and as the preacher was preparing to dunk him in the creek, Scrap spied a snake curled up in an exposed tree root on the creek bank. With that thought in mind, he felt something wiggle into his overalls as Reverend Bunch submerged his head in the water. Reverend Bunch was nearly drowned as Scrap scrambled wildly out of the creek, arms flailing, shouting unintelligibly. Many on the creek bank thought he was speaking in tongues. Others thought he was just plain daft as he ripped off his overalls and a twig fell out of the pants leg. That was the last time he attended church or any associated function.

"I like to catch up on my chores on Sundays," said Scrap, slurping the remainder of his coffee and sitting Harley on the table in front of him.

"That's a poor excuse," said Margaret, and Benny agreed but wisely kept his mouth shut.

Fearing a blowup between Margaret and Scrap, Benny changed the subject.

"I was wonderin' if ye could point me in the way of a job. Ye got any idees?" said Benny.

"I already got ye a job," said Scrap nonchalantly, as he gently placed the baby on the floor.

Before his startled son-in-law had a chance to reply, Scrap continued. "It ain't much, and ye'll be a workin' with me on the saw. Ye ain't afeared of work, are ye?"

"I'd work anywhar, jest as long as I can draw enough to feed my family," said Benny, trying but failing to contain his excitement.

"I'm jest gittin' started, and my hepper quit, so ye kin help me build the business. Ye won't be fer from home, and I figger ye kin make bout forty dollars a week in good times," said Scrap.

"That's fine with us," interrupted Margaret. "By the way, how much will we owe ye for rentin' this place, Daddy?" she asked. Scrap feigned being offended. "What do ye mean 'rent'? You'uns is family. All you'uns got to do is feed me ever once in a while, and I'll even chip in on the groceries," said Scrap as he slapped some leftover bacon on a cold biscuit.

"Lord!" thought Benny, "that'll put us in the poorhouse!"

Scrap came through the front door, as he said he would, at 5:30 a.m. Monday. Benny and Margaret were already at the kitchen table.

"How long ye young'uns been up?" said Scrap. "Marg got up about four, and I got up about four thirty. The baby's still asleep," said Benny in the wake of a large yawn. Scrap was disappointed. He'd looked forward to seeing Harley. "Well, what we got fer breakfast, Margaret?" he said as she poured him a cup of coffee. "I made some tater biscuits from the mashed taters we had fer supper, and we got aigs and some of that sausage ye had in the 'frigerator and some sausage gravy," she said as she served Benny, Scrap, and then herself. "Ye like that sausage? Duck Parker made it, and it's got sage, ginger, and lots of red hot pepper in it. It'll burn ye from noggin to tail if'n ye eat too much of it," said Scrap, his comments filtered through a mouthful of food. Benny was just about to eat a large piece of the sausage, but after Scrap's pronouncement, he placed it back on his plate and cut a small piece of it. He had barely finished his breakfast when Scrap shoved back from the table. "Well, Benny, let's go. Luther Byrd is s'posed to be here any minute with a load of yallar pine that he needs cut and planed fer to make his wife some cabinets." Margaret scurried to the counter and grabbed an ancient Coca-Cola cooler. "You'uns is welcome to come back to the house fer dinner; but if'n yore busy, I fixed ye some food," she said, placing the cooler in Benny's hands. "I got some ice in thar, some water; a couple of RC Colas, some samwiches, biscuits, and sausage," she said as the two men headed for the door. "We'll see ye soon. Thank ye, honey," Benny said as he ran to catch up with his father-in-law.

Chapter 8

BAND SAW ENTREPRENEUR

Luther Sharp was waiting for the men as they arrived at the site.

"I thought ye said you'uns would be here by six," said Luther irritably. Scrap fumbled in the watch pocket of his overalls and pulled out his Waltham. "Good Lord, Luther, it's three minutes till six by my pappy's watch, and it ain't never been wrong." Luther pulled out his timepiece, which was tethered to his belt by a long copper chain. "Well, I didn't git mine from my pappy, got it from Sears, and it says six twenty," said Luther, poised for an argument. "Never mind," said Scrap. "Let's git that pine cut. Luther, back yore truck up to the saw, and we'll unload the timber. Give me a hand, Benny." "Who's he?" grumbled Luther as he started his truck. "That's my son-in-law, Benny Baird. He's my new employee and a good'un," boasted Scrap. "I'm right behind ye, Scrap," said Benny as a rush of prideful warmth spread through his body.

Luckily Margaret had anticipated Scrap's ravenous appetite and packed the cooler with an abundance of sandwiches, the fiery sausage, biscuits, pickles and tomatoes, and boiled eggs, which Benny loved. By noon Scrap had consumed about half of their food store, but there was still plenty for both of them for dinner, especially since Benny didn't eat much.

"Whew, I don't thank we stopped fer one minute this mornin'," said Benny as they sat on a log and ate their lunch. "Well, it ain't like that ever'day, and some days it's worse. But it should git better with ye aheppin' me," said Scrap as he peeled an egg and ate it whole. Benny handed Scrap an RC and got one for himself. "Shoot, Marg didn't pack a can opener. How are we gonna open these?" "Like this," said Scrap as he placed the edge of his bottle on the corner of the saw bed and hit it with his hand. The bottle fizzed as the cap came off. Benny attempted the same maneuver but failed. "Here, give me that; I'll git it fer ye," said Scrap, who performed the exercise with ease.

As Scrap gnawed on his fourth sausage and biscuit, Benny decided to take a bite of his second baloney sandwich. If he was unable to finish it, he'd wrap it up and eat it tomorrow. "Hey, Scrap, how did ye decide to git in the band saw business," said Benny as he washed the first bite down with a swig of his RC.

Scrap took a giant quaff of his soda and burped loudly. "I'll be glad to tell ye. If I don't mind sayin' so, it's purty interestin'," he said as he reached in the cooler for a pickle. "It happened some years back."

Many years before the arrival of his new family, Scrap had worked numerous coal fields in Campbell County. Because of his stature, he was too big to work in the labyrinths of deep mines, so he usually worked a bank mule or operated a coal tipple or a Joy loader. Since he had land of his own and a home, he wasn't a prospect for living in a mining camp, and that, along with his unmanageable attitude, didn't set too well with mining authorities. But he came to work every day, and his coworkers could always rely on him to pick up the slack for them or lend them a few precious dollars if he had the wherewithal. He was definitely his own man, and because of his rebellious nature, his tenure at mines like Block, Red Ash, Turley, Pee Wee, and Westbourne was short. He was terminated from his last mining job because of a unique incident. It was on payday on a Friday afternoon. Scrap later remembered it as a day so foggy and dark that "hoot owls were callin'."

"I'm athankin' that you'uns owe me 'bout fifty some dollars," Scrap said as he finally took his place at the head of the long, crooked

line of workers formed in the company store. Company Clerk Arvo McGhee sat regally on his throne behind the pay window and squinted at his register book. He shook his head and frowned in the way he imagined an important man might do.

"I'm afraid not, Hopkins. Yore total earnin's was $50.25, but yore total deductions was $108.90. That means that ye owe us $58.65," he said smugly, tapping his pencil irritably on the desk. "The hell I do!" roared Scrap, causing the murmuring dialogue among the rest of the line of men to cease abruptly. "I worked eighty-four airs, and I wont my money!" he demanded, sending a tremble through the counter and a resounding echo through the store as he slammed his big fist down. Several of the "company men" suddenly appeared behind Arvo, including Scrap's boss, Stone Burress, an imposing figure feared by his workers, but smart enough not to raise the ire of Scrap Hopkins.

Burress scrutinized the register and turned it around for Scrap to read. "That's what's recorded here, Scrap. Read it fer yoreself." "Dammit Stone, ye know I cain't read!" whispered Scrap, but his words were spoken loud enough for everyone to hear. "OK, I'll read it to ye," said Burress. Scrap listened in disbelief along with his coworkers, as in a loud, sermonizing tone, Burress read the list of charges on the account. When he was finished, Burress startled Arvo, slamming the register down on the desk before him. "So thar ye have it, Hopkins. Pay up, or ye kin git issued more scrip to keep ye goin' fer a while. In the meantime cut out yore bawlin' so's we kin git ever'body paid," said Burress. Arvo and the company men stared a hole in Scrap.

Scrap stepped back a foot or two and sighed deeply. He was white as a sheet, and he spoke in angry, measured tones. "What ye got thar on that paper is wrong. I've had four sick young'uns; three with measles and one with the croup so bad we had to put her in the hospital. But I paid the hospital and the doctor and fer the medicine with earnin's from odd jobs I've worked. Ye read on that paper that I owed fer rent and usin' the bath house. I don't live in one of yore shitty little camp houses..." "Maybe ye should," shouted one of the company men, secure in the protection of the pay office. Scrap paid no attention to the barb. "And I worsh at home. I ain't got no overdraft, and I don't owe ye fer nothin'. And ye owe me fer eighty-four airs of machinin' coal. Now hand it over, and I'll put my mark in yore little book signifyin' that ye done the right thang!" said Scrap, stretching out his hand. Burress responded from his bully pulpit with a gravelly chortle, and his sycophants, including Arvo, followed obedient suit. The men in line were somber. "Why don't ye go home to *yore* house and clean up in *yore* bathtub. Ye kin come back tomorry when yore in a bit better frame of mind," said Burress sarcastically, as the remaining line of men braced themselves, expecting all hell to break loose as Scrap went through the wall. Instead he turned on his heels and stomped out of the store.

The last two workers waiting to be paid darted out of the store like scalded dogs when Scrap returned later with a double-barreled shotgun resting in his arm. Burress and the company men scrambled about like Keystone Cops, and Arvo fell off his throne when the barrels of the 12-gauge were shoved through the window. "Hold on thar, boys. Don't ye move another speck, except fer ye, skinny," Scrap said, low and throaty, as Arvo regained his perch. There was silence, then a collective gasp as Scrap cocked one of the triggers.

"I promise ye, this thang ain't filled with rock salt." He directed the barrels at Arvo. "Skinny, I wont ye to roll up fifty dollars and stick it in one barrel of this shotgun. Ye kin keep the twenty-five cents fer yore trouble. If'n ye don't do what I tell ye, I'm agoin' to pay all of you'uns off with both barrels," said Scrap, wagging the weapon at the frightened bunch. "Do what he says," said Burress in a less boisterous voice than usual; then he directed his comments at Scrap. "Hopkins, don't thank ye kin git away with this. Ye've done lost yore job, and the constable will be on ye afore ye know it." None of Burress's flatterers made a gesture in agreement as Arvo shakily rolled up the money and stuffed it in the right barrel opening of the gun. "That's fine with me. I hated this shitty job anyways," said Scrap, snaking the gun out of the pay window and backing quickly out of the store. "Now I gotta git to the house, my house, whar I'm agoin' to take a bath in my tub. Ye tell the constable he kin find me thar. I might even let him scrub my back," said Scrap, his hearty laugh trailing behind as he fired up his truck and sped out of the camp.

Scrap waited, but neither the constable nor Sheriff Bob Dossett came to his house. He was hailed as a hero by his former coworkers who, through no fault of their own, continued to suffer under the boot of the ruthless mining masters. The story of the "shotgun payout" would be told forever. It was also fortuitous for Scrap that he was fired because the mine, like many other mines of the time, soon closed, its seams of coal worn out. His dismissal from the mine hardly put a dent in Scrap and his family's lifestyle. That summer they lived off the cornucopia of Haley June's lush garden, and Scrap finally found a job at a local sawmill that he thoroughly enjoyed. In addition to his job at the mill, Scrap did a lot of "moonlighting."

Scrap and Melvin Cross labored in the deep woods. They were bathed in sweat, spotlighted by a stream of moonlight illuminating the small, leafy clearing. Melvin could hardly be heard above the hum of crickets carried on the cloying summer breeze. "Scrap, ye might wont to stir that corn a little slower; we don't wont to make sodie pop out of it," said Melvin as he hefted a sack of milled corn and sat it next to a tree near the tub. "When do ye thank this stuff will malt?" said Scrap as he wielded the big paddle in the swirl of corn and water. "'Bout five days, then we can git rid of it easy," chuckled Melvin as he bent to sniff the contents of the tub. Melvin had a reason to chuckle. State liquor prices had driven the price of hooch to all-time highs, which enabled him to ask premium prices for his "shine," which folks were more than happy to pay. Another boon to his business was that he'd redesigned his still and was receiving higher yield for his diligence. The still was skillfully made from copper sheeting, molded with a wooden mallet; and the furnace was made from nearby creek stone, which Melvin and Scrap had expertly chinked with clay. They fastened the pieces of the still together with brads. Later Scrap soldered the whole shebang together with tin. They were assured of no leaks between the top and bottom halves of the contraption. Working two jobs and getting little sleep, Scrap lost a lot of weight that summer, but he gained a lot of "jingle" in his pockets. By mid-fall he'd saved enough money to put his plan into action.

Haley June was tending a boiling pot in the yard when Scrap came rolling in.

"Ye look like a witch makin' a brew," said Scrap as he hugged her tightly. "That's right, and when this brew is finished, I'm goin' to turn ye into a big ole warty toad," said Haley June as she picked up a tub and dumped about six pounds of hog grease into the spiraling concoction. "That lye's about dissolved; now it'll begin to git as thick as jelly, and tomorry, it'll be hard, and the girls can hep me cut it into bricks," she said. "That's good. I'm sick of scrubbin' my hind end with a teeny piece of soap," said Scrap as he took off his hat, mopped his brow with his forearm, and followed his nose to the house where the girls were placing a pot roast on the table.

After supper the pair returned to the pot, and Haley June stirred the mixture one more time. "Homer, hep me pour this stuff," she said. Together they dumped the liquid soap into shallow pans to harden. She put her arms around his neck. "Let's go sit on the porch and talk about yore day," she said, placing her tiny hand in his and leading him across the yard to the house. "I'll be right back. I'm gonna hep the girls with the dishes," said Haley June.

Scrap plunked himself down in one of the rockers. He was taking his first drag off a cigarette when Haley June joined him with glasses of iced tea.

"That shore was a good supper, Haley June," said Scrap in the midst of sipping the refreshing beverage. "Ye cain't thank me fer that. The girls did most of the work." "Ye mean Margaret did most of the work. She's jest like ye, honey," said Scrap, blowing a perfect smoke ring in the air. Haley June said nothing, but she was pleased at the comment and a little embarrassed at the flattery. She changed the subject.

"Well, how did it go at work today? Anythang excitin' happen?" "Ye might say it did. I quit," said Scrap, as he crushed the remains of his cigarette beneath his work boot. Haley June said nothing as she rose from her chair and walked to the corner of the porch. Scrap got up slowly and approached her cautiously. He stood a few feet behind her, fearful that she might suddenly take a swing at him "Now, Haley June, don't git all crybaby with me," he said and was glad he'd maintained a distance, because she turned on him like a wildcat. "Crybaby? How in God's name do ye expect me to act when ye do somethin' like this?" she cried, her arms folded across her chest. "Ye got to listen to me, darlin'; it's not as bad as it sounds," pleaded Scrap as he guided her back to the rockers. She sat stiffly, avoiding his eyes as he told his story.

"I got us a job. Ye know Abe Tuttle, the feller that I've been workin' fer at the sawmill up on Davis Creek?" Margaret didn't answer. "Anyways, he's agoin' to shut down in a few months. The old man don't have the stomach fer the work anymore, and his son, Junior, is movin' to Kentucky to work fer his father-in-law. I offered to buy all the equipment from them, but I got to move it off'n the property," he said. He almost gasped for air because of the deluge of words that had spilled out of his mouth without his taking a breath. Haley June's shoulders relaxed a bit, but she was still furious. "Then whar did ye git the money, and whar are ye agoin' to put yore new business?" she demanded. "I've saved about four hunnert dollars, and I'm shore I kin git a loan from the bank. Thar's still a lot of band saw business to be had, even though most of the mines are shuttin' down. "That's all fine and dandy. But whar are ye goin' to put ever'thang?" she demanded. Scrap grinned. "Right here, down thar by that big white oak in the corner of the yard. It's flat down thar and close to the road. Perfect for bringin' logs in to saw," he said. Haley June placed her hands in a prayerful position and rested her chin on them. "Ye wouldn't ever be fer away from me, would ye, Scrap?" she said, a note of positivity in her voice. "Jest hollerin' distance," he said, relieved that she might be coming around to his way of thinking. They sat in silence for a while, and finally, to his great relief, she came to him and sat on his lap. He patted her back as she snuggled her head into his neck and spoke softly. "I could always git a job in town at the shirt factory. They need women who kin sew good, and I can. Besides, the girls are big enough to do chores and git supper ready when they come home from school," she said, sitting up and wiping the tears from her face with a corner of her apron. "Let's hope it don't come to that," said Scrap as he stroked her hair gently. They rocked for a while till Scrap broke the stillness.

"I hope ye and the girls have a lot canned; we're goin' to need it this winter," he said. "I got that covered. And I hope ye don't git tard of beans. Now how about a piece of pie while we still got it," said Haley June as she scooted off his lap.

The sun was high overhead when Scrap finished his tale, and Benny sat mesmerized by the story. "Yore right, Scrap, that's a good story, and it all worked out good fer ye!" he said. Scrap grinned, proud of his accomplishment, as Benny continued. "I shore wished I'd knowed Haley June; she seemed like a good woman." Scrap looked sad but only for an instant. "Ye do know her, Benny. Yore married to the image of her." Benny was moved. "Thank ye, Scrap. I cain't thank of a higher compliment." They didn't talk for a moment, and Benny thought that he noticed a tear in Scrap's eye. Scrap groaned as he hefted himself off the log and looked at Benny with deep concern on his face. "What's a matter, Scrap? Ye all right?" said Benny worriedly. "I was jest wonderin' if ye was goin' to eat the rest of that samwich, son." "Ye kin have it, Scrap. I was full anyway," said Benny, handing the sandwich over to his new and respected mentor.

Chapter 9

BEULAH LAND

"I'm kind of homesick for a country to which I've never been before. No sad good-byes will thar be spoken, and time won't matter anymore."

Margaret sang with passion as she worked, and the wringer washer took on a life of its own as it chugged and swished in cadence with the tune. "Beulah Land, I'm longin' fer ye, and someday on thee I'll stand. Thar my home shall be eternal in Beulah Land, sweet Beulah Land."

Margaret was happier than she could remember. Each day was a new dance in which she stepped lightly in time with the sweet, uncomplicated rhythms of her new life.

Since moving back to Cumberland Mountain, it seemed that her Maker smiled benevolently on her and her loved ones. Benny had a job right across the yard. She had reconnected with her sisters, who visited often but only when Scrap was absent. To her knowledge Scrap hadn't drunk a drop of shine since he'd made such a jackass of himself on that first evening, and Harley and Scrap had developed a deep affection for one another. She and Benny were never in need of a babysitter; as a matter of fact, they often had to challenge Scrap for possession of the tyke, who truly thrived on the attention of all. The child entertained them for hours with his antics, and his vocabulary was increasing by leaps and bounds. He was even attempting to sing a little bit, which delighted everyone. He was the light of their lives.

As Margaret went about her duties on a sun-splashed corner of the front porch, Harley watched her from his front-row seat, a quilt spread out on the ground in the yard. The child turned his attention to his few toys scattered about the surface of the quilt; some blocks carved by Benny, a sock-puppet contributed by one of Margaret's sisters, and a corncob doll fashioned by Scrap.

Harley's eyelids fluttered like the delicate wings of the butterfly that landed briefly on the doll and then floated away on the sweet, springtime zephyr. The buttery warm afternoon sun melted over his neck and shoulders, and the soft breath of the breeze caressed him tenderly, announcing that it was naptime. He was out before he knew what hit him, curled in a prenatal position on his quilt bed.

Harley's dreams naturally did not consist of complicated plots but bright and colorful visions of his most recent discoveries in his small, yet expanding world. His imaginings were mostly of being cradled, smothered with kisses, and spoken to with words slathered in love.

On this day his dreams began with the bluebirds he'd observed checking out the house Benny had built for them and nailed to a dogwood tree. The male, bluer than Harley's eyes, flittered from the peg doorstep of the house and landed on Harley's outstretched hand. The bird cocked its tiny head quizzically from side to side, and Harley mimicked the action as the two studied one another closely. Harley wondered if the creature would taste good and attempted to pop the feathery morsel in his mouth, but the bird flew away.

"That was bad, Harley! Bad!" warbled the ruffled bluebird angrily from his front porch. Before Harley could determine for himself if his actions were bad or not, he heard a thumping noise, and he was kneeling in a bed with bars in a semidarkened room.

"Shaddap, Bobby Ray! Stop it!" came the harsh, muted voice. Harley was frightened of being alone, and he cried for someone to come for him. He stretched out his arms for someone to pick him up, but no one appeared. His cries became desperate, and he was gasping for air when the door opened, flooding the room with brilliant sunshine.

"Baby, baby, baby, what's wrong, honey? Did ye git stung by a bee or somethin'?" cooed Margaret as she lifted him off the blanket, pressing the hysterical child close to her breast, rearranging the curls on his sweaty head, checking him for stings and bites.

Harley clung to her with a ferocity that was precious, yet troubling to Margaret. She sung her baby back to sleep, accompanied by the bluebirds who trilled their delight with their new home.

The boy fell back to sleep quickly, squirming to find a more comfortable position as she sang softly to him. So did the new life in her womb.

Part III

BABY LOVE

Chapter 10

EARLY

The thunderclaps were huge, commanding the little house in the swale to tremble and Margaret's treasured tea set and sparse collection of crockery to chatter defiantly in the cupboard.

There was no relief from the chaos, and as one bombardment rolled seemingly endless through the hollers, a new wave of monstrous claps followed.

Adding to the dissonance were Margaret's banshee screams, Harley's piercing cries, Benny's frail attempts at calming his family, and Scrap's expletives. "Hellfire! Whar is that woman?" yelled Scrap as he peered anxiously out the front door into the inky night.

When Margaret went into labor, Scrap raced up the hill to his house and called Dr. Minford down in LaFollette. "It's rainin' to beat the band down here, and we hear there are mudslides up on the mountain," said the doctor's wife. "Wait a minute," she said as a muffled voice in the background gave her direction.

"Harold says to call Nola Ruggles; she lives near you, doesn't she?"

"Who? Maw? 'Bout a mile up the road. Ye got her number?" Scrap hung up and quickly dialed Nola, known as "Maw" to all of the neighbors. She was an accomplished midwife who'd delivered many of the babies on this side of the mountain for over fifty years. Luckily Scrap got through to her. Maw questioned him about Margaret's condition.

"She warn't due fer two more months. Yep, this un's her first baby. Whut's contraptions mean? Well, git here as soon as ye kin, please. Thank ye...how long do...," said Scrap as the line went dead and the lights went out. He hurried out the door and slipped and slid back down the hill in the pouring rain.

"I called Maw Ruggles, and she said she'd be right here as soon as she finished settin' a broke arm," gasped Scrap as he stumbled into the little house. "That's good, Daddy," said Margaret weakly, producing a wan smile.

Benny said nothing, troubling Scrap with the tortured stare of a wounded animal.

Margaret moaned again, and Scrap left the room, unable to cope with his daughter's agony.

Was this the anguish suffered by Haley June when he wasn't present at the births of his four daughters? Was this the price Margaret should pay for not forsaking his sorry ass?

Scrap checked on Harley in his crib in the corner of the living room. The child was sleeping deeply, unaware that the storm was raging both inside and outside the house.

"Sleep tight, honey. Pappy Scrap is right here," he said, covering the boy with a quilt.

Despite the flashes of lightning that illuminated the yard periodically and the aroma of ozone in the air, Scrap walked out on the front porch and performed a long lost ritual. He prayed.

It had been hours since his conversation with Maw Ruggles was cut short.

Maw Ruggles had weathered many storms in her lifetime, one of the most formidable being her marriage over fifty years ago. Her husband was a natural-born wifebeater and a drunk. One night she sent him packing with nothing but the shirt on his back and a load of rock salt in his backside. She never remarried and was childless, though in her mind every child she delivered was partly hers. She regaled in the euphoria when a healthy child was delivered; and she grieved along with parents and relatives for the stillborn and the weak, who were soon to be cradled in the arms of God. In addition to her prodigious skills in midwifery, Maw was also revered as an herbalist and a powerful medicine woman in the mountain communities.

"This is a real gulley washer," she spoke aloud, maneuvering her ancient truck carefully around a fallen tree. She squinted her failing eyes through sheets of driven rain. "Thank ye, God, fer all this lightnin', otherwise I wouldn't be able to see a dadblamed thang," said Maw, hunkering over the wheel with fierce intensity, a fragile old woman intent on achieving her goal.

She wasn't always fragile. But her commitment to helping give life and dedication to the service of others in this hardscrabble environment had taken its toll. Her mind was as sharp as a tack though, fueled by the wonderful memories of a good life and the joy she brought to the world.

She had traveled this road innumerable times, almost had it memorized. But the memory was being erased by the pelting rain and black-as-black night. Suddenly a white light pierced a hole in the blackness. Maw slammed on the brakes, thinking she might be on the railroad tracks or the distinct possibility that she might be going to meet her Maker.

"Whoa thar, Maw! It's me, Scrap Hopkins," said a booming voice behind the light.

"Git in here, Scrap, afore ye ketch yore death of cold," yelled Maw out of the window. She almost laughed at the soaked and frazzled big man as he squeezed himself into the passenger seat. "Scrap, ye look like ye've been rode hard and put away wet." "I've felt better, Maw," he said, directing her down the branch- and leaf-littered path.

"The house is only a few more yards down the road. Slow down. Turn here," ordered Scrap as Maw wheeled the truck into the yard.

Maw grabbed her little carpet bag and laughed out loud as she hobbled up the steps. "I thought that light ye was holdin' was God fer a minute," she said, bewildering Scrap with the comment.

Maw made her way through the darkened house to the bedroom, which was dimly lit by an oil lantern.

Benny snapped to attention as she nodded sternly in his direction. "What's yore name, boy? Are ye the daddy?" Benny nodded and mumbled his name. "All righty then, Benny, don't jest stand thar lookin' like a hooty-owl. Ye and Scrap make yoreselves useful and git some hot water, clean beddin' and linens, towels, any clean cloth ye got. I will start makin' air little lady here comfortable. Scrap, why don't ye git that chair and that little stool out of the back of my truck and bring 'um in here." Both men rushed to their assignments.

Maw turned her attention to Margaret who had thrashed about in her pain, tangling herself in sweat-drenched sheets. "Hidey, honey. Ye 'member me, don't ye? I'm Maw, and I'm afixin' to hep ye brang yore blessin' into this world." With great effort, Margaret reached out her hand, and Maw took it gently between her own gnarled fingers. "It's nice to see ye, ma'am," Margaret whispered sweetly.

"It's my pleasure, darlin'. I delivered yore maw and, if my memory serves me right, one of yore sisters. Yore very purty, the vision of yore maw," said Maw as she gently untangled the sheets and removed them from the bed. Benny appeared with a fresh bowl of hot water, clean sheets, and some towels.

As Maw gently cleansed Margaret, she plied her with questions about her pregnancy.

"I was told that this was yore first young'un. Who is that little feller in the front room?"

Benny quickly stuck his head in the doorway. "That's my sister's boy. We're keepin' him fer a while," he jabbered and disappeared again.

Maw dried Margaret's body and covered her with a clean sheet.

Scrap came in with the stool and the chair, a straight-backed piece of furniture with arms and a hole cut smack dab in the middle of the seat. "Here ye go," said Scrap, who asked about the design of the chair.

"It's a birthin' chair. That stool is fer me to sit on. We'll see if we need 'em to induce labor," said Maw matter-of-factly. "Oh," said Scrap. "Uh, I'll go hep Benny," he said as he flew out of the room.

Margaret whimpered as another contraction assailed her body.

"God love ye, honey. Yore so tuckered out. I'm goin' to burn some lavender oil to try and relax ye," said Maw, producing the oil and a small oil burner from her bag. "We don't want to be dangerin' yore young'un's life because ye used up all its oxygen, do we?"

As the room filled with the sweet, calming aroma of lavender, Maw performed a cursory examination of Margaret's progress, or lack thereof. "Honey, yore young'un's crownin', but ye've plum wore yoresef out, and yore goin' to need some gravity to hep git it borned," said Maw, cautiously lifting Margaret to a sitting position. "Let's wrap ye up in this sheet, and I'll git Benny to hep us put ye in the birthin' chair. Benny, git yore hooty-owl sef in here and hep us git yore baby borned!"

Benny awakened on the kitchen floor. Scrap was kneeling over him. "Ye all right, boy?"

"What happened?" said Benny, lifting himself upright on his elbows, then wincing as a razor-sharp pain ran through the back of his head. "Ye was heppin' Maw and Margaret born the baby, rubbin' Margaret's back as she pushed, then ye jest fell out like a sack of rocks. Ye must have hit yore head on the bedpost or somethin' 'cause ye've got a knot as big as a goose aig back thar."

Benny felt the back of his head. Scrap wasn't kidding. The knot was as big as a goose egg. Then his fuzzy thoughts turned toward the drama unfolding in the bedroom.

"How's Margaret? Did she have the baby?" said Benny as a vigorous squall filled the tiny home.

"What do ye thank?" grinned Scrap. "We got us a big ole baby boy, Benny!"

Benny hardly had time to think about the good news when Scrap picked him up and squeezed him in a tight bear hug. The new father's feet dangled comically off the floor as Scrap whirled him around the kitchen. Benny was groggy but elated too and hoped his throbbing head wouldn't pop off his shoulders before he had the opportunity to see his child.

Once Maw had cut the umbilical cord and cleaned the mucus from the baby's nose, ears, and mouth, she wrapped the boy in a towel and reluctantly handed him to Benny.

"Now ye hold on to him tight, Hooty. Scrap, help me git Margaret back into bed."

Once that chore was done, she took the baby from Benny. Scrap and Benny followed as she hobbled to the front porch, child at her bosom. Maw lifted the baby skyward. "Oh, Master of the universe, here is yore sweet, blessed child, borned to Margaret and Benny Baird this night. Thank ye fer the miracle of his arrival to this planet. Pertect him and guide him through life withYore precious hand, and give his mommy and daddy the wisdom to pervide him with a lovin' home filled with the love and the words of Jesus. Amen." The men followed timidly, like submissive yard dogs, back to the bedroom, but Maw turned them away at the doorway. "We got more to do here. You'uns git fer a minute."

As Margaret slept soundly, Maw tended to the baby.

"Look at that black har! Ye must be part injun or somethin'," said

Maw as she soaked up the birth residue, washed and rinsed the child, and powdered him. The babe whimpered as she wrapped him in a clean towel, and Margaret awoke from her exhausted slumber. Maw placed the child at Margaret's breast, instructing her on the fundamentals of feeding and bragging on the newborn. "He's a perfect young'un, ten fangers, ten toes, and ever'thang. He shore is a biggun for comin' early."

Margaret's eyes brightened as she drew her son close to her breast.

"Early. That's what I'll name ye," said Margaret, tracing her son's hungry lips with her finger.

As the child began to feed, Benny appeared timidly in the doorway. "You'uns need anythang else?" "Why don't ye wake up little Harley and innerduce him to his cousin," said Maw, with innate wisdom that told her Harley was more than a cousin.

Chapter 11
THE CHURCH OF MAW

As time went on, Margaret and Maw formed an inextricable bond. Maw would visit periodically, babysit the boys, and assist Margaret with the many chores it took to manage a home inhabited by four males. But the most rewarding times were those when Margaret escaped for a while with the boys in tow and visited Maw. Early was content to sit on the kitchen floor and play with pot and pan lids as Margaret and Maw collaborated on a number of tasks, such as canning, and discussions of the plethora of folk remedies residing in Maw's expansive memory and pantry.

Maw's house was perched nicely on a hillside with a sweeping view of the yard and gardens below. As they visited, the women kept Harley in sight as he played in the yard and swung on the swing under the shady arbor at the foot of the garden. Occasionally he would make himself useful by watering the plants from several of the watering cans Maw had left by the garden for his convenience. The watering usually didn't last too long as Harley, bored with the task, made himself a mudhole in which to wallow.

"Let's go set on the porch," said Maw, after they'd put the boys down for a nap. It was raining steadily, beating a tattoo on the tin roof. The slight breeze rattled the chandelier of gourds she had hung on the porch roof beam. The women sat on the settin' chairs, with the rear posts bending backwards from the woven seats. The chairs were extremely comfortable, even though the frayed seats had been reseated more times than could be counted. The rain increased, and the breeze, inspired by the downpour, was refreshing.

"Ain't this nice? It's jest like church," said Maw, taking a deep breath. "Well, it ain't like my church. It's usually hotter'n a poker in thar, winter and summer," laughed Margaret, breathing deeply of the fresh-washed mountain air. The rain came harder, the drumming on the roof drowning out any attempts at conversation. When the downpour slackened a bit, Margaret offered an invitation.

"Ye know, Maw, yore welcome to come to church with us sometime. Do ye go to church somewhars?"

"I go to the Church of Maw," laughed Maw. "What do ye mean?" "'Zactly what I said. I believe church is right here," she said, thumping her chest above her heart. "I believe a piece of God is in us, and it was put thar in ever'one of us by the universe, which we're a part of. I believe that we are all borned knowin' right from wrong 'cause we are God." Margaret stared at her friend in disbelief, the word "blasphemy" ringing in her head as her fundamentalist doctrine was challenged. Finally she found her voice. "Maw, how kin ye say that we're God? The Bible don't tell us that." "Yes, it does. I figger I've read the Bible through and through 'bout four times. And I'm not shore I believe what common mortals writ about Jesus six hundred yars atter his death. But I do believe in Jesus, his words, and the words of some of his disciples, 'specially John. They tell us tharselves that God is in us and that we should thank like we're God 'cause we are godly. They tell us that air spirits are ferever. And we're here on this earth in our human body to serve others. And that's what I believe."

"Lordy, I don't know," said Margaret, gulping down her chamomile tea, glancing surreptitiously at the gray sky for lightning to disintegrate the porch at any moment. Maw cackled. "Don't ye fret 'bout it, honey. Thar's lots of folks in these hills who jedge me 'cause I don't believe the way they do, but I don't let it bother me. Thar entitled to make thar path to heaven as well as I am and ye are, as long as we don't stray from the meaning of this universe." "What's that?" "Love, love, like I love ye and those two babies in thar sleepin'," said Maw as she stood and hugged Margaret's neck. Margaret relished the affection; but she wasn't sure she believed totally in Maw's philosophy.

It was true that some folks shunned Maw, labeling her "one of the lost" because her beliefs didn't jell with their religious dogma. But most forgot about those differences when they were made miserable with an ailment. Some days and evenings there was a steady stream of patients flowing into Maw's "church," parishioners with a wide array of complaints. When she could Margaret helped out, grinding herbs with a mortar and pestle, mixing pastes for poultices, steeping teas comprised of leaves and roots.

Spring and summer were the busiest times for Maw, when the men were out in the logging woods, children were romping in the fields, and women were elbow deep in their gardens. Bites and infections from injuries were rampant. Many of the victims would try remedies passed down through their ancestors, but scores of the remedies failed because of their roots in superstition: placing a handful of salt on a head to ease a headache; putting an ax under the bed to cut the pain; and for a toothache, rubbing a splinter around the gum until it drew blood and driving the splinter into a tree. "All that's hogworsh," Maw told them as she applied tried-and-true remedies for their afflictions. And their afflictions were plentiful: toothaches, for which she used a tincture of sassafras root steeped in moonshine (a payment for successfully treating one of her patrons), boils, spider bites, snake bites, cuts, colic, diarrhea, gout, arthritis, gallbladder problems, dandruff. Maw had the prescription for just about every ailment known to man and many animals.

Sometimes her patients suffered from nothing but hunger, and she would feed them from her food pantry, which was always full. And one would wonder how she enjoyed such plenty, especially when she asked nothing for her services. But she was paid in full when folks reciprocated by plowing her garden every spring, replacing shingles on her roof or a board on her barn, chopping wood, or providing her with an occasional bag of cornmeal, chickens, milk, ginseng, and the roots and herbs she was unable to acquire.

"It's the way of the world. It's the way thangs is s'posed to be," said the rector of the "Church of Maw." And according to the laws of the universe, she was undeniably a godly woman.

Chapter 12

SISSY

There was a great hiatus before Margaret gave birth to another child, seven years and several miscarriages since the stormy night that Early was born. During this time, in a gesture of love and generosity, Scrap insisted that he trade houses with his family. "It's a lot bigger than yourn, and besides, mine's got extry bedrooms and indoor plumbin'. I ain't too proud to use an outhouse."

Margaret gave birth in the big house, and Maw oversaw this delivery also. The event was the antithesis of Early's frenzied arrival into this world. Cecilia Margaret announced her mother's easy delivery with a healthy squall that spelled relief for everyone, especially "Hooty" and Scrap. Harley and Early were delighted with their little sister too, bickering with each other for the opportunity to hold her. When it came his turn, Early seriously examined the newborn's features. Then he touched her lightly with his chubby hand and brushed her thick hair back from her temple. He smiled sweetly at the baby and spoke in his soft way. "I love ye, Sissy," he whispered, cradling her as if she were his own. From that point Cecilia was "Sissy" to her family and most everyone else. She was practically worshipped by members of her immediate family. From the moment she could talk, the precocious child assumed that it was her responsibility to look after everyone. She would often parade up and down the porch, issuing orders to the men and boys operating the saw and performing chores around the yard; "Harwey, put on yore shirt, ye git sunburn! Pappy, ye quit spittin' bakker juice aw over! Earwy, be keerful with them aigs! Daddy, yore fangers too close to that saw!" she would command, unaware that she was imitating her mother. Everyone would laugh but respected her self-proclaimed authority.

One day, as she was instructing Benny from her command post, she worked herself into a frenzy and fell off the porch, hitting her head on the well-pump handle. Benny witnessed the accident and rushed to find her covered in blood, a deep gash over her left eye. "Marg, git some clean towels; Sissy's been hurt," he said as he ran cold water on his daughter's forehead. "Wake up, Sissy, wake up," he yelled frantically, lifting her seemingly lifeless body in his arms. "Git in the truck, Marg; we got to take her to the hospital." Margaret complied, running to the truck and waiting with arms outstretched to receive her severely injured child. Benny drove like a demon, and Scrap, Early, and Harley wondered what was going on as they paused from their labor on the hillside tobacco patch. They figured out the scenario quickly though, when they saw the pool of blood by the pump.

Later the family sat huddled in a corner of LaFollette Community Hospital, waiting for news of Sissy's fate. Victims of auto, mining, and farm accidents and a fistfight also waited their turns to be seen. The family stood as one when the doctor who was treating their girl approached them.

"She's got a severe concussion…" "What's that?" Scrap asked. "It's a mild brain injury, Mr. Hopkins. But she's going to be all right. We'd like to keep her in the hospital overnight for observation." Again Scrap interrupted. "I don't thank so, doctor. We kin take keer of her at home." Frustrated, the doctor tried to reason with him. "Mr. Hopkins, I'm sure that your family will agree that it's best that we observe her here. Besides, she also has a deep cut in her forehead that needs looking after." "He's right, Scrap. We should let her stay here tonight," said Benny. The boys and Margaret nodded their heads in agreement, and Scrap relented. "Well, when kin we see her?" Scrap asked, unable to conceal his deep concern.

"She's awake now and a little antsy, but we've given her something for pain, so you can see her in about thirty minutes. I'll send someone to get you," said the doctor, who turned on his heels to attend to another emergency.

Later, when a nurse guided them to the pediatric ward, Margaret was stoic, but her menfolk were a mess when they viewed their Sissy lying in the hospital bed with her head swathed in bandages, curls sticking out of the wrapping like a turnip top.

Sissy cried when she saw them but only for a moment. "Momma and Pappy and Daddy and yore brothers are here, honey. Yore goin' to be all right, ain't she, fellers?" said Margaret, stroking the little girl's arm. "That's right," said Benny, "We're goin' to git ye out of here tomorry, and the first thang I'm goin' to do is buy ye some of that candy ye like. Ye know, those little wax bottles with juice in 'em. What do ye say to that, littleun?" She smiled a drawn smile in answer. Then she glanced sternly at the foot of the bed where Benny, Scrap, and Harley stood like mourners at a funeral and wagged her index finger at them. "You'uns stop at frettin', or I whoop yore tails." At that comment they were assuaged that Sissy would be all right. But she wasn't all right. The gash above her left eye was horrendous, marring her perfect beauty. In addition the doctor, or whoever stitched the wound, must have had something else on their mind that day because the job was performed sloppily.

When Sissy returned home, Maw applied various remedies to assist her healing and make the child more comfortable. "Here's some willer bark tea fer yore headache, darlin'; it's a lot more easy on yore belly than aspern," comforted Maw as she forced the bitter drink, sip by sip, into the youngster's mouth. Eventually the headaches went away, but Sissy's wound was a different story. She experienced several infections, which were tended successfully by Maw. But once the stitches were gone and the scab healed over, the scar remained an ugly, jagged red line, directly above her left eyebrow. Maw treated this with lemon balm and a mixture of bergamot, chamomile, geranium, lavender, and other essential oils. Sadly, when healed, the scar remained prominent. As she got older, the scar faded gradually but not enough to keep her classmates from poking fun at her. The derision came to a quick halt though when Harley threatened to thrash some of them. Because of the scorn, Sissy became shy and withdrawn in public and had her mother cut her hair with exceptionally long bangs that overhung her forehead, covering the scar. However, she was the same delightfully bossy mother hen on the home front.

Part IV

CRIMINAL BEHAVIOR

Chapter 13

A WOMAN SCORNED

Treva couldn't believe that Lonnie had the audacity to move around town and country without the slightest fear of being caught. It had been several months since he and a con named Willie had escaped from Rock Quarry Prison in Georgia. They had driven a laundry truck right through the front gate. Willie went his way, and as usual Treva had been there to chauffeur Lonnie to wherever he wanted to go. Much to her chagrin, he wanted to return to Knoxville, where he had friends to put them up. This time their refuge turned out to be a ramshackle farmhouse on the outskirts of Knoxville. During the daylight hours, the couple maintained a low profile. But when darkness fell, they went honky-tonking at numerous bars around town. Everyone knew Lonnie, and he was hailed as a hero by patrons in every dive they visited. "Hey, Lonnie, let me buy you and your lady a beer" was the phrase heard often, and Lonnie always tried to please his admirers.

He had chosen to move in the daylight this day, to meet some friends who might have a job for him. "Lonnie, this is right downtown. Are you sure this is a smart thing to do?" said Treva as she pulled to the curb on Gay Street. "Nobody goes to bars during the day, Treva, and besides, it's only going to be for a little while. I'll give you a call, and you can come back and get me."

"All the way from the house?" she complained. "Just go back, and I'll call you. These boys have a big plan and want to make me a part of it. When you pick me up, I'll take you out to dinner; maybe we'll go to Regas," said Lonnie. Even the thought of going to a fancy restaurant didn't curb Treva's suspicion of what was transpiring. "Well, I don't like it." "Just behave, Treva. I promise, this will be a good day and an even better night," he said, giving her a big smooch on the lips. "If I don't call in a couple of hours, I'll call you later," he said as he slid across the seat and hopped out of the car. He never looked back as he walked briskly down a side street toward his destination.

Treva decided to hang around a bit, just for curiosity's sake.

Her suspicions were correct. Lonnie had become stir-crazy cooped up in the little house. Treva was getting on his last nerve, and his craving for "extra companionship" was escalating. In a normal relationship, he would have told his companion that he needed some time to himself, but being a congenital liar and fearful of Treva's response to the truth, he lied about the meeting.

Sisters Kathy and Charlotte Queener couldn't believe their luck. They'd stopped in the bar to cash paychecks from their third-shift jobs at the knitting mill when they were accosted by the good-looking man in the gray flannel suit and expensive tweed coat. His name was "L.C." He carried a sizable wad of cash and insisted that the sisters tuck their meager earnings away. This afternoon was "on him." What the hell? They didn't have to be at work for hours; they had plenty of time to sober up if need be.

After several beers the trio moved to a booth, where L.C., loose-tongued from the brew, brashly confided that he'd been on the lam for nearly two months after escaping from Rock Quarry Prison. "You ever heard of Lonnie Cavanaugh?" he said, glancing slyly around the room. The sisters nearly spoke in unison. "Who in East Tennessee hasn't heard of him?" "Well, I'm him," grinned Lonnie as Kathy squealed and Charlotte covered her mouth. Lonnie chugged his beer. "You all got a car? Some people were supposed to meet me here, but it looks like they're not going to show up. Maybe we can go for a ride or something until my other ride picks me up." "I've got my car waitin' outside with a full tank of gas; let's go!" said Charlotte who, along with her sister, could not believe she was in the company of greatness. "Where are we goin'?" asked Kathy as she slipped out of the booth. "Let's go to the Pit Stop. It won't be too busy there this time of day," replied Charlotte, visions of a high time forming in her mind. The trio laughed like old friends as they left the tavern, and bartender Arnold McCluskey, desperately needing the business and the company, was sad to see them go. Treva was not laughing though as she saw them enter the Olds.

Arnold was startled as the door flew open. The door stuck on the carpet, allowing bright daylight to infiltrate the semidarkened tavern. "You want to close that door, lady? You're ruinin' the atmosphere," he said. Treva paid no heed to his request and sat at the bar. "What atmosphere? Close it yourself, but before you do that, get me a beer," she demanded, and Arnold obeyed. She downed the beer in the time it took him to close the door and return. "Give me another," she said, tapping her bottle on the bar top. "Another beer?" asked Arnold as he slid the cooler top back. "Yeah, another beer, dumbass." "I don't like that kind of talk, lady." "Excuse me. I'm kind of pissed right now. What's your name?" she asked, pushing a five-dollar bill his way and murmuring, "Keep the change." "Arnold," he said, delighted with the five dollars, probably the only money he would receive for the rest of the afternoon. "Arnold, I'm lookin' for a guy. He's about six one, six two, good-lookin', and dressed real nice. Have you seen him?" "You betcha. He left here about ten minutes ago with two...uh, two people." "You know where they went?" "I heard 'em say they was goin' to the Pit Stop out on Chapman Highway." Treva knew the location from her younger days. She shoved another five dollars at Arnold. "Give me another round, Arnold. Give me change for the jukebox and the phone booth, and keep the rest." Arnold happily complied. Treva scooped the handful of change off the bar, slid off the barstool, and made a beeline for the gaily lit jukebox.

It was dinnertime, and the woman already sounded a little tipsy. It was also obvious from the background noise that she was calling from some honky-tonk. Sheriff Ruford Boling held the phone away from his ear as "Volare" bellowed from the jukebox. "Wait a minute," slurred the caller; then the noise was muted as the squeaky phone booth door closed. There was a slight rustling, and she was back. "Anyway, as I was sayin', if you still want Lonnie Cavanaugh, I know where he is."

Boling had received a lot of tips regarding Lonnie Cavanaugh's whereabouts lately, all of them false. He answered calmly, in a bored monotone, "OK, ma'am, who am I speaking with?" The woman's voice level increased to a hysterical screech. "Who is this? Who is this? I'll tell you who it is! You're speakin' to nobody! At least that's who I am as far as Lonnie Cavanaugh is concerned!" Boling sat upright, interest suddenly peaked. A woman scorned? This could be a good one. He waited patiently for the woman to compose herself, then he continued. "I'm sorry you're upset, ma'am, uh, how do you know where he is?" "'Cause some sluts picked him up, and they're with him now." "Where are they, ma'am?" said Boling, putting pencil to a piece of scrap paper. "How in the hell should I know? But I know where he'll be later." "Where's that?" "Stay by the phone. It'll be about three or four hours from now. When he's there, I'll call you with the address," she said. "Did you get the name of the women who picked him up?" "What the hell difference does that make?" "It's just for the record, ma'am." "When you see him, give Lonnie a big ole hug from me, will ya?" said Treva as she hung up the phone. Boling made a few phone calls, including a couple to the FBI, and settled back in his chair for the long wait. One thing he knew for sure; he was eager to accommodate the scorned woman, to give Lonnie Cavanaugh a "big ole hug", to embrace him tightly in the strong arms of the law.

Treva powered down another beer and, before she left, asked Arnold for a favor.

"Hey, Arnie, you got somethin' I can bang on my carburetor with? It gets stuck every once in a while, and I have to take a hammer to it." Arnold pulled a short billy club from beneath the counter. "I ain't got a hammer, but this club might work. It's got lead in the tip." She leaned across the bar and snatched the club from his hands. "I'll bring it right back. Appreciate you, buddy," she said as she hurried toward the door.

Kathy, Charlotte, and Lonnie sat parked in the beat up sedan in a far corner of the Pit Stop Drive-in parking lot. They'd been there for some time, drinking beer, smoking, and telling stories, while the girls alternately necked heavily with Lonnie. That's why the windows were steamed up. And it was why they didn't notice Treva's car as it idled slowly through the parking lot. Although Lonnie was a pretty good kisser, Charlotte was glad he was having his turn with Kathy. The beer was wreaking havoc on her bladder, and she had to go to the little girl's room. She was scooting across the backseat when suddenly, the driver's door opened, and Lonnie, who was sitting behind the wheel, was pulled from the vehicle. "Meetin' with friends, huh?" said Treva, threatening him with the club. Lonnie tried to make an excuse. "Honest, Treva, I was just..." She waggled the club at him again. "Get in our car. I'll be with you in just a minute," she said, climbing into the front seat and closing the door behind her.

Kathy cringed in the passenger seat and had no time to defend herself as Treva knocked her out with a fierce blow to the temple.

Charlotte, frozen in horror, screamed in the backseat. "Shut up and take your medicine," said Treva as she slithered over the seat like a weasel in a hen house. "Don't hit me, please! We didn't know he was married!" screamed Charlotte. "Evidently he don't know it either," said Treva as she straddled the woman and delivered brutal blows to her head and body.

Lonnie sat in the passenger seat of their car, hanging his head like a truant schoolboy, when Treva hopped into the driver's seat. Oddly she seemed happy. "Let's go home, loverboy, so you can clean all that stink off of you," she said, starting the engine and backing out of the Pit Stop.

Billy Duncan, manager of the Pit Stop, noticed the car speeding away as he and several employees came out to determine the source of the commotion. "Always somebody makin' trouble," he said as he pecked on the passenger side window of Charlotte's car. When there was no answer, he opened the back passenger door and gasped at the ghastly scene before him. "Somebody call the cops! Call an ambulance first!" he said as Charlotte's bloody arm flopped out of the passenger door.

"What did you do to those two girls?" Lonnie finally had the courage to ask. Treva grinned as she turned into the yard of the little house. "Just gave 'em a couple of bumps and bruises. They won't try to screw you or anyone else for a while, maybe never," she said as she hurriedly got out of the car. "Whew, it's starting to get cold; let's get in the house," she said as she beat him to the door. Lonnie followed, perplexed and wary of her calm, almost cheery attitude.

She was taking her clothes off as he entered the home. "You want to do the wild thing before I take a shower?" "No thanks, Treva, I'm not in to it tonight." "I guess not; those two hussies wore you out, didn't they?" Lonnie didn't reply; he was afraid it might set her off again. She started up the stairs. "I'm going to take a shower. Maybe that will help change your mind later," she said as the bathroom door closed.

Later, as Lonnie showered, she went to the kitchen wall phone and dialed the number she had secreted on a piece of paper in her robe pocket. The phone rang many times before someone answered.

"Ruford Boling, what can I do for you?" "Is this the man I talked to earlier this afternoon about Lonnie Cavanaugh?" "Sure is, ma'am." "Listen up. He'll be at this address tomorrow morning. Dawn would be a good time to come get him." Boling hastily scribbled the house number on a tablet. "How do I know I can trust you?" She laughed in a low tone. "You don't know. See you at dawn, honey," and she hung up. Since Cavanaugh was wanted on federal charges, Boling made another call to the FBI, and together they set their plan into action. Back in the house, still excited from her sadistic encounter with the Queener sisters, Treva made her own plans for a night of wild lovemaking with Lonnie. It would be their last time for a long while.

The fog was soupy thick as the two cars sped down the pike. As they were passing through the sleepy little burg of Maloneyville, the lead car, a Knox County Sheriff's vehicle, slid catawampus on black ice and, after a few fishtails, straightened itself. Despite the conditions, the drivers did not lessen their speed as they continued their journey.

It was about 6:15 a.m. Sunday morning, and the low sky was a wintry shade of pewter when the small caravan turned onto the side road. They doused their headlights as they made a right onto the gravel lane leading up to the place. After about a fifth of a mile, the automobiles pulled off to the side of the lane, coasting to a halt on a hoarfrost-blanketed hill overlooking the home. Four men, appearing sinister in their long, dark trench coats, exited one of the automobiles quietly and walked to the trunk of the car where they retrieved their weapons.

The two policemen joined them, and as the group surveyed the white frame, two-story farmhouse below, a lean hound came scrambling up the hill at a dead run, baying for all he was worth. Having anticipated this occurrence, agent Haynes hastily reopened the trunk and grabbed the sack of bloody steak bones. Squatting on his haunches, he pulled a meaty tidbit from the sack and offered it to the hound as it approached warily.

Momentarily placated, the yard dog hunkered down with its prize, gnawing noisily on the bones. One of the trench-coated men, Arvil Gardner, turned to Ruford Boling and whispered, “Chief, have your deputies keep that mutt occupied. We’ll yell if we need you.” Then several of the FBI agents moved stealthily toward the house, wincing as their galoshes crunched noisily on the frozen grass. They hurried, for it was only a matter of time before someone would mosey out to the porch to investigate the racket.

Lonnie had just gotten up to relieve himself when he heard the dog bark, as agents Haynes and Swann skirted the house and posted themselves at prominent vantage points behind the toolshed at the rear of the place. The two agents slinked to either side of the porch and, via a prearranged signal from Gardner, moved toward the steps, shotguns at the ready.

At the top of the hill, Agent Gardner exhaled deeply, his breath pluming heavily in the frosty morning air. “Greg, there are two more shotguns in the trunk; issue them to the deputies, and let’s take this punk down.”

Ringed blood red from the first reflections of the sun, which was rising quickly over the crests of the distant Smokies, the dark, menacing clouds resembled smoldering coals. Gardner rechecked his weapon and did a quick mental recap of the facts he’d learned about

Cavanaugh during the investigation. Other than knocking out a guard in the Georgia escape, the man had never committed an act of physical violence. But the veteran agent wasn't about to throw caution to the wind. He also knew that nobody loved their freedom more than Cavanaugh, and a man desperate for freedom was liable to do anything to preserve it. He cocked an eyebrow as he queried his partner. "You ready, Greg?" "Ready as I'll ever be," said Agent Hughes, exhaling a cloud of smoke and flicking a just-lit cigarette in the wet grass, where it sizzled. They walked shoulder to shoulder down the hillside.

Lonnie stood at the window weighing his options, which were few. He should have run, should have run out the back door when he first heard the warning bark of the dog. True, he wasn't a spring chicken. He was thirty-two going on thirty-three, and he'd put on a few extra pounds during his recent two months of glorious freedom. But he could still run pretty fast. Now, as he gazed wistfully out the upstairs window, he envisioned himself racing, darting like a fleet jackrabbit over the dun-colored fields beyond.

"Dammit, get up, Treva," whispered Lonnie as he quickly donned his clothing. Treva, semicomatose from her night of heavy drinking, groaned and pulled the covers over her head. Lonnie crossed the room, which was lit eerily by the pinkish, ambient light from the one small window. He tried to awaken Treva again but without success. He returned to the window, watching the light flow from gradients of pink and lavender to sudden, shimmering gold as the morning sun peeped over the barn roof. He watched too, dismayed, as a shard of sunlight ricocheted off a gun barrel at the corner of the toolshed. He shook his head regretfully as "shoulda run, shoulda run" bounced around in his brain.

He managed to awaken Treva, who knew what was going on. She was pulling a sweater over her head when heavy footsteps sounded on the front porch. Lonnie reached in his coat pocket and withdrew a .38 caliber, nickel-plated pistol. He knelt, lifted the furnace grate, and placed the weapon on a narrow ledge. Replacing the grate, he stood and wrapped Treva in his arms. "If they don't find the gun, you come back and get it if you ever need it, do you understand?" he whispered in her ear. She nodded, quivering with fright, flinching as the front door opened. As a rush of frigid air flooded the stairwell and surged into the little bedroom, Lonnie kissed her deeply. "It's going to be all right, darlin'," he said. As he led her to the landing, they were startled once more by a loud crash.

Stealth was part of the plan as Gardner and Hughes entered the home. But a herd of cattle could have slipped in more quietly. No sense in trying to surprise anybody; the house was old, cold, and every board creaked and groaned with each step. To make matters worse, Hughes tripped over a shoe as he crossed the darkened living room and fell, flattening the coffee table. Embarrassed, he quickly lifted himself from the floor and limped to the corner of the room, giving Gardner a weak "high sign" as he leveled his shotgun at the stairwell.

Gardner's prayer of thanks that Hughes's weapon had not discharged was interrupted when a man's voice called down the stairs. "Everybody all right down there?" the voice asked, chuckling. Hughes braced himself in the corner as Gardner answered. "Lonnie Cavanaugh?" he yelled from his position in the kitchen doorway. "That's me" was the reply from the top of the stairs. "Lonnie Cavanaugh, this is Agent Gardner of the FBI. We have a warrant for your arrest, charging unlawful flight to avoid confinement, escape from a penal institution, and suspicion of bank robbery. Come down with your hands in the air." There was silence, except for the labored whisper of the aged oil furnace and the soft crying of a woman. The man's voice came again. "It's just me and my wife. We have no weapons. I'm coming down peaceably." Silence again. Finally footsteps from upstairs, then on the landing, a pair of highly polished wing tips appeared.

He waltzed down the staircase smiling as if he were welcoming long-lost friends. His wife, pale, trembling, hands in the air, followed close behind him. Gardner noticed immediately that Lonnie Cavanaugh was good-looking, better looking than his prison photos for sure. He was impeccably dressed, tall, wavy-haired, with a confident smile that Gardner thought could be disarming, even to hardened officers of the law. As he reached the bottom stair, the fugitive shot a glance at the demolished coffee table, then at Agent Hughes. “Y’all right, buddy?” he asked with mock concern. His warm eyes crinkled mischievously, and he smiled kindly, even as Hughes shoved him roughly against the wall and handcuffed him. As Lonnie was frisked, agents Haynes and Swann appeared and ordered Treva to take a seat on the couch. “She’s innocent. I made her help me,” said Lonnie over his shoulder. “Shut your piehole,” ordered Hughes.

The sun was bright now, the frost rapidly melting. The high, wet grass sopped their trouser legs as Gardner, Haynes, Hughes, and Swann led their prisoners up the hillside. When the group crested the top, Lonnie turned to the agents. “Could I see my wife one more time before we go?” he asked. “Sorry, we’ve got to get going, Lonnie,” answered Gardner brusquely, chastising himself for addressing the prisoner by his first name. Lonnie nodded, watching dejectedly as the sheriff’s car spirited Treva away. Then he grinned as he made another request. “So do you think I could get a voucher for the price of that coffee table?” All of the agents laughed aloud, even Greg Hughes.

Chapter 14

HOT DAY ON MARKET STREET

More than a few heads turned as the attractive blonde, fashionably dressed in a blue skirt, white summer blouse, hose and heels, flounced down Market Street. Oddly enough, despite the soaring mercury, Treva was also wearing a light sweater draped over her shoulders.

It was hard to believe that nearly two months had passed since that fateful afternoon, when in a fit of jealous rage, she had reported Lonnie's whereabouts to the authorities. Now here it was mid-May, and the temperature was in the high 80s, unusual for springtime in East Tennessee. The sun was high now, reflecting fiery white in her windshield as she approached the Ford. She reached for the door handle, which was griddle-hot, and cried out, jerking her hand back. Using her sweater sleeve potholder fashion, she grasped the handle cautiously and entered the automobile.

Treva inserted the key in the ignition and gunned the engine. She turned on the air conditioning. As the cool air gradually inundated the interior of the automobile, she leaned her head back on the seat and closed her eyes. The hum of the idling engine and the fan whisper from the air conditioning unit effectively hushed the outside noise, and her throbbing headache subsided by degrees as the encroaching coolness gently caressed her body. She was nervously envisioning her task when the bell from the First Baptist Church on Main Street rang one sonorous note, the muted gong penetrating the metal walls of her safe haven, signaling that it was time for the last visit. With gargantuan effort, she raised her head from the seatback. As her headache was reborn, she wearily massaged her temples. She sighed heavily as she reached in the glove box and withdrew the gun.

She got out of the car and adjusted her sweater in an effort to cloak the pistol she'd concealed in her oversized bra. It was hot, god-awful hot, as she headed down Market Street in the direction of the Knox County Jail. However, Treva Cavanaugh was chilled to the bone, the .38 caliber, nickel-plated pistol burning icy-cold against her bosom.

Lonnie reached through the bars and hugged his nearly hysterical wife. "Everything is OK, honey; it won't be long before they allow visitation at Reidsville," he said. Her shoulders convulsed violently as he consoled her, and her sweater tumbled to the floor. Turnkey Sam Barnes observed the couple from a discreet distance while the guard, John Cooley, embarrassed by the whole situation, pretended to sort mail at the desk by the door. Barnes and Cooley knew they were breaking the rules by allowing contact between the prisoner and his wife. All of Lonnie Cavanaugh's visitors were supposed to be flanked by two guards and stand against the wall opposite the cell. But hell, this was her last visit. The Georgia prison officials were supposed to come for him tomorrow, and it could be a long time before she would see her husband again. Barnes walked quickly across the room, scooped up the garment, and returned it to the shaken woman. "Here you are, Miz Cavanaugh," he said chivalrously. "You dropped your sweater." She turned, dabbing at her eyes. "Thank you, Mr. Barnes," she replied graciously, allowing him to wrap the sweater around her thin shoulders. He murmured a shy "You're welcome" and back-walked awkwardly to his post. The couple embraced once more; then she left abruptly. "I'll see you soon, Lonnie," Treva spoke tremulously, never looking back as Cooley ushered her out the door.

Barnes continued to observe as the prisoner flopped disconsolately on his bunk, shoulders slumped, back to the bars. He was going to miss Lonnie. He'd taken a liking to the boy from the very beginning. How could you not like him? Always joking, polite, clean; never heard him cuss, not once. He'd also miss the visits by pretty Treva and Paulette, Lonnie's mother. He chuckled to himself. What a character! What a cook! His mouth watered when he remembered the delicious victuals she'd cooked up for Lonnie over the past two months, and there was always plenty extra for him and John. His thoughts were interrupted as Cooley reentered the room.

They were reviewing the duty roster when Lonnie called softly, "Hey, John, Sam?" Cooley set the clipboard on the desk and walked over to the cell. "Whatcha' need, buddy?" he inquired, eager to address the request for he had a liking for Lonnie also. "Do you suppose I could get a shower?" Lonnie asked. Cooley tipped his hat and scratched his head. "Damn, Lonnie, you just had one a few hours ago." Lonnie grinned sheepishly, raising his arms to show huge wet spots. "I know, but this has been a rough morning, and I've been kind of nervous, you know?" "Well, I don't suppose it'd hurt anything. Besides, those Georgia boys will be here real early tomorrow morning, and you might not have time to take a shower," said Cooley, resituating his hat on his forehead. "Not that your being stinky makes a difference to them. Those crackers probably haven't had a bath in months," quipped Barnes as he sauntered over with the keys. The three had a good laugh at the expense of the Georgia Department of Corrections as Sam opened the cell door.

Lonnie exited the cell shirtless, towel and soap in hand. Then Cooley led the way to the elevator, his back to the prisoner. He rambled on good-naturedly, but his chatter was cut short when he heard Barnes yell, "Hellfire, Lonnie!" When he whirled around, he saw to his consternation the towel and soap on the floor and Lonnie, pale as a sheet, pressing the gun to Barnes's head. "Hold it right there, John!

Don't make a move, boys. I'm desperate, and I'll kill you if I have to," Lonnie cautioned as he snatched the keys from Barnes and prepared to shove him in the cell. "Throw me that shirt, Sam. Now get over here, John and into the cell with your buddy!" Hands in the air, Cooley trotted to the cell entrance where Lonnie nudged him inside, slamming the door with a resounding click. Barnes sat on the bunk with his head in his hands as Cooley stood at the cell door. "Lonnie, think about what you're doin', son," he pleaded, grasping the bars in a white-knuckle grip. Lonnie tucked the pistol in his waistband. "I've been thinking about it for over two months, John, and I've come to the conclusion that I'd rather die than go back to Georgia," he said, pocketing the keys. Barnes stood up quickly. "Uh, Lonnie, do me a favor, will ya'? Why don't you leave the keys on the desk? It's the only set we have." Cooley jerked his head toward Barnes. "Are you shittin' me?" he asked incredulously, as Lonnie donned his shirt and sprinted for the elevator laughing.

One eye shut completely, the other at half-mast, Claude Rainwater was digesting one of his wife's scrumptious meat loaf sandwiches, verging on full doze when the jangling bell rudely jolted him back to consciousness. "Brrang, brrang, brrang." The bell rang three more times as Claude strolled to the elevator. "Hold your horses, you dadblamed idjits," he muttered under his breath as he entered the cubicle and slid the door shut. He burped and yawned widely as the rickety lift rattled and clanked in its ponderous ascent from the basement to the fourth floor of the Knox County Jail.

Claude was wide awake now and pretty pissed. The bell sounded a least ten more times during the tedious climb, echoing harshly throughout the shaft and his nervous system. "Brrang." The bell rang again, and Claude leaned hard on the lever, as if the extra pressure could make the car go faster. By God, he was going to give Cooley and Barnes a piece of his mind when he arrived.

The elevator groaned to a halt, then bounced twice as Claude jogged the car even with the fourth floor ledge. He'd begun castigating Cooley and Barnes before the door was half opened. "What in the dadblamed hell are you in such a hurry for...Lordy mercy!" he exclaimed as he stared down the bore of the .38.

Claude immediately threw his hands in the air as Lonnie bounded into the elevator. "I'll kill you if you make a move," Lonnie threatened, advancing malevolently toward the startled operator. From down the hall, Barnes's voice pleaded from the cell. "Claude, ask him to leave the keys!" "Shut up, Sam!" Lonnie shouted over his shoulder. He wagged the gun in front of Claude's nose. "Take me to the basement. Is there anyone down there?" "No, nope," said Claude, hand quivering as he closed the door. Lonnie backed off a few steps, leaning against the wall. His arm remained outstretched, unwavering as he continued to draw a bead on Claude's head with the pistol. "You'd better hope you're telling me the truth." "Swear to God," said Claude as he set the car into gear. As the elevator descended slowly down the shaft, Claude's stomach gurgled loudly. He prayed to his Lord and Savior that the prisoner wouldn't kill him for upchucking meat loaf all over the place.

The elevator jiggled to a halt at the basement level. Trembling, Claude moved to open the door. "Hold it!" snapped Lonnie, brandishing the weapon close to the back of the captive's sweaty neck. "What's your name?" "Claude...Claude Rainwater, Mr. Cavanaugh." "You can call me Lonnie," he continued in a calm and even tone, as if he were giving instructions to a second grader. "Now listen closely, Claude. I don't want to hurt you, but I will if you don't cooperate with me, understand?" "Yes, Mr....yes, Lonnie." "Good. Now we're going to walk out the door together, and if there's no one down here like you said, I'm going to let you go. But if you've lied to me, I'm going to put a bullet in your ear, you got me?" Claude prattled on so fast his words were barely intelligible. “Yes sir, there won’t be nobody down here ’cause they can’t get in without me openin’ the door.” Lonnie patted him on the shoulder, and Claude flinched so hard his right foot shot out and kicked over his JFG spit can in the corner. Lonnie deftly sidestepped the can as the slimy contents oozed onto the elevator floor. Then he commended his hostage. “Good. I trust you, Claude. Let’s go.”

Claude was delighted to be correct. No one greeted them as they stepped guardedly out of the elevator. As he pocketed the key to the elevator control panel, Lonnie praised his prisoner once more, prodding him gently toward the door leading to the outside. “Very good, Claude. I just need one more favor, and I’ll leave you alone.” He gestured with the .38 toward the door. “Unlock that door; step outside into the yard. Just act natural, and let me know if the coast is clear, all right?” Claude answered shakily, fumbling with the huge wad of keys attached to the ring on his belt loop. “Yep, yep, I’ll do it,” he said as he miraculously found the right key. Regrettably, he was trembling so much he had difficulty finding the slot, pecking a tattoo all around the keyhole. Lonnie stepped to his side and grabbed the key. “Here, let me give you a hand with that,” he said, sliding the key smoothly in the lock and opening the door. Standing partially behind the door, Lonnie half-bowed to Claude. “After you,” he whispered, unsmiling.

Lonnie cringed as Claude stepped into the brassy sunlight and meandered stiffly around the yard, craning his scrawny neck left, then right, on Market Street. He did an about-face toward the open door. Standing at attention, he stated in a clear, loud voice, “It’s OK!” “So much for acting natural,” Lonnie thought as he slipped out of the building. He walked swiftly up to stiff-as-a-board Claude and spoke kindly to him. “Thanks for your help, ole buddy. Good luck to you.” Then he was off, running on the double up Market Street. Claude watched as Lonnie turned and disappeared on West Main. “Good luck to you too,” he said, not knowing why. He ran as fast as his wobbly legs could carry him toward the front entrance to the jail.

Ruford Boling watched despondently as the aged locksmith worried with the cell door lock. “This is goin’ to take a while,” said the locksmith, an employee of the Smoky Mountain Safe and Vault Service. Boling was about to ask a question when the reporter for the Knoxville Journal beat him to the punch. “How much longer do you think it will take?” The locksmith continued, never looking up from his tinkering. “Oh, I s’pose about two or three hours…give or take a few minutes.” “Shit!” exclaimed Barnes and Cooley in unison from inside the cell. There was a pop and a flash, and the Journal photographer cheerfully goaded the two inmates as he poised his camera for another shot. “That was good fellers; now can we have one with the two of you smiling?” It looked as though Barnes was attempting to squeeze his head through the bars as he spoke through gritted teeth, “The only smile you’ll get from me is when you kiss my…” He was interrupted as a deputy charged into the room. “Hey, Rufe,” he shouted. “They’ve got Cavanaugh’s wife down on Market Street!” “Keep at it!” Boling shouted at the locksmith as he chased the deputy and photographer down the stairs.

The blonde, well-dressed woman stood on the periphery of the gathering crowd. From the Journal photographer’s perspective, she seemed gracious, almost frail as she calmly addressed the numerous, rapid-fire questions from the phalanx of detectives. From her bearing, he found it difficult to believe that she played any role whatsoever in the escape of the notorious Lonnie Cavanaugh. The detectives backed off for a moment, their heads together in a secretive caucus. She seemed relieved for the respite and scanned the crowd, locking eyes with the photographer, smiling sweetly at him. He took advantage of the moment and popped a photo. She continued to smile demurely, and he moved closer for a better angle. As he stepped off the curb, he twisted his ankle on the sewer grating and fell, camera flying from his hands, scooting across the pavement like a hockey puck. As he writhed in pain at the curbside, she knelt and spoke to him eye to eye. "I hope you broke your leg, you son of a bitch," she said serenely. As she was escorted to the police car, the photographer hobbled about the street, gathering pieces of his camera, pondering the likelihood that Treva Cavanaugh was not completely innocent.

They pulled out all the stops in an effort to apprehend the escapee. The state patrol ordered its helicopter back from assignment in Kingsport; bloodhounds were sent in from Petros. Knoxville's mayor even made a special appearance on WATE- TV. "I know this boy," he stated with crusty charm. "He was a good boy when he started out, and he's not a dangerous boy now. What I'm afraid of is that somebody will think he's dangerous and shoot him." The mayor closed the broadcast with a personal appeal. "Lonnie, I give you my word. If you surrender and serve the required amount of prison time, I will do everything I can to get you paroled."

The sheriff offered a one-hundred-dollar reward for information leading to the capture of Lonnie Cavanaugh, and he received a lot of tips. One caller reported seeing the escapee leaving Knoxville in a blue 1955 Ford sedan, traveling in the direction of Maryville. He was seen at a Maryville Pike tavern, getting into a car with a red-headed woman. He left a bootlegger's place on Belt Road with two women. Another tipster gave an account of Cavanaugh and a woman in a gray 1957 Oldsmobile convertible on the highway between Elkmont and Townsend. Deputies and state patrol officers blockaded roads everywhere. They almost caught the fugitive at his uncle's home, about eight miles south of Maryville. Scores of deputies and state troopers chased him from the farmhouse to a barn to the woods just off

Highway 411. But the fleet-footed bandit eluded them, vanishing like a phantom. Two days later Treva received a phone call from Lonnie. “I know it was you who turned me in,” he said and hung up. She never saw him again.

Exasperated and embarrassed, Sheriff Boling curtailed all visits to the county jail except by special permission. There was no evidence that Treva Cavanaugh was culpable in her husband’s escape. Besides why would a wife help her husband escape so he could run around with other women? She was released. As the continuing search for Lonnie Cavanaugh proved futile, Sheriff Boling focused his wrath on recently liberated employees, John Cooley and Sam Barnes. They suffered quietly.

Part V

INTRODUCTIONS AND EXITS

Chapter 15

PENNYWHISTLES, EGGS, AND ITALIANS

Early watched intently as Benny rolled a cigarette. The boy was interested in everything and learned very quickly. "Daddy, will you teach me to roll a cigret?" said Early as Benny tapped the tobacco into the creased paper, rolled it expertly, licked the edge, and smoothed it. "No, yore not agoin' to larn that nasty habit," said Margaret, who sat next to Benny stringing and breaking beans for supper. "Now, Marg, I started smokin' when I was nine, and it hasn't hurt me one bit," he said, lighting a kitchen match with his thick, yellowed thumbnail and touching the flame to the end of the tightly rolled cylinder. He inhaled deeply, coughed a little, and continued speaking, smoke flowing plentifully through his mouth and nose as he spoke. "Yore momma's probably right, Early, but I'll teach ye somethin' else. Come over here and sit by yore daddy."

Early scrambled to his father's side, eager to see what was in store. "Now lookee here, son, I'm afixin' to show ye how to make a pennywhistle. Ye ever heared of one?" "No, sir." "Well, I thank yore 'bout to," grinned Margaret, not looking up from her bowl of beans. Benny gave her a sideways glance and continued. "Anyways, let's make a pennywhistle," he said, pulling a green stick from his overalls pocket. Before he could begin the lesson, Early had a question. "Why they call it a pennywhistle, Daddy?" "Well, it's probably 'cause folks like us cain't 'ford to spend the money on a regler whistle, so we make 'em airselves." "If we make 'em airselves, how come it costs a penny?" questioned Early.

Margaret giggled into her bowl as Benny was stumped for an answer. “Anyways, see this willer stick I fount down by the creek? It’s jest right fer a pennywhistle.” He handed the stick to Early, who studied it closely. “Now make shore the stick has green bark, a stick ’bout as thick as my fanger but not as crooked—smooth and straight, and ’bout eight inches long. Hand me that stick, will ye?” Early obeyed as Benny pulled out his pocketknife. “Now as ye can see, this willer stick has green bark, and that’s a good thang. I’ll show ye why in jest a minute.” Benny cut a small notch about three inches from the end of the stick, then cut a ring around the stick about two inches further in. “Now what ye have to do is take off the bark, and that’s why it’s good to have the green bark ‘cause it’s wet underneath,” said Benny as he tapped the bark hard with the handle of his knife all around. He twisted the bark tightly and removed it in one piece, much to Early’s delight. Then he deepened the notch about half way through the twig and planed the twig flat with his knife at the beginning of the notch. “Now here’s the finishin’ part,” said Benny, slipping the bark back on the twig. “Lookee, Early, nary a break in the skin,” said Benny as he passed the whistle to his child, who was wide-eyed in wonderment. “Sometimes this whistle will attrack a nosey ole cat or a deer. It’ll be good if’n ye ever get lost in the woods; jest blow on it, and I’ll come runnin’,” said Benny. Early blew through the narrow opening, and a shrill note came from what used to be a plain old willow stick. “Thank ye, Daddy!” said Early as he took off around the house to find his brother and sister. “Don’t be runnin’ with that thang in yore mouth,” yelled Margaret behind him.

Later Benny and Margaret heard the whistle blown repeatedly and the excited laughter of their children. “Yore goin’ to be sorry ye did that,” admonished Margaret. “It’s better than givin’ him a cigarette, ain’t it?” grinned Benny as he took out his pouch of tobacco and rolled himself another smoke.

The Baird kids hitched a ride on the bus from Westbourne and hopped off at Iveydale. "Kin we git off here, Mr. Wilder? We wont to try to find some pop bottles to trade in at Sullivan's," asked Sissy politely. "Shore, honey," said Wilder as he pulled the bus over to the side of the road. "Now young'uns, be keerful; this road is dangerous. I'll be comin' back in 'bout an air, and I'll be looking fer you'uns," he said as the children tumbled out the door. "Ye don't haf to; air Momma's meetin' us in town atter we see the movie," said Early.

"Lookee! Thar's one in the ditch, Early. Kin you git it? I ain't got no shoes on, and thar might be glass down thar!" "I'll git it, Sissy. Early's got the aigs, and he might break 'em," said Harley, scrambling into the deep ditch that ran alongside 25W. As he emerged from the ditch with his prize, a gleaming Nehi Orange bottle, a big Buick Roadmaster veered toward him on the shoulder and swerved away quickly. "Get outta the way; you're gonna get killed!" yelled the driver in a strange, intimidating voice. "Ye were on the shoder!" Harley shouted at the Buick, which was followed by a stream of automobiles bearing non-Tennessee license plates. "Damn Yankees," Harley muttered under his breath, but Sissy, who had an uncanny knack for hearing things she wasn't supposed to hear, caught the remark. "I'm telling Momma, Harley. You ain't s'posed to talk like that." "If ye tell Momma, ye ain't gittin' no candy," replied Early, shifting his small basket of eggs and cigar box full of pennywhistles from one hand to the other. Early's warning quieted Sissy; she wasn't going to miss out on candy. The Baird trio braved the onslaught of vehicles from the north that traveled down the highway through Campbell County on their way to other Southern vacation spots, especially the Great Smoky Mountains. Many of the visitors had no inkling that Campbell and adjacent counties harbored a fabulous secret: nestled in the hills beyond the highway was deep, blue-green Norris Lake, with eight hundred fifty miles of pristine shoreline. The children couldn't conceive of the idea of a vacation. But they were excited about their destination today. They were on their weekly trip to Sullivan's store, where they would cash in scrounged pop bottles and trade Early's hen eggs and pennywhistles for candy. Early had become quite proficient at producing the whistles and hoped to sell them to Mr. Sullivan for a nickle apiece. Mr. Sullivan got the best of the deal, especially the trade for Early's beautiful, brown hen's eggs. But it didn't matter to the children, who shared a junkie's ardor for the candy counter.

They stopped by Tank Springs, across from Big Creek, to rest. Sissy cupped her little hands, filling them with cold water that gushed from a pipe in the hillside and ultimately flowed into the creek. "Whew, that feels good," she said, splashing her bare feet in the cool water that pooled at the foot of the pipe. Early bent and drank directly from the pipe, and Harley did the same. When they were refreshed, they continued their journey down North Tennessee Avenue. As they approached The Tradin' Post, one of many souvenir shops popping up along the highways and byways, they noticed the offending Buick parked in front of the shop. "Hey, ain't that the car that almost hit ye, Harley?" said Early. Before Harley had a chance to confirm, a voice came from inside of the car. "Yeah? So what's it to ya?" said a teenager, emerging from the Buick. He was dressed oddly in a striped, boat-necked shirt, a clean blue cap with a big "B" on the front, white knee-length pants, and some sissy-looking canvas shoes. Except for the hat, he reminded Early of an Italian he'd seen in a magazine, poling a long, narrow boat down a water-filled ditch. "So what ah ya? Hillbillies?" smirked the visitor. "What'd he say?" Early whispered behind his hand. "I think he asked if we were hillbillies," said Harley, a dark rage welling up from the center of his being. "Are ye an I-talian?" asked Early, and the boy seemed surprised. "Yeah, name's Anthony (he pronounced it 'Antony') De Pasquale." "We're the Bairds; we live up yonder," said Sissy, pointing up the mountain. "Whar do ye live?" "I'm from Woostah, Massachusetts," said Anthony, puffing out his chest proudly, as if Worcester was the center of the universe. Sissy had difficulty deciphering the alien tongue but tried her best to be hospitable. "My brother, Early, has a rooster named Ralph and three settin' hens: Lula, she's a purty Rhode Island Red, and she lays brown aigs; and we got Patsy and Janet Sue too." Anthony cocked his head, then laughed aloud. "You dumb hick, you guys ah right out of a Lil' Abnah cahtoon!" Harley was on point now, fists clenched in tight balls. He took a step toward Anthony, but mercifully Early intervened, saving the visitor from a butt whooping. Anthony screeched as an egg, tossed with precision by Early, smacked him square in the forehead. The Bairds stood transfixed as Lula's embryonic progeny ran down Anthony's forehead and into his eyes And they were appalled as the cuss words, including abuse of the Lord's name, flowed from his filthy mouth "Run!" Harley commanded, and his brother and sister did as they were told. Sissy chastised Early during their mad dash to the store. "Dadburn yore hide, Early, that aig ye throwed was worth about three sticks of liquish!"

Later, as the three of them moseyed contentedly out of the store with a sack full of candy, the Buick zipped past them on its way to the Great Smokies. Anthony leaned out the back window and showed them his quivering middle finger. "Bye-bye," said Sissy, waving gaily back. Then she and her brothers sauntered off to the theater on Central Avenue.

The Bairds would meet a lot of "Italian boys" as their lives progressed, especially when tourists from up north and around the country became aware of Norris Lake and the cheap land available at that time. Many of the tourists were former Campbell Countians who'd returned home after making a living in the factories in Ohio, Indiana, and Michigan; pulled by the primordial tug of the mountains, with visions of the simple life they once enjoyed, and reuniting with their precious families. But other visitors were rude and poked fun at the barefoot children, farmers, miners, and townsfolk, ridiculing their way of speaking. Little did they know that much of the dialect they derided as inferior, lazy, and unsophisticated was actually a derivative of Shakespearian or Old English, brought to this frontier by the Scots-Irish and Anglo-Irish forebearers—a marvelous legacy that, unfortunately, many sons and daughters of Appalachia were unaware.

Chapter 16

INCIDENT AT THE CHEROKEE

It was cool in the theater, just like the sign with the penguin out front said.

Harley and his sibling entourage were a little late, so they bypassed the concession stand, racing into the dark theater as the opening strains of the Looney Tunes theme song began. Later Sissy drew the short straw, and as Harley and Early were reveling in the antics of Sylvester and Tweety, she raced up the aisle to fetch some popcorn at the concession stand.

She savored the first few kernels from the tall, skinny sack of popcorn she'd purchased for a dime, delighting as the warm, buttery corn melted in her mouth.

"Needs salt," she said aloud. She was standing on tiptoe, reaching for the big canister of salt on the counter when a rough, grimy, hand took hold of her wrist. "Give me a bite of that popcorn, Frankenstein," growled Florence Jenkins.

Florence was a thirteen-year-old boy housed in the body of an eighteen-year-old, which was governed by the brain of a four-year-old. He was continually looking for ways to update his bully resume, and he had a mean streak in him thicker than his skull. Of course any boy was apt to develop a mean streak if his parents named him Florence.

"Ye ain't getting none of this corn; it's fer me and my brothers," Sissy responded sharply, cradling the sack protectively in the crook of her thin, sunburned arm. Florence pondered smacking the little runt, but had second thoughts because better bullies than him didn't hit girls, especially if they were scrawny like this one. So he decided to verbally punch the daylights out of her.

"My daddy says that you'uns is nothin' but a bunch of Portygee niggers, and that ye should all be run out of the county," sneered Florence. Sissy didn't know what a "Portygee" was but knew that "nigger" was a bad word. Pappy Scrap said it once, and Momma scolded him for it. "Ye better watch yore mouth, or my brother Harley will whoop up on ye," said Sissy, turning back toward the flickering lights in the theater. Florence grabbed the back of her dress, ripping the collar. "That little bastard? My daddy says that he come from a white man that hid in yore woodpile and poked yore momma," said Florence. "Now give me some of that popcorn, Frankenstein!"

Harley was headed for the men's room when he saw the big boy grab Sissy from behind, nearly jerking her off her feet and spraying popcorn all over the lobby. He forgot that he had to pee, didn't remember what transpired between that moment and the moment he was on top of Florence. "Stop it, ye little hooligans," shouted Mrs. Chadwell, the popcorn and candy lady, from behind the counter.

"Whoop 'im, Harley!" exhorted Sissy, as Harley and Florence rolled around the popcorn-strewn lobby floor. "I'll kill ye, ye little bastard," grunted Florence as he spun on top of Harley.

Harley answered with a head-butt to Florence's face, and as Florence's nose gushed blood, Harley struggled to escape the powerful clutches of the much bigger boy. Florence screamed, not so much from the pain, but from the fact that his smaller opponent had drawn first blood.

"I'm gonna bash yore head in," swore Florence as he pinned one of Harley's arms with his knee and poised his huge fist to strike. "No, ye ain't!" wailed Sissy as she bounced the canister of salt off Florence's shaggy skull.

As Florence used his fists to rub salt from his eyes, Harley used the diversion to slide his arm from beneath the bully's knee. "Ye ain't goin' nowhere," yelled Florence as he threw himself on the smaller boy. "Get back!" yelled Mrs. Chadwell as she dumped a large fountain drink on the wriggling combatants. The tactic might have worked on hung-up dogs, but the fighters paid no heed to the bath. The usher, a skinny boy named Burl Humphrey, attempted to break up the melee but ended up getting his glasses broken for his efforts. Every manner of intervention failed as the boys, locked in battle, continued to roll in the salt, blood, and Coca-Cola, coating their sweaty bodies with spilled popcorn. Attending to his usherly duties, Burl opened the door to allow the huge ball of popcorn-covered humanity to exit the Cherokee into the street.

A sizable crowd had gathered, made up mostly of farmers on their Saturday trip to town. No one bothered to break up the fight, mainly because the ragged little boy was getting the best of the bigger one. In those days, and in that place, it was rare to see the little man win at anything. *Gunfight at the OK Corral* was long forgotten as Early and Sissy cheered on their hero.

"Jerk a knot in his tail, Harley," squealed Early, imitating a phrase he often heard used by his mother. Indeed, Harley, in a controlled rage, was jerking knots all over Florence's body, pummeling the bully with well-placed punches, kicks, and elbows. Florence was obviously losing the battle, covering his head with his arms, when Sheriff Bob Dossett snatched Harley off the cowering form.

"Whoa thar!" said Dossett, who was alerted to the commotion as he exited the drugstore down the street. Dossett was rough as a cob, rough enough to garner the fear and respect of the bootleggers, wifebeaters and husband beaters, street fighters, lowlifes, and outlaws that plagued Campbell and surrounding counties. He was also widely respected by the good folk because he made sure their young ones behaved when they weren't around.

"Ain't ye Cecil Jenkins' boy?" said Dossett as he shoved Florence into the front seat of his patrol car. Bowed and bloodied, Florence nodded his head. "And who do you'uns belong too?" growled Dossett to Harley and his two wide-eyed companions huddled in the backseat. "Our momma, daddy, pap, each other, and Jesus," said Early anxiously.

"I know that," said Dossett, his craggy face softening. "What's yore name, son?" "Harley Baird," mumbled Harley. "Boy, do ye know how many Bairds there is in this county? Which clan ye from?"

"Air momma's name is Margaret. She's sellin' her taters and stuff. Our daddy is Benny Baird, and our papaw's name is Scrap; they cut logs," offered Sissy.

Dossett smiled, which resembled a grimace. He knew Scrap Hopkins well and Benny slightly.

"Good. After we take Mister Jenkins home, I'll take ye to yore momma. Is she s'posed to meet you'uns at the theater?" asked Dossett. Harley nodded his head. "Ye mean we ain't goin' to jail?" said Early as he hugged the back of the driver's seat. "No." "Kin we run yore siren then?" "Maybe some other time," said Dossett sternly, doing his best to suppress a smile.

The excited chatter of the children filtered through the broken back window into the truck cab. Mimicking the action in *Gunfight at the OK Corral*, Sissy and Early fired their thumb and forefinger six-shooters at each other making "peekew, peekew" sounds with their mouths. Mortally wounded, Sissy feigned death on a sack of potatoes in what she considered a grotesque pose. Harley sat up front with Margaret.

"Ye should have seen 'em; they fit all over the place! Are ye goin' to jerk a knot in his tail?" said Early, sticking his head through the hole where the window should have been. "Sissy, keep yore brother in the back of the truck; git out of here, Early," said Margaret, slapping at the air where Early once was. Margaret was about to say something to Harley when Sissy stuck her head through the opening.

"Momma, what's a Portyghee?" said Sissy. "I believe it's a ferner, somebody from a differnt country; now git back thar with yore brother, honey," said Margaret. "What's a bass turd, Momma? Florence called Harley a bass turd." "Did ye hear me? I said git back thar with yore brother," said Margaret.

Sissy obeyed, still wondering what a "bass turd" meant. Harley gazed sullenly out the window.

He knew what it meant.

Harley sat on the steps watching the dogs, Whitey and Spike, cavort in the yard, dreading the "talk" he knew was coming from Margaret. He cringed when the screen door creaked, and her footfall vibrated the rickety porch. "Here," she said curtly. "Put this on that pumpknot; it's big as a duck egg," said Margaret, placing the stone root poultice on his swollen forehead. He said not a word, leaning his head against the railing so the foul-smelling concoction would not slide off.

"That poultice will take that knot down in no time, and it might even hep yore headache," said Margaret, her snappy brown eyes going soft in concern for her boy as she sat at his feet. "Harley, honey, I appreciate ye fer standin' up fer Sissy; yore a good brother and son," she said, wrapping her arms around his calf and leaning her head on his knee.

"I'm sorry, Momma." She shushed him. "But ye listen to me, Harley Baird. Even though ye whooped him, that boy outweighed ye by fifty pounds. If'n he would have got a lucky punch in, he could have killed ye. He...," she stammered, and her voice cracked.

"He could've killed ye, Harley," she continued, wagging her finger in front of his face as she rose from her seat. "Benny and me wont to talk to ye atter yore brother and sister go to bed. Now get on in here fer a bite of supper." She paused at the half-open screen door.

"And remember, honey, 'bastard' is jest a nasty word, jest like the other words that bully used. They don't mean nothin'," she said softly as the door closed noisily behind her. As Harley stood to go in, he noticed the steps below where Margaret was sitting were wet with tears.

By the time the De Pasquales and their sticky son arrived in Gatlinburg, the Baird children were just sitting down to supper and sharing the story of their day with Margaret and Benny. They made a pact earlier not to speak of the egg bombardment, and nothing more was said of the fight at the Cherokee. Harley's appearance spoke volumes about that episode; plus the children sensed the volatility of the subject.

"Momma, we fount a whole bunch of bottles, and Mr. Sullivan give us a big sack of candy in trade fer 'em and Early's aigs and pennywhistles. We got some left to share with ye and Daddy," said Sissy proudly. "Yep, and we met an I-talian boy from Rooster up north; we could hardly unnerstan' him," chimed in Early. "Well, I hope you'uns didn't eat too much and spole yore supper," said Margaret as she set a bowl of steaming collard greens on the table. "Ye know, a long time ago, there used to be a lot of ferners here," said Benny. "The I-talians lived in a place called Tallytown in LaFollette. They worked in the coke ovens…" "We've seen them down in Iveydale; thar all growed over," interrupted Harley. "What? I-talians?" said Early. "No, ye knucklehead, coke ovens," replied Harley sarcastically. Benny paused politely at the interruptions, then continued. "They was good stone masons too. They built a lot of bridge supports and that little church on the hill on Central Avenue," said Benny admiringly. "Did they war striped shirts, shrunk-up white britches, and have aig on thar faces?"

asked Sissy, sending Early and even his semi-morose brother into gales of laughter. “Cut the tomfoolery, boys. Harley, I believe it’s yore turn to say the blessin’,” said Margaret as she scooted up to the table.

“Night, Daddy; night, Momma; night, Papaw,” said the two younger children as they kissed and hugged their elders. “Night, babies,” said Scrap as he prepared to leave. “Well, I’d better be gittin’ down to the house; we got a big day ahead of us tomorry, ain’t we, Benny?” “Shore do,” replied Benny, who seemed especially tired this evening. As a matter of fact, he’d felt worn out for some time now, and he was losing weight, which he couldn’t afford to do. When the screen door had slammed behind Scrap, Margaret got up to go to the kitchen. “I’ll cut us a piece of cake. If Pap knowed we was eatin’ cake, he’d a stayed all night,” she laughed. Benny’s laugh was cut off by a ragged cough. He reached for a pre-rolled cigarette in his shirt pocket, lit it, and yelled to the kitchen, “No cake fer me, Marg.”

Harley dreaded what was coming, mainly because he had no idea of what was coming, but his dread was softened when Margaret returned with pieces of cake and glasses of cold milk for all of them.

‘Harley, first of all, I wont to tell ye how I appreciate ye for how ye pertected Sissy today. Yore momma tole me she scolded ye fer takin’ a chance; but I respeck ye as a man, which yore gittin’ to be. Now I wont to tell ye somethin’ that ye might have figgered out already, but if’n ye ain’t, we figger ye have a right to know, honey,” said Benny, taking a deep drag from the cigarette and knocking the ash into the cuff of his pants.

As Benny told the story, Harley listened intently. But he already knew the story, a story told to him by his distinct differences from others, whispers from behind hands at church, cruel remarks from those like Florence Jenkins, and a visceral feeling of deep sadness and loneliness at times that he couldn’t explain.

He asked one question when Benny finished the tale.

"Do ye have any idee who they was?" Benny started to answer, but Margaret cut him short. "It don't matter who they was, honey. Yore a part of us as any blood kin, and we are blessed with ye, ain't we, Benny?" "We shore are," said Benny as he pulled Harley to his thin chest. "Yore momma's right. It don't matter who they are."

It mattered to Harley. He suffered, unaware that his suffering came partly from being deprived of a primitive relationship with his biological mother. As he grew, at times he would become aloof or angry, endure depression, and feel incomplete. And every time Margaret and Benny told him lovingly that "We picked you out of all the babies in the world," it reminded him that his real parents didn't want him, that he was damaged goods. That's why they threw him away.

Chapter 17

ELLA DEE AND LOUIE B.

The following day Margaret visited Maw. As they sat in Maw's sunny kitchen, Margaret told the story of the previous day and the brawl at the Cherokee. She was not prepared for Maw's outburst when she mentioned Florence Jenkins and the filthy epithets that spewed from his mouth; especially the racial slur demeaning Negroes.

"I hate that word. And I ain't quite happy with anyone that uses it. It ain't fit fer air language and should never been invented." She got up from the table and busied herself around the kitchen, scrubbing counters furiously and deadheading hanging plants. "I know I've said this to ye before, Margaret, but I cain't hep repeatin' it. We are made to love...to love ever'one, regardless of color, 'cause we are all family, brothers and sisters. And those that don't foller that rule, those that try to douse life's sacred fire is destined to pay fer it some way, and those that foller the rules enjoy the fruits of thar goodness," said Maw as she knocked over her sugar bowl in the process of pouring coffee for her guest. "I'll git it," said Margaret, grabbing a dishcloth off the counter to wipe up the spill. The morning sun poured through the kitchen window as they returned to their seats at the table. It highlighted Maw's wispy, white hair and wildly scattered tendrils, accentuating her manic expression. But she eventually settled down as Margaret quietly sipped her coffee, reticent to further stoke Maw's uncharacteristic rage. Maw continued the conversation, her voice still a bit shaky. "Do ye know any colored folks in LaFollette, honey?" "No, thar ain't many," answered Margaret. "Well, thar used to be. When minin' was big business, they come from all over to work, along with I-talians, Polacks, China people, people from places that I never heared of. They was mostly good people, in many ways gooder'n the rest of us." The sun went behind the clouds, and the lighting in the kitchen took on a sepia tone as Maw bent forward as if to whisper a secret. "Let me tell ye 'bout people of color that's made my life and the lives of a lot of other folks more worthwhile."

Ella Dee and her nephew hitched a ride in the back of a truck from LaFollette. It was minutes after the farmer had dropped them off when they were accosted by a truckload of less kindly travelers. "Why don't ye git off air road, woman, and take that little tar baby back home with ye?" said a smaller boy, who seemed to be spokesperson for the group. "Yeah, go back to yore watermelon patch," said another boy, who laughed heartily at his own pitiful attempt at humor.

Maw was headed back from town with a bale of chicken wire riding in the back of her clattering truck. "Ain't no hens and chicks sneakin' out from thar coop, and no slinky fox gonna satisfy his appetite atter today," she spoke aloud. As she rounded a curve, she beheld the disturbing scene. Some boys in a truck had stopped, and it seemed as if they were harassing a black woman and a child, who was also black and appeared to be about six years old. The woman and child were dressed decently, and the child hid behind her skirts as they were harangued by the hooligans. Maw stopped her truck on the roadside and reached into the back.

The smaller boy was in the process of hurling another insult when the roar of a shotgun filled the air. Everyone flinched, and the black boy almost fell into the roadside ditch.

"Ever'body duck fer cover and git yore self goin', or I'll fill that truck and yore sorry tails with number three buckshot," said Maw. Everyone in the back of the truck obliged Maw's request, and the driver laid the best patch of rubber possible on bald tires as the truck disappeared around the curve.

The boy remained hidden behind the woman's skirt as Maw approached them. "Thank you, ma'am, for intervening," the woman said. "Ye mean fer breakin' that bunch of ignernt young'uns up? It's my pleasure, honey. What's yore name?" The woman, slight of build, fought to keep the terrified youngster from pulling her into the ditch. "My name is Ella Dee," she said, offering her hand graciously. Maw shook her hand firmly. "Well, glad to meet ye. And what's yore name little feller?" Wide-eyed and trembling from the former encounter, the youngster remained silent. "His name is Calvin. He's my nephew," said Ella, dragging him out from behind her skirt tails. "Nice to meet ye, Calvin. What are ye two doin' way out here in the hinterland?" "Calvin has a medical problem, and we were told to look up Nola Ruggles, who might have a remedy," said Ella. "Well ye've found her. That's me, and I would be happy to hep ye. Git in my truck; my house is jest a few miles away." Maw walked back to the driver's door and noticed that Ella had lifted Calvin into the back of the truck, and she was following. "Now don't ye do that! Come on up front, and sit with me. I've got plenty of room, and we kin git to know each other better." When they were settled, with Calvin in the middle of the bench seat, Maw looked down at him and placed her hand gently on his head. "Let's go, Calvin, and see what we kin do fer ye, awright?" "OK," he said barely audibly, as they headed for the house.

Calvin had a boil about the size of a golf ball in the middle of his back, fiery-red and angry looking.

Maw came over from the stove, where she was boiling milk in a pan. "Let's see what ye got here, young'un," she said as she gently probed the infected sphere. "Hmm, don't have no red lines comin' from it, and a head's startin' to form; ye ain't got no fever or chills, so ye ain't infected, honey." She looked at Ella, who sat concerned at her nephew's side. "It's a good thang it ain't a carbuncle, but ye see them mostly in old fellers. I'd say it's a furuncle; lots a people call 'em boles," she said as she walked back to the stove, shut the fire off beneath the pan, and dropped a piece of bread in the milk. Once it had soaked for a while, she removed the bread and placed it on the boil. Calvin squealed but stood his ground. "The warmth draws blood to the bole, and the blood fights infection. How does that feel, Calvin?" "Feels good, not as sore," said Calvin, his eyes closed in relief. When Maw removed the bread poultice, the head on the boil had become more pronounced. Maw placed a gauze pad on the boil and taped it to Calvin's back. As Ella helped him put his shirt back on, Maw went to her cupboard and picked three sizeable onions from a storage bin.

"Now when ye git home, cut a big slice of onion and put it over the bole. Wrap it in a cloth, and change it in about three airs. It should come to a head and drain. If ye got alcohol, rub it on the bole, and wrap it up. He'll be awright," she said, hugging Calvin gently. "Ye was a good patient. How 'bout a nice cold glass of Kool-Aid fer yore trouble, honey?" "That would be nice, Miss Ruggles, but we have to get home before dark. How much do I owe you?" said Ella, rummaging through her purse. "Ye don't owe me a thang. I should pay you'uns fer lettin' me serve ye," said Maw as she mixed up a pitcher of grape Kool-Aid. Ella looked surprised because of Maw's kind comments and the fact that she was preparing Kool-Aid when Ella had said they had to be leaving. "And it's too late fer you'uns to walk home. Whar do ye live?" "We live off Ore Street in LaFollette." "I know whar that is. I'll take you'uns home myself. Ye cain't trust nobody to pick a body up any more. Now here, try some of this grape Kool-Aid; it's my favert," said Maw, topping off three jelly glasses of the cool drink from the pitcher.

As Calvin enjoyed drinking his second glass of Kool-Aid and playing with Maw's parakeet, Maw and Ella talked. "Ye talk good, Ella honey. Ye got a lot of schoolin'?" "Yes, I graduated from Tennessee State University in Nashville. I have a teaching degree." "Lordy mercy, that's wunnerful. Do ye teach in LaFollette?" "As a matter of fact, I used to teach at the colored school; but since they closed and the schools are integrated, I'm at LaFollette High School." "What do ye teach thar?" "Actually, I don't teach anything—I'm the librarian. I don't make as much as most of the teachers, but I make more than I did at the colored school," said Ella without enthusiasm. Maw shook her head. "I'm sorry, honey, about ye not bein' treated fairly." "That's OK. I'm discovering that all women, and especially black women, are the underdogs of this world. But I'm hoping that I can play some role in changing that," said Ella, failing to hide her bitterness. Maw wisely changed the subject. "Well, how did ye come by gittin' to little ole LaFollette, all the way from Nashville?" "Some of my family and friends settled here from Dayton, Tennessee, many years ago when there was work in the mines and coke ovens. You may have heard of my friend, Howard Armstrong?" Maw clapped her hands. "Lord yes! I heared him and his band play one time. He told stories and sang and played about five music instruments. What is it they call him now?" "Louie Bluie," said Ella proudly. She went on with her story. "Anyway, I had my heart set on teaching at a school in Ohio, but my cousin who lived in LaFollette died suddenly and left three children, Calvin, who is six; Juanita, who is four; and Florida, who is 12. Florida is watching over Juanita now."

"Well, why don't we git ye home to 'em," said Maw as she took Ella's glass and put it in the sink. "Come on, Calvin, let's git ye home to yore sisters," said Maw as she shepherded the little fellow toward the door. "Ye got yore onions, Ella? Then, let's go if'n yore ready."

The sky was just darkening as Maw and her new friends pulled in to the yard of the tiny home. The two girls raced out of the house to greet their aunt and their brother. "Did Calvin get fixed?" said Juanita. "Yes, he did, thanks to Nola. Juanita, Florida, I'd like for you to meet our new friend, Nola Ruggles." The girls, unaccustomed to the company of white people, hung their heads shyly. Maw knelt and hugged them both to her. "Ye kin call me Maw, babies. It's nice to meet ye both," she said as she stood. "You all take Calvin out of that mudhole over there and go in the house. I'll be in soon to cook supper for us," said Ella. "Juanita and I have already started supper, Aunt Ella," said Florida as she and her little sister ran to herd Calvin into the house. "Would you like to stay for supper, Nola?" "No thank ye, but I do have a favor to ask," said Maw, diffident for the first time since she met Ella. "Anything, what is it?" said Ella, delighted to be of help. "Well, I cain't read that good, and I was wonderin' if ye could hep me git better," said Maw. "I would be honored, Nola. Is there any reading material you'd like to start with?" Maw got into the truck and spoke out the window. "I've got a book that a friend give me. It's a book of pomes by a man named Robert Brownin'," she said as she backed out onto the road. "I think we can do that," said Ella happily, as Maw's taillights became tiny specks of brightness at the end of Ore Street hill.

Ella started Maw off with some third grade primers. Maw proved to be a good student and progressed rapidly, but she was very eager to start reading the Robert Browning book and asked Ella if she could start with a particular poem, "Meeting at Night." "OK, you read it first, then I'll read it aloud with you, and then you can read it again, Nola," said Ella as the lessons continued on a cold Saturday afternoon. Maw eagerly opened the book and began, "The gray sea and the long, black land, and the yallar half-moon, large and low..."

After months of tutoring, Maw was becoming quite proficient with her reading. Today she looked forward to beginning *Little Women* as she hurried to Ella's home. As she pulled into the gravel lane, she spied a shiny, black, late-model Oldsmobile parked beneath the pin oak in the front yard. The children, now lacking any shyness, rushed to greet her. "Come on in, Maw. We've got company," said Calvin as the girls took her packages and he grabbed her hand.

When the parade of children led her into the living room, she was greeted by Ella and a man, who was sitting in a rocking chair by the fireplace. "Nola! Welcome!" said Ella as the man rose from his chair. "Nola, this is my good friend, Howard Armstrong," said Ella, bursting with pride. The man was distinguished looking and wore a colorful shirt. She noticed his beaded bracelet and beautiful trousers, of a material unknown to her, and exquisite leather sandals. He held out his hand and bowed slightly to her. As she took his hand, he spoke in a mellow voice. "Enchanté," he said, grasping her hand with his long, beautiful fingers, which were adorned with many rings. Maw blushed. "I hope that don't mean somethin' bad," she giggled. Howard, tall and dark, with the noble, sharp features of an Indian chieftain, laughed a deep, rolling laugh that made the room feel good. Ella bubbled. "Howard just returned from France." "Was that France talk that ye jest said to me?" Maw marveled. "Yes, it was. It means that I'm glad to meet you, as a matter of fact; it means I'm enchanted to meet you, and I am," he said, offering her his rocker and seating himself in a threadbare club chair opposite her and Ella.

As the afternoon wore on, Maw's *Little Women* tutorial was forgotten, but she thoroughly enjoyed a lesson that she never imagined she would receive. "Did you know that Howard speaks seven languages?" said Ella as she served them coffee in the demitasse cups he'd brought her from Europe. "I heared that. Did ye learn 'em from overseas?" Howard chuckled in mid-sip of his coffee. "I learned a little over there, but I learned most from immigrants here in LaFollette. When

I was a youngster, I used to play in bars where they gathered, and I learned that they appreciated my music more if I spoke their language and learned their customs." Ella interjected a comment of her own. "In those days, and even today, local people were suspicious of outsiders and cultures other than their own. Many folks felt it was beneath them to learn another language," she said as she brought a platter of freshly baked cookies into the room. "Well, I ain't like that. I shore wisht ye could play some music fer me," said Maw, hands clasped in eager entreaty. "Your wish is my command, lady. I shall return," said Howard gallantly as he left the room. Directly he returned carrying two cases: one that housed his cherished fiddle, the other his mandolin. Later the children danced, and the adults clapped and sang as Howard entertained them with ragtime, gospel, work songs, and blues. He introduced each tune with an interesting and oftentimes funny anecdote that had to do with the origin of the song, his travels, and the people he befriended on several continents. Maw particularly loved the songs he sang in Polish, Italian, and especially Spanish. They were beautiful and sentimental, and the listener knew that the song was about love without even knowing a word of the language. The hours flew by, and finally the concert was completed. "Oh, Haird, ye must be tard atter all that playin' and singin'. I'm tard from clappin' and laughin'," said Maw. "I'm not tired, Nola. It's what I do; it's who I am. And when I feel enjoyment from people like you, I feel honored." "Well, yore an honorable man, and I'm so glad I got to meet ye," said Maw, rising from the rocker. Howard stood, and Maw grabbed his hand in hers. "In shanty," she said warmly, and Howard smiled a beautiful smile in return. As Howard, Ella, and the children saw her to the door, she took the opportunity to ask him one more question. "Haird, I'd like to know. What's yore 'pinion of all the folks ye met that warn't from here?" He answered without hesitation. "Nola, I can safely say that they're just like us, with all the hopes, fears, and joys that we experience," he said, opening the driver's door to the truck for her. She smiled and sighed. "Jest like family, right?" "Just like family," he replied, patting the door with affection meant for her.

As Maw drove home, her mind was bursting with thoughts of amazing people in the wide, wonderful world far beyond her mountain microcosm. "I'd love to travel and meet some of those folks. After all, thar my family," she said as Howard Armstrong's vibrant tales and tunes echoed through the corridors of her mind.

When Maw had finished the tale, Margaret had a number of questions. "What happened to all of them? Do they still live here?" "No, I'm 'fraid not. Atter a time Ella moved back to Nashville and got her a good teachin' job at the same school she gradgeated from. Florida become a doctor and works somewhars in South America, and Juanita and Calvin are both perfessors at a school down south." "How about Haird?" "I never seen him agin. But I'm told he become more famouser. They say thar even thankin' 'bout makin' a movie 'bout him," said Maw as she poured seed into the dish clamped to the parakeet's cage. "I'll probly never live to see it, but I'll never forgit him, Ella, and the children, and the dreams they set in my head," said Maw as the tiny bird trilled a song of thanks in return for her loving care.

Chapter 18

BENNY'S CONFESSION

Benny coughed all night.

Knowing he was keeping the household awake, he finally rolled out of bed and walked out on the porch to smoke a cigarette. He sat on the glider, rolled two, and lit one cigarette. The first deep drag of smoke seemed to calm his lungs as well as his nerves, which were shot lately. His appetite had waned, and he was becoming skinnier every day. Maw had prescribed several remedies for coughs and for weight gain but to no avail. And Scrap hinted, with little subtlety, at his weight loss as they worked at the sawmill on Monday. "Here ye go, take this," he ordered, plopping a short log in Benny's arms. "Whatchee wont me to do with this?" Benny asked. "I wont ye to put it in yore britches so ye won't float up and hit yore head on the roof," said Scrap.

Benny was lighting the second cigarette off the mostly finished first when he heard the front screen door complain as it was opened and closed. "Brrr, it's cold out here, honey," said Margaret as she shuffled across the porch floor, sat on the glider, and scooted almost on top of her husband for warmth. The glider creaked beneath the weight of them both, mingling with the eerie hoot of a barred owl from somewhere in the deep woods beyond. "I'm sorry if I woke ye, Marg. I thought I'd come out here and settle down a little bit. Ye all right?" "I'm fine, honey, jest worried about ye. I was thankin'...I got some butter and aig money saved up, and I was hopin' that we could make an appointment with Dr. Minton; maybe he kin give ye somethin' fer that cough. What do ye thank?" said Margaret, snuggling closer to Benny. "It'll go away. Besides ye worked too hard fer that money; ye should spend it on yoreself." He took another deep drag, and he noticed the look of worry and dismay on her face in the fiery glow of the tobacco. “Let me sleep on it, and I’ll let ye know in the mornin’,” he said, flicking the cigarette out into the yard. “Let’s go in, honey. I’ll try not to cough no more tonight.” “Ye don’t bother me, honey,” she lied as they entered the house arm in arm. Benny looked forward to the warmth of Margaret’s body as they climbed into bed. As he reached up to turn out the light, he was startled by the blood specks on his pillow. Trying not to appear alarmed, he turned his pillow over and spoke softly, “Marg, why don’t ye give Dr. Minton a call tomorry.”

Big Creek Holiness Church was full as usual on Sunday morning, and Pastor Oddus Bunch was on a roll, delighted to be scaring his congregation out of hell.

“And the devil that deceived them was cast into the lake of fire and brimstone, where the beast and the false prophet are, and shall be tormented day and night for ever and ever.

“But the fearful and unbelieving and the abominable and murderers and whoremongers and sorcerers and idolaters and all liars shall have their part in the lake, which burneth with fire and brimstone, which is the second death,” quoted Bunch loudly from the Book of Revelation.

Red-faced, veins bulging in his neck and prominent forehead, Bunch paced back and forth like a caged bear, working himself into a frenzy, punctuating each sentence with a doglike bark, and identifying his people as “sinners in the hands of an angry God.”

When he completed his sermon, he was sweating profusely and so were some members of the congregation. Some of the older children were biting their nails for they had certainly told a few fibs in their young lifetimes. Now they pictured themselves paddling around in a lake of fire for eternity. Later, after the offering was collected, the sopping wet Pastor Bunch made a plea for members of his congregation to testify their sins.

Benny raised his hand weakly and, with the help of Scrap, made his way slowly to the altar.

Margaret followed sorrowfully behind and sat in the front pew, ready to catch her desperately fragile husband if he collapsed. The cancer had taken its toll, spreading from his lungs to his throat, and each breath taken, each word, was uttered with painful difficulty.

Benny told the congregation of the doctor's morbid prognosis a month earlier, that he was to die sooner than later. He confessed his sins, which were small and few compared to most mortals: a stolen chicken when he was a starving youngster (he'd probably given away several flocks of chickens to his neighbors over the years, not in atonement, just because he wanted to help), harsh words spoken to his worthless siblings, regret that he didn't help Margaret more with the chores, apologies to neighbors for not being more neighborly. And he thanked his Maker for his blessings in life: Margaret, Early, Scrap, and Sissy. Lastly, he spoke of his eldest son.

"I fount him acryin' in a basket on the steps of a church house over in Morgan County, and me and Margaret kep him. I ask the Lord's fergiveness for never tellin' nobody, and I hope nobody's lookin' fer him, fer if they was, Lord fergive me, we wouldn't give him back.

"Me and Margaret thank the Lord fer air boy," croaked Benny as tears pooled deeply in his hollow eye sockets. He coughed hard, a rattling cough that shook his entire body.

"We thank the Lord fer air Harley, the finest gift we've ever been give," Benny repeated. He swayed and would have fallen if not for Scrap's and Margaret's intervention. The congregation sat in shocked silence as the Baird brood scrambled out of the pew to the aid of their daddy. As Scrap half-carried Benny out of the church, Harley felt as if all eyes were on him.

Benny went straight to bed when they got home, and although

it was hot in the house, he asked Margaret for an extra quilt. When Margaret returned from tucking him in, the little ones questioned her about Benny's confession; but she shushed them, giving them a hard look that meant they'd better be quiet or she would "cut the blood out of their legs with a hickory switch."

(Margaret never would have cut the blood out of their legs with any kind of switch; however, the mere image of blood flowing from their limbs was enough to make the children think twice about misbehaving.) Margaret offered a dish pan to Harley, who was sitting on the stoop picking burrs off the dogs.

"Harley, go out to the garden and pick me some maters, honey," she said as she donned an apron and grabbed a meat clever off a hook beside the stove.

She laughed as the children fought to get out the back door, fearful that she would ask them to run down a chicken for supper and chop off its head.

Harley grabbed the hoe leaning against the house and headed toward the garden, which at this time of year was bursting forth with all kinds of earthy delights.

The perimeter of the bushy green plot was planted with bright yellow and orange marigolds. This, according to Margaret, was an efficient snake repellent.

But Harley was mistrusting of the remedy, fearful that a Copperhead might gather the courage to cross the marigold border in its hunger for insects, mice, or other rodents that found sustenance in the garden. He always treaded cautiously down the narrow garden rows, fearful of stepping on an exquisitely camouflaged pit viper, which unlike a rattler that warns interlopers with its buzzing tail, will strike out immediately when it feels threatened. He'd picked a whole pan full of juicy, red tomatoes and threw in some cucumbers and onions, hoping to marinate them in Margaret's apple cider vinegar and eat them for supper, when he felt the presence of something other than the sweet summer critters that sang just to be living in this garden paradise.

Sissy and Early stood a short distance away, observing him from behind the beans. "What are ye starin' at?" said Harley, peeved at the intrusion. No one said a word. Finally Sissy broke the silence.

"Are ye 'dopted, Harley?" "No, I was just fount," he said, trying to appear nonchalant as he tossed another tomato into the pan. "Did somebody throw ye away?" asked Early as he wielded a popsicle stick, jousting with a big yellow and black tomato spider. With each jab the feisty arachnid swung its web toward him menacingly "I guess they did; I was too little to walk away on my own," said Harley, walking toward his siblings. "Why would anybody throw a little biddy baby away?" said Sissy, almost to herself.

"I guess they jest didn't wont me," said Harley. Suddenly Sissy threw herself at Harley, grabbing his waist and burying her head in his hip. "Oh, Harley, I'm glad they throwed ye away; we'd never of had ye if they didn't," she blubbered. Early hugged Harley's neck. "It's all right, Harley. Don't ye never mind if they throwed ye away," he said in a trembling voice. "I don't mind," said Harley as Whitey and Spike, sensing the commotion, darted around the corner of the house. The gangly shepherd jumped on Early, knocking him to the ground, where Spike waited eagerly to lick his face. Crying turned to giggles as the two mutts herded the children to the house.

Much later, after they'd scrubbed up, the children sat down to the table, which was laden with bowls of mashed potatoes, green beans, cornbread, all kinds of vegetables, and the hapless hen that Margaret murdered earlier in the afternoon.

"Sissy, go fetch Daddy, will ye, honey?" said Margaret as she sat a sweating pitcher of cherry Kool-Aid swirling with ice cubes on the table.

"Momma, why was Harley throwed away," said Early as he reached for a steaming fried chicken leg. "He wasn't throwed away. Now I don't want to hear another word about it," said Scrap as he scooted his chair noisily to the table. Margaret was about to admonish Harley for petting the dogs after he'd washed his hands when Sissy returned.

"Momma, Daddy won't wake up," she said, her once sunny-bright summer face blanched gray with dread.

Chapter 19

THE HOME GOING

The funeral home prepared Benny's body, and at the request of Margaret, returned it to the house where it was laid out for visitation in the living room.

During the hours before the day of visitation, Margaret cried herself into a stupor. By the time mourners started to arrive the next day, she tried to present a semblance of composure, standing sentry at the casket with Harley and Early, while Scrap and Sissy greeted visitors in the yard.

Benny's useless brothers and sisters and other kin got word of his passing and came over from Morgan County to pay their respects. In reality they were present to ask if he'd left them anything or if there were any family valuables they could claim.

"Margrit, we're so sorry 'bout yore loss. Don't he look skinny," said one of Benny's grossly fat sisters as she peered into the casket. She wore a brightly colored muumuu. "And who's these young'ns?" she said, examining Harley and Early up close, as if they were hanging meat.

"That's our boys, Harley and Early," said Margaret, taking hold of Harley's hand. The sister stepped back a couple of steps, placing her hand on her hip, not taking her eyes off the boys. "Whichun's Harley and whichun's Early?" she demanded.

"I'm Harley, and this is Early," Harley answered politely, saving his mother the burden of further conversation with this trash. "Well, Harley, ye don't look like nobody, not a Baird, that's fer shore, and not a Hopkins either. Early, yore the spittin' image of Scrap out thar, and that little girl in the yard looks a lot like Margrit and Benny," said the woman, eyeing Harley suspiciously as she moved on. Margaret squeezed Harley's hand as the line of curious relatives and sympathetic neighbors filed past the casket, some remarking about the physical differences between Harley and the rest of his family. As the day progressed, Benny's relatives discerned that there was nothing for them to profit by from Benny's death, so they bid adieu and returned to Morgan County. It was a blessing to Margaret, who dreaded the thought of putting them up for the night.

The night was cruelly long as the family sat up with the remains of their beloved Benny, talking, dozing, and crying intermittently. "You'uns go on to bed," said Margaret as she cradled Sissy's comatose form in her arms. Early and Scrap gladly did as they were told, and Early scooped the little girl out of Margaret's arms as he headed for bed. "I'll tuck her in, Momma." "See you'uns in the mornin'," said Scrap as he stopped to kiss his daughter and gaze at the shell of the gentle, kindly man whom he considered a son. "God bless ye, Benny; I love ye, son," he said, and he wept as he shouldered his way out the door.

Margaret hadn't really stopped crying the entire day, but the tears flowed heavily as she observed her heartbroken father. Harley, seated on the couch next to her, put his arms around her shoulders. "Ye go on to bed, honey," she said between hitching sobs. "I'll stay up with Benny." "That's all right, Momma. I'll stay with ye," said Harley, dabbing at her face with a clean handkerchief.

As the hours passed, Harley was unable to keep his eyes open and drifted off to sleep in the corner of the couch. About three in the morning, he was awakened by his mother's soft voice. She was standing by the casket, brushing Benny's hair. Harley was devastated as he listened to her heartrending words.

"Oh, my precious Benny, do ye 'member when we was courtin', and ye bought that ole dried-up cake of mine at the cakewalk? Ye won my heart that day, not 'cause ye bought the cake but 'cause of yore sweetness. And ye know what, honey? That sweetness jest got sweeter as the days and years went on. I never doubted yore love fer me, and I always knowed that ye was true to air vows and more true to me than I ever deserved. Ye always worked and pervided fer me and the three precious children ye give me. I know that we will live together ferever, honey. Jest stand by me, and wait on me as ye done in life, and I will join ye when the time comes. I jest hope I don't go crazy in this life without ye," she said as she bent to kiss her husband's forehead. Harley buried his head in a pillow in an effort to stifle his sorrow.

For those who slept, the first light of morning brought the realization that Benny's death had not been a nightmare—such as it was for Harley, who was awakened by Sissy's musical voice and the aroma of biscuits and fried country ham floating from the kitchen. Feeling drugged, he forced himself from a prone position to the edge of the couch, and once his sandy eyes cleared, he focused on his mother who had nodded off in a chair next to the casket. Someone had wrapped an afghan over her shoulders. He could not imagine how she must feel. He decided not to awaken her, to allow her the blessed intercession of sleep for a little while longer.

As he dragged his feet through the darkened house into the kitchen, the fluorescent ceiling lights drew him further into a wakeful state. "Well, lookee what the cat drug in," said Scrap, who sat at the table sipping coffee. Harley stooped to hug Scrap and Early, who looked as though something had dragged him in too.

Sissy ran and jumped into his arms. "Me and Maw's cookin' us breakfist, Harley! Now why don't ye sit down and have somethin' to eat?" "I will," he said as he walked over and hugged Maw, who was bustling around the stove. "How are ye feelin' this mornin', honey?" she said as she bent to take a tray of golden-brown biscuits out of the oven. "I've shore felt better." "I'm shore ye have. I laid awake all night thankin' 'bout poor little Hooty." Everyone smiled at the remark, which featured the nickname Maw gave Benny the night Early was born. "Now why don't you'uns eat while I go and check on yore momma?" she said, wiping her hands on her apron. They ate in silence, each consumed with their thoughts and fears, each dreading the events that would lead later to their farewell, the final good-bye to the earthly remains of Dwane Benny Baird.

The shiny, black Cadillac Fleetwood hearse arrived from the Harper-Woodson Funeral Home precisely on time, at eleven o'clock. Harley felt relief and guilt for feeling that way as the men from the funeral home closed the lid to the casket, placed it on a gurney, and wheeled Benny's remains out of the house. Later other members of the procession arrived, and the funeral home employees organized cars and trucks in an orderly line, placing little magnetic funeral flags on the roofs of their vehicles.

The family sat silently, huddled together in the strangely empty living room, when a knock came at their door. "Are ye ready, Mrs. Baird?" said the funeral attendant. "I guess I am," said Margaret as Scrap helped the exhausted widow out of her chair. She was attired neatly in a black A-line dress that someone had purchased for her at a second-hand store in Jacksboro. Early and Harley wore clip-on black ties and borrowed sport jackets—a striped seersucker for Harley and a herringbone design for Early that was way too small for him. Scrap was dressed in his usual dress-up duds: clean overalls, a kind of white shirt, and a paisley tie. Sissy outshone them all in a black skirt that Maw had fashioned for her, a white blouse, and shiny, black, patent leather Mary Jane shoes.

As the hearse led the procession slowly up Jellico Highway, vehicles on the other side of the road stopped in respect for the deceased and the mourners.

The circuitous line of cars and trucks stopped traffic as it turned off the main road onto the lane leading to Calgary Cemetery. The fog was burning off, and the sun burned brightly against the bluest of skies, announcing the prospect of a beautiful day. But the Bairds were unaware of that prospect. Enfolded in grief, Margaret and Sissy were led to the front row of chairs inside the tent, facing a mound of dirt at the freshly dug grave. As was common, the grave was dug east to west, so Benny would face the rising sun in preparation for judgment day. Harley, Early, and Scrap joined the other pallbearers, solemnly transporting their adored Benny to the bier overlooking his resting place.

After the gospel group sang Benny's favorite hymn, "Precious Jesus Hold My Hand," Reverend Bunch delivered an excellent sermon from John 11, describing the raising of Lazarus, one of the signs that illustrate the provision of life through the death of the Son of God. But his sermon was vastly overshadowed by the heartfelt words of an unscheduled speaker.

"Reverend Bunch, if ye don't mind, I'd like to say somethin' about my daddy," said Harley toward the end of the service. "Shore, Harley, come on up here and say yore piece," said Bunch, walking forward and placing his guiding hand lovingly on Harley's shoulder.

Harley took his place at the foot of the grave and, with trembling hands, withdrew a piece of wrinkled paper from his inside coat pocket. He was a little quivery at first, but his resolve strengthened as he continued with the words he'd written during the early morning hours.

"My daddy warn't a fancy man. He didn't travel over the world. He went to work, he went to church, and he come home ever night. We always knowed whar he was, and it made us feel safe. He didn't dress in fine clothes As a matter of fact, he had vury few clothes; I thank he had one set of shoes that we'd take turns cleanin' up and shinin' ever oncet in a while, two sets of overalls, and a couple of shirts. Shoot, even the suit he's awearin' today was give to him. He loved air momma and showed her and us how much he loved her ever day. Him and my momma taught me and my brother and sister that ye don't need much to be happy, that thar's a difference between bein' poor and bein' sorry. And I thank that the most important thang he taught us was to love one another, and that to have love of a family is one of the greatest gifts ye could ever have. Daddy, I appreciate ye for the love you give to Momma, Scrap, Early, and Sissy, fer they deserved it." He turned and spoke directly to the casket. "And I appreciate ye fer the great love you give to me...I hope I deserved it...I tried to deserve it."

As he walked back to the tent, Sissy applauded lustily for him. When the men from the funeral home signaled that it was time to leave, Margaret stayed behind for a moment, her family waiting not far from the grave. Margaret unwrapped the cloth that housed the object she had brought with her. She knelt by the grave and casket and placed the rock at the head of the grave. "This ole rock's the one I brung from that tumbledown shack we lived in over in Petros. It's a reminder of how good air lives have become, honey," she said as Scrap came over to help her up.

There was a sense of relief when they returned home, shed their fancy clothes, and greeted mourners who came back to the house with bowls of food and to partake of the delicious spread Maw had prepared for everyone. The house, porch, and yard were packed with folks. Harley stood by the window observing Sissy, Spike, and Whitey, and children chasing one another; Early and Scrap sharing stories about Benny and eating off paper plates. He was feeling like an intruder, oddly disconnected from them, when a hand lightly brushed his shoulder.

Margaret, drawn and fatigued, smiled—the first smile he'd noticed on her face in a while. "Harley, I was awful proud of ye today, and I knowed Benny was proud, proud to have ye as a son." He was unable to say anything in response but buried his head in her chest. She held him gently, rubbing his back as he wept. They were both unaware that his tears were shed for the loss of more than Benny.

Part VI

RITES OF PASSAGE

Chapter 20

PHYSICAL ABUSE

Of all the Baird clan, other than Margaret, Harley's grief over the death of Benny was the heaviest and most damaging. It was especially tragic for Harley because he viewed the passing as having been abandoned again. It reopened his wounds of being thrown away, and with his evolving adolescence, he became fretful, bitter, and sometimes enraged. He was not about to be thrown away again, and he began to provoke family members with the silent commitment of "If I'm abandoned again, at least I'll be in charge of making it happen."

"Dammit, Early! Git off yore hind end and hep us with these logs," Harley yelled as Early sat and whittled while on a break. "I'll be thar when I'm ready," Early replied defiantly. "I started up the saw and come to work at least an air before you'uns did this morn...," Scrap cried out as Harley dove and knocked Early off the log. "Git off him, Harley," said the old man as he limped over to break up the two. Scrap was surprised to see that Harley's arm was bleeding, and Early was horrified. "I couldn't hep it, Pappy; he dived right on the blade! I'm sorry, brother," he apologized as Harley got off him and returned to the job. "What in the world's got into ye? I don't wont to see that kind of actin' agin, or I'll use a heavy hand on ye," said Scrap. Harley was wrapping a handkerchief around his arm and stopped what he was doing. "I wouldn't try that if I was ye, Pappy," he said, wiping blood off his arm with his hand. He continued working as Scrap and Early stared at him with disbelief and sadness. Later that evening Harley looked directly into nowhere as Margaret cleaned the wound with calendula tea, then coated it with aloe vera gel. "I thank ye kin git by without stitches, but I'll put this butterfly tape on it," she said. "Keep it on, and it will heal in no time, honey," she said, cleaning up the clutter on the kitchen table. "Yore gonna be all right, brother," said Early kindly, but Harley failed to respond in any way. "Ye should have never done that, Harley. Early loves ye," rebuked Sissy. Harley was quick to react to her comment. "Why don't ye shut up, Sissy, and mind yore own business." Crushed by the harsh words from her hero, Sissy ran from the room crying. Early departed in silence, and Margaret kept mum too.

The rush of testosterone did nothing to remedy Harley's anger and frustration. And it fed his dreams at night with blurry visions of his biological parents, images of his real mother and father, who pleaded with him for forgiveness, asking for his devotion and gratitude. He never did get a look at the physical characteristics of the specters as they began to dominate his life. He kept them secret from his adoptive family for fear of them feeling offended by their presence. His out-of-control moments came more often, and Scrap and Early were on tenterhooks when they worked with him at the saw. One day, while Scrap was in town on an errand, Early bravely endured Harley's occasional berating and his sullen attitude. At a convenient moment, Early shut the saw down and stood face-to-face with his brother. "What's the matter now?" demanded Harley. "I'll tell ye what's a matter, Harley. Yore meanness is about to git aholt of me and all of us!" shouted Early. Harley sneered. "Us? Ye mean all ye Bairds that looks alike? Well, Early, that's tough shit! If I have my way, I'm gonna move out of here when I graduate. I'll git me a job in Knoxville or maybe even move up north and work in a factory," said Harley, bracing himself for a vehement response. Instead Early put his face in his huge hands. "Please don't leave us, Harley. Momma and Scrap would die, and it would break me and Sissy's hearts. Yore the one we all look up to, 'specially since Daddy died." Early stumbled over to the sitting log and continued as Harley stood by, dumbfounded. "I knowed that ye was hurt by his passin', and I knowed that ye was his favert; but I also knowed that he loved all of us, and we loved him. Ye said that yoreself. It don't matter who was his favert; it jest matters that we was loved." Early removed his cupped hands from his face, and his tormented appearance broke Harley's heart. "I really cain't unnerstand what's botherin' ye, brother, but I'll wait it out. 'Cause yore my brother, and even if'n ye beat me into the ground, I couldn't stand to live without ye," he said, shaking his head sadly. Harley walked, as if in a trance, over to the log and sat by his brother. He was suddenly aware of the essence of his anxiety and anger. All of his grief, sense of loss, and fear of abandonment were washed away in the deluge of his brother's tears and his frantic plea of "don't leave me." Harley put his arm around Early's shaking shoulders and spoke quietly. "I won't ever leave ye, Early. That would be too hurtful. And I know all about that," he said, offering a clean bandana to him. "Now go ahead and clean yoreself up afore Scrap gits back," he said. He patted Early's broad shoulder as he rose to restart the saw.

Thanks to the band saw, Margaret and Maw's gardens, and the help of the rapidly growing children, the Baird clan managed to thrive in the years following Benny's death. Harley grew exponentially, in body and spirit, and it saddened Scrap and Margaret to see him become a man so quickly. But the government was pleased with his progress.

It wasn't long after he graduated from high school and celebrated his eighteenth birthday that he received a present from Uncle Sam: a letter inviting him to be a registrant for the draft. A few weeks later, he received more correspondence. He hastily tore open the letter addressed to him from the Selective Service System and read aloud as he walked the lane back to the house. "Harley Baird, Selective Service No. 35-9-49-664, Duff, Tennessee, Campbell County; you are hereby ordered to present yourself for Armed Forces Physical Examination by reporting to the Knoxville Federal Building on August 7, 1968, at 9:00 a.m." The letter went on to say that a bus would be available to deliver him to the destination and bring him back home, and that he must be at the Fleet Building in LaFollette at six thirty that morning to meet the bus.

"Maybe ye won't pass the physical," said Margaret, dreading the thought that her son might be sent to Vietnam. "I'll knock 'im upside the head with a shovel if'n you wont me to, Momma. That should fix it," said Early. "Jest don't stab me agin," retorted Harley. Scrap, who normally had something to say about every subject, was silent as he walked out on the porch.

He was also silent on the morning of August 7 as he drove Harley to LaFollette. When Harley got out of the truck in front of the Fleet Building, Scrap gave him some advice. "Try not to be too healthy down thar, honey; I don't wont to see ye go either."

There was a crowd of young men, mostly graduates of LaFollette High School, waiting as the bus arrived, a beat-up old school bus leased by the government to ferry young East Tennessee conscripts to destinations in preparation for service to their country. The driver, who appeared hung over, stepped wearily off the bus, his potbelly preceding him by several inches. Frog Harvey, a classmate of Harley's, stood at attention when the driver appeared. "That's just the bus driver," Harley whispered. "Shit," said Frog, who relaxed immediately. Frog's real name was Millard, but he garnered the nickname from his habit of jumping and yelling whatever was on his mind at the time when startled. This affliction prompted many of his male classmates to goose Frog at every opportunity, just to experience his hilarious reaction.

The driver studied a clipboard. "OK, gentlemen, when I call your name, signify your presence by saying 'here'." Someone goosed Frog when his name was called, and he screamed, "Germany!" When the laughter died down, the driver reprimanded Frog before continuing. "One more outburst like that, smart-ass, and I'll leave you behind, you understand?" "Yes sir," said Frog respectfully.

Later, when they boarded the bus, Frog sat next to Harley. "What in the world did ye yell 'Germany' fer?" asked Harley. "That was what was on my mind when somebody poked me. That's whar I wont to be stationed. Not that I'm a chicken, but I'd rather go to Germany than Vietnam." "Who wouldn't?" thought Harley.

The bus crept along, stopping to pick up other young men down the way. It caught fire in Caryville at Cove Lake State Park. Harley and the rest of the passengers cheered loudly as they disembarked, at the prospect of not taking their physicals that day. But the driver used the phone at the park ranger station, and another decrepit vehicle was dispatched to transport them to their destination.

On arrival at the Federal Building, the passengers were ushered in to a big, airy room on the fifth floor. The room was set with about one hundred chairs, and decorations were sparse. Some recruitment posters for all branches of the armed services and a large photo of Lyndon B. Johnson glowered down on the assembly. "Be seated, boys, and I do mean boys, because none of you look like men to me," said a squat, barrel-chested sergeant as he strutted into the room. "Now I want all of you to behave today. Cooperate with the doctors and corpsmen, and we'll get out of here as soon as we can. If I catch any of you screwin' around, I will personally kick your ass." The comment didn't settle well with most of the Campbell County contingent, who didn't cotton to threats; but they wisely kept their mouths shut, all except Frog. "Hey, that ain't no way to talk to nobody!" he spoke in a squeaky voice. Enraged, the sergeant slammed his clipboard on a table, quickstepped to Frog's chair, jerked him up, and threw him against the wall. Frog slid to the floor and trembled as the sergeant continued his tirade. "You little piss ant, I'm gonna stomp…" Harley blocked his way as he moved toward the boy. "That's enough, mister. He cain't hep it." "You stay out of this, and you call me sergeant!" screamed the aggressor, blood red, his neck veins bulging. "I'll call ye sergeant when I'm 'fischally a soldier. But I ain't yet, and neither is he or anybody else in this room," said Harley in a cold, hard voice, accompanied by a look of intention that spelled big trouble to the sergeant. Without uttering a word, the sergeant whirled about-face, stomped out of the room, and was not seen again.

Soon a corporal entered the room. His demeanor was much nicer than the previous instructor's. "OK, gentlemen. Take off all your clothes except your drawers, fold them neatly on your chairs, and line up here at the door as I call your names…please." The group followed the directions quietly and, at the corporal's instruction, lined up alphabetically at the door. Harley was relieved that Frog's last name didn't begin with the same letter as his.

The room on the other side of the door was about the same size as the first room. There were a few folding chairs in use by clerks at various stations on the perimeter. The clerks took information from the young men as they were allowed in, five at a time. When the information was taken, the group filed through the other stations where doctors and corpsmen ogled, poked, probed, pinched, and in general embarrassed boys who'd never been to a doctor in their lives. Harley was being examined for flat feet when he heard the unmistakable voice of Frog scream, "Betty," startling the hell out of the corpsman tapping lightly on Frog's knee with a rubber hammer.

Everyone had climbed back into their clothes when Frog came

through the door. He'd been referred to a psychiatrist who, after brief examination, pronounced him unfit for military service. "He said I had some kind of sindrum, 'turnips sindrum' or somethin' like that. He said that I cain't be trusted to handle a rifle. I mean, why would I even need a gun in Germany?" he said glumly as he slipped his britches on.

On the way back home, those who'd failed their physicals (with the exception of Frog) sang and joked around. Harley and the others that passed were pensive.

Chapter 21

ATTACK OF THE LITTLE MAN

The pipes on the Mercury were so loud they could be heard above the band saw.

"Who's that?" said Harley as he shut the saw off, and it whined gradually to silence. "That's Bucky Goodman. I don't know him, but I know his car. He goes to LaFollette High School. Family owns Goodman Body Shop and Auto Repair," said Early as he took off his safety goggles. The driver of the Mercury gunned the car one more time before shutting his engine down. "Guess that feller wonts to be heared," said Harley as the roar echoed through the holler. They watched with mounting interest as the driver's door opened, and a diminutive fellow hopped spryly out and walked briskly to the passenger's side to open the door. Early gasped as Sissy emerged from the car. "Good Lord! What's Sissy doin' with him?" "Let's go see," said Harley, pulling his shirt on.

"Hey, Harley, Early, you'uns know Bucky Goodman?"said Sissy cautiously. "Bucky, these are my brothers." "You'uns shore don't look like brothers," said Bucky, grinning widely, displaying the overbite responsible for his nickname. "What ye doin' in this neighborhood?" said Harley, ignoring the remark. "He picked me up as I was walkin' home from Triple-Trio practice. Ain't that nice?" said Sissy, nervously attempting to diffuse the palpable tension in the air. Early joined her. "I shore like yore car, Bucky. That's a purty paint job." Bucky swelled with pride. "I painted it myself, got three coats on it," he said proudly, buffing the hood with his shirt tail. Sissy took the opportunity to slide out of the awkward conversation and fled into the house. "Well, bye-bye, Bucky, and thank ye agin fer the ride!"

"Yore welcome, Sissy, maybe I'll see ye agin!" There was an awkward pause, then Bucky made an improper overture. "Hey, fellers, look what I got," he whispered, reaching into his back pocket and producing a pint of bourbon. "It's Old Crow! Let's have a snort!" he grinned an evil beaver smile. Early was mortified. "Put that thang away; if our momma and Scrap sees that, they'll raise Cain." "If Bob Dossett catches you with that, ye might as well say goodby to yore car," said Harley, stone-faced. Realizing that he had no takers on his offer, Bucky slid the pint back in his pocket. "I ain't worried about Bob Dossett; my daddy's a county commissioner." he abruptly turned to leave. "Well, don't wont to war out my welcome. I got to git to the house. Maybe I'll see you'uns some other time," said Bucky, his last words drowned out by the commotion as the engine came to life. Harley and Early clamped their hands over their ears as he gunned the engine several times, backed onto the main road, and squealed his tires as he sped away.

Sissy was angry. "Harley, what's wrong with ye and Early? You'uns was rude to him. The whole time he talked to ye, you'uns looked like mules eatin' sawbriars," said Sissy as Harley and Early came into the house. "Ooh, sounds like Sissy's got herself a feller!" chided Early, who ducked behind the couch when she threatened to chuck one of Scrap's boots at him. "Hesh up, all of ye," scolded Margaret. She didn't like the idea of her little girl riding in cars, but she was wise enough to keep her mouth shut, knowing full well that a chastised girl with raging hormones could rebel at the slightest provocation. Harley spoke pseudo-contritely, "I'm sorry, Sissy. I was jest worried that if you'uns got married, you might have a tribe of pygmies," he said and barely made it out the door as Scrap's boot came sailing dangerously near his head. Early rolled on the floor behind the couch, laughing like a hyena, as Sissy marched off to her room.

As time passed, the Mercury could be heard driving past the Baird house in the wee hours of the morning, and Bucky found reasons to visit the house throughout the daylight hours; bringing presents to Margaret and attempting to butter up Scrap. Scrap was more unkind to him than either Harley or Early, calling him "Little Man." "Little Man, what in hellfire are ye doin' out ball-hootin' on the roads, drivin' past this house at one o'clock in the mornin'?" "I jest like drivin' around," replied the unflappable Bucky.

"Well, drive around somewhars else," snarled Scrap. "Thar ain't nobody has any business out atter eleven o'clock; nothin' good happens atter eleven anyways." Bucky pondered the advice and wisely refrained from continuing the conversation.

Like many males of his stature, Bucky got his way through tenaciousness, wearing folks down till they gave in to his wishes. Eventually the Bairds bowed to his persistent ways, tolerating his presence, mainly because they knew that Sissy cared for him. After a while they allowed Sissy to go out riding with him but only after Sunday dinner during daylight hours.

"You'uns be keerful now," said Margaret. "We will, Momma," replied Sissy as Bucky started the "Bellerin' Merc" (as Scrap named it), and the couple drove slowly out of the yard. Scrap and the boys conveniently disappeared at the couple's departure, glum over the fact that their "baby" was courting the cocky little banty rooster.

"Let's go swimming in the lake," said Bucky as he steered the Mercury wildly around the curves leading into LaFollette. "But I ain't got no swimmin' suit," said Sissy, grasping the door with a death grip but enjoying the rush of the experience. "Who needs a swimmin' suit?" said Bucky as he lit a cigarette. "We do", said Sissy, a bit put off with the remark. "What if'n I tole you that I brought mine, and I have one for ye too?" "You bought me a swimmin' suit?!" cried Sissy, twisting around to look in the backseat. "Well, I kinda' borried my sister's. It's in the trunk." "Oh, Bucky, do you thank it'll fit? It's such a hot day, I'd love to git in the water." "Well, if'n it don't fit, we kin always go skinny-dippin'," he said, and threw his arm up as she slugged him in the shoulder.

They drove for a long while on back roads until they arrived at Panther Point, an unusually flat piece of land bordering the lake. "Ooh, Bucky, ain't this the place whar people saw the Painther Man?" said Sissy as he flipped open the trunk of the car. He snickered and reached way back in the trunk, past a cooler that he'd filled with ice, Nehi's, Cokes, and snacks. "We don't have to worry 'bout a half-man, half-painther, darlin', not when we got this," said Bucky, proudly brandishing a .44 magnum pistol. "Put that thang away; yore agoin' to hurt somebody!" Sissy cried shrilly. "Ye won't be sayin' that when the Painther Man tries to grab ye," said Bucky as he tossed her his sister's swimsuit. "Now go ahead and put this on; I'm warin' mine under my dungarees." "OK, but turn yore head. Wait a minute, I'll go behind those bushes over thar," she said. "Whatever makes ye feel good," he said, returning the weapon to the trunk. As Sissy was changing, he found the bottle of bourbon he'd also stashed in the back of the trunk. He congratulated himself on planning an excellent afternoon as he took a swig.

Sissy emerged shyly from the bushes and placed her neatly folded clothing in the backseat. "Does this look all right?" The suit was a bit tight, which thrilled Bucky to no end. "It's perfect, darlin'; now let's git in that water. Come on, I'll race ye," he yelled and took off toward the lake as fast as his pale little legs would carry him. It was all he could do to contain his anger when she beat him.

They had the lake to themselves, which wasn't uncommon in those days, and they splashed around in the cool, clear water for an hour or so. Sissy flopped down in the grass and felt pleasantly tired as the breeze and hot sun dried her body. She looked back as Bucky returned to the car to get the cooler. His affection and painstaking attempts to please touched her, and she had developed more than a liking for him, despite his occasional obnoxiousness. She rolled over on her back. An eagle "screed" somewhere in the vastness of the deep blue sky, and she shielded her eyes against the sun in an effort to find it.

Bucky lifted the cooler out of the trunk, then rummaged around for the bottle of bourbon, grinning at the success of the day and his prospects for the rest of the afternoon.

"Ye wont a Coke?" he asked as he sat the cooler down in the grass. "Thank ye, Bucky, I thank I will," answered Sissy, giddy with the beauty of a perfect day. "All righty then, I'll fix ye a special one," he said, filling a cup with ice, pouring a double shot of bourbon in, and filling the rest with Coke. "I'm really thirsty after that swim," said Sissy as she took the entire drink down in one gulp. She choked hard, and Bucky had a good laugh as he patted her on the back. "What in the world did ye put in that?" sputtered Sissy, wiping her mouth disgustedly with the back of her hand. "Jest a little bourbon, it'll relax ye. See I've got some myself," he said, taking a swig out of his cup. "Heck fire, Bucky, I was already relaxed," said Sissy, her head swimming from the effects of the double shot. "My momma would kill me if'n she knew I drunk whiskey." Bucky corrected her. "It ain't whiskey, it's bourbon." He filled her cup again with Coke and another shot of Old Crow. "C'mon, darlin', have one more with me, then we'll quit," pleaded Bucky, thrusting the cup at her. For some reason she accepted the cup and drank the contents down. "Thar, now are ye satisfied? Put that bottle away," she said, noting to herself that the second drink didn't taste as bad as the first.

Despite the fact that it was parked in the shade, the interior of the Mercury was hot, and Bucky and Sissy perspired profusely as he struggled to take her virginity. “Ouch, Bucky, be keerful. That hurts,” squealed Sissy as Bucky poked and prodded with the finesse of a rapist, which in essence he was. When the act was completed, Sissy cried as she squirmed back into Bucky’s sister’s swimming suit. “What’s a matter?” he panted as he pulled his suit back up from around his ankles. “I don’t know why I did that. My family would die if’n they knowed I done that,” cried Sissy as she exited the car. “Don’t worry about it; they’ll never know,” he answered glibly, lighting a cigarette. “Here, ye wont a drag?” “What are ye tryin’ to do to me?” she said, slapping his hand away as she sprinted toward the lake. “Whar ye goin’?” “I’m afixin’ to clean myself,” she said.

Later they arrived at Sissy’s home before dark. “My momma and Scrap is goin’ to be mad. I was s’posed to git home in time to go to church; thar all there now.” “Don’t worry about it. Now you got time to clean yourself up a little bit before they come home. Tell ’em I had a flat tar.” “OK,” she mumbled as she raced up the porch steps. “Sissy,” he yelled as she opened the front door. “What?” “I love ye.” She smiled sadly at the remark but didn’t answer. Somehow it was of no consolation to her.

Reliving his conquest Bucky grinned a toothy grin, and as he pulled out of the yard, he made a mental note to wash his sister’s swimsuit.

Scrap and Margaret were not pleased that Sissy didn’t show up in time to attend church. But the “flat tire” story, vouched for by Bucky, worked, and she was forgiven. She and her paramour were allowed to continue their rides on Sunday afternoons, which they often used as an excuse to continue their shenanigans at Panther Point. She was beginning to like the trysts, even without the aid of bourbon. Although her affection for Bucky was becoming truly genuine, Sissy was experiencing considerable guilt for deceiving her family and offending God. And it manifested itself in her personality, which, at times, was brooding. Margaret chalked the difference up to hormonal changes, changes that she had experienced as a young woman. The men were purely mystified and kept their distance from Sissy, cutting a wide swath around her on her bad days.

Chapter 22

DECISIONS

Sissy didn't feel well, especially in the mornings. Her breasts were tender, and her back ached terribly. She was bereft of energy and could barely make it through a day of school. Early, in his infinite kindness, volunteered to do her chores in the evenings but only if she'd "spell" him with his chores when she felt better. When she missed her period, she was certain there was a new life within her. She was petrified at the thought of being pregnant but told no one, not even Bucky. Despite her deep religious faith, she even thought of aborting the child, an action considered so abhorrent that folks rarely talked about it. She'd heard stories about folk medicine and the herbs that would make an unwanted child "go away."

"Take Spike 'n' Whitey with ye; they'll take keer of any snakes on the road or any other ornery critters," said Margaret as Sissy walked out on the porch. "OK, Momma," said Sissy as Early's dogs came scampering, knowing that someone was going for a walk, and they were taking part in the adventure. It was dusk on a beautiful Indian summer evening. The wind was up, but it was still a comfortably warm, if not a perfect, temperature. Sissy had wrapped one of Harley's faded flannel shirts around her shoulders in the likelihood the weather turned cooler later. "I might stop by Maw's and visit fer a while," shouted Sissy as she walked onto the road, the two mutts frolicking ahead of her. Margaret shouted a reply that was drowned out by the wind, which rustled the dry leaves in the trees and scattered the fallen ones along the road.

Maw was concocting a remedy when Sissy tapped on the edge of her screen door.

"Come on in if'n yore friendly," yelled Maw from the kitchen. Earlier she had gathered a large bunch of jewelweed that grew by the stream that meandered through her property. Now she was adding the bunch to a pot of boiling water, from which she would later strain the concoction.

"Well, hidey, Sis! I was jest makin' up a balm for little Haird here. He got hisself into a mess of pizen ivy or maybe sumac." Sitting patiently on the two chairs in the kitchen were Howard, an eight-year-old boy who looked as if he'd been burned badly, and a concerned woman, obviously, his mother.

Maw strained the juice into a jar and capped it. "Here ye go, Wilma. Rub it on his blisters tonight. If'n ye got a 'frigerator, pour some of the juice in a ice tray so it will be soothin' when ye rub it on him tomorry mornin'. He should be healin' up by tomorry night. I wisht ye'd have come earlier; we could have worshed him off with soapwort, and he'd be better afore the night was over." "Thank ye, Maw," said the woman, clutching Maw's hand in her own. "What do I owe ye?" "I'll tell ye what, have this little feller pick me some black-burries when they come into season agin. Put a kerosene-soaked rag in his belt to stave off the chiggers, and make shore he stays away from pizen ivy," laughed Maw as she Dutch-rubbed the victim's head. "He'll do it, pon my word and honor," promised Howard's mother as she ushered him out the door.

"Now, little sister, set yoreself down, and let's talk awhile. It's been a time since I seen ye, honey," said Maw as she eased her old bones into a chair. Sissy attempted to speak but burst into tears.

"I knowed somethin' was wrong the minute I seen ye," said Maw, rising to envelope the girl in her wizened arms.

It took a while for the story to be told, but Maw listened patiently to the tormented girl.

"Lord, Lord, Lord, little Hooty would have had a conniption fit over this," Maw exclaimed and immediately regretted the statement that set Sissy into another fit of weeping.

"Now, now, thar ain't nothin' we cain't handle with the hep of God, and God is in us, so we got to thank positive 'cause that's what God does. God is love, and he don't thank no negative thoughts," Maw said. "Now what's yore plan, honey?" she said as she brewed some chamomile tea for the both of them. Sissy fell to pieces again. "I only got one, Maw. That's one of the reasons I come up here," said Sissy, attempting to stifle a sob with no success. Maw's wrinkled face formed into a pucker, somewhat like that of a dried apple doll. "Ye ain't thankin' 'bout makin' it go away, are ye?" Sissy couldn't speak but nodded her head affirmatively. "Have ye tole yore momma 'bout this?" Sissy shook her head "no." "Then why don't ye stay with me tonight? I'll call yore momma and ask her if'n ye can," said Maw as she reached for the telephone on the wall behind her.

The chamomile tea and Maw's tender mercies had a calming effect on Sissy, who fought a fit of hiccups between sips. Maw gazed out the window at the harvest moon that had risen. "Lord have mercy, that moon is shinin' on my yard like a lamp. Let's go outside and soak up the magic," said Maw, pulling back Sissy's chair. "Grab yore cup, and I'll git the teapot, honey."

Maw led Sissy down to her garden, which was pretty much picked over for the season, and they sat in the swing together. Sissy scolded the dogs as Whitey and Spike chased one another between Maw's sheets, which were illuminated blue-white in the bright moonlight, snapping and popping in the wind. "Don't ye worry 'bout them pups; thar havin' a good time. And if need be, I kin worsh those sheets agin.

What I wont ye to do is lissin to me and what I have to tell ye."

"I was jest 'bout four or five yars older 'n ye. I'd run my no-good old man off, and I was on my own. I was able to keep the house and the land 'cause my momma left it to me, and it was paid fer. And I swore that I would not disrespeck her memry by lettin' this little farm fall down aroun' me. I planted corn, herbs, taters, maters, onions, and beans in a garden that would feed two families. My second yar alone, I planned on settin' a bakker field up yonder in that pasture," said Maw, gesturing with a bony finger to the hillside above the house.

"I planted my seeds in May. They's little biddy seeds, and I planted 'em in float trays like it said in the almanac. I worked the field with my ole mule, Bill, and by June it was time to put my plants in that bed of beautiful, groomed earth. Onliest thang was that I warn't really shore 'bout how to go 'bout it. I talked to ole Bob Morton, who's growed bakker all his life, and he lended me his boy, Wesley, who was home from collige in Kentucky that summer. "He's gittin' aintsy fer somethin' to do, and he'd be plum tickled to hep ye. He's planted with me and his brothers since he was a young'un," said Bob.

Maw paused to take a sip of her tea and continued. "Well, shore as shootin', Wesley showed up the next mornin' towin' a two-row bakker setter with his daddy's tractor. We worked hard, even with the setter, but we got the patch planted in a few days. I thought he was a mite quare 'cause he hardly spoke to me, and when we would rest a spell, he would pull a book out his knapsack and read the whole time. I'd never knowed nobody that finished high school, much less somebody that was agoin' to college, so I s'pose he thought I acted purty quare too. But direckly we got used to each other, and purty soon we was talkin' up a storm. I fixed him dinner and supper as part of his pay, and durin' those meals he would tell me wunnerful stories 'bout school and his classmates that come from ever'whar, even France. And he tole me jokes that made me laugh, and it felt good 'cause I hadn't laughed fer a while. When we warn't tendin' bakker, he hepped me aroun' the farm with other chores. Later he hepped me cut and stake the bakker. We were both brown as burries from workin' long airs in the sun; and he was a sight to behold with those broad shoders and ripply muscles that shined with sweat and that purty, curly har bleached by the sun.

"When it was time, me and him hung the bakker in an old shed, that ain't thar no more, to use as a firin' barn. When we put leaves on the floor and lit 'em to smolder, he hepped me seal the shed, and air work was purty much done.

"We went back to the house to eat what we called "air last supper" 'cause Wesley had to leave fer school the next day. We were both vury quiet at the table. Finely he looked at me with those purty green eyes and spoke so sweet. "This has been the best summer of my life, Nola. I wisht I could take ye with me to make all my seasons beautiful." My eyes filled with tears, but I couldn't find any words. He got up and come 'round the table, picked me up, and curried me to my bedroom. It was a beautiful night, even more beautiful than this'n. He stayed with me until the wee airs, and I woke up to the sound of the tractor sputterin' out of the yard. When the sun come up, I found a book of his on the kitchen table, it was his favert by Robert Brownin', and he used to read to me from it. Wont to hear my favorite pome? I memorized it." Transfixed by the tale, Sissy nodded dumbly. Maw cleared her voice and spoke solemnly, "Meeting at Night," by Robert Brownin'. "The gray sea and the long black land, and the yaller moon, large and low, and the startled little waves that leap in fiery ringlets from thar sleep. As I gain the cove with pushin' prow and quenched its speed into the slushy sand. Then a mile of warm, sea-scented beach, three fields to cross till a farm appears, a tap at the pane, the quick sharp scratch, and blue spurt of a lighted match, and a voice less loud, through its joys and fears, than them two hearts beatin' each to each!"

At the end of the recitation, Maw and Sissy sat mute, as if contemplating a fervent prayer. Their trance was interrupted by a screech owl's mournful call in the deep woods. The dogs, curled up at their feet, raised their heads briefly but worn out from their game of tag, decided not to investigate the source of the sound.

"I ain't never seen the sea, but I'd like to thank that farm was mine, and that pome was 'bout Wesley and me," said Maw wistfully. "Ye gittin' cold, young'n?" "No, Maw, this is fine," said Sissy, wrapping Harley's shirt tightly around herself. "Go on with yore story, if'n ye wont to."

"Well, I fount mysef with child," stated Maw matter-of-factly. Sissy gasped, and Maw held up her hand, knowing she would receive this reaction to her confession.

"I experienced all of the signs, and I was skeered. It was bad enough that a growed woman lived alone in those days, and I would have been shorely scorned if'n folks knowed I was pregnint.

"Even though my belly warn't showin' yet, I started a warin' clothes that was too big for me, like dresses and sech that would cover my belly. I was a might juberous about goin' to church 'cause that seems whar the most nosiest and condemin' folks is. And I seldom, if ever, went to town. But the fear in me caused me to conjure up a plan, a plan like the one that's torturin' ye, darlin'." Sissy leaned forward, hands clenched tightly in a ball, a supplicant with hopes of receiving an answer to her dilemma.

"I was at my wit's end, and had no whar to go if'n I was run out of Campbell County. One rainy night I mixed up a tea of black cohosh and Angelica leaves. Ye ever been to Jellico, young'un?" "A couple of times," answered Sissy. "Well, it's named after the Angelica root, which they used to make spirits out of. Anyways, as the tea steeped, I prayed that when I drunk it, the concoction would git rid of my baby. Then a vision of Wesley come to my mind, and he said one line from the pome, "Two hearts, beatin' each to each." "I thought of air baby's heart, abeatin' like the heart of a little bird, and I thought of my heart, abeatin' fer the two of us. I busted into tears and throwed the tea away. Right then and thar, I was obliged to keep our child, and I wasn't afeered of the future," said Maw. She continued in a sorrowful tenor.

"That child was the first one I ever delivered. She came early in April. She was tiny as a dolly, and she was beautiful. She had the makins' of the purtiest green eyes ye ever seen, and she hardly made a sound. Even her cry was like the tinklin' of bells. But she died the next mornin'. As I held her at my breast, she died in my arms, and I figger it was my punishment fer my wayward thoughts."

Weeping, Sissy rushed to help Maw as she struggled to get out of the swing. "I appreciate ye, darlin'. Come over here, and I'll show ye whar I laid my little angel to rest," she said as she waddled along. "Lookee here," said Maw as she cleaned off a stone in one of her rock gardens. The stone, which could be easily read in the bright moonlight, was inscribed with the roughly chisled word, "Glory." Sissy had noted the stone many times as she visited and figured that "Glory" was just a rock, placed in the garden in homage to the Maker.

"That's my little girl, Glory, a gift from God, and I'll be ferever thankful for the decision I made and the short time I had with her," said Maw, changing the subject quickly. "C'mon, honey, let's go to the house. Ye'll feel better 'bout all this in the mornin', and ye'll find that yore more loved than ye ever knowed ye was."

Sissy was worn to a frazzle as she and Maw prepared for bed." "I only got one bed, youngun. If ye mind me asharin' it with ye, then I'll make me a pallet on the floor." "Oh, I don't mind; sometimes I sleep with Momma, and I like it," said Sissy as Maw handed her an ancient dressing gown. "That was mine a long time ago. Ye kin war it, and ye kin keep it, honey; I ain't got no use fer it. Now hop in here, and keep yore Maw warm."

Maw lay awake listening to the wind, which was quite high now, soughing, prompting the old house to speak in a grating voice. Sissy complained in her sleep and rolled over, slinging her arm over Maw's chest and eventually snuggling into her neck. "God bless yore sweet heart, chile. It's agoin' to be OK. Air Creator will make it OK; He always does," said Maw, who was soon lulled to sleep by the murmur of the wind and of the rhythmic breathing of the sleeping girl. Later, in her dreams, she heard the voice of a man beckoning to her from the window. He was beautiful and robust in his youth, as was she. She sighed as he gathered her effortlessly in his strong arms and carried her through the open window. Her nightgown whipped around her knees in the breeze as he led her through the yard to a waiting ship that was rocking gently in a sandy harbor. They held each other tightly as the ship set sail, sails popping like sheets on a clothesline. "I ain't never been on the sea, Wes," said Maw as the prow of the ship rose and fell on the swells. "We're going to do a lot of things that you haven't done, Nola. It won't be long; isn't that right, Glory," he said to the curly-headed little girl with the emerald-green eyes, snuggled in the crook of his right arm. Glory whispered sweetly, "Umm hmm," and reached out to lovingly trace Maw's features with her tiny fingers. The three drew close, swaying together on the rolling deck; three hearts beating, each to each, mesmerized by the full yellow moon, enchanted by the presence of one another.

Chapter 23

PROUDLY PRESENTING MR. AND MRS. BUCKY GOODMAN

Even after a pep talk by Maw, Sissy was unable to find the courage to go home and tell her family about her condition. "Maw, they'll kill me. Worser, they'll disfigger Bucky!" "Ye've got to tell 'em, honey; then ever'one kin git on with thar lives and ye kin brang a sweet little life into this world. Now whyont ye go on home. Ye cain't stay here fer the rest of yore life." "Kin I tell Bucky first?" said Sissy pitifully, her face ravaged from crying and hormonal chaos. Maw yanked the phone from its cradle on the wall. "Go ahead, call 'im and tell 'im to git his hind end to my place as soon as he kin," said Maw, placing the phone in her hand.

Maw peered out the window at Bucky and Sissy as they sat in his car, talking animatedly. Sissy hadn't mentioned what the problem was on the phone but expressed great urgency that he should see her. It was Saturday morning, and he didn't have to work at his daddy's shop, so he showed up about an hour after she had called.

"Shit, shit, shit! Why did this have to happen?" yelled Bucky, pounding the dashboard with his fist. "Stop it, Bucky. It ain't nobody's fault; it jest happened. Now what are we goin' to do?" cried Sissy, wringing her hands till they were red. "Shut the hell up and let me thank fer a minute," screamed Bucky with a wild look in his eyes that frightened her. He was silent for a moment; then he spoke excitedly. "I got it. Ye don't have to tell 'em at all! We'll git married; and when the baby comes, we'll jest let 'em figger it out. We'll say it come early or somethin'! How does that sound to ye?"

It came time for the Sunday courtship ritual. Shaking like a leaf, Bucky stood at the dinner table and asked Scrap if he could marry his granddaughter. The room roared with stillness before Scrap responded, “Hell no!” Harley and Early laughed heartily. Sissy began to cry, which immediately deflated their bravado. “Honey, yore jest ’bout to finish high school, and ye’ve never courted nobody but Little Man here. Don’t ye wont more out of life?” Disregarding Scrap’s obvious disdain for her boyfriend, Sissy spoke her piece. “All I know is that I love him,” she said tragically. There was a brief silence, which was interrupted by Margaret. “Bucky, honey, let’s thank ’bout this. What does yore momma and daddy have to say about it?” “Thar fine with it,” he lied, knowing in his heart that when he did tell them, they would be thrilled at the prospect of getting him out of the house. “Sissy, are you shore you love him?” said Harley, pointing his finger rudely at Bucky, as if the boy were road kill. “Yes, I do,” she said pleadingly. “Bucky, we’re goin’ to have to thank on this fer a bit. Come back tomorry, and we’ll have a answer fer ye,” said Margaret, whose heart broke at the sight of her daughter’s tragic posture. Margaret knew that there was more to this situation, something that escaped the sensibilities of her menfolk.

After Bucky left, the family discussed the situation way into the night. Sissy stubbornly refused any attempts to dissuade her from matrimony. When an impasse was reached between her and her family, she threatened to run away in order to get married.

The Community News section of the local paper was filled with photographs of engaged couples announcing their upcoming nuptials. A few of the photos featured starry-eyed girls with visions of life with Prince Charming. They were usually held in a hammerlock by a redneck with a vacant stare and a hole in his T-shirt, wearing a ragged ball cap with a slogan on the bill. So much for Prince Charming. Sissy and Bucky were not included in this week's illustrious group. Nor would they ever have their photo in the paper, because their marriage was an impromptu event being that Sissy was carrying a child—and that child was growing every minute.

Bucky and his kin insisted on having the wedding and reception at his parents' home but acquiesced to having Reverend Bunch perform the marriage ceremony instead of their own preacher.

The guests parked their cars in the yard alongside junked vehicles of every year and type, rusting patients waiting to be parted out by the Goodmans for various automotive repair projects. As Bucky's friends horsed around with him in the yard, the Bairds attended to Sissy in the kitchen of the Goodman home.

"Are ye shore you wont to do this?" said Scrap, who appeared the vision of misery in his new overalls, crisp white shirt, and tie, fashioned into something that barely resembled a Windsor knot. "Pappy, don't start that again," said Sissy as Margaret and Maw fluttered like little birds, picking at the roomy bodice of the little white dress that Margaret had lovingly sewn for her daughter. Harley and Early leaned glumly against the kitchen counter, and although they agreed heartily with Scrap, they kept their mouths shut.

Margaret stood back to admire her handiwork. "Thar now, don't ye look purty! I wish Benny could see ye," she exclaimed, clasping her hands tightly in front of her. Maw held her hands in the same position and beamed broadly. "I feel like a toad," said Sissy, voice quivering. Early made a weak but sincere attempt at comforting her. "Momma's right, Sissy, ye look beautiful." "Besides, the only toads around here are the ones croakin' in the front yard," added Harley, at which point everybody laughed.

"Oh, my little Doney Gal, don't you guess, better be makin' yore weddin' dress, weddin' dress, weddin' dress, better be makin' yore weddin' dress," sang the older folks as Bucky's cousin, Caleb, (whose repertoire was limited) played that and other wedding-related tunes on his accordion. Bucky and his groomsmen were lined up and lit up from numerous trips to the trunks of their cars and trucks, and snickered behind their hands as Caleb finished the song. Reverend Bunch climbed the steps, signaling the beginning of the wedding, and the guests took their seats, which were stenciled on the backs, "Property of Harper-Woodson Funeral Home." After bridesmaids Margaret and Maw took their places at the side of the porch steps, the reverend nodded solemnly to Caleb, who played a lively, polka-style version of the "Wedding March."

"Well, let's git this thang agoin'," said Scrap sadly. "Stop it, Pappy!" scolded Sissy as she slipped her arm through his. Harley and Early led the way for the bride-to-be and her reluctant escort.

Mercifully, Caleb's snappy rendition of the "Wedding March" ended, signaling Bucky to join Sissy on the front porch with Reverend Bunch. When Scrap, Harley, and Early had taken their seats in the front row, Reverend Bunch began the service.

"Dearly beloved, we are gathered here today, in the presence of God and these witnesses, to join Cecilia Margaret Baird and Roland Radcliff Goodman..." At the mention of Bucky's given names, his wedding party burst into guffaws. Most of them knew him only by his lifelong moniker of "Bucky." Bucky's ears turned bright red as Reverend Bunch paused for the laughter to fade. Then he continued. "We are here to join these two in matrimony, which is commended to be honorable among all men; and therefore, is not by any to be entered into unadvisedly or lightly but reverently, discreetly, advisedly, and solemnly. Into this holy estate these two persons present now come to be joined. If any person can show just cause why they may not be joined together, let them speak now or forever hold their peace."

"I kin!" yelled Bucky, eliciting raucous laughter from his friends and mortifying Reverend Bunch, Sissy, and most of the guests. "Just kiddin'," said Bucky, smirking at his groomsmen, who were falling all over one another. Perhaps it was the accordion music combined with the disrespectfulness of Bucky and his inebriated cronies that caused the reverend to shorten his normally lengthy wedding sermon that day. He raced through his reading of 1 Corinthians 13:4-13, a verse selected specially by Sissy: "Love is patient and kind; love does not envy or boast. It is not arrogant or rude; it does not insist on its own way; it is not irritable or resentful. It does not rejoice at wrongdoing but rejoices with the truth. Love bears all things, believes all things, hopes all things, and endures all things. Love never ends. As for prophecies, they will pass away; as for tongues, they will cease; as for knowledge, it will pass away. For we know in part, and we prophesy in part, but when the perfect comes, the partial will pass away. When I was a child, I spoke like a child, I thought like a child, I reasoned like a child. When I became a man, I gave up childish ways. For now we see in a mirror dimly but then face-to-face. Now I know in part; then I shall know fully, even as I have been fully known. So now faith, hope, and love abide, these three; but the greatest of these is love."

Right before the vows were said, the best man acted as if he'd lost the wedding rings, then Bucky planted a sloppy kiss on Sissy's mouth, and Reverend Bunch introduced the couple as man and wife. Caleb played the "Wedding March" again as Bucky proudly escorted his queasy bride down to the line of junked cars on the perimeter of the yard, where he was met by his friends, who ripped him away from Sissy and hoisted him on their shoulders. Reverend Bunch departed before Scrap had an opportunity to pay him.

After the exit of the clergy and most of the guests went into the house to put on the feed bag, Bucky and his buddies danced. They danced with any woman or girl who remained in the yard, and with each other, as Caleb played "The Beer Barrel Polka," "In Heaven There is No Beer," and other songs that glorified drinking, which the boys did copiously.

Finally Caleb slowed the pace with "Are You Lonesome Tonight?" and the wedding party cheered as Bucky staggered toward Sissy, who had been sitting on the edge of the porch, casually observing the mayhem.

"May I have this dance, lady?" he said, outstretching his hand regally, prideful that everyone was watching him. "Jest one dance, honey. I really don't feel too good," said Sissy as he grabbed her around the waist and drug her off the porch. Unfortunately Bucky's entourage decided that it would be funny to cut in, one by one, stepping on the toes of her white slippers and whirling her clumsily around the yard. Sissy managed to get away from the last suitor who fell down, almost taking her with him. As she staggered back to the porch, nauseated to the point of vomiting, Bucky intercepted her. "Let's take one more turn around the yard, darlin'," he said, his boozy breath igniting her gag reflexes "I'm sorry, Bucky, I'm 'bout to throw up," said Sissy, covering her mouth with her hand. "C'mon, one more time," slurred Bucky, when a hand tapped him hard on the shoulder.

"Ye wont to dance? I'll dance with ye!" said Scrap as he hoisted the Little Man up in his arms and squeezed him in a bone-breaking bear hug. Bucky's friends cheered as Scrap continued to squeeze the breath out of Bucky, whirling him around the yard. Bucky's face was red, and he didn't have the breath to speak. But Scrap spoke through gritted teeth that appeared to be a smile to the spectators. "I'll tell ye what, ye little piece of shit. If'n ye ever hurt that little girl, we'll stomp a mudhole in yore backside and walk it dry." Again Bucky's cadre of friends decided to get in on the act, and one of them tapped Scrap on the shoulder to cut in. They continued to whisk Bucky around the yard until finally he vomited on one of them.

Early and Scrap escorted Sissy into the house, where Margaret, Maw, and Mrs. Goodman took the shaken girl into the bathroom to clean her up. "When you'uns finish with air little girl, bring her to the truck; we're agoin' home," said Scrap in a manner that was not to be argued with.

Harley brought the truck around, drove it right through the revelers, and up to the front porch. "What ye thank yore doin'?" shouted Bucky, puke running down the front of his checkered sport coat. "I'm takin' my sister home. Ye kin come and git her when and if ye sober up," said Harley. "Ye cain't do this to me on my weddin' night," demanded Bucky, weaving back and forth as if he were standing on a rocking boat. One of the drunken crew found what he thought was an opportunity to be clever. "Thass all right, Buckaroo, ye've already started yore family, she..." His remark was cut short, the smacking sound and repulsive bone crunch reverberating around the yard, as Harley knocked him out with one punch. Some of the boys and men moved to their fallen friend's aid, and others crept toward Harley but thought better of it when he turned on them, poised to destroy, dark primal rage manifesting itself in his taut body. "Ye wont a piece of me? Well, come on; I'd be glad to oblige ye," he said calmly, his fierce blue eyes darting from one to the other of them, as if he were making up his mind which one of them to tear apart next. There were no challengers, and they were quiet as Early escorted Sissy out of the house, along with Margaret and Maw.

Margaret got in the driver's seat, and Sissy and Maw sat up front as Scrap, Harley, and Early climbed in the back. "I'll come and git ye later, Sissy!" shouted Bucky as the truck's taillights dimmed in the gathering dusk. Then he stumbled over to the side of the porch, where his father and several men were attempting to revive the hapless victim of Harley's wrath.

Bucky arrived the next afternoon with Bob Dossett. He stood behind Dossett as they entered the Baird home. They were greeted grimly by Scrap. "Wont some coffee or tea, Bob?" said Scrap, offering him a seat at the kitchen table. "No thank ye, Scrap. I'd as soon as git this business over with and git out of yore har," said Dossett, settling uneasily into his seat. Bucky remained standing behind Dossett's chair. "Hidee, Sheriff," said Harley as he came in the room and sat beside Scrap. "Hey, Harley. Ye know what we're here fer, don't ye?" "I'm guessin' it's about that fracas I got into last night, Sheriff," said Harley, eyes fixed on the tabletop. "Well, son, it was more than a fracas. That boy you whooped up on is in the hospital with a wired-up jaw and a broken nose. I'm glad he's a stout feller; ye could have kilt him," said Dossett as Bucky fidgeted behind his chair. Scrap started to speak, but Harley silenced him. "That boy made a bad remark about my sister, and I won't stand fer it…I won't stand fer anyone sayin' a bad word about any of my family…they're all I've got…and I'll pertect 'em," said Harley, standing and rapping the table with his knuckles to punctuate his remarks. Dossett didn't answer, but silently he respected the boy's allegiance to his family. "I'll pay fer the hospital bill, Bob. Will they take payments?" said Scrap. "I'm purty shore they will, Scrap. But Harley's got to pay somehow. Ye jest cain't go beatin' someone to a pulp like that," said Dossett. Harley answered quickly. "I'm agoin' in to the service in a few weeks, and I promise I will pay fer the damage, and I will apologize to that boy and his family face-to-face," said Harley sincerely. "Ye goin' into the service, huh? What branch?" "Army, sir." "I was in the Marines in Korea. 'Bout froze to death at the Chosin Reservoir and almost got my hind end shot off too. Anyways, since yore goin' to serve yore country, I ain't goin' to arrest ye. I thank it's purty brave of ye to face the boy and his family, and I'll go with ye. Wont to do it now?" "Let me put a clean shirt on; I'll be right back," said Harley. As he left the room, Bucky stepped from around the chair.

"Kin I git my wife now?" Dossett answered for Scrap. "Why don't ye wait a couple more days, son, till thangs cool down a bit." As Bucky stormed out of the house, the sheriff stood and shook Scrap's hand.

Chapter 24

SOLITARY MAN

MaryAnne McKenzie was a spoiled brat who considered herself at the top of the food chain when it came to status in the county. Her old man owned the successful McKenzie's Auto Dealership, so had her grandfather and his father before him. Her father ensured that MaryAnne had the very best of everything, and she felt entitled to the pampering. Good looking, endowed with a beautiful body, and well-dressed, she was known to eschew anyone who was not within her small socioeconomic circle. However, she didn't allow class issues to interfere with her overactive libido and occasionally selected someone outside of her sphere to fulfill her needs. He had to be handsome and virile though, and pickings were slim.

Since she was old enough to drive, Daddy dressed her up with a new car each year. This year, her senior year, she gamboled around Campbell County in a turquoise Thunderbird convertible, with turquoise and white, rolled and pleated, leather seat covers. It was the vehicle she was driving today on her way back from a visit to her cousin in Jellico. The top was down, and her shiny, raven tresses were tied up with a bright blue ribbon as she pulled into The Snack Shack for a cold drink. It was typical Indian summer weather: hot sun, cooling breezes, low humidity. Her sundress blew up as she got out of the car, exposing for a moment her silky, tanned legs and snow-white panties. She didn't bother to hold the dress down, hoping that she might give some hayseed a thrill. "Whew, I'd like to take that fer a ride," said Early as she wiggled into the store. Harley had been funneling peanuts into his Coke and almost spilled the sleeve of Planter's. "Dang, Early, I never heared ye talk like that," he said with fake astonishment. Early turned red. “I was talkin’ ’bout that T-Bird, smarty-paints!” Harley danced around the parking lot, bending over occasionally to chortle, while Early leaned back, one foot on the running board of Scrap’s truck, and shook his head in mock exasperation. The two had just finished baling hay for Dormus Caldwell and were discussing how they would spend the extra money they’d earned. “I’m gonna give ten dollars to Momma, and I’m gonna spend the rest on myself,” said Early as Harley skipped back to the truck. “Man, are ye cheap! I’m gonna give Momma ten dollars and Scrap five dollars and Sissy five dollars,” said Harley, pulling a wad of money out of his pocket and waving it in the air for emphasis. “Yore nothin’ but a big ole brownnose, Harley,” said Early, hurling a rock at Harley’s feet. “Who’s a brownnose?” said MaryAnne as she strolled up to the brothers, sipping a cold Coke. Early stared at his boots. “We was jest kiddin’ around,” said Harley as she came closer. She boldly sized them up, focusing mostly on Harley. Embarrassed at her brashness, Harley introduced himself and Early. “I’m Harley Baird, and this is my brother, Early.” “I’ve seen ye in town,” said Early politely. She ignored Early’s comments, and instead of introducing herself, Maryanne sidled very close to Harley, close enough to make him step back. “You don’t wear a shirt that often, do you, Harley?” Harley stuttered, “Uh…I take it off when I’m a doin’ field work. I jest fergot to put it back on.” “Well, you shore are brown, and it looks like you do a lot of liftin’,” said MaryAnne as she took another swig of her Coke, not taking her dark eyes off of him. Before he could answer, she asked another question. “Do you have a shirt?” “Yep, I got one in the truck cab. It ain’t vury nice though.” “It don’t have to be nice. Just put it on, and I’ll take you for a ride. It’s getting’ close to dark, and it is s’posed to cool off this evenin’. I don’t want you catching a cold.” Harley knew that this vixen was not going to take “no” for an answer but hedged for a moment. Early came to the rescue. “Here’s yore shirt, Harley,” he said, tossing it to him from the truck cab. MaryAnne laughed. “Now that’s a good brother. Are you sure you two are related?" she said, turning tail and strutting back to the Thunderbird. She issued an order to Harley. "C'mon, Harley, let's roll," she said as he obeyed and slid into the passenger seat. "Wait a minute," yelled Early, trotting over to the passenger side of the car. He handed Harley a wadded up piece of currency. "Here's ten dollars if'n ye need it, brother," Early whispered and backed away. "I'll have him back here in a couple of hours," said MaryAnne. "Don't worry about it, Early. I kin walk home from here or catch a ride," yelled Harley as she sped away.

Harley tasted good to MaryAnne: salty, sun-burnished skin; musky, clean, honest sweat; and soft lips that cooperated when she kissed him and when she placed her breast into his mouth. Breathing heavily, she broke away from him, stood up in the front seat and removed all of her clothing with the exception of her white panties, which shone like a beacon in the harvest moonlight. She slipped out of the panties and jumped nimbly over the side of the car into the tall grass at the roadside. "Let's go for a swim," she said, opening the door for him. Harley followed, as if hypnotized, peeling his clothing off and placing it in a pile in the back floorboard of the Thunderbird. "You'd better take 'em with you. We don't want to come back in our birthday suits," she said, scooping up her clothing and reaching into the glove compartment for her purse. "You ain't takin' yore pocketbook, are ye?" "No, I just had to get something out of my purse," she answered, stuffing the purse back into the glove compartment.

The creek was fairly deep, fast flowing, and refreshing. "Damn, I thought it was supposed to cool off tonight. This feels good, don't it, Harley?" she giggled as they frolicked in the cool water. Harley didn't answer. He was mesmerized by the sight of her: her curvaceous body and especially her breasts that shone in the moonlight, shiny wet, enticing, as they bobbed in the water. "Let's get out for a minute; I don't want to get my hair too wet. I've got to meet some people later," she said as she scampered up the embankment to a flat rock, where they'd left their clothing. She turned to him, her mons pubis a perfectly coiffed "V" of curly black hair. "C'mon up here, Harley, I've got somethin' to give you." Harley didn't have to be asked twice and was soon standing over her as she knelt beside him. "This rock's still warm from today's sun. C'mon down here with me," she said huskily, pulling him down beside her. As he sat down, she straddled his legs. "Before we git started, we've got to be ready," she said, biting at the edge of the pack of Trojans and extracting the condom. She slid it on him. It was a good ride, but the journey didn't last too long. She leaned over him, breathing heavily into his neck. "This is your first time, ain't it?" Harley could only grunt. When both of them had settled down, she slid the condom off and replaced it with another. "I see yore ready to go agin," she giggled, and they performed the act once more, but this time the routine was more controlled and lasted much longer. They sat on the rock, necked, and fondled one another for a time, then she glanced at her watch in the moonlight. "Shit, we'd better be goin'. Git dressed, Harley," she said as she slipped into her panties, bra, and sundress. They skirted the creek and ran back to the T-Bird, happy to find that there wasn't a crowd waiting on them.

The radio blared, and the wind felt good as it caressed their bodies and dried their damp hair. MaryAnne and Harley sang along as she whipped the vehicle around the curves. "Don't know that I will but until I can find me. The girl who'll stay and won't play games behind me. I'll be what I am. A solitary man." When the song was over, she turned the radio down and lit a cigarette. "Want one, Harley?" "No thanks, never took it up," he said. He leaned his head back on the headrest, closing his eyes, relishing his first time with a woman. He was on the verge of telling her that he had feelings for her when she interrupted. “Maybe we kin do this agin sometime soon,” she said. “Well, we’d better make it quick ’cause I’m goin’ into the service in about a week,” he replied. She laughed. “I know what you mean. I’m goin’ off to school in Johnson City, ETSU, in about two weeks.” As they came upon the lights of The Snack Shack, MaryAnne shrieked. “Git down, git down on the floorboard!” she demanded. Not knowing what the emergency was, Harley followed her orders. As the lights of the store faded and the road was dark again, she made a sharp turn in a wide spot, the car pointed back from where they came. “You can git out now, Harley,” she said with a tinge of urgency in her voice. “What’s goin’ on?” “There are some friends of mine back there at The Snack Shack; I don’t want them to see me with you,” she said, looking at herself in the lighted mirror, applying touches of lipstick and makeup. “All I kin say is that yore not like me…or them. They just wouldn’t git you, Harley. Now please git out. It’s only about a half a mile back, and we’ll be gone by the time you git there,” she said. Thunderstruck, he opened the door and exited the car. “Good luck in the war,” she said as she raced away.

Early was sitting on the running board of the truck whittling, a pile of shavings around his feet, when Harley came walking around the bend into the garish neon lights of The Snack Shack’s parking lot. “How long ye been here, brother?” said Harley, a bit winded after the steep climb. “Oh, I’ve been here about an air,” said Early as he arose from the running board and hugged Harley. “Well, thank ye fer comin’ back. Did ye see her?” “Yep, I saw her. She acted like she didn’t see me though. She tolt those people that she got stuck at her cousin’s house in Jellico and fergot the time. They all took off to a party down at some creek.” Harley hung his head. “Let’s go home, little brother,”

he said as they climbed into the truck. They were both quiet for a while. Early, knowing that Harley had been humiliated, continued his silence. Finally Harley reached into his pocket and handed a crumpled ten dollar bill over to Early. "Here ye go; thanks fer the loan. Sorry it's a little bit wet." Early smoothed the bill out on the seat with one hand, then he placed it on the dashboard to dry. "Wont to tell me about how it got wet?" he grinned. "Not really," said Harley, the lyrics to "Solitary Man"* resounding in his head with specific meaning.

* *"Solitary Man" by Neil Diamond*

Part VII

AIRBORNE

Chapter 25

THE CHICKEN MEN

As he told Bob Dossett and MaryAnne, Harley did leave for the service soon. He had hoped to be sent to Fort Campbell, which was close to home, sitting astraddle of the Tennessee/Kentucky line. Instead he was sent across the country to Fort Leonard Wood, Missouri. He weathered abuse by despotic drill instructors admirably. And having spent most of his no-frills life performing hard physical labor, romping in the woods and hunting, he excelled on the firing range and came in first in all physical training exercises. He was intelligent and willing to please, following orders to perfection. He impressed his drill instructors, particularly on the day someone screamed "Snake!" on the PT field.

As his comrades, including the drill instructor cowered on the sidelines, Harley calmly picked up the shiny reptile that unfortunately had made a wrong turn out of the Ozark outback. The snake curled around his arm as he walked to the edge of the field and tossed it in the underbrush. His fellow recruits clapped and shouted his name when he returned. The DI, Sergeant Hibby, called the group to attention and approached Harley. "What the hell did you think you were doin', Baird?" said Hibby, nose to nose with the recruit. "Gittin' rid of that snake, Sergeant." Hibby moved even closer. "Why in the hell did you choose to get rid of the snake, Baird?" he shouted, his breath revealing the contents of his lunch. "'Cause I didn't wont ever'one to be afraid, and it was jest a big ole bull snake," replied Harley, still at rigid attention. "At ease!" shouted Hibby, shaking his head disgustedly. "OK, fall out, and let's see how many pushups you sissies can do." As the instructor counted slowly, and the recruits struggled in the dust, the post commander observed from the PT tower at the edge of the field.

As time went on, Harley was viewed by his superiors as a natural leader, and he was the impetus for several of his comrades to survive the grueling regimen. “Come on, Barclay, ye kin do it,” he yelled at the struggling, overweight recruit as they ran the track and did calisthenics together at the end of the day. Barclay stopped and bent over, his hands on his fat knees, his face fiery-red, and white around the lips. “I can’t go any more, Baird,” said the portly boy who was in danger of getting kicked out of the service because of his weight. Harley put his arm around Barclay’s shoulder. “Buddy, ye’ve already lost eight pounds, ye got two more to go. Ye don’t wont to be throwed out or set back. Now I’ll slow down, and ye jest foller me.” Barclay reluctantly obeyed as they continued to trudge around the track. Sergeant Hibby watched from a distance.

Six weeks into the ten-week training period, Harley was summoned by Sergeant Hibby to the dayroom. He walked briskly to the table, where Hibby was seated. “Sergeant, Private Baird reporting as ordered, Sergeant!” “At ease, Private Baird,” said Hibby, who went directly to his point. “Baird, I ain’t goin’ to pussyfoot around. I think you’re goofy as shit, but someone higher up has recommended that you attend the United States Army Airborne School. You know what the 101st Airborne is, boy?” “I thank so, sir.” “Well, let me tell you that it’s one of the most elite units in all of the military services, and for some reason you’ve been selected to attend. Do you agree that you want to go?” “I guess so, sir…” “Don’t call me sir, boy; that’s for officers.” “Yes, Sergeant. Kin I ask how long the training is?” “Providing you don’t flunk out, it’s four weeks.” “Kin I ask whar it is?” “It’s at Fort Benning, Georgia.” “Kin ye tell me what I have to do?” The sergeant sighed and fumbled through a folder that held a sheaf of papers.

"Well, the first week you're there is called Ground Week. Before you get to jump out of a plane, you are loaded up with fifty pounds of combat and reserve equipment; you'll jump from a two-story tower attached to a static line. The second week is called Tower Week. You will practice jumping from a two-hundred-fifty-foot tower, and you'll learn all about how to exit an aircraft when jumping and all of the stuff about parachutes and aiming for the point of impact in the drop zone. If you pass the test, you will move on to Jump Week. That's when you jump from a real aircraft, probably a C-130 at twelve hundred feet. You must complete five jumps, one at night, to graduate Airborne School. "There's a lot more to it, but I ain't got time to explain it all to you," said Hibby, snapping the folder shut. "What do you say, Baird? Are you game?" It all sounded exciting to Harley. "Yes sir, Sergeant. Whar do I go atter Airborne School?" Hibby shook his head. "You'll be given thirty days leave; then I can guarantee you that you'll be sent straight to Vietnam. You won't be jumping out of planes though You'll probably be dropped in by choppers." "When do ye wont me to git?" "Pack your grip; you're leaving at 0800 tomorrow morning." "Yes, Sergeant, I appreciate ye," said Harley as he turned about face and almost ran toward the dayroom door. "Baird!" Sergeant Hibby's voice echoed in the empty dayroom, as Harley opened the door. "Yes, Sergeant?" "See if you can learn how to talk while you're there." Harley had never seen him smile before.

It was supposed to be a peaceful time. But the North Vietnamese Army utilized Tet, the traditional Vietnamese New Year celebration, when normally all fighting ceased, as a red herring to catch the Americans by surprise. On January 31, the NVA committed thousands of their regular forces to capturing the ancient capital of Hue, just north of the Perfume River, driving out the occupying South Vietnamese forces. It was considered a major coup for the NVA, having a prestigious hold on the former Imperial Capital of Vietnam. Subsequently the 101st Airborne and the First Calvary were dispatched to recapture the city, where thirty-three thousand soldiers of the People's Army were waiting with baited breath.

The National Liberation Front's flag, red with a bright yellow star, fluttered and popped authoritatively from the Citadel's massive flag tower as it had for nearly the past three weeks. The sporadic chatter of AK47s, M-16s, grenades, helicopters, rumbling tanks, and other war machinery drifted upward to the spot where Captain Vo Tan Nguyen and his machine gunner, Corporal Duong Thu Ninh, were settled in. Ngyuen focused his field glasses on the squad of US soldiers slinking cautiously, door-to-door, on the streets of the severely damaged city. "We've got chicken men," said Ngyuen as members of the 101st Airborne ducked out of range. Ngyuen frowned, even more than was his usual countenance. Most North Vietnamese had never seen an eagle, which is why they bestowed the name "chicken men" on members of the 101st Airborne, whose arm patch bore the image of an eagle. He was frowning too because his commanders had cautioned their troops to avoid the enemy at all costs, because they would surely lose any engagement with the daunting "Screaming Eagles."

Sergeant Harley Baird had not slept for nearly two days, since rappelling along with his comrades from Huey Helicopters on the outskirts of Hue, duckwalking through the elephant grass, and slogging through rice paddies and junglelike terrain. Harley and his fellow soldiers from the 101st and the First Calvary were assailed by cleverly positioned snipers just about every step of the way into the city. The Americans suffered many casualties. Once they managed to enter the city, they found the going much tougher. Many of the troops had never been trained in urban warfare. It was an agonizing task, fighting the fiercely dedicated enemy door-to-door, often in hand-to-hand combat. Most of Harley's fighting prior to the siege of Hue involved taking potshots at the enemy from far away, firing at toy soldiers who appeared among the distant trees and faded like shadowy ghosts into the jungle. In this new scenario, Harley was forced to use his Ka-Bar knife more than once to dispatch an enemy troop. He wasn't a proponent of hand-to-hand, although he was always the victor. He actually felt sorry for his victims, who writhed in pain from their wounds, taking a long time to die. Most times if stealth wasn't the issue, he would put a bullet in their heads to end the suffering. The frightful images would remain in his heart and mind long after the war. On finally entering the city, he ducked inside an ancient building, hunkered down in the corner, and despite the sound of bullets richocheting in the courtyard and off the building, the famished GI attempted to stuff some "Charlie rats" (C rations) down his gullet. "Lord, I wisht I had some of Momma's chicken and dumplin's right now," he said to himself, as he ravenously polished off some "turkey loaf" and crackers. The smell of death hung in the air like incense; even his C rations had the taste of death, and he gagged as he swallowed the remainder of his meal. A machine gun opened fire, and he grabbed his M-16 as three of his squad came diving through the door amid a hail of bullets. "Holy shit, Sarge, it's dangerous out there," shouted Corporal Frank Spotted Warbonnet, a full-blooded Comanche from Enid, Oklahoma. Robert Washington and Delayne Greathouse, two black recruits who shared the same hometown of Vicksburg, Mississippi, crawled over to Harley. Washington slapped him on the back. "We thought you was dead, redneck," said Washington as he and his buddy wore wide, warm grins. Harley grinned back. He had an affinity for the two as well as the Native American. They were a lot like him: different in culture and values, and possessing a toughness and goodness that was fast vanishing in the big cities from which many of their fellow band of brothers hailed. Harley loved it when Frank told tales of his noble plains ancestors, and he never tired of hearing Washington and Greathouse pronounce the name of their hometown, "Vicksboig." He replied to their greeting. "I ain't dead yet, but I'm afraid I will be if'n I keep eatin' these C rations," he said, running his tongue disgustedly over his teeth. They waited for over an hour for more members of their platoon to join them, but none arrived.

Darkness was falling, and Harley made a hard decision to move on. "Well, let's move on into town. We got to meet up with the rest of our unit. Listen up, boys," he said, gesturing out the door. "I'm agoin' to run to that church house down the street. I figger it's about one-half a klick," said Harley as he crouched and prepared to race out the door. "Hold it!" said Frank. "That's a pagoda, you hillbilly. Let me lead the way this time; you take too many chances for bein' a short-timer." "OK, Geronimo, be a hero," said Harley as Washington and Greathouse laughed nervously at their banter. The Indian was two or three steps out of the door when he was cut down by the machine gun. He crawled a few more feet in an attempt to get back through the door; then his body jumped and quivered as it was sliced to pieces by an additional spray of deadly fire. "You motherfuckers," screamed Greathouse, spittle flying from his mouth as Washington pulled him back from the doorway. Through his despair, Harley managed to settle them both down. "I saw whar that come from, in that tare up thar below the flagpole. You'uns cover me. I'll head fer the church... pagoda," he corrected himself. "Then I'll backtrack to the tare and blindside them fuckers," said Harley, who rarely cursed. Washington took his position by the only window in the building, and Greathouse lay on his belly, his M-16 resting on a backpack, pointing out the doorway and upward, as Harley poised at the door's edge. He whispered to Greathouse. "Now don't you'uns shoot me in the hind end. I don't wont people thankin' I was runnin' away from somethin'. You'uns stay here, and I'll come back for ye when I finish with the machine-gun nest in that tare," he said as he scampered out the door.

A burst of machine-gun fire came at once, but it was darker, and the target was lightning-quick. Return fire from Greathouse and Washington was also helpful in Harley's safe race to the pagoda, located just a few yards away from a demolished Buddhist temple. The street, illuminated by the waning lunar moon, made pedestrians an easy target for the sniper. But the temple, which lay on the same side of the street as the tower, was in shadow. Harley melted easily into the shadows and hugged the temple wall as he inched his way back to the tower. He stopped in his tracks as a burst of machine-gun fire stuttered from the tower; then there was silence. He continued on his mission.

"The chicken men are easier prey than we've been told," chuckled Ngyuen, though his face remained fixed in a natural frown. "I agree, Captain Ngyuen," said Corporal Duong as he took a brief respite from his position, standing and stretching. Then after replacing the ammo belt, he returned to his seated position behind the gun. "I must urinate. Keep your eyes on the building, although I don't think we have to worry about any more 'chickens'," said Ngyuen sardonically, as he headed for a far corner of the room to do his business. Duong was thinking about his family in Ha Tay Province, west of Hanoi, when Harley sent him homeward with a deft slice from his Ka-Bar.

When Ngyuen returned from his pee break, he immediately chastised the corporal, who was slumped over the gun. "No time for resting, Corporal; we must be vigilant," barked Ngyyuen, tugging roughly at Duong's shirt. Ngyuen gasped as Duong fell over, a pool of blood drenching the machine gun. He bore a crimson slit from ear to ear, which was highlighted by the moonlight. As Ngyuen fumbled for his pistol, Harley emerged from the darkness and sunk the seven-inch knife blade to its hilt in the base of the captain's neck. As Ngyuen fell in a heap like a string puppet, the knife, still gripped by Harley, was dislodged. "That was fer the Comanche Indian Nation," said Harley as he wiped the blade on Ngyuen's uniform.

Harley heard gunfire from distant parts of the Citadel as he returned stealthily to the building where Washington and Greathouse were waiting. But with the dispatching of the occupants of the machine-gun nest, it was quiet. He grabbed Frank Spotted Warbonnet's collar as he neared the building and announced his arrival as he dragged the body back through the open doorway.

"I'm back, boys! They won't be botherin' us no more," said Harley as he propped Frank's body gently against the wall. There was no reception, and his blood chilled. "Whar is ever'body?" he whispered. He heard a bubbling sound from a corner of the room. Cautiously he followed the sound and came upon Washington, lying on his back. The soldier had a sucking wound in his chest and was bleeding profusely from the wound and from the mouth. "Damn it, Robert, what happened?" said Harley, reaching for the canteen in Washington's backpack. "No water. I'm afraid I can't swallow," whispered Washington. He continued weakly. "We tried to follow you when we thought you'd reached the pagoda. But they had a bead on us," said Washington. "DeLayne got hit first, and we both crawled back inside. Delayne's dead; he's under the table," he said, gesturing weakly in that direction. Devastated, Harley stuffed gauze from his medical kit in the gaping wound, knowing all along that his efforts were useless. "Ye jest hold on thar, Robert. I'll git ye to safety, buddy," said Harley as he stroked Washington's sweaty forehead. "I don't think so, Sarge," he gasped. "But there is one last thing I'd like to say to you." "What's that, brother?" said Harley, bracing himself for the death rattle. Washington mustered all of his strength and raised his head. "Vicksboig," he whispered.

Harley eventually ended up with his command. They were reinforced by the Fifth Marine Regiment, and Hue was liberated from the North Vietnamese at the cost of many thousands of lives. As they departed the Citadel, Harley and members of his unit returned to the house near the pagoda and claimed the remains of his comrades. Several months later, he and his unit were deployed to the A Shau Valley, where they fought intensely, capturing several hundred tons of enemy supplies. Harley was flown out of the valley early to Saigon. His time in hell was up.

Chapter 26

LEONARD SPEAKS HIS MIND

Leonard Tatum loved his grandkids; but he was glad to say goodbye to them, his daughter, and son-in-law. After a week of entertaining the rambunctious youngsters—taking them to the zoo, on piggyback rides, a trip to the museum, and sightseeing in Chicago, plus tucking them in every night—he yearned for his slower pace of life; his Lazy-Boy recliner, and the comforts of his small home in West Knoxville. A widower, Leonard wasn't the least bit concerned that no one would greet him when he landed at McGhee-Tyson Airport. He had finally become accustomed to his lonely existence, years after his beloved wife had died.

The plane wasn't due to depart for about an hour, but Leonard didn't mind the wait. He enjoyed people- watching, and airports seemed the best venues for that pastime. He didn't even mind when some rowdy college students sat across from him at the gate. Both of the boys wore blue school sweaters with big, yellow "M's" emblazoned on the fronts. A dyed-in-the-wool Vols fan, Leonard took an immediate dislike to them, not for their choice of a non-SEC school, but for the fact that they were making off-color remarks about every female passerby.

"Check the caboose on that one!" said the larger boy, jabbing his finger in the direction of a woman who was shepherding two unruly children. The young woman reminded Leonard of his daughter-in-law; the kids were reminiscent of his grandchildren and the memorable week he had experienced with them. Leonard was about to say something to the obnoxious students when they were joined by two excited girls, who swarmed them out of nowhere like cawing crows.

"Roger, Danny! Are you guys on spring break too?" "Yep. We're going to Knoxville. My dad has a cabin in the Smokies," said Roger as he and Danny stood reluctantly to receive the chatterboxes. "Oh, that sounds great," said the redhead with the ridiculous Howdy Doody smile. "Lynn and I are going to Fort Lauderdale," said her brunette companion excitedly. "That sounds great, but I don't think we're allowed there after last year," Danny lied. "Well, listen, you guys have a good time. We have to hurry; our plane leaves in about fifteen minutes, and we're twenty gates on down," said the brunette. They hugged the boys awkwardly and took off, giggling inanely as they ran. "Hope you all get laid," smirked Roger. "I wouldn't lay them with your tool," said Danny as Roger reproached him with a punch in the shoulder. Disgusted with their dialogue, Leonard folded his paper, picked up his carry-on, and moved a couple of seats down from the clowns.

They'd told Harley when he mustered out in Seattle that it would be prudent for him not to wear his uniform home, because of the antiwar sentiment. Harley refused, prideful of his service to his country and because the few civilian clothes he had didn't fit him. Despite harsh conditions, he'd gained about twenty-five pounds, mostly muscle, since basic training. And he was an imposing figure as he strode through O'Hare Airport in his dress greens. His chest glittered with an array of medals, and his deep green blouse was decorated with a blue braid strung through the right shoulder epaulette. The right shoulder of his uniform bore the Screaming Eagle patch, and his trousers were bloused beautifully in his combat boots, shiny as wet sealskin. He was lean and chisel-jawed, and his deep tan went well with his heavily starched tan shirt and black tie. He carried his heavy dufflebag with little effort and sat it down at the reception desk.

"We're pretty full on the trip to Knoxville today, sir; let me write your name down on the standby list. "There are two other standby passengers in front of you; good luck," said the pretty attendant, who barely looked his way. "Thank ye," said Harley quietly as he picked up the dufflebag and turned to be seated in the waiting area. He dropped his ticket, which was stamped "Standby," and thanked one of the students, as he returned it to him.

"Ye don't mind if I sit here do ye?" said Harley as Leonard hastily moved his carry-on bag from the chair. The college students looked up as Harley spoke, and Roger whispered something to Danny out the side of his mouth. Leonard was glad the GI chose to sit next to him. "Have a seat, son; glad to have you. You on your way home?" "Yes sir, I live in Campbell County actually, on Cumberland Mountain in a place called Duff," said Harley. Leonard nodded his head. "I'm from Knoxville; name's Leonard Tatum," he said, offering his hand. Harley shook his hand, and Leonard was immediately aware of his steely grip. "Harley Baird's my name, pleased to meet ye." "I'm really glad to meet a comrade. I was in the 101st in World War II, 501st Parachute Infantry. Fought in the Normandy invasion and ran the Krauts out of St. Come-du-Mont." Harley loosened up a bit. "I've heard stories from some of the lifers about that. You fellers were real heroes, still are," he said, and Leonard glowed with pride. "Well, I'm sure you've seen some action too." "Yes sir; Cam Rahn Bay, Khe San, Hue, A Shau Valley. I probably would have ended up on Hill 937 if my tour hadn't ended," said Harley. "Hamburger Hill? I heard that was brutal. I'm glad you missed it," said Leonard as Roger yelled down the aisleway. "Hey soldier! What you got in that dufflebag, a body?" Leonard flushed crimson, but Harley just stared at the two who were bent double in hysterics. Leonard put his hand on Harley's shoulder. "I'm sorry, son. Don't do anything that will get you in trouble. You've come all this way." Harley didn't appear to be angry, but his eyes were deeply sad. "Don't worry, Mr. Tatum. I've had enough violence to last me several lifetimes. All I wont to do is git home to my family."

The desk attendant interrupted with an announcement. "I'm sorry to say that the plane is full. All standby passengers please report to the desk, and we will try to get you on the next available flight," she said, but she didn't sound sorry. She immediately made a boarding call for first-class passengers to get on the plane. Roger and Danny's parents had sprung for first-class tickets for the boys, and they got in line. Before they disappeared through the entrance, Roger turned toward Harley and waved daintily with his fingers. "Bye-bye, baby killer," he sang as he disappeared through the door. Harley had to restrain Leonard as he leaped out of his seat. "Damn that punk! If I were twenty years younger, I'd whip his ass!" said Leonard as Harley gripped his arm. "As a matter of fact, the day is young, and I might try him on for size before it's over!" "Hold on thar, Mr. Tatum, we don't wont ye to git in trouble either. They ain't worth it". Harley reported to the desk and placed his name on the next standby list. Leonard got up and talked briefly to the attendant at the desk, then returned to his seat next to Harley. The desk attendant announced last call for the flight, and when it was Leonard's turn to leave, he looked as though his heart were breaking. "Son, I asked them if you could have my seat, that I wasn't really in a hurry to get anywhere; but for some reason, I'm not allowed...I'm so sorry," said Leonard as he shook Harley's hand warmly. Harley smiled and placed his hand on Leonard's shoulder. "I'll never forgit ye, my brother; yore a good troop!" Leonard's eyes watered at the comment as he turned to go.

The first-class passengers were already comfortable in their seats as the rest of the passengers filed down the aisle. Roger and Danny were opening their little bottles of vodka when Leonard grabbed the front of Roger's sweater and nearly pulled him out of his seat. Leonard didn't mean to, but he spit in Roger's face as he berated him. "You son of a bitch! You don't know how lucky you are! That boy—that man out there—could have turned you and that little bastard next to you inside out and stuck your heads on sticks before you had time to think about it. You should be ashamed of ridiculing a person who has laid his life on the line for your sorry asses and for your right to do whatever it is you do, you pieces of crap!"

Had it been another time, Leonard would have been arrested. But as it was, passengers who'd witnessed Roger's despicable actions broke into applause.

After the plane landed, Roger and Danny, amid baleful stares, made sure they stationed themselves on the other side of the baggage carousel from Leonard Tatum.

Chapter 27

GROUND TRANSPORTATION

Harley spent the night in the airport, and his plane left at two o'clock the next afternoon. He was disappointed that he didn't appear as spit and polished as the day before, but he was happy to be on the last flying leg of his trip. The ride to Knoxville was bumpy, and several times he was reminded that he would rather be jumping out of planes than riding in them. The plane landed right on time, 4:00 p.m. Harley had gotten little sleep the night before and was a little grumpy. Dead tired, he lugged his duffelbag up the gangway. But his spirits were buoyed when he saw his welcoming party at the gate.

"Hey, man!" yelled Joe Boy and Wayne Jackson. Wayne waved a misspelled sign with crude printing that said "Welcome Home, Haley!" The Jackson brothers were friends that Harley had run the woods with as a youngster. Both had already served in Nam at different times, and now they were linemen at the electric company. They'd put in a good word for Harley, and he hoped to gain employment there.

"Hoo boy, you got fat over thar," said Joe Boy, attempting but failing to pinch some fat on Harley's flat stomach. "Yep, I gained some weight, eatin' too much rice and fish," kidded Harley. "Bull," said Wayne.

"Ye were probably guzzlin' lots of cold beer in Saigon!" he said as he struggled to get a good grip on Harley's dufflebag. As they walked through the terminal, Harley asked about his family. "They were disappointed when ye called last night, but when we volunteered to pick ye up today, Scrap acted kind of relieved. I don't thank he was lookin' ford to drivin' in Knoxville and Alcoa traffic," said Joe Boy. "We've checked ever' plane that come in from Chicago fer the last four airs," said Wayne as they strode out of the terminal. "What's yore car look like?" said Harley, after they'd wandered around the full parking garage for a while. "It's right in front of ye," said Joe Boy. Harley's shoulders slumped a little as he beheld the two Harley-Davidsons parked side by side in one parking space. "Boy, I'm glad I didn't brang a steamer trunk," said Harley, taking off his garrison cap and scratching his head. "It's all right. Ye kin ride with me, and Wayne kin take yore duffelbag," said Joe Boy. Wayne was already in the process of securing the bag to his sissy bar. "I feel kind of funny with this thang ridin' in back of me," said Wayne. "I've seen ye carry a lot uglier bags than that on the back of yore bike," said Joe Boy. "Hop on, Harley; we'll git ye home in one piece." Both men started their bikes, and the rumble repeated throughout the garage.

Joe Boy and Wayne were comfortable at the helms of their bikes, and the trip from Alcoa onto I-75, northward to LaFollette, was fast as they zipped in and out of traffic. Harley and Joe Boy laughed hard at the stares Wayne received from motorists as they beheld his odd passenger, strapped to the sissy bar. Although he wondered if he would make it home alive, Harley was in ecstasy when he saw his mountains loom just outside of Clinton. Later, after passing Clinton, Lake City, and crossing the Campbell County line, Joe Boy followed Wayne up the mountain and off the 134 exit into Caryville. Much to Harley's happiness, they sped even faster once they were on the road home. After whizzing through Jacksboro into LaFollette, a police car pulled up beside Joe Boy and motioned him to pull over. Wayne caught the action and followed suit. Bob Dossett turned on his flashing lights and walked toward the cyclists.

"Wayne, what in the world have ye got on the back of that thang?" said Dossett, examining the dufflebag closely. He fingered the stencil on the bag. "Baird? Who's Baird?" "That's Harley Baird. He's on Joe Boy's bike," said Wayne. Dossett walked slowly back to Joe Boy's bike. Harley had dismounted and was stretching his bones. "Harley? Is that you?" said Dossett, removing his hat, perhaps in a gesture of respect. Harley stuck his hand out. "How are ye, Sheriff? It's good to see ye agin." Dossett shook his hand firmly. "I guess it's good to see anybody without slanty eyes," said Dossett. "Hey, Joe Boy," said Dossett, eying his bike with suspicion. "Ye know how fast you'uns was goin'?" "Purty fast," said Joe Boy. "We was tryin' to git Harley here home to his folks." Dossett put his hat back on and spoke over his shoulder as he walked away. "Well, jest git him home in one piece," he said as he entered his car, shut the lights down, and took off.

Scrap and Early were waiting at The Snack Shack. "Durn, I thank this little pecan pie is better 'n what Margaret makes," said Scrap as he popped the last crumbs of the pie into his mouth. "Purty good," said Early as he hurriedly polished off his piece before Scrap asked him for the remainder. The two had been there for hours, waiting on Harley's arrival. Early stood up and looked down the mountain. "I thank I hear 'em comin'," he said, cupping his hand to his ear. Scrap cocked his head. "I cain't hear as good as I used to; are ye shore?" Early didn't bother to answer as the unmistakable thunder of the bikes became audible, and the Jackson brothers came hurtling around the curve, bearing the gift of Harley.

As they pulled up in the dusty parking lot, Early helped Scrap off the tailgate, and they both walked as quickly as Scrap could walk over to the bikes. Harley swung off the seat to greet them. Scrap opened his arms and yelled, "Whar ye been, boy? We thought the hogs had ate ye!" Harley fought from tearing up as he received the old man's hug and buried his head in his shoulder. "Ye knowed I'd be back, Pappy; hogs got to do thar business jest like we do." "Lord, Lord, brother, I'd forgot how tall ye was," said Early as he hugged him, then worked his hand repeatedly like a pump handle.

Wayne and Joe Boy stood by, thoroughly enjoying the reunion. Joe Boy decided it was time to leave Harley in the arms of his family. "Wayne, why don't ye untie yore girlfriend from yore sissy bar, throw 'er in the back of Scrap's truck, and let's git to the house," said Joe Boy as he threw his leg over the saddle of his bike. "Harley, ye take keer, and we'll talk about that job as soon as ye git settled," Wayne said as he tossed the duffle bag into the truck. They took off dramatically, as usual, in a spray of gravel and a cloud of dust.

Early started honking the horn long before their arrival at the big house, and the family—Margaret, Sissy, Glory, (whom Harley had never met), and Maw—waited like keyed-up puppies by the roadside when Early pulled in. Sissy handed Glory to Maw and jumped into Harley's arms before anyone else had a chance to greet him. "Oh, Harley, honey, we missed ye so much!" she said, knocking his hat off as she flung her arms around his neck. Then she took Glory from Maw's arms. "This is yore niece, Glory," she said proudly and placed the little girl, the image of herself, into his waiting arms. "Come here to Uncle Harley, little'un, and give me some sugar!" said Harley, reaching for the child. The dark-haired babe complied and gave him a drooly smooch on the cheek. Maw hugged him gently. "Welcome home, soldier. We're so grateful that the Master seen fit to brang ye back," she said, tapping lightly at her eyes with the corner of her shawl. As usual Margaret waited till everyone was fed before she ate. "Harley, Harley, Harley," was all she could say, as he took her in his arms and held her for a long while. When he finally released her, she found her voice. "Honey, ye must have gained fifty pounds, and fer the life of me, I never realized how tall ye was," she said, touching his sleeve. It had been nearly two years since he'd seem them last, and they had also changed. They all seemed to have aged, especially Scrap and Margaret, whose hair was streaked with gray. “I thought he was taller too,” said Early as they all walked, arm in arm, back to the big house. Harley didn’t notice, or care, that Bucky wasn’t there to greet him.

Part VIII

HOMEFRONT

Chapter 28

BUCKY BUYS THE FARM

Bucky and Sissy's marriage had lasted a lot longer than the Bairds had expected. The couple was still together after two years. What the Bairds didn't know was the abuse that Sissy was suffering.

Bucky had a lot of free time and spent that time with his buddies, who seemed to have a lot of free time also. He came home drunk and surly, ignoring Sissy's questions about his whereabouts, ignoring his precious daughter. He'd become fat over the past couple of years and meaner, especially when he drank moonshine. When he was on "shine," he would open-hand Sissy at the slightest provocation and slug her in the shoulders and thighs so the bruises wouldn't show. He refrained often from using his fists for fear of Harley, who had been home from the war just a few months, and Scrap finding out. He even threatened to kill Glory once, when after a particularly nasty altercation, Sissy threatened to tell her family of his nastiness.

Sissy stood on the porch waiting for Bucky to arrive. He was two hours late for his daughter's second birthday party, which was being held at Margaret's house.

She heard the rumbling pipes before she saw him; then the Mercury appeared in the yard. "Whar ye been, honey? We were s'posed to be at Momma's two airs ago?" said Sissy as Bucky came clomping up the porch steps.

"Git off my back, and fix my supper," said Bucky, evading her question.

"Honey, we don't have time fer supper. I'm shore that Momma will have somethin' to eat at the house," said Sissy in a pleading voice edged with fear.

"Don't argue with me, bitch! Git my supper, and then you'uns kin go to the damned party. I'm tired from workin' all day," said Bucky, rubbing his bleary eyes.

Sissy brushed past him toward the kitchen, noting that he reeked of booze.

"Good. I'll fix yore supper, and we'll go to the party without ye," said Sissy. Unfortunately she followed under her breath with a whispered, "Ye fat son of a bitch."

"What did ye call me?" said Bucky, grabbing Sissy by the throat and pinning her against the refrigerator. She was unable to answer, and he slapped her hard, once, twice, three times.

"Call me a sumbitch?" he shouted as he topped off the vicious beating with a backhand to her temple, causing her to hit her head on the counter as she fell to the floor.

"Don't ye never, ever, call me a sumbitch, bitch," railed Bucky, cocking his arm back as if to hit her again. Sissy lay in a spreading pool of blood, dazed and unable to decipher his words through the fog of her pain. She did hear Glory though, who was screaming her lungs out in the other room.

Bucky hurled a dishrag at her. "Clean y'ass up, stick a sock in that damn kid's mouth, and git me some supper," he ordered, as Sissy rose to a wobbly elbow, pressing the rag tightly against the deep gash in the corner of her eyebrow, on the scar from so long ago.

"I think my eye's hurt bad whar ye hit me," said Sissy weakly.

"I didn't hit ye in the eye; ye bashed it on the counter on yore way down," said Bucky as he took a swipe with his boot at the chair she was using to pull herself upright. Sissy fell again face first into the mess, matting her hair with sticky blood.

"I'll shut the squealy kid up; ye get me some supper," he snarled, giving a kick at her ribs but missing his mark as he stumbled to the bedroom.

"No, no, please, Bucky, I'll get the baby, and I'll get yore supper; ye just sit down. I'll get it quick," she said, her addled brain fueled by a hefty shot of panic-laced adrenaline, commanding her body to rise from the linoleum.

"Then do it," slurred Bucky. "Call me a sumbitch, I'll kill yore ass," he mumbled as he took a long pull out of the jar of moonshine he'd retrieved from under the cabinet. He hitched his trousers up importantly, thumbs through the belt loops.

Early heard the commotion when he was about twenty yards from the house.

"Shoot, he's at it again," he said to himself, and as he quickened his step, the string puppet he'd carved for Glory danced merrily at his side.

Through his ranting and Glory's screaming, Bucky didn't hear Early come into the house.

Early was stunned at the sight of blood and scattered chairs as he entered the kitchen.

"I said shut that kid up, or I'm gonna deal with both of ye!" shrieked Bucky.

"Bucky, what happened? Where's Sissy?" demanded Early.

Startled, Bucky shut his mouth for the first time since he arrived home. Then he resumed his tirade.

"Jest foller the noise of that screamin' young'un, and ye'll find the bitch," he sneered.

"Now come on, Bucky, ye don't have to be callin' nobody no names," said Early, concern surging at the evidence of Bucky's rage and for the well-being of his sister and her child.

"Ye ain't comin' into my house and tellin' me what to do, fat boy.

How ye like that for name callin', huh, fat boy? How ye like that?" taunted Bucky.

"C'mon Early, let's git outta here," said Sissy as she appeared at the kitchen door, holding Glory. Glory quieted at the sight of her uncle, her cries reduced to sniffling and whimpers. "Ye ain't goin' nowhere, bitch. Yore gonna git my supper, ye hear?" screamed Bucky, slobbering on his shirt front.

Early beheld in horror his sister's swollen face; split lips, and the blood streaming from the wound in her eyebrow. "It ain't as bad as it looks. The bitch hit her head when she fell in the kitch..." Bucky lacked the wherewithal to finish his sentence, as Early roared and punched him between the eyes with his huge fist.

Bucky's response was to become airborne, careen off the butcher's block in the corner, and splinter the kitchen table on his way down. He lay in Sissy's and his own blood, moaning as if he were giving birth.

Seething, Early moved toward the prostrate form, but Sissy tugged at his arm.

"C'mon Early, we'll go to Momma's. If he follers, he'll have you'uns, Harley, and Scrap to face," said Sissy, hefting Glory on her hip and leading the way out the front door.

Bucky felt as if he'd been hit by a coal truck, but he was too stupid and too drunk to let it go. He was humiliated. He'd be the laughing stock of the county when it was known that he'd been laid out by gentle Early Baird.

"I'll kill that fat bastard," he croaked, as blood flowed freely through his broken nose. He rummaged through the kitchen drawer for his pistol.

"You'uns walk on ahead of me, Sissy," said Early, caressing his sister's arm tenderly, his heart breaking at the sight of her.

Sissy obeyed, hastening her step at the thought of the monster in the house coming after them.

She and Glory were about ten yards in front of Early when the shout came from the porch.

"Hold on thar, fat boy. Turn around; I don't want to shoot ye in the back," shouted Bucky, his threats bouncing off the mountain.

"Keep movin', Sissy; he ain't goin' to do nothin'," said Early, who picked up his pace too.

"Awright, ye asked fer it!" screamed Bucky. The .44 boomed. The sound was still echoing around the holler as Early stumbled, then went down heavily.

"Run, Sissy, run!" said Early, thinking he was shouting. But the warning, issued in a mere whisper, went unheard.

Balloons and crepe-paper streamers festooned the house, and a homemade red velvet cake with two candles graced the kitchen table.

"Don't even think about it, Pap," admonished Margaret when she caught Scrap eying her cake longingly. "I warn't doin' nothin'," whined Scrap sheepishly. "When's this party gettin' started? I'm hongry." "Why don't ye go out in the yard and play horseshoes with the boys? Early's gone down to Sissy's house to git 'em goin'," said Margaret.

"Ye know Bucky's probably been drankin'; that's why thar late. That boy is worthless, I wouldn't give him air if'n he was stuck in a jug," said Scrap, swiping a handful of potato chips on his way out the door. Margaret felt the same as Scrap about Bucky and rued the day Sissy had ever set eyes on him. And although today was designed for celebration, she dreaded the thought of Bucky showing up all "Saturday drunk" and ruining her grandchild's birthday party.

The ice cream carton on the counter was beginning to sag a little, and she was placing it back in the freezer when she heard the report of Bucky's pistol.

From the kitchen window, she could see Scrap and Harley hurrying toward the truck.

They were out of the truck before it stopped rolling.

Early was lying in a heap on the ground. Sissy, her face disfigured and bloody, knelt beside him, his bloodied head in her hands. Glory, seemingly catatonic, stroked Early's hair awkwardly, petting his still form as if he were a puppy.

About twenty yards up the road, dust hung in the air, a sign of Bucky's quick departure.

"Lord, Lord, Lord, what's he done to ye?" said Harley as he took a clean handkerchief out of his pocket and dabbed at Sissy's wounds. She continued to cradle Early's head in her hands, while permitting her grieving big brother to comfort her. "Early sleepin'," said Glory as Harley knelt beside his beloved brother. Tears filled his eyes, and he was preparing to take Early's pulse when Scrap tumbled into the midst of all of them, frantic, out of control with anguish.

"What's happened to my babies?" he cried, falling to his knees. The big man was more awkward than the child as he stroked the innate form of Early and pawed Sissy clumsily on her shoulder. "Oh, Early, son, please be alive," cried Scrap, crocodile tears flooding his cheeks.

"I thank he's gone, Pap," sobbed Sissy as she and her baby buried their heads in Scrap's heaving chest.

"No, I ain't, but I feel like it," moaned Early weakly, from the pile of wreckage that was him.

Glory stood back, confused, as Scrap and Sissy rolled Early over, thanking Jesus for His mercy.

In their jubilation, they failed to realize that Harley had taken off in the truck.

Bucky laughed when he saw Scrap's truck in his rearview mirror. "Ye'll never catch this Merc in that piece of shit," he screamed as he spun out onto the gravel road and later onto the Jellico Highway blacktop. Bucky pushed the Mercury to its limit, squealing around the curves and across a bridge. He slowed down briefly to turn on Stinking Creek Road, which led to Walnut Mountain where, in his drunken and confused state, he planned to hide out in a remote cabin.

"Fat fucker should have knowed not to mess with Bucky Goodman. I'm drunkern Cooter Brown, and I still got 'im with a head shot at forty yards," laughed Bucky as he reached into his visor for a Camel. As he bent his head to light the cigarette, he ran off the road and collided with a tree. The Mercury exploded into a fireball that quickly engulfed the automobile. Bucky, trapped beneath the dash, screamed himself sober as the flames licked hungrily at his body. Luckily he could move his arms and found his pistol lying conveniently on the floor beside him; a gift of sorts. "Fuck it!" he cried as he placed the pistol under his chin and pulled the trigger.

Harley saw the smoke and heard the gunshot, leading him to the site of the accident. He pulled off to the side of the road as the conflagration raged—flames shooting up the oak tree, the silhouette of the Mercury shimmering at the base, a ghastly mirage. Harley walked back to Scrap's truck, his boiling rage at Bucky Goodman cooling, as his sorrow for his siblings took precedence. He picked up the pace, hopped in the truck, and took one last look at the flaming, skeletal remains of the Mercury and the entombed body of his brother-in-law.

"Hell cain't be much hotter than that Bucky, but I hope it is," he spoke through gritted teeth, as he made a U-turn and sped back to Sissy's house.

Bucky's interment was no big deal.

The general feeling among the mourners on that cold, rainy morning seemed to be, "Let's get this thing over with and go home." The Baird clan shared the feeling more deeply than most and were in attendance only in support of Sissy, who bore the resemblance of a boxer who was sorely unmatched to his opponent. Early was also an unwelcome example of the rage of Bucky; head bandaged over the wound that would forever manifest itself as a permanent part in his hair. They stood on the perimeter of the funeral tent, covering themselves with umbrellas provided by the funeral home.

The antediluvian rule in these mountains was that there would be hard feelings between the Goodman and Baird clans for generations to come, over who was responsible for Bucky's demise. Unbeknownst to everyone, including his own family, Scrap had secreted a pistol in his coat pocket. And it was a given that members of the Goodman clan were packing iron also.

As the rain increased in intensity, The Clear Branch Sons of God sang an appropriate song, "Oh They Tell Me of an Uncloudy Day." When they were finished, they retreated quickly to the back of the tent for protection against the elements. Reverend Bunch delivered an uninspired sermon, based on scripture from the book of John, and later attempted to comfort Bucky's family by saying, "God has a room reserved for Bucky and all of you'uns in His mansion." As Bucky's mother wailed and threw herself over the casket, Bucky's father, Morely, approached the Bairds. "I ain't apologizin' fer nothin' that Bucky ever done, jest as you'uns would do fer yore kin," said Morely, oblivious to the rain pouring off his hat brim. "But we'd shore like to ask you'uns a favor." He waited for a reply, which didn't come. The Bairds just stared blankly at him.

"I...I'd like to ask if you'uns would allow us to see Glory ever' little bit?" Remarkably Sissy reached out and hugged the old man. "Shore ye kin, Morely, but only at air house." Morely nodded his head and walked back to the casket to comfort his wife. As the Bairds made their way through the muddy graveyard to their vehicles, Scrap took his hand out of his coat pocket.

Chapter 29

FORTUNATE SON

"Listen, kin ye hear it, Early?" said Scrap as he cupped his hand to his ear. "I thank so, Pap," said Early, grinning broadly. Every day at around 5:00 p.m., they would shut down their saw, whether they were finished or not, and listen for the sound of Harley rumbling home through the hollers.

About three months ago, he'd accepted a job at the electric company as a groundman. The pay was decent, there were good benefits, and he was a perfect candidate for lineman, which was dangerous at times but one of the highest paid jobs in Campbell County. "Hell, it cain't be any more dangerous than workin' a band saw day in and day out go fer it," counseled Scrap when Harley asked his blessing. Besides, work had slowed down some at the saw, and Harley could help on the weekends if needed.

Harley was eventually accepted by the clannish linemen and other workers, absorbing their criticisms and pranks good-naturedly. There were many veterans among the crew; and there were even a couple of younger men who served in Vietnam, like Harley's friends, brothers Wayne and Joe Boy Jackson. They were responsible for getting Harley the job. Both of them were considered ornery but "good" ornery. Wayne had been blessed with the ability to play every instrument that he picked up, especially the guitar. And Joe Boy had an innate knack for feeding people. Renowned for his barbecue recipes, he was also known for his baby face, for which he received the moniker, "Joe Boy." It was a good face, but he elected to cover it up with an unkempt, flowing beard that gave him the appearance of a ZZ Top guitarist or a Muslim cleric, take your pick. The brothers were cut from the same cloth as Harley: strong as oxen, combat veterans, young, and full of piss and vinegar. Wayne and Joe Boy nicknamed Harley "Bike," because he shared his given name with the name of their prized "hogs." "Hey, Bike, we found ye a good deal on a Harley," said Wayne one morning as they were loading up their truck. "I ain't lookin' fer a Harley, Wayne. How many times I have to tell ye?" "Lissin', Bike, this feller needs the money bad, and he'll sell ye this Harley fer a song. Tell 'im, Joe Boy!" "It's air cousin Willard, 'member him? He went up north and got some girl in a family way, and now he's gittin' murried. He's home fer a little while, and he rode the Harley back down here." "What's it look like?" "It's cherry, buddy, a '66 FLH Electra Glide. It's a Shovelhead with sixty horsepower; it needs it 'cause the SOB weighs about eight hundred pounds, and it'll fly. Rode it myself." After a bit of cajoling, Harley's friends finally convinced him to look at the bike, and he fell in love with it immediately: red and white, with white sidewalls, and Joe Boy was right, it could fly. Although it put a dent in his wallet, he got a good deal, paying fifteen hundred dollars toward Willard's shotgun wedding.

"Is that Harley?" yelled Margaret from the porch. Scrap and Early nodded their heads, and she returned to the kitchen to put the finishing touches on supper. Harley was quite a sight as he made a noisy entrance into the yard on the big hog. It was a hot day, and he'd folded his work shirt into his saddle bags. He wore only his work pants, boots, a bandana tied around his head, and aviator sunglasses that were given to him by a helicopter pilot. His lean, sinewy body was deeply tanned from riding shirtless on the weekends, his forearms and biceps heavily muscled from the challenges of the service and of his current lifestyle. The Screaming Eagle tattoo on his left shoulder spoke loudly of his service to his country and announced that he was probably a badass.

"What's fer supper?" he asked as he slid out of the saddle and dug his shirt out of the saddlebags.

"I thank it's pork chops," said Scrap as he performed the ritual he started the day Harley brought the bike home. He walked slowly around the bike, investigating every feature in minute detail. He'd take his bandana out and rub at a spot here and there; then he would pat one of the handlebars and walk away. Harley had once offered him a ride, but he refused. "Hellfire, I'd break that thang in haif," he said and quickly walked away, looking back tentatively as if someone would force him to climb aboard. Early was fond of the bike too, but also spurned any opportunities to ride the beast. Sissy, however, was in love with it and pestered Harley constantly to give her a ride. When he did, she encouraged him to go fast and to travel far. Margaret would not go near the machine.

"Ye got time fer me to take a share afore supper, Momma?" "If ye stank, I'll make time," laughed Margaret as she set the table. Harley sniffed under his arm and blinked. "Then take yore time, and I'll hurry." Later the family sat at the table, a little miffed that Harley wasn't ready to eat. "Hit's about time!" complained Scrap as Harley came into the room. "Well, don't he look purty," kidded Early as Harley sat down, wet hair slicked back, and freshly scrubbed from the shower. "What ye goin' to do tonight, honey?" said Margaret as she filled Harley's plate. "Well, I'm goin' to meet Wayne and Joe Boy down at the pool room, and later we're goin' to ride up the valley to a bonfire at Booger Partin's farm." "Ain't he one of them Sons of the South?" said Margaret, scrunching up her face at Booger's distasteful handle. "Yep, he belongs to the club. But he's a good feller, and most of the rest of 'em are. Some of 'em are vets," said Harley, heaping a spoonful of chowchow on his beans. "Well, ye'd best be keerful with that bunch; they thank thar Marlow Brandon," sniffed Scrap, who'd recently watched *The Wild Ones* on television. "That's Marlon Brando, Pap," laughed Early, nearly spraying his lemonade all over Margaret. "Whutever," said Scrap, laughing good-naturedly at his own faux pas.

Wayne and Joe Boy's bikes were parked in front of the pool room when Harley arrived. They played nine-ball at ten cents a game for about two hours, with Joe Boy reigning victorious. Bored of winning, Joe Boy hung up his cue stick. "I'm a gittin' thirsty, fellers; let's head on up to Booger's."

It was dark by the time they pulled into Booger's farm. They parked their bikes on a grassy hillside, heard music down by the barn, and saw the silhouettes of people dancing around a big bonfire. As they stepped into the amber light, a giant blocked their way. He stood about six foot six, sported bushy red eyebrows, sideburns, and a thick handlebar moustache. "That'll be ten dollars, gents, all the beer you can drink and all the hot dogs and chili you can eat. Cough it up." He stuck his massive paw out and wiggled his fingers. "Who in the hell are ye?" said Joe Boy, bristling at the disrespect. "I'm the guest of honor, you fuckin', buffalo-lookin' motherfucker," said the big man, dropping his hands, adjusting his spiked wristbands, squaring his shoulders for a fight. "Well, come on, Yosemite Sam," said Joe Boy, assuming a tae kwon do pose. Somebody stopped the music, and Booger Partin came running out of the barn. "Hold it! Hold it, boys!" he yelled as he ran between the combatants. "Joe Boy, Harley, Wayne! It's good to see ye fellers! This here's Rodney Partin, my cousin. He's from Vandalia, Ohio, and he's down here fer the weekend to party. I asked him to collect money for the beer and vittles." "We was ready to pay, but we ain't used to bein' treated this away," said Joe Boy, dropping his open-handed guard. Harley and Wayne said not a word but stood ready to defend their comrade. "Say yore sorry, Rodney," said Booger. "Fuck you," said Rodney as he walked away sullenly. "That's Rodney's way of sayin' he's sorry, boys; now I'll shave two dollars off fer bad manners, and you'uns have a good time!" They each gave him eight dollars and walked over to the tubs filled with iced-down beer.

As the evening wore on, Wayne and Joe Boy did their best to get their eight dollars worth, pigging out on the food and drinking all the beer they could get their hands on, at times two cans at a time. Harley wasn't too interested in the food; he'd eaten quite a bit at home, but he was working hard on the beer. He'd never drunk beer before he went into the service, but he learned quickly and practiced diligently in Vietnam, where he drank plentiful amounts of Budweiser on base and treated himself to cold bottles of Vietnamese-brewed Bier La Rue in Saigon. It was good beer, cheap, helped beat the heat, and cushioned his longing to go back to the "world" for a little while. Tonight the Budweisers were going down smooth and fast, and Harley was enjoying the buzz, the music, and a bit of dancing. He'd never danced before he went into the service either, but the B-girls in Saigon taught him some excellent moves. "You Numbah One, Hary," they would say as they bumped and grinded, and he bumped and grinded right back. Someone put on *"Fortunate Son,"* by Creedence, which brought back memories, and Harley couldn't help himself, gyrating around the campfire like a lunatic to the cheers of the Sons of the South. They liked Harley because he didn't judge them and because of his name. "Get down, Bike," they yelled, and Harley complied with their wishes. He was still dancing to *"War,"* by Edwin Starr, when a comely little beauty in cut-off shorts, a T-strap blouse, and cowboy boots joined him. "Mind if I join you?" she asked in a Yankee accent, batting her eyes, and bumping and grinding, even better than the B-girls in his memory. "Don't mind if ye do," replied Harley, who did as he was taught. He was twirling her around when her hand was snatched from his, and Yosemite Sam stood before him in a rage. "That's my woman, you fuckin' hick!" he screamed as he took a mighty roundhouse swing at Harley's head. Harley ducked and, before Yosemite could regain his balance, took him out with simultaneous judo chops to both sides of his neck. "Yea, Bike!" cheered the Sons of the South as the big man went down hard and out for the count.

"Why don't ye git outta here, Bike. Me and Joe Boy'll make shore he don't foller ye," said Wayne as Booger tended to Yosemite. "We'll meet ye later at the pool room." Harley agreed it was a good idea that he vamoose.

A light rain was falling as Harley zoomed down Old 63. He was sorry the evening ended the way it did, and hoped Yosemite was OK. He did enjoy the dance though, and he yearned for more female companionship. Maybe he would call a prospect from the pool room and ask her if she'd enjoy a ride tonight. Yes, that sounded like a good idea. Imbued with visions of romance, he sang at the top of his lungs. "It ain't me, it ain't me, I ain't no fortunate one. It ain't me, it ain't me, I ain't yore fortunate son …" His vocal act was cut short when a cow upstaged him. He swerved to miss the cow and laid the bike down on the wet pavement. The big Harley went skittering down the road in a shower of sparks as little Harley hit the macadam hard, shedding lots of skin along the way and breaking bones until he came to rest in a deep ditch on the left-hand side of the highway. He had just time enough to contemplate the irony before the pain set in. He couldn't believe he faced death in Vietnam and got away without a scratch. Now he was royally screwed by a cow in Claiborne County. He laughed as he struggled to pull himself out of the ditch.

Luckily Joe Boy and Wayne decided to leave the party soon after Harley's departure, noting that Yosemite was done for the night. The rain was falling harder now as they made their way slowly down 63.

Wayne held up his hand as Joe Boy pulled up next to him. "What's a matter, bro?" "Look at those taillights down thar. It looks like thar in a ditch. Oh man, I hope it ain't Bike," said Wayne as he pulled away quickly.

Harley had only one good arm and, in his shocked state, was attempting to pull the heavy bike out of the ditch. "Sit down, you idjit, yore hurt," said Wayne, and the brothers helped Harley to a half-sitting position on the side of the road. "Damn, Harley, yore a sight. Are ye all right?" said Joe Boy. "I'm about a numbah ten right now," said Harley. "We'll figger out how to git ye to the hospital. Is thar anythang we kin do to make ye feel better?" said Wayne. "Ye got yore pistol on ye, Joe Boy?" "Yep." "Then shoot that cow over thar, then put a slug in me," said Harley, pointing a shaking finger in the direction of the Holstein that was contentedly munching grass on the side of the road. Joe Boy and Wayne laughed their asses off. Harley would have joined them, but most of his ass was on the pavement.

Chapter 30

BRENDA

Harley wasn't laughing the next morning either when he awoke in a bed at University of Tennessee Hospital. His arms and legs were bandaged heavily as was his back. A nurse was bustling around his bedside, jotting stuff down on a clipboard. "Well, am I goin' to make it?" he asked, startling her. "Uh…yes sir, you're going to make it, but you're hurt pretty bad. You dislocated your shoulder and broke your elbow, and you've got third-degree burns on a lot of your body from sliding along the road," she said as she checked his vital signs. "Road rash. I didn't scrape off my tattoo, did I?" "That depends on where it's located. If it's on your hind end, it's gone." "It's on my left shoulder. Will ye look?" asked Harley. "Let me see. Is it a parakeet that looks angry?" "It's s'posed to be a Screamin' Eagle," replied Harley, not understanding her attempt at humor. "Oh yes, it is an eagle, and it says 101st Airborne underneath it. It's completely undamaged, Harley, if I may call you Harley," she said, adjusting his bandages gently. "Ye thank I'll be in here long?" "I can only guess, probably at least a week or more. My name is Brenda, and I'll be looking after you on the night shift," she said. "You get better, Harley, and think good thoughts," she said sweetly as she walked briskly out of the room. "I will," he said. And he thought about her.

South Pittsburg

Named in honor of Pittsburgh, Pennsylvania, (without the "h" on the end of Pittsburgh), South Pittsburg is located in Marion County, Tennessee, close to Chattanooga and the Alabama border. It's the birthplace of Lodge, world-renowned manufacturer of cast-iron skillets and the less renowned, US Stove Company. South Pittsburg is also the birthplace of Brenda Luttrell, RN.

Brenda was the only daughter of Ewell and Hughetta May Luttrell, who both died in a car wreck soon after Brenda graduated from high school. Her mother was a homemaker, and her father made a meager living, casting skillets at the foundry. Despite near poverty conditions, the frugal Luttrells managed to sock away some money, which Brenda inherited. It wasn't a large sum but enough, along with her full- and part-time jobs, to put her through nursing school in Knoxville, where she also received help with the assistance of a scholarship. Upon graduation she had no desire to work in South Pittsburg. She had no other relatives there (or anywhere else that she knew of). She'd worked at the hospital in town as a candy striper, but the building was rumored to be haunted and gave her the creeps. She had been haunted enough by the deaths of her parents and tossed into the maelstrom of adulthood and self-preservation at the tender age of seventeen. During her schooling, she experienced a disastrous affair with a young intern, which soured her view of men for a while. She had few friends, and despite the fact that she was beautifully cute and amiable, she distanced herself from a busy social life, spurning the advances of horny interns, older doctors, and a variety of medical professionals interested in a tryst. She was definitely not husband hunting. However, she was searching for something, or someone, which at this point was unidentifiable. She happily accepted a job at the University of Tennessee Hospital in Knoxville, a city that she had grown to love, along with the Tennessee Vols.

Scrap was doing his best to inspire Harley. "Yore bike is as purty as new. Joe Boy and Wayne stopped by the house atter work last week with a whole sack full of parts. They fixed that thang in no time, and

Wayne took it fer a test ride. Me and Early have been polishin' on it, and yore goin' to like it," said Scrap proudly. "I been tryin' to git them to sell that blamed thang," said Margaret scornfully, as she smoothed back Harley's disheveled mop of hair.

It was Margaret and Scrap's turn to visit Harley. Early was running the saw, while Sissy worked her job at the shirt factory, and Maw was watching Glory. Harley was mending, albeit, slowly. It was important that he stay in the hospital for a while in order for his wounds to heal and avoid infection. Margaret and Scrap had difficulty keeping their hands off their boy but managed restraint.

"Are they takin' good keer of ye, son?" said Margaret as she poured him a cup of water. "They seem to do a good job, 'specially at night. The night nurse lets me sleep, and she's always there when I need hep with anything," said Harley, who was feeling poorly and secretly wished that his well-wishers would leave. Margaret and Scrap sensed his impatience and were preparing to go at the shift change when Brenda entered the room. "Oh, I'm sorry, I'll come back when your company leaves," she said and turned to go, but Margaret stopped her. "Oh, honey, are ye the night nurse?" "Yes ma'am, my name is Brenda." Margaret came at her with arms spread and wrapped them around her as if she had known her forever. "Oh, thank ye, honey, fer takin' care of air boy. He says yore so kind to him, and that means the world to us," said Margaret. "That's right. We're obliged," said the big man with her, as he patted her shoulder affectionately. Harley looked a little embarrassed as he struggled to sit up on the bed. "This is my momma, Margaret, and my papaw, Scrap." Brenda hesitated before answering, recuperating from the outpouring of sincerity she had just experienced. "Well, thank you all. I don't get too many 'thanks' from people, and that means a lot to me. Harley says a lot of nice things about you all too; it's evident that he loves his family, and that you all love him," she said, turning her attention to her patient. "How are you feeling today, Harley?" "Like a bird on a war," he said, grinning faintly. She knew just by looking at him that he was feeling feeble. Patients with severe injuries always seemed to suffer more when night came on. "I'll be right back, Harley, with your medications. It was nice meeting you all," she said as she exited. "Dang, Harley, she's a purty thang," giggled Scrap, resisting the urge to hit Harley on the shoulder. "I jest wish I was in good enough shape to do somethin' about it," said Harley, and they both laughed at the innuendo. Embarrassed, Margaret grabbed Scrap's arm. "Hush now, both of ye. C'mon, let's git outta here, Daddy," she said. "Love ye, Harley," their voices echoed in unison as they walked down the hallway.

Brenda admired Harley's muscular butt as she removed gravel from his backside. Harley lay on his stomach as she performed the nightly ritual and considered himself lucky that barely any part of his front side had been injured in the accident. "This is healing nicely, scabbing over well," said Brenda as, after gravel duty, she gently washed him down with a medicated soap and applied soothing zinc oxide to his wounds. There was a bit of pain involved, but all in all, Harley loved her cool, healing touch. "How does that feel, honey…I mean, Harley," said Brenda, chastising herself for the Freudian slip. "It feels good, sweetie pie…I mean, Brenda," he replied. She was embarrassed and didn't bother to answer. It was quiet in the room since Harley's roommate, a man whose hands were burned as he attempted to start a trash fire with kerosene as an accelerant, was discharged that afternoon. "Ye thank it would be OK if we turned that radio up a little bit, Brenda? I like that song." "No problem," said Brenda, upping the volume on the little transistor radio at his bedside. She nodded her head in time with the music as Gregg Allman wailed "Statesboro Blues." She gave Harley a little pleated paper cup that contained his pain meds, made sure he took them, then helped him onto his side and covered him with a clean sheet. "I know that you're uncomfortable, Harley, but the medication will take effect soon, and I'll be in to check on you throughout the night. Remember, just press the call button, and I'll be here. "Thank ye, Brenda. Ye shore do make me feel…better," he said groggily, the medication taking almost immediate effect. "Sleep tight, Harley," she said as she left the room. She had just reached the nurse's station when she saw the light flashing above his room number. "What do you need, Harley?" she said as she reentered the room. Harley's eyes were heavy-lidded as he replied with a few words. "Jest ye, Brenda." Then he slipped into unconsciousness. Moved by the sweet remarks, Brenda rearranged Harley's sheets and turned off his night-light. She was glad to see that he was recuperating and would return home soon, but she hated to see him go. He was released three days later, on a Friday morning. "Too bad ye didn't git to say bye to Brenda," said Scrap as one of the day nurses propelled Harley down the hallway in a wheelchair. Harley didn't answer, but his thoughts deeply echoed Scrap's sentiments.

Early drove him back a month later to have the cast removed from his arm. He chauffeured Harley in Harley's "new" old car, a '55 Chevy Bel Air. The car had belonged to Wendell Goins' widow, who literally, drove it only to church on Sundays and Wednesdays, and garaged it on other days. It had low mileage, impeccable interior and exterior, and a sweet V-8 with plenty of power. It was red and white, just like Harley's bike that he sold for a fair price to one of the Sons of the South, much to Wayne and Joe Boy's sorrow. "It's jest like fallin' off a horse; you git back on and ride," pleaded Joe Boy. "I ain't skeered; I jest need somethin' that I kin court in," said Harley. "Hell, you cain't git a girlfriend anyways," said Wayne. Harley hoped differently.

Early was amazed at how much Harley's previously casted arm had shrunken. "Shit fire, Harley! Yore arm's no biggern Glory's." "The doctor said that it would build back up in no time, and it's healed nice. He said that it would be good if I could git therapy fer it, but if I couldn't afford it, he'd give me some exercises," said Harley, scratching his scaly limb. Harley quickly changed the subject. "Hey, if ye ain't got nothin' going on, ye wont to stop by Blue Circle and git a sack full of hamburgers? I'm buyin'." Early was always game for a meal, especially if it was free. "Shore!" he said excitedly, as he turned on Broadway. The two sated their appetites, splitting a sack of twelve hamburgers and washing them down with big Cokes. "Shoot, those burgers are so little I could eat another whole sack of 'em. Thank ye fer buyin'," said Early, patting his stomach. "Well hell, I'll buy ye some more," said Harley, rolling over on his good hip and reaching awkwardly into his back pocket for his wallet. "No, no that's all right. I need to lose weight anyways. The next time we come back, the sack is on me," laughed Early as he reached to stop Harley from opening his billfold. "I'll tell ye what ye kin do. Will you drop me by the hospital fer a few minutes? I'd like to say hello to Brenda," said Harley, almost shyly. Early shook his head sadly. "What I won't do fer a sack of hamburgers. We'd better git another sack to go; I'll need somethin' to do while I'm sittin' thar waitin' on ye," he said, reaching out the window and pushing the call button for a carhop.

Harley felt his breath quiver in his chest as he rode the elevator up to the third floor. He'd never really had to chase a girl before. Enamored with his good looks and his easy way, they came to him. He chuckled to himself when he remembered the advice Scrap gave to him as a youth. "Ye jest 'member, a man chases a woman till she ketches him." But Brenda was different. She was beautiful, educated, and confident. She didn't have to lay a trap for a man. They probably came to her like bass to a bright light. He shook his head from side to side. Who in the hell did he think he was, this redneck mountain boy trying to woo a woman of such sophistication? She'd probably laugh in his face or, worse, get angry with him for even trying to see her. When the elevator finally reached its destination and the doors opened, he thought seriously about pushing the down button, but he regrouped and stepped off the elevator just as the doors were about to close.

Brenda was at the nurse's station, reviewing doctor's orders for treatment of a patient, when Harley came sauntering up the corridor. "Hey," he said in a whisper so as not to startle her, but he did. "Harley! What's wrong? Is someone in your family sick?" she said, touching his arm concernedly. "No, no. I was jest in the neighborhood. I got my cast off today, and I thought I would drop by and see ye, if ye don't mind." "Let me see that arm. Goodness, it's atrophied quite a bit, but that's not unusual. Are you taking therapy?" "I'm s'posed to. I hate to cry poor mouth, but I don't thank I kin afford it. But don't git me wrong; I didn't come here to bit…gripe about that, I come here to see ye," he said, staring at the floor like an embarrassed schoolboy. Brenda was awkward too but impressed by his bravery. She knew that it wasn't easy for him to take this step. "Well, it's good to see you. I was just about to take a break, and I can spend a few minutes with you. Is that all right?" "Shore!" he said happily, as she linked her arm through his and escorted him to the lounge.

She laughed hysterically when he told her that Early was out in the car making love to a sack of hamburgers. And she was still giggling as she poured more coffee for them. He relaxed. She excused herself and returned with a towel and a jar of something. "Lay that arm on this towel, and let me rub some cocoa butter on it," she ordered. Harley sighed as she massaged the damaged limb with the ointment. "Oh man, does that feel good!" "I'm sure it does. It's still a little crooked at the elbow. The tendons have shrunken, but if you stretch it and exercise it, your arm should straighten out nicely," said Brenda as she placed her hand on the front of his shoulder and pulled gently on his wrist. "Ow! That's not vury nice of ye," he joked. "If you're like most men, you won't take the time to have someone do this for you. When do you go back to work?" "In about three weeks." "Then let me make a suggestion. I'm off work on Fridays and Saturdays and all day on Sundays. Why don't you visit me at my place on one of those days, and I'll give you some therapy for that elbow?" "Uh...whar do ye live?" She took a pen out of her pocket, scribbled some information on a napkin, and handed it to him. "I live in Maryville on Old Niles Ferry Road. The house number is on there and also my phone number. I'd appreciate it if you'd call before you decide to visit, so I can clean the place up a little bit," she said. Harley didn't know how he dredged up the courage for his next question. "Well, do ye mind if I drop by this Saturday?" "Not at all, how about four o'clock?" "Great. What would ye like fer me to brang?" "I'll have everything we need. And come hungry," she said as she stood up. He caught the hint that it was time to leave and stood also. "Brenda, thank ye fer yore hep. I'll see ye on Saturday," he said as he turned to go. "Wait a minute, you forgot something." "What's that?" She glanced furtively around the empty room. "This," she said and kissed him lightly on the cheek. She turned scarlet at her brazen act, and he grinned as though he'd won a million dollars as he pushed the down button for the elevator.

When he got to his car, he found Early asleep in a pile of empty hamburger wrappers. "Scoot over, big boy; I'll drive ye home," he said, tapping on the window. As Early slept, Harley sang to himself and ate the two remaining hamburgers in the sack. He wasn't sure how far this thing would go, but he was sure that Brenda was just the therapy he needed.

Chapter 31
THERAPY

Brenda had been surprised to see Harley and was overwhelmed by his bright good looks, his refreshing lack of pretentiousness, and his evident admiration for her. But she was most taken by the fact of how much she had missed him. She still wasn't convinced that she had done the right thing by inviting him to her home; but she forged ahead with her plan to help heal his arm and to get to know him better. She'd dug out some old orthopedic reference material and arrived at work early in the afternoons for several days to visit her colleagues in the rehab center. They allowed her to monitor their work on patients, especially those patients with shoulder and elbow injuries.

Harley had called on Friday and asked if he was still welcome on Saturday. "It's a done deal; see you about four o'clock," she said cheerfully. When she hung up, she spent some time untangling the phone cord that she'd nervously twisted in a knot. She was awakened early on Saturday morning to the glaring light of apprehensiveness. But she soon overcame her doubts about the agenda to follow. She hopped out of bed and headed for the local A&P store, where she rounded up all of the ingredients for her meal, and hurried back home to prepare the feast.

The entrée for this evening would be Chicken Piccata with Angel Hair pasta, and the first step was for Brenda to beat the dickens out of the chicken breasts, flattening them with a rolling pin. She loved to cook, which reflected her nurturing side. She had learned a lot of what she knew from waitressing in diners and road houses. Her favorite job was at a small Italian restaurant called D'Amico's. She spent as much time in the kitchen with Mamma D'Amico, learning how to prepare authentic Italian dishes, as she did waiting on tables. The D'Amicos adored her and came to her graduation bearing a mouth-watering box of Italian cookies. She visited them often, and they kept her supplied with bottles of their homemade Dago Red wine, which was produced with loving care in their basement.

After wrapping the chicken breasts in waxed paper and placing them in the refrigerator, Brenda mixed together flour, black pepper, and cayenne pepper in a shallow dish in which to dredge the chicken. She decided to cook the chicken in a mixture of white wine, chicken stock, garlic, butter, capers, and lemon zest right before Harley arrived, so he would appreciate the delicious aroma in the house.

Fall was coming on. The wind was up, and a slant-driven rain was falling when Harley arrived at Brenda's house. He was impressed with the little rented bungalow that looked as if it were built entirely of stone; sturdy enough to stand for an eternity. He glanced in the rearview mirror and punished himself for not getting a haircut. But he was proud of his new, long-sleeved madras shirt, pleated slacks, and brown penny loafers, which he'd recently purchased at Miller's Department Store in Knoxville. Margaret and Sissy thought he looked nice, but Early and Scrap gave him down the road. "Ye look like one of them Yankees on the TV," said Scrap as Early pinched his own nose. "What's that stank?" Harley wasn't about to tell him that he'd bought a bottle of English Leather and walked out the door without answering. He sighed deeply, picked up the bouquet of hardy mums that Margaret had arranged from her garden and an apple pie that she insisted he take, and walked to Brenda's front door.

For Harley, stepping across Brenda's threshold was like walking onto a movie set. She had a nice little fire flickering, throwing shadows on the walls. There was a bright light in the kitchen, where the aroma of something good wafted, filling the entire house. But the living room was lit warmly with several shaded lamps around the perimeter, while Gordon Lightfoot crooned, "If You Could Read My Mind" from a phonograph in the hallway. Brenda reached gratefully for the bouquet. "Oh, flowers! How sweet of you. I love mums!" "I brought ye a pie too. It's apple, I thank," he said shyly, handing over the pie. "That's great; I didn't make dessert. You take your coat off and hang it in the hallway, and I'll put these flowers in water."

She wore tight bell-bottomed jeans and a flannel shirt. He admired what she did for the outfit as she walked away from him. He was about to sit down on the couch when she returned with the flowers arranged nicely in a vase. "Now why don't you take that pretty shirt off, and we'll get started," she said, leading him by the hand into the dining room. She sat him down at the table, which was covered with an assortment of items: two heating pads plugged into wall sockets, tubes and jars of creams, towels, tape, a five-pound dumbbell, and a tennis ball. "Here, let me help you with that shirt," she said, peeling the garment off his shoulders and hanging it across one of the dining room chairs. "Is it too cold in here for you?" "No, it's jest right actually," he said, but he was perspiring lightly. "Well, let's start with that elbow. Would you like something to drink?" "What ye got?" "Not much; how about a little wine?" Harley had never drunk wine but was not taking a chance of offending her. "Shore, why not." She left and returned quickly with two glasses of the D'Amicos' prized product. "Cheers," she said and clinked her glass against his. Harley drank half of his glass down before she stopped him. "Whoa there, boy!" she laughed. "This isn't beer. You've got to take it easy." "Yore right, it's purty strong, but it's purty good," he said, eyes watering.

She took the hand at the end of his injured arm in hers. "Now let's put your elbow on the table, like you're going to arm wrestle someone," she said, seating herself across from him and reaching for a jar of cream. She applied the cream from his hand to his shoulder. "When you've had a cast on your arm for as long as you have, it can cause stiffness and severe loss of mobility and strength. Turn your hand with your palm facing you, and try to touch the towel on the table with the back of your hand." He tried but was unable to complete the process, his hand stopping about five inches from the tabletop. "See what I mean? Let's loosen those tendons, ligaments, and cartilage," she said, massaging his arm strongly, bending his elbow at angles he hadn't tried. Then she wrapped his elbow in heating pads and taped the pads in place. She dabbed at his sweaty brow with another clean towel. "I know that hurt, but it'll get better as time goes on. Now how about another sip of wine?" Harley gladly picked up his glass. "Cheers," he said, and she giggled.

While the heating pads were on, she had him squeeze the tennis ball. He hardly put a dent in it. "That's OK. In the next few weeks, you'll be able to tell a huge difference," she said as she unwrapped the heating pads. "Now stand up and hang your arms by your sides." He did as he was told, and she placed the five-pound dumbbell in his injured hand. "Hold on to it as long as you can. You have an injury in a hinge joint, which contains ligaments, cartilage, and even little fluid sacs. This will help to stretch them out." He couldn't hold on long, but she didn't harangue him. "That's good. Now let's see how well we've done." She had him place his arm in an arm-wrestling position again and bent his elbow so that his hand was about two inches from the table. The pain was excruciating. "Look at that! You're making progress already!" "Thank ye," he said through gritted teeth. "Kin I have another sip of wine?"

When they were finished, she helped him put his shirt back on. "Why don't you take all of this stuff in the laundry room, and I'll finish getting supper on the table." "Shore," said Harley as he gathered up as many items as he could. When he was finished, he joined her in the kitchen, where she was salting the water in a pot that was just beginning to boil. Then she added the angel hair pasta. "I ain't never seen pasta that skinny," said Harley. "Wait till you see what I'm going to do with this," she said, removing the pasta from the water and draining it. She removed the chicken from the pan onto a serving dish and spooned some of the capers and the sauce onto the pieces. Then she added the pasta to the skillet, and tossed it with the remaining piccata sauce to coat it. "You want your pasta on the chicken or on the side?" she said as she placed the pasta in a serving bowl. "On the side, I guess." "Then follow me," she said, leading the way to the dining room. Harley was amazed how she transformed the table from a physical therapy room to a fine dining area. The table was dressed with a fresh white cloth, napkins, the few pieces of fine china and silverware service that she owned, lit candles, and the flowers that he'd brought as a centerpiece. She seated him at the end of the table, and before she sat catty-corner from him, she poured them both full glasses of wine. "I'll be right back; I'm going to change the record," she said. She returned to the mellow tones of Cat Stevens. "You like him, Harley?" "I'm afraid I don't know who he is." "That's Cat Stevens; it's one of my favorite songs of his. Isn't it nice?" "Here's to you," she said, touching her glass to his. "Cheers. Yore nice too, Brenda," he responded, turning up his glass.

After they dug into the pie, he helped her with the dishes. "Do you do this at home?" "Nope, I've tried, but Momma won't let me. Lord knows, I owe her. I try to do as much as I kin fer her and the rest of my family. I owe them all…" Brenda paused in the midst of wiping a bowl dry. "But Harley, why do you think you owe them?" "I owe 'em fer takin' me in," he said but changed the subject. "Hey! Do ye have any soul music? When I was in Nam, the brothers played a lot of it, and I got to likin' it." "Well, let's see, I have some Marvin Gay, Temptations, and…" "Well, put 'em on and let's daince. Do ye daince?" "I'm not very good..." "Ye don't have to be; ye jest got to move and feel good about it!" She laughed, a deep throaty laugh, and it went all over him. "You roll back the rug while I put the records on, and we'll boogie," she said.

They must have danced for an hour straight to a variety of music: Junior Walker's "Shotgun," The Temps' "Can't Get Next to You," and Marvin Gaye's "Ain't Nothin' Like the Real Thing." When she became tired, she sat at the table and clapped for him like a delighted child as he continued to circle around the room, flailing his arms wildly. "That's probably good for your elbow; keep it up!" she hollered over the music. He was glad she'd put on a Delfonics album because he was getting pretty tired. His madras shirt was bleeding with sweat, but he pulled her off the chair, and she gladly joined him for a slow dance to "La-La Means I Love You." "I love this song," she said, pressing tightly against him. "I'm sorry I'm sweatin' so much; do ye mind if we daince this close?" "Not at all; I think you smell good," she whispered in his ear. "English Leather and lye soap," he whispered back, proudly. She stepped back and laughed out loud at his comment. "What's the matter?" "You're just so damned sweet," she said as she left the room to turn off the record player. He wisely caught the clue and glanced at his watch. Ten-thirty, time to leave.

"Now, Harley, you've got a long way to drive; please be careful," she told him at the door. "I'll be keerful if I can come back agin next week," he said. "How about a little earlier? You've got such a long way to drive. We'll get that arm of yours in good shape," she said. "OK then. Well, bye," he said, bending to hug her. She grabbed his face in her hands and kissed him long and hard on the lips. "I can't remember when I've had such a good time, Harley." "Me either, he said, finding it difficult to catch his breath. "I'll call ye tomorry," he said as he ran out into the rain to his car. He was allowing the Chevy to warm up when she tapped lightly on his window. "Git out of that rain; yore gittin' soaked!" "Just be careful, Harley. We drank a lot of wine." "Hey, I'm purty shore I dainced it off; I'll be all right. Now git in the house afore ye ketch yore death!"

Harley beeped the horn as he headed up Old Niles Ferry Road. He felt good all over: his arm felt good, he had a full belly, his head was pleasantly buzzing, and his heart was overflowing with love for Brenda Luttrell.

Chapter 32

LITTLE BEE

With Brenda's help and the healing power of youth, Harley's arm began to heal and regain its original appearance, straight and muscular. Margaret and Sissy helped him with treatments one night a week, and he travelled to Brenda's house on Saturdays. "What kin she do that we cain't do?" said Sissy petulantly, as he prepared to leave one Saturday morning. "Nothin', cain't ye see that he's usin' it as an excuse to court and spark?" laughed Early. "Leave him alone; he's jest gittin' what he needs," said Margaret, rubbing his shoulder. "I'll bet he is," said Sissy as she stormed out of the room. "Don't ye never mind," said Margaret as Scrap and Early hid in the kitchen, giggling at Sissy's insinuation. "Why don't ye brang her up here fer Thanksgivin'; it's jest around the corner. She kin stay all night if she likes." "Yep, and she kin sleep at my place; she'll like it since we put in a bathroom and share, and I'll sleep up here. How's that sound, son?" said Scrap as he moseyed out of the kitchen. "I don't know if I wont her to come up here if Sissy's goin' to act like that." "Like I said, don't ye never mind, honey; Sissy jest loves ye, and she's a little bit jealous," said Margaret as she shooed her son out the door.

Brenda was happy that Harley's arm was healing and that she played an important role in the process. But she figured it was time to quit using therapy as a façade for their affair. She had come to believe she loved Harley Baird, and she had a feeling that he loved her, though neither one had mentioned the fact. Unbelievably they hadn't become "intimate" yet, other than some heavy necking on the couch and in the doorway before he had to return to Campbell County. They spent most of their times together sight-seeing in the Smokies, going to football games, and visiting the East Tennessee History Center in Knoxville and the Museum of Appalachia in Anderson County, which butts up to Campbell County. Harley was fascinated with the history of East Tennessee, a history that belonged to him, a history that he lived and breathed. "Lookee here, my daddy carved a dulcimer that looked jest like this!" he told Brenda. "He never did strang it up before he died, but Momma still has it. Maybe I'll put some strangs on it one day."

One night she took him to D'Amico's for an early supper. "You said you thought I was a good cook? Wait till you taste Mamma D'Amico's food!" said Brenda excitedly. Her excitement was founded on more than just the food. She was thrilled at the prospect of showing Harley off to her friends. He looked especially handsome this evening, and she was proud. "Brens, welcome! This must be your boyfriend, no?" said Mamma as she hugged them both tightly. "This is Harley Baird, Mamma. Harley, this is Mamma," said Brenda as a young man took their coats. "It's a pleasure to meet you, ma'am," said Harley. "Nobody answers? Are you her boyfriend?" said Mamma, with her hands on her hips. Brenda saved him from answering, much to his delight. "Yes, he is." "He's so handsome. You done good, bambina!" she said, smooching Brenda heavily on the cheek. "Giuseppe, sit these two lovebirds inna nice booth!" she ordered an olive-skinned young waiter.

As they perused the menu in the glow of a candle that was stuck in a wine bottle, with rivulets of wax that had flowed down the side, Harley hesitantly asked her a question. "Did ye really mean it?" "Mean what?" "That I'm yore boyfriend." "Why, yes, I assumed…" "Well, that's how I feel too. I was afraid to ask if ye felt the same way. Thank ye," he said humbly. "Oh, Harley, thank you. No one…no man has ever made me feel as important as you do. You're so honest, so unpretentious…" "What's that mean?" "It means you don't try to be anyone but yourself, and that's rare," she said, reaching across the checkered table cloth to touch him. "Hell, I don't know how to be anyone else," he said, squeezing her hand.

"So, whatcha decide? Tonight the special is saltimbocca. And if I do say so, it is delicious!" Mamma said, kissing her fingers with a loud smack. "What's that?" said Harley. "In Italiano, ita means 'jumps in your mouth'!" Mamma said with a flare. "It's veal with prosciutto and sage. It's marinated in wine and cooked in marsala and butter," said Brenda. Harley had no idea what prosciutto and marsala were, but everything sounded pretty good to him. "Then that's what we'll have," he said authoritatively. "And can we have some wine to go with it?"

As they finished their giardiniera and sipped their wine, Brenda asked Harley a question that had been weighing on her. "Harley, what did your daddy die of?" "He had somethin' wrong with his lungs. They thank it was cancer." "I'm sorry," she said, clasping his hand in both of hers. "Did he look like you?" "No, nobody looks like me," he said. Then he told her the story of Benny finding him on the church steps. When he was finished, she wiped her eyes with her napkin. "What's wrong?" he asked. "Now I know why you feel as if you owe everyone," she said, kissing his hands. He started to say something but was interrupted when the waiter brought their entrées.

Later, when he dropped her off at the stone house, he offered an invitation before kissing her good night. "What ye doin' fer Thanksgivin' next week?" "I'm off work for four glorious days in a row," she said. "I knowed that, but what ye doin'?" She thought he was wrangling for an invitation to dinner, and it pleased her. "Well, I could cook a small turkey...make that a large turkey, knowing how you like to eat; and we could watch some football." "I've got another idee; why don't I pick ye up on Wednesday and drive ye up to the house so ye can eat

Thanksgivin' dinner with us? Ye could stay all night if ye'd like or longer." Brenda was flustered at first. "Well, are you sure?" "Shore I'm shore. My family and I have already talked about it, and they'd be plumb tickled if ye come!" "Well…OK, if you're sure…" "Yahoo!" he shouted and bumped his head on her gutter as he jumped in the air. "Are you OK?" "I'm OK," he said, rubbing his head and kissing her fervently on the mouth. "I'll pick you up next Wednesday afternoon." "But Harley, I can drive; just give me some directions." "Ye'd never find it. Besides, this way I kin hold ye hostage," he yelled as he backed out of her driveway.

He kept his promise and was there to pick her up the day before Thanksgiving. And she was dismayed at how long it took to get to their destination, only because she hadn't realized how treacherous some of the roads were and how far it was to come to see her in Maryville.

As they pulled into the yard of the little house, Scrap waved excitedly to them from the front porch. "Thar's my Pappy Scrap; you remember him, don't ye?" said Harley "We live up thar on the hill, but Scrap's givin' up his place down here so ye kin have some privacy," he said as he lifted her luggage out of the trunk of the Chevy. They'd barely had time to climb the steps before Scrap enveloped her in a shy embrace and welcomed her into the house.

"Welcome, Brender, to air place. Did Harley tell ye that ye was stayin' here, at my house? Well, come on in, and let me show ye around." Harley grinned as he took Brenda's overnight bag into the bedroom, and Scrap started the royal tour. "As ye kin see, this is yore livin' room. Me and Harley and Early and Sissy put up this knotty pine panelin' that we cut and finished airselves. We put it in ever' room in the house; nice, ain't it? The livin' room's not vury big, but it's comferble, with a couch and a telephone next to it that you kin use any time, and we'll come runnin'. And over thar in the corner is yore lazy feller char that the family give me fer Christmas. The TV's over thar in the other corner, and I'm sorry but we only git one station. Now lookee here, I got pitchers of ever'body on this little table," he said, pointing to a stand filled with frames of images of children, couples, and himself. Brenda started to mention something about the family, but Scrap motioned her into the kitchen. "Now this here's yore kitchen," he said, flinging open the refrigerator door. He repeated the speech that he had given to Benny and Margaret many years ago. "I've stocked it with ever'thang ye need: baloney, bacon, hot banana peppers, maters, aigs, mustard, mayonnaise...ever'thang ye need, and thar's bread in this little box on top of the 'frigerator. Margaret stuffed this here cookie jar with peanut butter and chocolate chip cookies, probably yore favorites," he said, helping himself to a cookie." "This is very nice, Scrap. I'm sure that..." He interrupted again, waving her to follow him. "Now come on in here, and I'll show ye somethin' ye'll really cotton to," he said, leading her into the bathroom. "We didn't put a tub in 'cause the room is too small and I'm too big, but ye've got a nice share and a sank and a toilet; and we've got lots of toilet paper under the sank, plus some towels, soap, and worsh cloths.

"Now lookee here," he said, gesturing for her to follow him into the bedroom, in which most of the space was taken up by a huge four-poster. The bed was covered with a worn but pretty blue chenille spread, and there was a photo of a woman on the nightstand that bore a significant resemblance to Margaret. "That's my Haley June; we was murried for over twenty-eight yars," said Scrap affectionately. "Well, that's it. Me and Harley has to go now and tell the family that yore here. Ye jest make yoreself comferable, and when yore ready, come on up to the house on the hill, and we'll have a big time," he said and walked out of the room. Harley smiled sweetly at her. "Thanks fer puttin' up with that. He's been excited as a young'un, waitin' fer ye to arrive. Here's the number fer ye to call when yore ready, and I'll come down to git ye." She looked incredulously at the slip of paper on which he'd written the number. "Holy cow, I feel like I'm at the Ritz!"

"Ain't that a cracker?" he asked. "Never mind, give me about forty-five minutes, and I'll be ready."

It was only about thirty yards from the little house to the big house, but Harley drove down to pick her up. "Ye ever rode in an old truck before? This'un's a doozy," said Harley as they bumped out of the yard, up the road, and into the yard of the big house, where Scrap, Margaret, Glory, and Early stood on the porch waiting for them. "Does this thing have any shocks?" said Brenda, rattled from the short but jarring trip. "Kinda' rough, ain't it?" laughed Harley as he took a bag that Brenda was carrying away from her. "What's in this? It's kinda heavy," he said as they neared the porch. "Just some gifts for your family that we bought in Gatlinburg and some food for dinner tomorrow," she answered as she was welcomed warmly. She was embarrassed as Scrap blurted out, "Ain't she purty, Early?" "What's in the sack?" said Glory, after she was introduced and hugged Brenda hello. "We have a present for you, Glory," said Brenda, pulling a box of saltwater taffy out of the bag. "Your Uncle Harley and I bought this for you in Gatlinburg. "Whar's that?" said Glory as she tugged on the ribbon tied to the box. "It's in the Smoky Mountains," said Harley as he bent to untie the ribbon for her. "Is it up thar?" said Glory, pointing her finger at the top of their mountain. "Nope, thar a little south of here, and thar a lot bigger than airs," said Harley. "We'll take you there someday," said Brenda as she reached in the bag for another item.

"Mrs. Baird, Harley said that you suffer from arthritis and that sometimes it hurts your hands when you're tending to your plants. So I thought you might like to use these pruning shears. They've got smooth ceramic handles, and they're spring-loaded; they'll be easier on your hands," said Brenda, handing her the package. "Oh, how kind and thoughtful," said Margaret, caressing the shears. "Please, honey, call me Margaret."

As she approached Early, he grinned broadly, knowing that she had brought a gift for him too. "Early, Harley told me how good you were with whittling and woodcarving, just like your daddy, and I thought you might like this," she said, presenting him with a book on woodcarving. Early was unable to repress his excitement over the book. "Lookit that picher on the front! It's a wood chain, and I've always wanted to carve one! Thank ye, Brender!" he said and hugged her without restraint.

She walked over to Scrap, who shuffled his feet nervously. "Scrap, this present isn't enough to repay you for giving up your home and bed for me. But I hope it's enough to help you catch that big old large-mouth you've been fishing for down on the lake," she said, handing him a packet of fancy lures. "Lord have mercy! I could slay a lot of hawgs with these!" he said, admiring the lures. "Thank ye, Brender!"

"Now where's Sissy? I've got something for her too," inquired Brenda.

"She's in the kitchen gittin' supper," said Margaret excitedly. "Let's go fetch her."

It was a typically gray November day in the mountains, dusk was falling, and Brenda appreciated the glowy-warm home as she entered. Every piece of overstuffed furniture in the large living room beckoned "snuggle in to me," and the Warm Morning woodstove in the corner radiated soothing heat. The equally large and airy kitchen, about five times the size of the kitchen at the stone house, featured a long wooden table that seated about eight, and was the venue for ages of nourishing meals, hated homework, serious and joyous family discussions, and all manner of Margaret and Maw's handiwork. It was definitely the gathering place and the engine of the house, as most kitchens were in the mountains. A woodstove, about the size of a ship, stood sentinel along the far wall at which a darkly beautiful woman-child, with silken, ebony tresses, was stirring a bubbling pot.

"Momma, Momma! Look what Brender brought me!" said Glory, running to show her box of taffy. Sissy turned to her daughter, and Brenda noticed the scar above her left eyebrow. To Brenda, the scar enhanced rather than flawed her beauty. "A badge of courage and character," she thought. "Don't eat any more of that, Glory; ye'll spole yore supper. Besides, it ain't good fer yore teeth," she said, wiping her hands on her shirt. "Hidey. My name's Sissy, Harley's sister," she said, greeting Brenda with noticeably less exuberance than did the rest of the family. "It's nice to meet you, Sissy. I've heard a lot of nice things about you," Brenda said cordially. "Brender's got a present fer ye, Momma!" Glory shouted with anticipation.

"She does? Well, it's Thanksgivin', not Christmas," said Sissy unenthusiastically. Brenda ignored the bad manners. "Harley said you enjoyed cooking, and I had this made for you in a store in Gatlinburg," she said, handing Sissy a beautifully made apron, with SISSY monogrammed on the front.

Sissy showed little enthusiasm for the gift. "I've got about a thousand aperns, but none of 'em have my name on 'em. I'll save this'un fer a special occasion," she said, hanging the apron on a hook on the wall beside the refrigerator. "Now if ever'body's ready, let's eat. Momma said that since we're afixin' to eat a heavy meal tomorry, we should probably jest eat soup and samwiches tonight," she said, hefting a huge platter of sandwiches off the counter and placing it on a lazy Susan in the middle of the table, which was already set with crockery and silverware.

They sat around the table for an hour, enjoying the assortment of sandwiches and Sissy's delicious soup, telling stories and enjoying getting to know one another. Sissy didn't participate in the conversation, keeping busy refilling bowls and replenishing drinks. "Harley, you 'member that night me and you and Joe Boy and Wayne was down at the lake bank fishin', and ye and Joe Boy decided to borry that motorboat?" said Early. "Ye don't need to tell that..." cautioned Harley, but Early was on a roll. "We was walkin' along the bank, atryin' to find a good spot to put out air trotlines, when we come upon this motorboat that was banked. It had a purty good-sized engine on it and some water skis in the back. 'Hey, you'uns wont to go skiin'?' said Joe Boy. Wayne said that he wonted no part of takin' a boat, so Harley left him with me 'cause I was little then…" "You ain't never been little!" interrupted Harley. "Anyways, they took off in the boat. The moon was real bright that night, and it was jest like daylight. Harley went first on the skis, and Joe Boy drove. It took Harley a few tries, but finally he got up on them skis and was havin' the time of his life. He saw what looked like a stump in the water and skied around it, and it spoke to him. 'Hey,' it said, and Harley realized it was Joe Boy. He had fell out of the boat atryin' to look at somethin' in the water. Harley let go of the tow rope and swimmed back to Joe Boy. It's a good thang 'cause Joe Boy couldn't swim that good, and Harley hepped him back to shore. We spent the rest of the night alookin' fer that boat and finally found it banked about a mile away. It wasn't hurt, and we drove it back to the same spot we found it and parked it thar," said Early as everybody laughed and clapped, with the exception of Margaret. "You'uns never tolt me about that," she said with a disdainful look on her face. "If'n he had, ye'd have worn more skin off'n his backside than the road did in that motorcycle crash," said Scrap to wild laughter.

Sissy put on her jacket. "Well, me and Glory had best be gittin' to the house. Momma, I'll see ye bright and early tomorry mornin', about six, if that's OK. We'll git that ole bird in the oven and start him acookin'," said Sissy as she bent down to kiss her mother. "Thank ye fer the taffy, Brender; we'll see ye tomorry, Mamaw," said Glory as she hugged Margaret. "Night, night, honey; I'll be waitin' fer ye," said Margaret, kissing her head. "Night, Brender," said Sissy as she went out the door, not waiting for a reply. Determined not to be iced out of the situation, Brenda took action. "I had best be getting to bed too, if I'm going to help with tomorrow's dinner. Margaret, what time are you getting up tomorrow?" "I'll be putterin' around the kitchen about five o'clock; I really like that time of day." "So do I. Do you mind if I show up around five thirty?" "Not at all, honey. I appreciate the company." "Good, then I'll be here, and you can show me what I can do to help you. Harley, do you mind walking me to *my* house?" she said, leaning over to touch Scrap on his shoulder. Scrap glowed as she and Harley walked to the door.

"Are ye shore ye don't mind sleepin' here?" Harley said at the door of the little house. "Of course not, I'm honored," said Brenda, kissing him affectionately. "I really love your family. I've learned a lot about you from meeting them." "I hope that yore not upset by Sissy. She's always been kind of bossy, and she has looked after us all, even though she's littler than all of us. If ye don't mind me sayin' so, she's kind of like you," he said, caressing her shoulder. "If she's anything like me, she'll get better as time goes on, honey." She kissed him sweetly. "I'll see you tomorrow, boat thief," she said and closed the door.

"Night, boys," said Scrap in the doorway of Early's bedroom. "Night, Pap," they said as he went to his room, located adjacent to Early's. Soon the wall was rattling with the sounds of his snoring. "God almighty, between you and Pap, it's agoin' to be a snorefest tonight!" said Harley from his cot in the corner. "I betchee Brender's got plenty of room in that big ole four-poster down at the little house, don't ye thank, Harley?" "Shut up and go to sleep," said Harley as Early snickered like a mischievous schoolboy for a while. Soon it sounded like a tractor pull was being conducted in the bedroom. Harley settled in for a sleepless night. He hoped Brenda was comfortable. He wished he were with her.

Brenda was under the covers by nine thirty, and if she hadn't drunk about a gallon of high-octane, iced tea, she would have slept through the night. She got up twice to pee. The first time she awakened, she was taken by the inky blackness and the tomblike quiet of the place. However, she wasn't frightened; the change from the cacophonous noise of the hospital and city life was quite comforting. The second time she woke, she didn't turn any lights on and, after relieving herself, walked out on the front porch. The weather had cleared, and the clouds moved out. It was refreshingly cold, and the canopy of stars overhead seemed brighter and closer than she'd ever experienced. Guided by the luminescent hands on the bedside Big Ben, which she'd set for four thirty, she made her way back to the bedroom and snuggled beneath the warm comforter. She wished she had Harley for her bedmate and hoped to accomplish that goal soon.

At four thirty on the nose, the reliable clock jangled her awake. She fixed herself a cup of coffee and ate a chocolate chip cookie, foregoing any of the "delicacies" Scrap had stocked in the refrigerator. After a leisurely shower, she donned a pair of jeans and a turtleneck. She took a sack full of goods that she'd put in the refrigerator the night before and made her way carefully up the frosted hill to the big house, from which one light shone from a window. When she reached the front door, it was open a crack, and she heard laughter filtering from the kitchen. She assumed that the door was left open for her, and she let herself in. As she entered the kitchen, she beheld Margaret and an older woman drinking coffee at the table. She could already smell the aroma of turkey cooking in the oven. The women looked up from their conversation and spoke to, but mainly about, Brenda. "Law, Margaret. She's jest like ye said she was, purty as an angel!" said the older woman. "Didn't I tell ye, Maw? Lookit them purty little pixie eyes and that shiny brown har! And don't she have a fine-spun frame?" said Margaret.

Both of the women rose from the table to greet her. "Hidey,

young'un, I'm Maw, and ye must be Brenda," said the older woman, who was shorter than Brenda by more than a few inches. She laid her head on Brenda's chest, hugged her tightly around the waist, and patted her hip as Margaret poured another cup of coffee. "Harley's told me so much about you, Maw, and how you help heal a lot of people up here," said Brenda. Still holding Brenda's hand, Maw responded sweetly as they sat down at the table. "I guess war in the same business but differnt," she said, faded blue eyes twinkling. "Maybe ye could teach me a few thangs while yore here." "I was hoping that you could teach me a few things," said Brenda, gently patting her thin-skinned, thickly veined hand. Margaret beamed. "Maw hepped me born Early and Sissy." "Yes'm, right down thar in that bed yore asleepin' in," said Maw proudly. "Ye delivered any babies, little angel?" "I've helped deliver several in the emergency room, but I'm not an obstetrical nurse," said Brenda. "Well, that don't make no never mind. If somebody needs hep bornin' a child while yore here, I'd appreciate if ye would hep me; I'm a gittin' too old fer that kind of thang." "I would be honored, Maw," said Brenda, and she meant it.

"I had Early git that old turkey that Scrap shot out of the freezer yesterday mornin' to thaw, and we got it in the oven right now; kin ye smell it?" "We plucked and cleaned it some time ago. I didn't realize how heavy that gobbler was. We liked to never got it in the oven," said Maw, and she and Margaret laughed hysterically. "We dropped the damn thang once on the floor," laughed Maw as Margaret doubled over and clapped her hands. "Don't worry, Brender, we worshed it off agin." They were all laughing as Sissy walked in.

"Well, what's goin' on? It sounds like yore havin' a party in here," she said as sleepy-eyed Glory stumbled zombielike to the comfort of her Mamaw's lap and immediately fell back to sleep. "I'll be right back. I'm agoin' to put her down on the couch," said Margaret. "Why don't you let me do that," said Brenda and took the child from Margaret's arms. "Remember what you did with the turkey? Don't want that happening again," she said, and Maw and Margaret cackled as she left the room. When she returned, Sissy had taken her seat so she took the seat next to her. "Well, tell me what you want me to do," said Brenda, directing her question to Margaret. "I figger us old birds will take keer of the cookin' the young bird and the pies; we got the fixin's fer punkin' and pecan. Sissy makes the best cornbread dressin' and sweet tater casserole and apple salad. Brender, do ye mind a peelin' taters fer mashed taters and fixin' them? Ye kin also peel the sweet taters fer Sissy's casserole. And we got some canned green beans down in the cellar and some frozen corn. Ye can do with 'em like ye wont. Oh, kin ye make gravy?" "I can handle all of that. Would you like for me to make some rolls too? I brought some Parker House rolls, and I brought some oysters too." "Oysters? What in the world do we need with oysters?" said Sissy. "Well, I thought I'd fix a little oyster dressing for Harley, I fixed it for him once before, and he loved it." "Well, don't git it near my dressin'; I don't wont it spoled." "I'd like to try some, honey," said Maw. "I heared that oysters are good fer yore sex life," she said as they scooted away from the table.

The women were in high gear as Scrap appeared in the kitchen. "Ye got any coffee brewin'?" he asked as he sat down at the table. "I'll get you a cup," said Brenda, who'd just finished peeling the sweet potatoes for Sissy's casserole and started peeling spuds for her mashed potatoes. "How're you feeling this morning, Scrap?" said Brenda, setting his coffee in front of him. "I'm ahangin' in thar, like a har in a biscuit," he said as he slurped his coffee. "Pap, ye know how I hate that sayin'," said Margaret. Brenda laughed as she opened her pack of rolls and began applying a mixture of Parmesan cheese, mayonnaise, Worcestershire sauce, and butter to them. "I'll be right back. I'm going to the cellar to get some frozen corn and a jar of green beans. Does anyone else need anything?" she said. She was back in a flash, picked up Scrap's mug, and served him another cup of coffee. "Lordy, ye buzz around this place like a little bee," said Scrap appreciatively.

"She's been a buzzin' since five thirty this mornin'; I never seen a woman with so much energy," said Margaret as she rolled out the dough for her pies. "I thank that's what we ought to call her from now on; it suits her, don't ye thank?" said Maw. "OK, 'Little Bee,' ye got those taters peeled fer my casserole?" said Sissy mockingly. "They've been done for about five minutes," said Brenda as she mixed up her oyster dressing in a little baking dish. Sissy didn't reply. "What'd I tell ye? She's jest like a little bee, buzzin' all over the place," repeated Scrap. When Early and Harley straggled in, Scrap told them his Little Bee story, and by mealtime everyone was addressing her by that nickname, including Glory.

When it came time to eat, Brenda had set the table and had the tapered candles she brought burning in holders at both ends of the table. She had debated about bringing a bottle of wine and finally decided to uncork a bottle of Dago Red. If nobody else drank it, she and Harley would enjoy a glass. "What's this?" said Early as he sat down at the table. "It's Dago Red wine. That's an Italian wine that's made here in America," said Harley, proud of his newfound knowledge. Margaret and Sissy were taken aback at the thought of spirits in the house, but Maw seemed pleased that there was vino on the table. "What's it say in the Bible? A little wine is good fer thy stomach?" said Maw, taking a healthy swig from her glass. "But a little shine is good fer yore whole body," said Scrap, who downed his glass in one gulp. "That ain't in the Bible," said Margaret. "I didn't say it was. Fill me up agin, will ye, Little Bee?" Margaret asked Harley to say the prayer, and when he finished offering the blessing, he stood with wine glass in hand. "I'd like to say a toast in honor of my guest and yore guest, Miss Brenda Luttrell. Ever'body raise yore glasses please. When they did, he recited the toast that he'd laboriously memorized: "Here's to the one and the only one, and may that one be she; who loves but one and only one, and may that one be me! Cheers!" he said and drank a sip of wine and everyone followed suit, with the exception of Margaret and Sissy. "To Little Bee!" said Early as he drank the remainder of wine in his jelly glass and helped himself to some more. Brenda was moved by Harley's toast and the warm response of his family, but was disappointed when Sissy questioned her brother. "Are ye shore yore in love, Harley?" "I'm purty shore, Sissy," he said with confidence. "It all depends if she loves me, and if she don't, I'll keep on workin' at it." "Cheers," said Early. "Cheers right back at ye," replied Scrap as he slurped down the contents of his glass.

Everyone seemed to enjoy Brenda's contributions to the dinner. Maw and Harley fought to clean up the oyster dressing. Sissy had hardly spoken during the meal, and when the chatter quieted down for a moment, she fired a mean-spirited salvo at Brenda. "Well, Little Bee, how do ye like eatin' with poor folks? Is it much differnt than eatin' with yore momma and daddy down in Chattanooga?" Brenda stared at her for a moment, then buried her face in her hands. Her shoulders shook as she cried silently. Glory immediately got out of her seat, rushed to Brenda's side, and crawled into her lap. "It's OK, Little Bee. Please don't cry." "C'mon, Little Bee, it cain't be that bad," sneered Sissy. No one said a word. Finally Harley spoke. "She ain't got no momma and daddy. She ain't got nobody," he said venomously, as he got up, moved to the side of Brenda, and clasped her hand in his. Sissy got up from the table and walked over to a corner of the kitchen, pretending to fiddle with the stove. Maw came over and comforted Brenda, rubbing her shoulder with her worn hand. "I'm sorry if we made ye cry, child," she apologized for Sissy. "I wasn't crying because of anything in particular. I was crying because of how kind most of you have been to me. I was crying because of how I've been made to feel a part of this wonderful family! I was crying because I miss my mamma and daddy. And I understand you, Sissy; I know how hurt you've been, and I know how important family is to you and Glory. I want you to know how important you are to me," she said, turning to face Sissy. At that remark the entire family attempted to comfort her with heartfelt remarks. Scrap patted Brenda with his big paw. “That’s OK, Little Bee; we’ll be yore family, even if ye and Harley don’t git murried.” There was palpable tension in the room as everyone looked at Scrap as if he’d just crapped his overalls. “Whut?” he said, causing the entire room to burst into laughter. “Pap, ye jest won’t do,” said Margaret. Sissy slipped the apron Brenda had given her off the hook and tried it on. She walked over and embraced Brenda’s neck from behind. “What kind of pie does ever’one wont? We’ll start with ye, Little Bee.”

Chapter 33

RETURN TO THE STONE HOUSE

They'd heard on the radio that some rough weather was moving in over the next couple of days: rain, sleet, and possibly snow. Brenda made the decision to return home on Friday afternoon for fear of being socked in and missing work. After they packed up the car at the little house, they drove up to the big house to say good-bye to the family. Margaret, Scrap, Early, and Glory were waiting on the porch as they arrived. Margaret had a sack in her hand. "I fixed you'uns some samiches, a thermos of coffee, and some cups to take with ye, Little Bee. I'm sorry, but thar warn't much left of that ole bird to give ye," she said, glaring at Scrap and Early. "Papaw and Early ate most of the turkey afore they went to bed last night," scolded Glory. "Don't be a tattletale, Glory!" snapped Early, and the little girl ran behind her grandmother for un-needed protection. "It's OK. I'm still stuffed from last night's meal. Where's Sissy?" said Brenda. "She's at work. They don't git much time off at the shirt factory," said Margaret. "She said to tell ye good-bye, and she looks ford to seein' ye agin." "I look forward to seeing her and all of you again. Thanks for the wonderful hospitality, and thanks, especially to you, Scrap, for giving up your place for a couple of days. "To be honest with ye, it'll be nice to git back thar," he said, jerking a thumb at Early. "This 'uns kep me awake fer two days." As Early stared incredulously at Scrap, Harley took the opportunity to say final good-byes. "Well, we got to git; those clouds look like thar rollin' in purty fast," he said, looking at the scudding clouds. "If the weather gits too bad, ye stay thar!" commanded Margaret. "Yeah! Stay thar in Little Bee's hive, Harley; ye'll be safe thar," Early taunted. Embarrassed, Harley ushered Brenda to the Chevy. "I'll be back when I git here," he said.

As they pulled out of the yard, Brenda asked Harley to go left instead of right. "I'd like to say good-bye to Maw, if you don't mind." "Shore, she's probably at home." Brenda was intrigued by Maw's property as they drove into the yard. "My! This place looks like an arboretum! Look at all of the plants, gardens, and that beautiful stream," she said as they got out of the car. "Harley, will you open the trunk for me? I need to get something out of my bag." When he popped the trunk, she unzipped the bag and extracted a bottle of Dago Red. "I brought this along just for you and me. But I've got more at the house," she said as they made their way to Maw's front door. She met them on the porch. "Lord, what a nice surprise! Come on in and sit a spell, Little Bee, Harley." Harley reluctantly refused the invitation. "I'm sorry, Maw. Thar's some bad weather comin' in, and we'd like to git her back to Maryville soon," he said, glancing again at the active sky. "What I wanted to do was thank you for your hospitality and give you this bottle of wine; you seemed to enjoy it." "Oh child, thank ye so much!" said Maw, holding the bottle as if it were a delicate treasure and hugging Brenda with great sincerity. "Well, my driver says it's time to go, so I'll say good-bye for now," she said, hugging the slight woman gently. Maw stood on the porch as they were starting to pull away and waved frantically at them. Harley shut the engine off and stuck his head out of the window. "What'd ye say, Maw?" She cupped her hands to her mouth. "I said, ye don't have any more of them oysters do ye?" She laughed at her own witticism. "Heck no, ye ate all of 'em yesterday!" he shouted back. She waved him away and walked back into the house, cackling like an old hen.

On their way to 25W, Harley turned left outside the community of Duff and climbed the treacherous gravel road to the top of McCloud Mountain. "This is one of my favert places. Thar's bars up here, waterfalls, caves, and all kinds of wildlife. But here's my favert part," he said as he parked below a hillside. They walked to the top

of the hill to the edge of the mountain, which featured spectacular views of the entire county and beyond that were gradually becoming obliterated by the clouds forming above them. "I can see why you love this place—not just this place but where you live. It's definitely God's country," she said, taking in the stunning vista. "Could ye live here?"
"I could live here if I could make a living here," she said wistfully.
"Well, those clouds are movin' in fast, and it shore feels like rain; we'd better be gittin' off this mountain," he said and took her arm as they climbed down the steep hillside.

A cold rain was falling heavily by the time they reached Knoxville, and the drops were becoming slushy as they hit the Alcoa Highway leading to Maryville. By the time they reached the stone house, sleet was peppering down. "Whew! I'm glad we left when we did!" said Harley, shaking the wet granules off at her door. Brenda busied herself turning lights on around the house. "Well, I might as well turn around and go back afore this gits any worse," he said as she came to him. "No you don't!" she demanded, grabbing his arm. "Now you get in the kitchen and call your mother. Tell her you're staying in a motel, that you're sleeping on my couch, anything you want. You're not going anywhere, buster!" she said, throwing her arms around his neck. "But I ain't got no clean clothes." "I'll wash your clothes." "But I ain't got no toothbrush." "I think I may have an extra one around here. If I don't, you can use mine. You don't need pajamas either," she said and kissed him long and seductively. "Now why don't we get these wet clothes off, and you come in here and keep me warm," she said, leading him to her bedroom.

Harley was afraid that he might hurt her, but Brenda accepted every bit of his ardor gratefully and gave it right back with great zeal and devotion to the act. When they had completed their lovemaking, she curled up in his arms, and they were quiet for a while, listening to the sleet peck at the sturdy stone house and nibble at the windowpanes. "I thank I kin do better than that, Brenda. I'll be better and go longer the next time," he said in the midst of an ecstatic sigh. "You were great, Harley, and I look forward to the next time. How about now?" She feigned an attack and crawled on top of him. When she stopped giggling, she laid her head on his chest. "Your heart sounds so strong, Harley," she said, massaging his pectoral muscle. "It beats jest fer ye," he replied and rolled her gently on her back. "Aren't you going to call Margaret?" she said, moaning as he kissed her neck. "I will in jest a minute. Make that an air."

Chapter 34

BETROTHAL

Walter Canady, general manager of the electric company, was a tall man. He was about Harley's height and frame as a younger man, when he was a lineman. But as the years advanced and he was promoted to a desk job, Walter had morphed into a "big man." He was going through his closet, inventorying clothing to give to his sons, nephews, brother-in-laws, and the church when he came upon the suit he'd bought when he was promoted—the same suit he wore when he got married to his second wife, Regina, and on other special occasions. "I'd look like a link sausage in this thang," he said to himself, examining the nice gray suit he'd purchased at an exclusive haberdashery in Knoxville years ago. "You're not going to attempt to wear that are you?" said Regina from the closet entrance. "Hell no, but I know jest who to give it to."

Walter and Regina thought Harley looked wonderful in the gray suit, although it was a little loose on him. They were also taken with the quiet beauty of his wife-to-be as she walked down the aisle on the arm of Scrap Hopkins, a vision of sartorial splendor, attired in a sports coat he bought at the Goodwill store that could have previously been worn by Sasquatch. The bride wore a simple white dress trimmed in lace as did her bridesmaids: Sissy, Margaret, and Maw, and the flower girl, Glory. Harley's entourage included Joe Boy and Wayne, beaming in crisp white shirts, bolo ties, and black pants. Best Man Early, wore a lime green leisure suit and a paisley, floppy-collared shirt he'd bought on sale at S.H. George & Son department store in Knoxville. He was well satisfied with his appearance, and it showed.

When Doris Blanchard, a friend of Sissy's from the shirt factory, completed the "Wedding March" with a flourish, Reverend Bunch performed the ceremony.

"Who gives this woman to be married," said Reverend Bunch as Scrap placed Brenda's hand in Harley's. "Missus D'Amico, Little Bee's momma and daddy, God rest thar souls, me and Margaret, and Maw, and Sissy, and Early, and Glory. Little Bee was family even afore she got murried here today," said Scrap as Brenda and her bridesmaids became dewy-eyed at his loving display of unpretentious sincerity. Scrap had to be reminded to sit down. Then Reverend Bunch performed the ceremony without a hitch, and everyone played their roles beautifully.

Later cake and punch were served at the big house, but Mamma D'Amico's food contribution ensured that the small gathering of wedding guests were fed extremely well. An assembly line of men gathered at the back of her station wagon to unload the food that she transported from her kitchen to Margaret's big kitchen table, which was eventually crowded with bowls of Zuchinni Parmagiana, sciatielli, bruschetta, and the most elegant wedding cookies ever to grace a table. Most of the guests were raised on standard fare and were tentative to venture on a gastronomic journey to Italy. But Scrap was in heaven, and Mamma was more than pleased with his zeal for her cooking. "What's this thang?" said Scrap as he picked up the bruschetta. He took a big bite and closed his eyes, an ecstatic look playing on his broad face. Mamma smiled and clasped her hands appreciatively. "Thatsa bruschetta, my Gianni's favorite." "Who's Johnny?" asked Scrap as he moved on to the next appetizer. "He wasa my husbanda; he died two years ago," she said sadly. She selected three pieces of ham from the meat tray—prosciutto, Genoa salami, and hot capicolla—and rolled them together. "Open uppa, Scrap; try this and then eata some of my olive salad," she said, popping the ham into Scrap's waiting mouth, following with a spoonful of the delicious salad. Scrap sampled everything on the table, including the biscotti and cheese cookies. Later he whispered, "Ye wouldn't happen to have any of that red wine with ye, would ye?" Mamma smiled and put her finger to her lips; then she grabbed him by the hand and led him out to her car.

Joe Boy and Wayne were getting thirsty too, and decided to leave rather than offend their hosts by bringing alcohol into their home. "Well, Bike, ole buddy, we got to be gittin' to the house," said Joe Boy as he and Wayne headed to the bedroom where coats were piled in a heap on the bed. Harley hugged him around the neck. "I know whar yore agoin'; yore goin' to the Bud barn!" Joe Boy shrugged and tugged at his beard. "Ye know, we hadn't thought of that, but it sounds like a good idee," he said. "Why don't ye join us later? Ye don't have anything to do tonight, do ye?" said Wayne as Joe Boy hee-hawed and elbowed him in the side. "You boys just be careful," said Brenda, unhooking her arm from Harley's and kissing them both on their cheeks. Embarrassed, the Jackson brothers said good night to all and retreated hastily. They stopped briefly at the station wagon to have a taste of Dago Red with Mamma and Scrap, then hopped on their bikes and roared off into the night.

Other guests, particularly the few from Knoxville, bade farewell to the couple and trickled out the door. The last of the local folk said good-bye too, including Walter Canady and Regina. "Best of luck to ye, son," said Walter as he helped his wife with her coat. "Thank ye, Walter, especially fer the loan of the suit. I'll have it dry cleaned and return it to ye next week," said Harley, shaking Walter's hand sincerely. "Why don't ye keep it, Harley? Ye might have other needs fer it someday," said Walter, and his wife agreed with him.

As Harley and Brenda were preparing for the trip to their rented home in Clinton, Early appeared after a brief absence. His leisure suit was disheveled, and his hands were filthy. "What ye been doin', brother? Better yet, what have ye tied to the back of my car?" said Harley, grabbing his brother in a headlock. "I ain't done nothin'!" yelled Early, slithering out of the hold. Brenda was appalled at all of the dirty dishes. "Would you like me to help you clean up?" she asked Margaret, who hugged her and sent her on her way with a gentle shove. "Naw, me, Sissy, and Glory will take keer of that, and Scrap and Early will hep. Now git on out of here!" "Speakin' of Scrap, whar is he?" said Early as he washed his hands in the kitchen sink. The front door flew open. "Here we are!" said Scrap, his arm around the shoulders of tiny Mamma D'Amico, who was giggling for all she was worth. It was obvious that the two were hitting the wine pretty seriously. "Where isa my coat? I gotta be gettin' home," said Mamma, her face beet red. Harley and Brenda found it a good time to disappear during the drama. Glory looked on in confusion at the antics, but Margaret, Early, and Sissy couldn't conceal their laughter. "Sissy, why don't ye make up a bed fer Missus D'Amico, and I'll find her some nightclothes." "I've got plenty of room at my place," burped Scrap. Early fell into a chair, while the women, including Mamma, laughed raucously.

As gales of laughter floated from the house, Harley paused from his work to listen and chuckle. "I'll be right thar, honey; I've jest got to untangle this mess that Early hitched to air bumper." Harley used the hawkbill knife that he'd fished from the glove compartment to separate the conglomeration of garbage that Early had affixed to the bumper: cans, a tree branch, a tin chamber pot, and pieces of discarded farm implements. "Now let's git outta here afore they come out and laugh at us," he said as he jumped behind the wheel. Brenda scooted across the bench seat and used her handkerchief, dabbing at his dirty hands as he drove. He curled his arm gently around her shoulder. "I'll try not to git anything on that purty dress, honey," he said as she laid her head on his shoulder. "You get anything on me you want, darlin', just love me." "Well that's an easy request; I'll love ye forever," he said as they stopped at the light on Central and North Tennessee. Harley pointed toward the pool room. "Look down thar at those boys' bikes in front of the pool room. I'll bet thar playin' nine-ball and guzzlin' beer," he said as the light changed. They caught another light at the top of the hill, and Harley pointed out Walter Canady's brick house on Ninth Street. "That's whar Walter and Regina live." "You don't think he knows we're staying in Clinton till I find a job at LaFollette Hospital, do you?" said Brenda. "I'm shore he does, but as long as I git to work on time and cover my on-call duties, he won't say a thang. Right now, the most important thang is that you have a safe drive to work, and I'm not that fer away from mine either," said Harley. Brenda grabbed him by the tie, tugging his head close to her mouth. "The most important thing is that we get to our house and get busy," she said, her breath hot on his neck. Harley stepped on the gas.

Part IX

HEROES AND SAINTS

Chapter 35

CLIFF HANGER

"I'll bet yore two matchsticks and raise ye three," Joe Boy said defiantly, tossing his wager into the middle of a pile on the table, a pile that would have served as igniter for a bonfire. "He don't bluff that good. He's got somethin' shore as shootin'. I'm out," said Wayne, flipping his hand disgustedly on the makeshift, barrel-top poker table. "Chickenshit! What'll ye do, Harley? Time's a wastin'," said Joe Boy, grinning from ear to ear. Harley, holding a full house, was about to call and raise Joe Boy's bet when the general foreman walked into the truck bay. "Boys, I hate to break up yore little party, but we got a problem up on Caryville Mountain at Round Rock," said Lendon Jordan. Lendon was getting a little long in the tooth, having worked for the company for many years. He was still strong as an ox though, and his knowledge of proper work and safety procedures far outweighed anyone else's in the company. His experience as an apprentice lineman and journeyman lineman, and his ten years of supervisory skills were the framework for his extensive understanding of a lineman's duties. Born and raised in Campbell County and an accomplished woodsman, Jordan knew the rugged terrain like the back of his tough, weathered hand.

"Round Rock? Dadblame it, Lendon, that's nigh onto the top of Caryville Mountain," griped Joe Boy, eager to rake in his mountain of matchsticks. "That's right, but folks ain't got no juice, and you'uns are the ones that is goin' to hook 'em up agin," said Lendon, used to dealing with a contrary breed of men, who quarreled just for the sake of pissing somebody off. As the three got up from the table, Jordan gave them instructions on the location of the transformer that had blown and a caveat. "You'uns git yore rain suits and foul weather gear on. It's rainin' to beat the band down here, but you kin bet thar's a chance of snow, sleet, and big wind up on that mountain. He turned to go, hesitated, and spoke again. "And ye might as well take the bucket truck. We're allowed to use it on Friday." "Whew, boy, I didn't cotton to havin' Bike shinny up a pole in this weather," said Joe Boy as Harley gave him a withering glance. "Ye won't be so high-and-mighty when we finish this poker game," he said. "I'm a lookin' ford to it," said Joe Boy, sure that his two pair of nines and threes would eventually garner him a pocket full of matchsticks. They wouldn't buy groceries, but they were certain to afford him bragging rights.

Anticipating rough weather, the crew quickly put chains on the truck tires and donned their hard hats and foul weather gear. They hadn't traveled a mile when the brothers began arguing.

"Hey, Wayne, I left my dip back at the garage; kin ye lend me a little bit of yorn?" "Ye know, ye do this ever' time we leave, and I'll bet ye that ye've gone through ten cans of my Skoal," said Wayne angrily, reaching into his hip pocket. "And ye eat up a whole pack of my Red Man ever' time we go fishin'," groused Joe Boy. Wayne flipped the can in Joe Boy's lap. "Here, it's cherry flavored—yore favert'". Joe Boy grinned as he placed a big hunk of snuff between his cheek and gums. "Thank ye little brother. Look, I brought along a spit cup fer us both to use," he said. Harley laughed. "It's goin' to be a long afternoon," he thought to himself as he turned on Central Avenue and headed for Caryville Mountain.

Lendon's weather prediction was spot on. By the time the bucket truck was near the top of the mountain, the weather had turned treacherous. "That's a good huntin' spot over thar," said Wayne, pointing to a copse of trees on the edge of a frosty field. "It's good if'n ye kin hit anythang. Remember when you missed that big buck, and ye fell out of yore tree stand?" jibed Joe Boy. Wayne didn't bother to argue back, speaking with a faraway look in his eyes. "That was a

Boone and Crockett buck fer shore," he said wistfully. Harley interrupted their conversation as he pulled over to the side of the icy road next to the field.

"Well, here's the pole. Let's git this transformer fixed and git back to the house," he said, opening the door and allowing a chilling blast of sleet to shower the truck's interior.

The trio repaired the transformer in no time. As Harley descended the pole in the bucket, his cronies created a scuffle with an impromptu ice-ball battle in the field. Wayne was deeply offended when Joe Boy knocked his hard hat crooked with a half-frozen horse apple. "If ye two are finished with yore shenanigans, we kin go to the house," said Harley as he closed and fastened the door to the equipment panel on the truck.

Joe Boy cranked up the heater, and as the warm air filled the truck, he scrunched up his face. "Shew, Wayne. Ye smell like horse-shit!" "When we git back, I'm gonna beat ye like a rented mule," said Wayne, doubling up his fist. "Well, until we git home, would ye mind a sharin' some more of that dip?" said Joe Boy as Wayne ripped off his hard hat and rubbed it in his brother's beard. "Why don't you'uns cut out the cavortin' and call in to the shop; let 'em know we got the pare back on," said Harley as he warily steered the truck around the icy hairpin turns on Stony Fork Road.

Joe Boy released his headlock on Wayne. "We cain't, Bike. We're high up on this rock and fer out in the piney woods. They cain't hear us now." After they'd traveled a few more miles down the mountain, reception improved, and Joe Boy called in to report their success. When he was hanging up the microphone, he was startled as both Wayne and Harley yelled in unison, "God Almighty!"

The sight of the faded orange school bus appeared surreal in the gloom, cloaked in a shroud of sleet. Skid marks painted the icy road, proving that the bus had skidded around the curve and plunged backwards through the guardrail. Now the bus hung precariously on the edge of a forty-foot drop-off. It seemed the only thing that kept the bus from plummeting into the deep, rocky ravine and the train tracks below was a huge boulder supporting the undercarriage, and the bus was leaning slightly against a big oak tree, blocking the entrance doors to the vehicle.

The three linemen jumped out of their truck, slipping and sliding as they raced toward the accident.

"Lookee thar," said Joe Boy, pointing to the ghostly figure of the driver as he waved feebly from his seat at the windshield. Wayne cupped his hands to his mouth. "You'uns all right in thar?"

The driver waved his hand and yelled weakly out of his side window. "We're all right. I got four young'uns on here, and thar purty skeered. We're afraid to move," he said, voice trembling.

Wayne looked at his companions. "You'uns know Rascal Orick? That's him," he said. Despite the desperate situation, Harley and Joe Boy grinned. They knew Rascal, whose real name was Virgil, but he earned the nickname by playing clever tricks on folks. "Hey, Rascal, this ain't no trick, is it?" Harley yelled. Rascal didn't answer but shook his head side to side furiously. "OK, you'uns, be real still; we're a comin' to git ye," said Harley as the brothers ran back to the truck.

After deciding that driving down a frontage road to the tracks, lifting the bucket up to the back end of the bus, and unloading the passengers into the bucket was too dangerous, the linemen decided on another tactic. "Why don't we park air truck on the road and hook air winch underneath the front of the bus. Thar's some big ole trees that we kin tie the truck to from the back. That won't make shore that, if the bus goes, it won't take air truck with it, but it will shore stabilize the bus as we try to git Rascal and those young'uns out," said Harley as he quickly unloaded equipment out of their vehicle. "Lord, Lendon will skin us alive if'n we lose this truck," said Wayne. "I don't mean nothin' by this, brother, but git yore head out of yore ass," said Joe Boy as they set to work.

When the winch was hooked and the utility truck was anchored to the trees, the linemen prepared to execute the next step of their plan. Harley produced a hand pick from the tool box. “I thought that we could break a hole in the front windshield with this, one chip at a time, so’s we won’t unsettle the bus. When we git a hole big enough, we’ll take the young’uns and Rascal out through it, one at a time.” Joe Boy started to reply but was interrupted by muffled sobs and cries of the youngsters trapped inside the bus. “I’ll tell ye what, Bike, it’s a good plan, but why don’t ye let me or Wayne do the pickin’? Ye and Little Bee got a baby on the way, and me and Wayne ain’t murried.” Harley grinned and patted Joe Boy on the shoulder. “You’ve gained a lot of weight lately, boys, from sittin’ around. I’m a lot skinnier than both of ye and less likely to stir that bus when I move around. “I don’t know, Harley, hit’s kind of skeery thankin’ about it,” said Wayne. Harley gave Wayne a slight punch on the shoulder. “Shit. We’ve been through a lot skeerier things in Nam, brother-man,” he said as he walked slowly toward the bus. Joe Boy stopped him mid-stride. “I need to know somethin’, Bike.” “What’s that?” said Harley, squinting as the sleet pelted his face. “What kind of poker hand did ye have when we left the garage?” Harley shook his head and walked on.

The bus groaned with its new burden as Harley cautiously climbed aboard the hood. He stopped his progress for a moment, then spoke to Rascal, whose eyes were as big as saucers. “Rascal, it’s me, Harley Baird. Why don’t ye move out of the way of the windshield, real gentle-like, but not too fer back in the bus. Are the young’uns up front too?” “Thar about the fourth row back; I’ll bring ’em up close if’n ye wont,” said Rascal, moving in slow motion away from his seat and the windshield. “Leave ’em whar they are fer the time bein’,” said Harley as he prepared to take the first whack with the pick at the windshield.

It was tedious, nerve-racking work, breaking out the windshield with a small pick hammer. With each strike to the glass, the bus creaked mournfully, and occasionally gravel would tumble from the boulder that supported the back undercarriage. Finally Harley succeeded in punching a hole in the windshield big enough to extract the youngsters, and hopefully Rascal. He hollered into the ragged hole. "OK, Rascal, ole buddy, hand me out one of them young'uns, the littlest first," said Harley, gaining better purchase on the hood with his feet and outstretching his arms.

Rascal obeyed, lifting a thin child with hair the color of straw through the hole and into Harley's strong, waiting arms. The child was fish-belly white, wearing a worn pinafore over a thin dress and sandals, woefully underdressed for the weather. "What's yore name, darlin'?" said Harley as he cradled her tightly in his arms. "Jamie," said the little one, who was trembling like a leaf. "Don't fergit my sissy, Jennifer; she's right back of me," she said as Joe Boy took her, and Wayne wrapped her in one of the blankets he'd brought from the truck. "I promise," said Harley, who received auburn-haired, freckle-faced Jennifer through the portal. Then the last of the children, sisters Joy and Kathy Sibert, were gingerly extracted from the disaster waiting to happen. When it came his turn, Rascal backed away from the hole.

"C'mon, Rascal, I'll hep ye out," said Harley, reaching into the hole. Rascal shook his head. "I cain't. I jest had my 'pendix took out, and I'm still purty weak. I don't thank I've got the gumption in me," he said, close to tears. Harley felt a pang of sorrow for the man. "Shoot, Rascal Orick not havin' gumption? Thar ain't nary a person would have the nerve to pull off some of the pranks ye pulled, Virgil. C'mon, I'll give ye a hand," said Harley, his face close to the window. He hoped Rascal would make up his mind soon; his legs were aching and getting numb after sitting on his haunches for a long period. Rascal didn't make a move. "Well, I'll tell ye what, why don't I come in and lift ye through the hole; will that help?" "Bike, don't go in thar;

he kin git out hisself," yelled Joe Boy, but Harley paid no heed to his warning. "Git up here and take my place, fat boy," he said as he slithered through the hole.

"I'm tellin' ye, I ain't got the gumption," said Rascal as Harley prodded him to climb out of the hole. Harley put his arm around the man's shaking shoulders. "Rascal, thank about yore wife and young'uns. This bus is a grumblin' and shakin'; ye don't have to go down with a sankin' ship. Ye've already saved all yore passengers," Harley pleaded. "My wife died two years ago and my young'uns have all moved up north," said Rascal, choking back a sob. Harley was overcome by compassion and hugged the quaking man. After a moment he found the proper words to speak. For some reason, he felt an uncanny kinship to the man.

"Rascal, I'm shore yore wife's spirit is with ye right now, and I'm shore she would wont ye to go on. Besides, if yore children don't keer enough to stay in touch, I'm shore these little girls and thar families will love ye forever fer savin' them; hell, they'll probably ask ye to move in with 'em. Now git out that winder, and Joe Boy will hep ye. He looks fat, but he's strong as a mule." Rascal broke from Harley's grasp and stared at him as though he'd experienced an epiphany. "If ye'll push, I'll squeeze through that hole," he said as Harley prepared to shove him to safety.

As Joe Boy and Wayne were assisting Rascal off the hood, the bus quivered. There was a loud "crack" from beneath the undercarriage, and the sound of gravel falling like rain.

Harley shouted as he was scrambling to the hole. "Untie and unhook air truck—fast!" he said as he dove through the hole and slid headfirst off the hood of the bus. He almost landed on Joe Boy, who was releasing the winch, while Wayne scrambled to untie the truck.

"Is ever'body all right?" asked Wayne, as the motley group huddled together, thanking the Lord, and staring forlornly at what might have been their tomb with the inscription, "Campbell County Schools."

Harley, Wayne, and Joe Boy loaded Rascal and the four girls into the cab and cranked the heat up to high. "Me and Joe Boy will git in the back and cover up with the tarp and blankets," said Wayne. "I'll snuggle up and keep ye warm if'n ye lend me another pinch of that dip," said Joe Boy as they clambered into the back, and Harley entered the cab. Rascal and the children were silent as they made their way down the mountain.

Eventually the sleet gave way to rain, and the roads cleared. In a state of shock, the group was silent. News had gotten around of the rescue, and several tow trucks were dispatched to save Rascal's bus the next day. Unfortunately, they arrived too late. The bus had given up the balancing act and plummeted to the depths of the ravine. Train traffic was rerouted until road crews removed debris off the tracks.

Harley, stiff and sore from the ordeal, was relaxing by the fire, alternately reading *Field and Stream* and watching Little Bee lovingly as she puttered around the house. She hesitated from dusting a table to glance out the window. "Who do we know that drives a green truck and a Chevy station wagon," she said. Harley shrugged his shoulders and sighed. He didn't feel like visitors today. Grudgingly, he put his magazine aside and prepared to answer the door.

When he opened the door, he didn't recognize the two men and a woman who stood at his threshold. But he was quite familiar with the two youngsters with them, Jamie and Jennifer, the girls he'd rescued. One of the men spoke. "Hidee. My name's Floyd McCarty, and this is my wife, Lillian," he said, putting his arm around the plain woman standing next to him. "We're the parents of Jamie and Jennifer," said the wife, beaming. The thin, bespeckled man standing behind them identified himself. "And I'm Sterling Peck, of the Press," he said, reaching to shake Harley's hand. Peck continued. "The McCartys are here to thank you for saving their daughters from the accident yesterday, and I'd like to write a story about it for our readers. Would you mind telling me about the incident and let me get a few pictures?" he asked.

"Sure. Come on in," said Brenda, before Harley could answer.

Harley and the girls, who fought to sit on his lap, told the story in great detail, and the parents lauded him for his bravery. Peck asked for a photograph. "I'll pose fer a picture if ye'll do me a favor," said Harley, sweeping both girls up into his arms. "What's that," said Peck, loading his camera with new film. "Make shore ye write somethin' about Joe Boy and Wayne Jackson and all they did, and especially Rascal Orick. He was the real hero, warn't he girls?" he said as the children agreed excitedly. "I can do that," said Peck, pointing the camera in their direction. "OK, everybody, say 'cheese'."

Chapter 36

MAW SETS SAIL

"How faist was that rabbit agoin' when it hit yore head?" said Scrap as he and Early took a break from cutting cedar planks. "That's real funny, Pap!" said Early as he adjusted the cotton in his ear. He was suffering from a fierce earache. That morning Margaret had poured some sweet oil in his ear and plugged the ear with a cottonball. Unfortunately the remedy wasn't helping much, especially with the noise of the saw. "I'll tell ye what. Why don't ye take the truck up to Maw's, have her take that rabbit out of yore ear, and fix it right," suggested Scrap. "I got plenty of thangs to do that only takes one," he added. Early was glad for the break and looking forward to Maw alleviating his constant pain. "I'll see ye in a minute," he said as he moseyed to the truck.

Maw was suffering more than usual from aches and pains that morning, especially in her head. To relieve the throbbing, she made herself a tea of a mixture of cinnamon, lemongrass, peppermint, and rosemary. The pain seemed to intensify, and she almost broke down and took a packet of Goody's powder for the ailment but decided to wait it out. It was a pretty day, and the temperature was probably in the high fifties; so she bundled up, hoping some fresh air would do her good. She took some shears and a trowel along, just in case the fancy hit her to clean out some of the dead plants in her flower beds.

Early clomped across the porch and into Maw's house; loudly announcing his presence. "Hey, Maw, it's me, Early! I got a furious earache, and I was wonderin' if ye could hep me." After poking his head into every room, he decided that she must be outside. Standing on the porch, he yelled again. "Hey, Maw, whar are ye?" Receiving no answer, he opted to look for her in the yard. That's where he usually found her when she wasn't tending to a sick person. He discovered her lying next to one of her rock gardens as if asleep. She had a trowel in one hand, and her arm was outstretched, with her other hand clutching a stone. "Oh, Maw! God bless ye!" he said as he knelt beside her. He lifted her head and cradled it gently in his arms, smoothing back the wisps of gray hair. "Maw, honey, war goin' to miss ye so much!" whispered Early. But Maw was unaware of his pain and grief; she was unaware of all earthly anguish, as she was absorbed into the golden light of pure love and the welcoming arms of a handsome young man and curly-headed, green-eyed little girl.

In her advancing age, Maw had prepaid for funeral arrangements, including a casket and a headstone, on which was simply carved "Nola 'Maw' Ruggles" and her birth date. She had also made arrangements to be buried in Calgary Cemetery and for there to be no viewing, no funeral, just words at her gravesite. The Bairds were appalled by her wishes but dutifully upheld them. The day before the interment and many days afterward, Early and Scrap stayed at her house in an effort to keep folks from taking household objects in remembrance of the extraordinary woman.

Reverend Bunch didn't speak at Maw's funeral. Some assumed his absence was because Maw didn't attend church. But Ella Dee was recruited for the honor. She and her nephew, Calvin, and niece, Juanita, had traveled far to attend the funeral of a woman they loved and respected. Florida couldn't make it but sent her condolences from South America. As Ella prepared to speak the heartfelt words that Margaret and Sissy had painstakingly written down, as well as words of praise from her own family, Margaret and the rest of the family huddled around the casket. "I can imagine how much this fine woman meant to you and just about every family this side of Campbell County," said Ella Dee. "She was wise and kind, and served her fellow man the best she knew how. And she served everyone without expecting anything in return. No one ever heard her say a bad word about anybody, even those who talked negatively about her way of thinking. She never judged anyone on this blessed earth, and if she's being judged herself, we are sure the judgment will be more than favorable." Ella opened her well-worn Bible. "Now Maw didn't have any children, and she didn't have a husband. But we're all her family—all of her children. And this verse from Proverbs 31:10-31 says so much about the angel she was to all of us on earth and the angel that she is in heaven:

"Who can find a virtuous woman? For her price is far above rubies. The heart of her husband doth safely trust in her, so that he shall have no need of spoil. She will do him good and not evil all the days of her life. She seeketh wool and flax, and worketh willingly with her hands. She is like the merchants' ships; she bringeth her food from afar. She riseth also while it is yet night and giveth meat to her household, and a portion to her maidens. She considereth a field and buyeth it; with the fruit of her hands, she planteth a vineyard. She girdeth her loins with strength and strengtheneth her arms. She perceiveth that her merchandise is good; her candle goeth not out by night. She layeth her hands to the spindle, and her hands hold the distaff. She stretcheth out her hand to the poor; yea, she reacheth forth her hands to the needy. She is not afraid of the snow for all of her household are clothed with scarlet.

"She maketh herself coverings of tapestry; her clothing is silk and purple. She maketh fine linen and selleth it; and delivereth girdles unto the merchant. Strength and honour are her clothing; and she shall rejoice in time to come. She openeth her mouth with wisdom; and in her tongue is the law of kindness.

"She looketh well to the ways of her household and eateth not the bread of idleness. Her children arise up and call her blessed; her husband also, and he praiseth her. Many daughters have done virtuously, but thou excellest them all. Favour is deceitful, and beauty is vain, but a woman that feareth the Lord she shall be praised. Give her of the fruit of her hands, and let her own works praise her in the gates."

After the casket was lowered into the ground, Ella, Calvin, Juanita, the Bairds, and other mourners tossed handfuls of dirt into the grave and walked quickly back to their vehicles. The weather had become foul, and the roads leading down the mountainside would soon become hazardous. "I'll be right thar, jest give me a minute," said Sissy. She knelt on the muddy ground next to the grave, pulled something out of her coat pocket, and scratched out a hollow at the base of the headstone. She placed the small, flat stone inscribed with the word "GLORY" in the hollow. "Ye were one of the biggest blessin's in my life," she said. "Ye are the reason I have my blessed child, and I hope that ye are with yore's now." Sissy rose, touched Maw's headstone reverently, and walked slowly back to the road and her waiting family.

Several days later Margaret received a phone call from a lawyer in Clinton. "Mrs. Baird, my name is Lowell Longstreet of the firm Bostic, Hammac, Tipton, and Longstreet. I would like to meet with you and your family in my office in Clinton at your earliest convenience. This is concerning the last will and testament of Nola Ruggles.

Can you make it tomorrow at 10:00 a.m.?" he said and gave her directions, which she wrote down. "We'll make it. Did she leave us somethin'?" inquired Margaret. "All I can say is that I believe you'll be very pleased," said Longstreet. "See you tomorrow." Knowing that tomorrow was Brenda's day off, Margaret called her that evening to let her know what was happening. "Anyway I was wonderin' if, since ye and Harley live in Clinton fer the time bein', will ye go with me and Early tomorry to the lawyer's office? Scrap kin stay here and run the saw, and Sissy cain't git off work, and we kin be back home afore Glory gits home from school. Ye can? Good, we'll pick ye up!"

"Dadgumit, Momma, I love whar we live, but it seems like it takes us a durn week to git wharever we're agoin'!" said Early as they drove through LaFollette. Early had his best clothes on this morning, and Margaret wore the dress she wore to Benny's funeral. Sissy was disappointed that she couldn't go, and Scrap was kind of peeved that he had to stay behind and deal with a persnickety customer. Harley couldn't get off work either, but Margaret was happy that Brenda could come. She'd convinced Harley and Brenda to come to the house tonight for supper. Harley could drive up from work, and Margaret and Early would take Brenda home with them from Clinton. They picked Brenda up at her house, and the three of them arrived at the office thirty minutes early for the appointment. At precisely 9:55 a.m., the secretary invited them into Longstreet's office. He stood to greet them, but one could hardly notice he was standing, he was so short and squat. They introduced themselves around, and since time is money, Longstreet got down to business.

"I've invited you folks here today to read the last will and testament of Nola Ruggles." He stopped for a moment and smiled. "She was a very charming lady and a real character, but I don't have to tell you that. I can tell you that she thought immensely of you all, and her will, although brief, spells out exactly what she wanted you to have. If I may," he said, opening a folder and clearing his throat officiously.

"LAST WILL AND TESTAMENT OF NOLA RUGGLES. I, Nola Ruggles, of the community of Duff, County of Campbell and State of Tennessee, being of sound and disposing mind and memory, do hereby make, publish, and declare this to be my Last Will and Testament, hereby revoking all wills and codicils previously made by me.

ARTICLE I: TANGIBLE PERSONAL PROPERTY

A. I give all of the tangible personal property that I may own at the time of my death, which is not otherwise specifically bequeathed under this will, including my home, forty-two acres of property, personal effects, jewelry, household furniture and furnishings, garden and lawn furnishings and equipment, books, silver, art objects, hobby equipment and collections of homeopathic medicine, wearing apparel, vehicles, and other personal articles, to my trusted friend and confidant, Margaret Baird, to do with as she wishes and to share with her wonderful family, who have been like a family to me.

B. I may leave a memorandum of my wishes regarding the ultimate disposition of some or all of my tangible personal property, and I would hope that my wishes as to the ultimate disposition of such property would be respected. However, such memorandum shall not affect the absolute nature of the bequests made under this Article l."

Longstreet pushed the folder toward Margaret and handed her a pen. "All I require is your signature, Mrs. Baird. I trust you've identified yourself with proper identification to my secretary." "Yes sir. But I need to understand exactly what all this means," said Margaret as Early and Brenda hugged each other.

"It means that everything Nola Ruggles had is bequeathed to you, including her land and her home," said Longstreet. "Kin I do what I wont to with it all?" she said. "Certainly, it's yours to do with as you like," he said, glancing at his watch. "Just sign these papers, and I'll turn over the deed, and we'll take care of other incidentals." With a shaking hand, Margaret signed the papers. When she had completed the task, Longstreet shook her hand. "Congratulations to you and your family, Mrs. Baird." "Uh, how much do we owe ye?" asked Early. "Not a penny. Nola ensured that my fee is already taken care of. Here's my card; if you ever require representation, just give me a call," he said, opening the door for them to exit before his next appointment showed up.

"Now, Early, don't kill us afore we git a chance to tell ever'body," said Margaret as Early drove like a wild man on the way home. "I cain't believe it, Momma! Kin you, Little Bee?" "I think it's marvelous, and no one deserves it more than you, Margaret," said Brenda. "I thank I know what I'm agoin' to do with Maw's property, since I'm the…what is it?" "Executor," said Brenda. "Yore not agoin' to sell it, are ye?" said Early anxiously. "No, honey, I'll let ye know at supper tonight."

It was like New Year's Eve at the big house when Harley arrived. Scrap and Early were taking turns dancing with Glory in the living room, while the women chattered gaily in the kitchen. "Hi, honey. Why don't ye let Little Bee tell ye about what's happened, and me and Sissy will go in the livin' room fer a minute." Sissy looked confused as Margaret grabbed her by the hand and led her out of the kitchen.

As Brenda told Harley about the events of the day and the family's good fortune, Margaret held a caucus with her father, son, and daughter. To her great satisfaction, they agreed wholeheartedly with her plan. "I was thankin' of that myself," said Early.

Supper was belly-warming: homemade beef stew, cornbread, and mustard coleslaw, finished off with German chocolate cake. At the end of the meal, Margaret stood, prepared to make a presentation. "OK, Little Bee and Harley. We've decided that since you'uns have to live in Clinton and drive that dangerous highway to yore work ever'day, we wont ye to have Maw's house…that is, if I kin have her herbs and medicine." Harley and Brenda's mouths flew open. "We can't do that!" said Brenda. "Why cain't ye? I've got a house, Momma and Early's got a house, and Papaw Scrap's got a house," said Sissy. "That's right; we kin all live close together and hep out each other when we kin," said Early. "Besides, Little Bee, ye've been talkin' about quittin' at the hospital in Knoxville and tryin' to git a job at the LaFollette hospital," said Margaret, handing the deed over to Brenda. "Little Bee, we won't take 'no' fer an answer, and Harley, ye jest do what she says," said Margaret, slapping her hand down on the table authoritatively. "Well, do ye mind if we talk about it fer a day and night?" said Harley. "Jest as long as ye don't say 'no' to the…what is it, Early?" "The executor," he said.

Part X

MADNESS DESCENDS

Chapter 37

THE HOLLER

It was 9:00 a.m. in the morning, and The Holler was still smoldering from the action the night before: three fistfights (two of them involving women), a drawn pistol, and the incident involving Henry Byrge who, drunk as a monkey, insisted on singing "Blue Moon of Kentucky" with the band, "Cecil Seiber and The Cumberland Cooners".

Unfortunately, when asked to leave the tiny stage, Henry refused.

"Play it again; I kin do better next time," slobbered Henry, tugging heavily at Cecil's leather guitar strap. You could tell it was Cecil's guitar strap because the name "Cecil" was burned along its length in huge letters.

"We've had enough of your actin' out, Henry," said Cecil, giving Henry a friendly shove. When Henry responded pugnaciously, Cecil dispatched him with a wicked swat to the noggin with the microphone stand.

Scenes like this were nearly nightly occurrences at The Holler, located, not in some Kentucky or Tennessee backwater, but at the lower end of East Fifth Street in Dayton, Ohio.

The Holler's exterior was emblazoned with an amateur painting, depicting a mountaineer taking a pull from a jug as he leaned against a boulder, while other characters in ragged clothes cavorted with skimpily clad "Daisy Mae"-type girls. But the most colorful part of the bar were the patrons, country boys and girls who'd migrated from down south with hopes of finding employment at Dayton's well-paying automobile assembly plants and at myriad other factories and shops. They gathered at The Holler to talk about "back home," to whoop up on some errant Yankee who stumbled into their lair, or to whoop up on each other when, during drunken conversation, an ancient feud between families was revisited. Bible Belt born and raised, these folks were taught from the get-go that if you take a drink, you'll act like a heathen. So that's what they did. Thus The Holler was visited frequently by the Dayton police.

"Jeanene, get me another cup of coffee," demanded the blonde-headed woman slouched on the barstool. "Let me finish moppin' up this blood. Henry bled like a stuck pig last night," said Jeanene, scrubbing furiously at a spot on the floor.

"Cecil should have stuck that microphone stand up his ass," croaked the blonde as she took a deep drag off her Marlboro, the filter tattooed with remnants of last night's lipstick.

"Ole Henry would have sung 'Blue Moon of Kentucky' even higher and lonesomer, and I would be cleanin' up somethin' worse than blood," said Jeanene as she plopped the mop in the bucket wringer and pushed the handle forward.

The blonde laughed mid-drag and broke into a spasmodic coughing fit.

"Damn you, Jeanene, you're gonna make me cough my lungs up," said the blonde, wiping her mouth with the sleeve of her cheap dressing gown.

When her spasms ceased, the woman did a double take when she was presented with the reflection of herself in the smoky mirror behind the bar.

Although she was only pushing the front side of forty, twenty years of bar smoke, hooch, little sleep, and all that goes with running with the seamy underbelly of society had wreaked mayhem on her appearance.

Deep lines gullied from the corners of her watery blue eyes, and beneath were purplish bags that became brown bags with the application of a lot of pancake makeup. Her prominent cheekbones overshadowed rough hollows in her cheeks, and there was a wattle forming beneath her chin that brought attention to the crepey skin on her neck. Her nose, once straight and pert, was a bit crooked and carried a small lump on the bridge.

She pushed a lock of hair back from her forehead and sadly examined her reflection. Her hair was still good, thick, and wavy; and her teeth, although yellowed from coffee and cigarettes, were still in fairly good shape.

Amazingly so was her body, which had retained its firmness despite lack of physical exercise.

"I get plenty of exercise," she smirked to herself, thinking of the young buck she'd enticed up to her apartment above the bar last night. He'd left early this morning—had to pull a Saturday shift at the Frigidaire plant.

He'd be back tonight though with plenty of jingle in his pockets. She'd ply him with a couple of on-the-house boilermakers, and in the dimly lit ambience—that, along with alcohol, masqueraded sometimes ghastly imperfections—whisper breathy compliments in his ear, referring to his sexual prowess. When he began getting sloshed, she would smile seductively as he showered her with huge tips.

She figured she'd fleece him for about eighty bucks this evening and reward him and herself with another roll in the hay, if he was able, after closing time. "Here's yore coffee," said Jeanene, placing the steaming cup of java on the carved-up bar top.

"Took you long enough," said the blonde as she thumbed through the *Journal Herald*.

Treva had owned The Holler now for five years. It had been left to her by the previous owner, an old greaser from Kentucky who still wore pegged pants and sported a dyed-black Elvis pompadour at seventy-three years of age. He died on Treva one night of a heart attack.

She had gravitated to The Holler from her previous position at another dive, The Doll House, right across the river from Cincinnati, in Newport, Kentucky.

She had arrived at The Doll House thirteen years ago with her newest beau, a guy named Dave who said that he would take her to California.

Like Lonnie, Dave said he had to stop to visit relatives, who owed him some money, before they could head west. Dave left one night to get some cigarettes and evaporated. When Treva's companion disappeared, she became a fixture at The Doll House, hustling drinks and money. The owner gave her a job as a barmaid, and soon she was made manager of the place, mainly because she didn't take any crap from anybody, and the other employees were scared to death of her volatile temper. She did a good job, despite the fact that she was descending into a quagmire of alcohol and drugs. She continued on a downhill slide until she met her savior, Carl Hatmaker. Carl was older than her by, perhaps, twenty years. Although he was a teetotaler, he stopped by the bar often, drinking coffee and joking with the other patrons—a desperate effort to dull the razor-sharp edge of the exquisite loneliness he endured as a recent widower. He owned a profitable machine shop and carried a huge roll of bills, to which Treva immediately took a liking. He took her in, made good decisions for her; and when she got into trouble, which was often, he bailed her out. The big wad of bills paid for an abortion, although the baby wasn't Carl's; bought her out of jail for stabbing the man she suspected was the father in the arm; turned her electricity on for the umpteenth time, and bought her a secondhand car, etc., etc., etc. Despite his influence, there was little Carl could do to curb her drinking binges, which included prowling the bars and spoiling for fights, usually finding one waiting.

She was in one of those nasty moods when she entered the bar one evening to find Carl casually drinking coffee at his corner seat and the new barmaid, "Bambi" something-or-another, leaning against him and tittering as she waited on an order.

"What the hell do you think you're doin', you little whore? Git the hell off my man!" screamed Treva as she fumbled in her purse for an implement, a nail file, anything to stick into the offending wench.

Unlike most of Treva's victims, "Bambi," whose real name was Dora, did not run at the anticipated assault of the madwoman but stood her ground. Raised in squalor in the backwoods of Manchester, Kentucky, Dora was no stranger to fighting, scraping, and scrapping for existence from the time she could walk. Dora knew "mean" and how to deal with it.

"Screw you, bitch," said Dora, locking eyes with Treva. This demeanor further infuriated Treva, who screamed at the top of her lungs and dove at Dora, slashing with a rat-tailed comb. With the grace of a matador, chunky little Dora deftly sidestepped her attacker and smacked Treva full in the face with her serving tray.

Treva's wildly flailing hand swept the bar top as she went down, taking ashtrays, a bowl of pretzels, a jar of pickled eggs, and an assortment of Schlitz and PBR bottles with her as she landed in a tangle of upended barstools and broken glass.

Dora backed off as Carl knelt beside the moaning, semicomatose Treva.

"Is she gonna be all right?" said Dora, tentatively approaching the bloody mess on the floor.

"I think so," said Carl as he pulled himself up to the edge of the bar. "We'd better call an ambulance though," he said worriedly, motioning to the bartender for a phone.

The thought of the arrival of ambulances and the cops made Dora anxious. She touched Carl's shoulder, intent on asking a question; but her face went white, and she dropped like a stone before she had a chance to utter the words.

"God damn you, whore, you broke my nose," screamed Treva as she jabbed the broken beer bottle upward, deep into Dora's inner thigh, severing an artery.

Dora fell into a seated position, blood from the wound immediately soaking the floor.

"Oh Lord Jesus, I'm dying," she cried as her life-blood flowed from the jagged gash.

"By God, you're going to suffer first. I'm gonna do a little surgery on your ass," was Treva's reply as she leaped on the girl, brandishing the broken bottle wickedly.

Treva made a jagged incision in her victim's cheek before Carl, the bouncer, and another burly patron dragged her off the helpless Dora, who was in shock, waxen and silent. Someone rushed to apply a tourniquet on her mutilated thigh and a handkerchief to her newly wounded cheek, the bone showing white through the crimson.

Blood was still flowing profusely from Treva's broken nose, and she looked like she'd wandered in from a train wreck. Carl took a hanky out of his pocket and approached her, appealing with Treva to calm down and take a seat.

"Don't come near me, you son of a bitch. I saw you…I saw you…" she screamed hoarsely, pointing a bloody finger in his face.

"I want everybody to know that this fat son of a bitch has never touched me. He's just a meal ticket…did you hear that? A fuckin' meal ticket! Fuck all of you," she yelled as she ran upstairs and hastily packed her meager belongings. She left town in a hurry that night, still cursing Carl and Dora, who would survive but barely. "I hope you bleed to death, you bitch," thought Treva as she lit a cigarette and flicked her high beams in retaliation against the bright lights of oncoming traffic.

As she headed north, she replayed the beer bottle-assisted surgical procedures she'd performed on Dora with satisfaction. Patsy Cline's "Sweet Dreams" floated out of the radio, and a tear came to her eye, not because of how she'd ruined Dora, but because of the man she blamed for ruining her life, Lonnie Cavanaugh.

"You son of a bitch," she muttered, snuffing out her cigarette in a shower of sparks in the ashtray. If she could, she would mutilate him—cut him up piece by piece and watch him writhe in glorious agony. But she never would have the opportunity. Lonnie was dead.

Chapter 38

AU REVOIR

Little stacks of money covered Louis Boudreaux's kitchen table, with the exception of one corner where Louis was hunkered, placing bills in envelopes and scribbling the names of his employees on the outsides. Louis, sovereign of Boudreaux's Rice Plantation, usually kept his money in a huge Wells Fargo walk-in safe, a sentinel in the corner of his bedroom. He didn't trust banks. A hateful, miserly curmudgeon, Louis Boudreaux didn't trust anyone.

He had arrived at the plantation from Bayou Lafourche over thirty-five years ago at the behest of his cousin, Guy ("Coozan Gee"), who was foreman of the plantation, then known as the LeBlanc Rice Plantation.

Guy had summoned his cousin's help because the plantation fields had been heavily salted by a recent hurricane, falling further into ruin via the apathy of owner, Justin LeBlanc, whose primary interest was partying in New Orleans, squandering his inheritance on Golden Hurricanes and exotic Creole beauties. While LeBlanc slept off hangovers in his suite at the Place d'Armes, Louis and Guy slaved, along with a tiny band of workers, to save the ruined ground.

They drained and plowed the fields, installed new gates on the levees, flooded the land, and planted a new, hardier strain of rice in March. In June they seeded crawfish in the rice field; in July and August they drained the rice field to harvest the rice, then re-flooded the field for the crustaceans to continue their growth, harvesting them over the following months. Fortunately for the Boudreauxs, before they could prove a profit for the plantation, the LeBlanc family intervened on Justin's hedonistic lifestyle and offered him a new opportunity, vice president of the family shipyard in Mobile, accompanied by a favorable salary.

Justin jumped at the prospect, knowing that he wouldn't have much responsibility in his new capacity; his brother was president of the shipyard, and Mobile was a lot like New Orleans, with its own carnival and Mardi Gras. He returned home, literally drunk with excitement about his new prospects. Eager to get rid of the plantation before the family could get involved, he offered the farm, kit and caboodle, to Guy and Louis for a mere pittance.

The two couldn't believe their ears and raced to the Crescent City Land Bank, which gladly provided them with the money for the place, based on a down payment from the profits of their first crop. When the deal was done, Justin took off to Mobile, wastrel visions dancing in his foggy head. Guy and Louis concentrated on becoming very rich. In five years the plantation was running superbly. Louis and Guy were well on their way to exceeding their highest expectations.

In the long years since their good fortune, much had transpired at the Boudreaux Plantation.

The cousins were blessed with decent weather and good crops, except the year of the next hurricane that salted and ruined their fields and killed their mudbugs. They recovered quickly though, and Guy counted his blessings; he wanted to share the wealth with the workers, the mainstay of their business, but Louis refused to hear of it. "Dey would steal us blind if dey could," Louis would say, spinning the dial on the safe for emphasis.

As Guy grew more altruistic, Louis became more selfish and callous, occasionally accusing Guy of misappropriation of funds and other business infractions. Fed up with the constant haranguing and meanness, Guy sold his half of the business to Louis and bid adieu to his partner of the past ten years.

"Au revoir, mon ami, I hope you find happiness," said Guy, who retreated to the French West Indies in Martinique, where he eventually settled, married, and fathered four children.

The departure of his business partner was of no consequence to Louis. Boudreaux Plantation and the profits rendered were all he needed. The fewer people involved in running the plantation meant more money for him, and he took on even menial tasks, including the tedious job of filling and addressing the payroll envelopes. "Good-for-nothing," snarled Louis as he reluctantly wrote the name on the envelope of an employee that he held in particular disdain. His diatribe was cut short by the sound of tires on his long, gravel driveway.

Despite his life of crime and occasional incarcerations, Lonnie Cavanaugh was an exceptionally lucky man. He'd managed to escape from Rock Quarry Prison in Georgia, federal facilities in Tennessee, Ohio jails, and the fearsome Angola Prison in Louisiana, where a guard shot him in the back with a scattergun on his first attempt to go over the wall.

His escapades earned him cult-hero status in Tennessee. And it was due to the efforts of high-ranking politicians and businesspeople in Tennessee, particularly Knoxville, that he was pardoned from his incarceration in Alcatraz, the only place authorities thought he was incapable of escaping.

"He's actually a good boy," said one of his chief advocates, a supermarket and broadcasting magnate, and mayor of Knoxville. When he was released, Lonnie reciprocated the kindness of his supporters, acting like a good boy—for a while.

When he was allowed, Lonnie took off to New Orleans, where he lived when he was on the lam from Angola. During that time he developed an affinity for life in the Big Easy—the women, the food, beignets, red beans and rice and beer bread, jambalaya, étouffée, gumbo, and the smorgasbord of easy "marks," especially unsuspecting tourists, from which he made a living at his various scams.

"Laissez les bon temps rouler" was definitely right up his alley.

But the good times were not rolling on track for Lonnie now, and he was ready to throw in the towel.

Unbelievably he had started a security business in New Orleans, called Cavanaugh Confidence, with the tag line, "Your Security Specialist." He *was* a specialist of sorts, with beaucoups on-the-job training.

Lonnie located his business on the outskirts of the Crescent City, in Harvey. He soon discovered that business was not going to come to him, so he set out on the road in his van to recruit customers, visiting numerous parishes along his path.

His modus operandi was to start in the small towns, and when all of the business owners had rebuffed him, he would ask if they knew of any residential folks who might require his services. He lucked out when a hardware storeowner gave him the name of a plantation owner on the outskirts of the town of Crowley. "He named Boudreaux, and be careful, the man bracque," said the clerk, twirling his index finger at his temple. "That's OK, I'm sure I can handle him," said Lonnie affably.

Louis squinted through the curtains at the dusty van parked in his driveway. "Cavanaugh Confidence—Your Security Specialist," he read with deliberation; then he limped from the kitchen to the living room, across the faded Persian carpet, to answer the knock on his door.

"What you want?" Louis spoke hatefully as he flung open the door.

"Name's Cavanaugh. I represent Cavanaugh Security," said Lonnie, mustering all of his charm.

"I know, I know, I read your truck," barked Louis. "I give you ten minutes; get in, get in!

Lonnie followed the old grouch into the dark, cool living room that was once opulently furnished. Now the furniture, acquired with the sale of the place decades ago, was musty, saggy, and a bit raggedy around the edges.

“What you got to offer?” said Louis with the cordiality of an angry badger.

Lonnie went through his spiel, all of the while studying the outlay of the home. He took a sharp intake of breath when his eyes rested on the money-laden kitchen table. And he jumped when he was interrupted by the old man. “Enough. I’ve got a safe an dat be enough for me; now be on you way.”

“Well, uh, do you mind if I leave some brochures for you? They’re out in the van.” “OK, ok, but I got to make my payroll; hurry up!” “Be right back,” said Lonnie as he hurried out the door.

One glance at the table stacked with money and the mention of a safe reignited Lonnie’s instincts, and he was shaking when he got into his van. “God almighty, there must be ten thousand dollars on that table and a lot more in the safe,” thought Lonnie as he reached into the glove box and withdrew the .38 caliber, nickel-plated pistol he’d used in the Knoxville escape. This could be the caper that would set him up for life, and he thought about going to Texas or maybe back to Tennessee, when the job was done. He pulled his shirt out of his pants and tucked the gun in his waistband.

Louis was startled when Lonnie walked back in, uninvited.

“Where da brochure”?” said Louis irritably. Then he stumbled backwards, raising his hands as Lonnie produced the .38 and a large Piggly Wiggly shopping bag.

“I’m out of them,” he said, directing Louis to the kitchen with a wave of the gun.

“Why don’t you scoop all of that cash into this bag, and then we’ll visit your safe, old man.”

“But I can’t pay my workers tomorrow,” Louis whined.

“That’s a pity; now start scoopin’.”

When the kitchen table loot was in the bag, at Lonnie’s forceful request, Louis reluctantly led him to the bedroom and the safe. "I've cracked these before, but to make things simple, why don't you open it for me...what's your name?" "Louis," said Boudreaux, who was frightened but equally livid that someone would take from him. "OK, Louis, let's get crackin'; excuse the pun," laughed Lonnie, jabbing the old man in the ribs with the weapon.

"Dere nothing in dere," said Louis unconvincingly, as he began rotating the dial. The dial clicked sweetly at the touch of the gnarled fingers, and Lonnie helped him swing back the door. It was pitch-dark in the interior. "You got a light or something in there?" said Lonnie, peering into the darkness.

"Yeah, I got da light," replied Louis, reaching in to the side of the safe. "Here it is," said Louis as he wheeled around and shot Lonnie in the shoulder with his .357 Magnum. The impact of the bullet knocked Lonnie off his feet, and he slid across the floor, knocking his head against the heavy armoire next to the bed. At first his head hurt more than his shoulder.

"Damn, Louis, you didn't have to do that. My gun wasn't even loaded," groaned Lonnie, raising himself up on his good elbow as the blood began to flow copiously from his shattered shoulder and arm.

Louis methodically closed the door and locked the safe, which harbored about forty thousand dollars, and turned to Lonnie. "Nobody take from me," he said malignantly, cocking the gun.

"Now come on, Louis, you've won. I'm not going to take..."

"Fais-dodo—go to sleep, fils de putain," said Louis. Another explosion rocked the room as Louis casually shot Lonnie in the chest and left to call the constable.

"I think I'll go back to Tennessee," whispered Lonnie Cavanaugh, with his last rattling breath.

Chapter 39

NO NEWS IS GOOD NEWS

"The paper come yet? Let's see if anybody got killed last night," said Treva.

"Here you go, came jest a few minutes ago,"said Jeanene, slapping the *Journal Herald* on the bar in front of Treva. "I got my paper from home; I'm goin' to take a little time to read it too," said Jeanene, sliding the rubber band off her hometown newspaper and spreading it out on the bar.

Treva perused the front pages, then glossed over the sports page, which, at this time of year, focused on the Dayton Flyers and their chances at winning the NIT. Then she moved on.

She turned to the entertainment section. "I might find somebody to take me to a movie tomorrow night."

"There ain't much. Let's see, *Blackbeard's Ghost* is on at the Belmont, Southland 75 features *Harper*, starring Paul Newman, oh, he's dreamy, that sounds..." Treva was interrupted by Jeanene's exclamation. "God Almighty, there's Harley!" she shrieked as she turned a page in the paper. Treva spilled her coffee and raged at her. "You dumb bitch! What're you tryin' to do, scald me?" "Lookee here, I know this feller...went to church with him!" babbled Jeanene, who slid off the barstool and brought the paper over for Treva's inspection. "Look! Look!" she said, stabbing with her index finger at the photo at the top right-hand corner of the page. The headline read. "Lineman Saves Children, Bus Driver." "*A lineman for the utility company, Harley Baird, is hailed as a hero for rescuing four children and a bus driver when the bus slid off the road and dangled precariously for hours on the edge of a cliff. While Baird and his crew risked their own lives to save them...*" "He's good lookin'," said Treva as she examined the photo of Harley more closely. He was holding two little girls in his arms as they both shyly smiled for the camera. Then Treva's chest tightened, and she gasped as she looked into the eyes of Lonnie Cavanaugh. "What's a matter?" asked Jeanene. "You stocked the coolers yet?" "Yes ma'am." "Then get me a damn beer." "But it's only nine thirty..." "Don't give me any shit, Jeanene; get me a damn beer!" Jeanene scrambled to get Treva a beer before the "darkness" came over her.

"Do you know him?" asked Jeanene as Treva chugged her third beer of the morning. "No, he just reminds me of someone I used to know. Now, tell me, what did you say his name was? Actually tell me everything you know about him." "But I already told you..." "I don't give a tinker's dam! Tell me again," shouted Treva. "Well, he went to my church, and he was a couple of years younger than me..." "How old are you?" "I'm 26. Anyway his name is Harley Baird, and he come from a real nice family, Benny and Margaret Baird are his momma and daddy. They was mostly dark, you know, like Indians, and he didn't look anything like 'em. They said he was adopted or somethin'. They lived down the road from me, off Cumberland Mountain in Campbell County," said Jeanene, fearful of her boss's unpredictable fury. "Do they still live in the same place?" "I'm not sure," said Jeanene, wary of the transformation she was seeing take place in Treva. "I'll be upstairs gettin' cleaned up. You'd better be ready to open this place by noon," she ordered harshly, and Jeanene scurried to do her bidding.

Treva trembled as she ran her bathwater and placed fresh clothing on her bed. The lineman in the photo had to be Bobby Ray, of whom she hadn't given a thought in a long time. It was a black-and-white photo, but she could tell the boy had crystal-blue eyes and a prominent brow, blondish hair, and the exact same cheekbones as Lonnie. Adopted? He appeared the age Bobby Ray would have been at this point in time. "It has to be Bobby Ray," she thought as she stepped into the tub, admiring herself in the mirror over the bathroom sink. "Bobby Ray! Well, I'll be damned! I think I might look you up, kid," she said aloud, as she slipped up to her neck in the soothing, warm water.

Chapter 40

REUNION

For weeks Treva had pumped Jeanene dry for every piece of information she knew about the Bairds and living on Cumberland Mountain. And as she drove across the Kentucky line into Tennessee, she remembered Jeanene's advice and took the Jellico exit off I-75 instead of going across Jellico Mountain, which she heard could be treacherous, even in good weather. She turned right on the Jellico exit ramp and to the nearest gas station. After filling her car, she went inside the station, found the pay phone, and leafed furiously through the local directory. "Baird, Baird...what the hell, there must be a thousand of them in here!" she thought. But she found who she was looking for right away. "Benny Baird, 232 Hopkins Lane," she read aloud. Instead of writing the number down, she ripped the page out of the phone book. The attendant started to say something to her, but she stared him down. "What the hell are you lookin' at, Gomer?" she snipped as she paid her bill and walked out the door. She thought briefly about turning right, to look for the place where she was briefly raised, but decided against it. There were no pleasant memories there anyway. As she turned left on 25W and headed south toward LaFollette, the attendant noted her Ohio license plate. "I knowed it had to be a Yankee," he muttered to himself.

As she turned on Habersham Road, she thought of her siblings, Elmer and Wanda, and wondered if they were even alive. It was brief wonderment for she had more important things on her mind. She rehearsed the planned scenario as she maneuvered the twisting curves leading to Duff: "Hello, Mrs. Baird? My name is Treva. I think I have some news for you about your son's birth parents. May I come by to tell you about it? You don't know what I'm talking about? You have a son named Harley, right? I read about him in the paper. I sure would like to meet him. Is that OK? When's a good time for you? OK, I'll drop by tomorrow morning at nine. Thank you."

It would be easy. When she met with the family, she would explain with tears in her eyes, how her despicable husband, a hardened criminal, supposedly took the baby to visit with his family in Morgan County and never returned. She imagined the worst but had continued her search for Bobby Ray off and on for the past two decades. She had seen the photo of Harley in the paper, and from his appearance, age, and other information, she had a strong hunch that he might be her son. She would mention that her baby had a small, strawberry-shaped birthmark on his shoulder, and the family would gasp. "Harley has a mark like that on his shoulder!" they would say. (If he didn't bear the mark, she would call it quits and say good-bye.) She would be reunited with Bobby Ray, and at the moment of reunification, she would fall to her knees in a near-faint and say how her life had been incomplete without him. He would lift her up and hold her and say, "I love you, Mom." Later she would convince him to pack his bags and return to Dayton with her, where she would proudly introduce him to all of her friends. She would use her connections to get him a job at one of the auto assembly plants, or maybe at NCR, building cash registers, where he would earn more money than he ever could have dreamed of in Hickville. And she would give him free drinks and snacks when he dropped in at the bar every night to see her. He'd eventually marry, and he and his wife could bring the grandkids to the bar, where she could show them off. Of course the Bairds could come and visit, but she didn't plan on issuing an invitation.

Her spirits were lifted when she came upon a road sign a few miles outside of Cotula identified as Duff/Davis Creek Road and finally upon a mailbox on which was printed *232 Hopkins Lane*. "I'll be here tomorrow, folks," she said, relieved at knowing exactly how to get to her destination. She followed the road, which led her back to 25W, and soon she arrived in LaFollette. Luckily Jeanene had apprised her that it was impossible to get a hard drink in Campbell County, so as Treva unpacked her belongings in her room at Flower's Motor Court, she pulled three fifths of vodka from her suitcase. "This should last me the few days that I plan on being here," she said as she placed the bottles on the top of the closet shelf. She filled a little bucket with ice from the machine that hummed outside of her room. When she was settled, she took the wrinkled page from her pocketbook, poured herself a drink, and dialed the number. The conversation didn't go quite as she had expected.

Margaret appeared waxen when she hung up the phone and sat down hard at the kitchen table, her hands trembling. "What's a matter, Momma?" said Sissy, pausing from frosting a layer cake for Early's birthday party the next day. Dazed, Margaret couldn't answer. "Momma? Ye all right? Ye look like ye saw a ghost." "I...I...didn't see no haint. But I thank I jest heared one." Sissy had to sit down too, when Margaret told her of the conversation. "Well, what did ye tell her?" said Sissy, barely able to contain her curiosity. "I tolt her I'd call her back," said Margaret, pushing the piece of paper with the phone number of Flower's Motor Court, room number seventeen, toward Sissy. "I thank we ought to call the family together to talk about this," said Sissy. "Well, they'll all be here fer supper direckly." "Even Harley and Brenda?" "No, they'll be here tomorry fer Early's birthday; Harley had to take her to the doctor in Knoxville, and I thank thar goin' to eat down thar."

Later, with the help of Sissy, Margaret shared the incredible story with the rest of the family. "I say ye jest don't call her back, and she'll go away," said Scrap as he helped himself to another heaping helping of mashed potatoes. "I agree with Papaw. Let's jest give it a couple of days. It could be somebody pullin' a prank—sounds like somethin' Bucky would have done," said Sissy bitterly.

"Just my luck, held hostage by a stupid hillbilly!" said Treva as she lit a cigarette and poured herself another double-shot of vodka. She turned on the television, which carried one station, WATE out of Knoxville, and cursed as the fuzzy image of the newscaster, "Sam" somebody, appeared on the screen. "This podunk, hillbilly heaven! You can't even get a TV station," she said as she stormed out of the room with her ice bucket. Treva Cavanaugh rarely tolerated not having her way. And at one o'clock in the morning, when she hadn't received a phone call, she was teetering on the ragged edge of reason.

She slept fitfully, awakening at noon the next day, experiencing the hangover of all hangovers. Sitting on the edge of the bed, running her hands through her Medusa mass of hair, she lit a cigarette and picked up the phone. "Yeah, where can I get a decent meal in this shithole? OK," she said to the stunned operator. As she soaked her hammering head beneath the cold shower, she planned her next move. After showering she fixed her hair, applied some makeup, donned a blouse and a pair of gold lamé toreador pants and high heels. There were many curious stares as she swaggered to the diner just a few steps down the street. After consuming mass quantities of coffee and food, she returned to her room and slept soundly till about four o'clock. Recovered, she took another shower, reapplied her makeup, and chose an outfit more appropriate for the trip she would make that evening.

"The doctor said that everything was all right, and it will probably be four more months before the baby is..." Brenda's eyes widened, and she failed to finish the sentence. "Get that nasty thing off Momma's countertop!" she ordered, and Harley obediently removed the spit cup. "I told ye I'd quit when the baby was born," he said contritely. "What's that got to do with anything?" "It'll be a gift fer ye and the baby," he said, approaching her, stooping to wrap his strong arms around her and gently pat her expanding belly. "Boy, are you whooped," laughed Early. "Yore gonna git whooped if ye don't watch out," said Sissy. Suddenly the lights were doused, and Glory's sweet voice rang out. "Happy birthday to you, happy birthday to you," she sang, her face lit up by the soft light atop a birthday cake, which was decorated with many candles. Everyone joined in the singing, including Early, as Glory marched into the room followed by Margaret. "Happy birthday, dear Early, happy birthday to you!" "Whew! That's a lot of candles," said Early as the cake was set in front of him. "Why don't ye come up here and sit on my lap and help Uncle Early blow 'em out?" Glory happily obliged. "Momma made it!" she said, and Early smiled appreciatively at Sissy before he and Glory extinguished the candles.

The lights were turned back on, and after the cake was mostly devoured, Margaret, Sissy, and Glory brought in Early's presents and placed them on the table before him. "Open that'un first," said Scrap, pointing to a package wrapped clumsily in newspaper. "Okeydoke," said Early. But he was interrupted by a knock on the front door. Margaret cringed. It had to be a stranger, because most neighbors would walk right in or stick their heads in the door and yell, "Hey!" "Go on, Early, open it before Pap explodes," said Harley as he got up to answer the door.

"Hi. What kin I do fer ye?" said Harley, opening the door for the woman on the porch. Treva was so taken with the nearly exact vision of Lonnie Cavanaugh that she gasped. "What's wrong, ma'am?" said Harley. "Bobby Ray!" she uttered weakly, collapsing on the floor before him. It wasn't an act. She didn't have to see a birthmark to verify his ancestry.

The men gently lifted Treva onto the couch, and Brenda placed a cool rag on her forehead. Margaret carefully compared her features to Harley's as Treva was revived and opened her eyes. "Same hair, same blue eyes," thought Margaret despondently. She would be further convinced that Treva was Harley's biological mother when and if she smiled; Harley had the most beautiful smile.

Treva was revived quickly and raised herself up on the couch. "Yore shakin', ma'am; ye better lay back down," said Scrap. "I'm… I'm OK," said Treva, who was shaking, primarily because she was in desperate need of a cigarette and a drink. "Oh, Bobby Ray, my darling! I've searched for you for so long!" she cried and smiled broadly as she reached for his hand. At that moment, Margaret was positive that Treva was related to her son. When Treva introduced herself, the Bairds shyly identified themselves. After a moment of awkward silence, Treva implored Harley, "Please come sit by me. I have so much to tell you—all of you," she said, pulling on Harley's hand and patting the couch for him to join her. Margaret cut in and sat on one side of Treva, while Brenda sat on the other. "When's our baby due, dear?" said Treva. "About five months," answered Brenda, without a hint of the shyness exhibited by the rest of the family. Everyone listened with incredulity as Treva spun the story she had so carefully practiced. "Your father was a lifelong criminal, Bobby Ray; he was very handsome, and you resemble him so much," said Treva. Harley attempted to break the ice. "No wonder I've always wonted to rob a fillin' station," he said, but the audience, with the exception of Early, was too stressed to appreciate the humor. As Treva rambled on, Harley listened with skepticism. He was embarrassed that someone professed to know so much about him that he did not know himself. But Treva's next remark took the sharp edge off his skepticism, almost making him a believer. "Do you still have that strawberry birthmark on your shoulder, honey?' "Yes," he stammered, touching his shoulder absent-mindedly. Treva started to say something else, but Scrap interrupted.

"Who was yore husbin's kin in Morgin County, and why didn't ye check with them about the boy?" he asked unsmiling. "They were Cavanaughs. I never met them. But when I drove down there a couple of weeks ago, people said they remembered them, and they moved to Michigan over twenty years ago. But no one remembered that a little boy was with them." "Is that my little granddaughter over there in the corner?" "Come here sweetie, and hug your grandma!" said Treva, opening her arms wide for Glory who, frightfully shy, stayed where she was. "That's my daughter, and she's her grandmother," said Sissy defiantly, pointing to Margaret. "Well, what's her name?" "Glory". "What a pretty name...so biblical-sounding," said Treva. Sissy detected a hint of sarcasm but didn't say anything. Margaret, who looked like the walking wounded, didn't forget her manners. "Would ye like a piece of cake and something to drank, ma'am?" Treva wanted to say, "No, but I sure could use a double shot of Smirnoff, you ignorant hick." "Please call me Treva. No thank you, Margaret. It's getting late, and I'm not familiar with the roads. I'd better be getting back to the motel. I'm sorry I dropped in on you like this, but I couldn't help myself. I'll be in town for a few more days. Do you mind if I come back and visit?" No one answered, and finally Harley spoke up. "Since I'm the reason fer yore visit, I guess it's up to me to invite ye back. Tomorry's Saturday, and I'm off work. Why don't ye come to me and Little Bee's house fer supper?" "I'd be glad to come to dinner." "Jest to let ye know, ma'am, dinner's what you'uns call lunch," said Early as Margaret interrupted. "If'n ye don't mind, why don't ye come to air house fer supper. I'll fix somethin' nice fer all of us, and we kin talk some more." "That sounds good! About five?" Margaret shook her head affirmatively. "Bobby Ray, do you mind walking me to my car? It's dark out there." "Should be, it's nighttime," muttered Early as Harley led the way to Treva's Crown Victoria.

"Mind if I smoke?" she said, opening the door to the car and reaching in the visor for a pack of Marlboro.

"No. Shore don't, Miss Cavanaugh; go right ahead." "Please, I'd rather you call me Mom, but if that won't do at this time, call me Treva." "OK, Treva." "I love you, son; I've always loved you. And I thank the Lord that He's brought us together." Harley said nothing, noting the silhouettes of heads gathered at the window observing his and Treva's every move. "Well, I thank it's a nice thang too. I'm lookin' forward to knowin' ye a little better." "I'm looking forward to knowing you a lot better and to sharing my life with you," she said, caressing the back of his neck. The porchlight came on, and she smiled sardonically. "It looks like they don't trust me. See you tomorrow, son," she said and drove the big Crown Vic out of the yard. Harley dreaded going back into the house.

There was a funereal silence in the home as Harley walked back in. The family, including Glory, sat at the kitchen table wearing hangdog expressions, with the exception of Margaret, who bore an expression of great sorrow. "Well, what do you'uns thank?" said Harley as Brenda rose from her chair to hug him. "It don't matter what we thank. All that matters is what ye thank," said Margaret, inviting him to sit at the table. Harley was contemplative for a moment and then spoke. "I always thought that I would be happy to know whar I come from... to know my roots. Ever'one should know whar they come from; that way they'll know whar thar agoin'. But fer some reason, even if she is my birth momma, I don't feel nothin' fer her." He reached his arm around Margaret's thin shoulders. "And I wont ever'one to know that she could never replace Momma or any of ye." Margaret hid her face in her hands as he kissed her head.

Treva was ecstatic. Full of herself, she cranked the volume on the tinny clock radio and danced around the room to Loretta Lynn's *Coal Miner's Daughter.* "I'm glad I'm not a coal miner's daughter. I'll be glad to get away from this stinkin' holler," she sang as she grabbed her ice bucket and opened the front door of her motel room. She was certain that she'd made a good impression on the Bairds, and she was delighted with her son. "He's as handsome as or more handsome than Lonnie," she said to herself, as she poured the first of a succession of many Smirnoff cocktails. As the evening wore on, she envisioned the sweet life that the two of them would share together. Later she became blubbery as "Close to You" played. Then she passed out in a dreamless stupor.

The next day Treva awoke to bluegrass blaring from the radio. She pounded the silence bar and knocked over the empty bottle of vodka on the nightstand. Squinting through blurry eyes, she discerned by the clock that it was three in the afternoon. "Shit. I'm supposed to be at the hillbillies' house in two hours," she thought and almost passed out as she jumped out of the bed. She lit a cigarette, reached in her purse, and popped two aspirin, realizing that she wouldn't have time to eat anything until she arrived at the Baird home. As she started the shower, she noticed the reflection in the bathroom mirror of the last fifth of vodka on the top shelf of the closet. "Nothing like a little 'hair of the dog' for what ails ya," she said, unscrewing the cap and filling a water glass full of the white liquor. She felt better immediately, having chugged down the contents.

She arrived at the Bairds at a little after six, exceptionally drunk. Fueled by nearly a whole fifth of vodka on an empty stomach, all of Treva's defenses were down and facades forgotten. She tripped up the porch with a bouquet of flowers in her arms. "Sorry I'm late, I got lost. Here Marge, these are for you, sweetie," she said, plopping the flowers in Margaret's arms. "Where's my Bobby Ray?" she demanded. "There you are, honey. I dreamed about you all night!" she said, enveloping him in a boozy hug. Then she circled the supper table, planting rocket fuel-smelling kisses on everyone gathered. Early resisted the urge to wipe off the smooch, but Sissy and Glory did not. She came to Scrap last and squeezed his arm. "Scrod, you're a big boy, I'll bet you're strong as an ox!" Scrap didn't correct her, but he was fire-engine red as she sat down at the table. "You know, Scrod, if you had any moonshine hidden in the barn, I wouldn't mind trying some," she giggled. "I don't, and ye probably wouldn't like it," he said almost inaudibly, ashamed of the way she was acting.

"Would you like some coffee?" said Brenda, hoping that Treva would accept her offer. "Nope, but I sure would like some vittles. Isn't that what you people call them? What we got for dinner…'scuse me, I mean supper tonight, Marge? Possum?" "We got chicken and dumplins, cornbread, soup beans, some kilt greens…" Treva cut her short. "How's about a steak, a big juicy porterhouse?" "Well, we bought some beef from Waymon Morton not long ago. I could see what we got in air freezer," said Margaret, who started to go out on the back porch, where the freezer was located. "Stop, Momma. What ye've got here is fine for all of us," said Harley, grim-faced. "What the fuck is this 'ye' shit, Bobby Ray? You're better than that. You've got a lot to learn if you're going to live with me," she said as she reached in her purse for her ever-present pack of Marlboros. "What in the world do you mean?" said Brenda, slapping the table hard, making the silverware jump and spilling a little of her water on the cloth. "She don't mean anythang. She's drunk as a skunk," said Scrap. "You're right, Scrod, I'm a bit tipsy. And you know what? If this girl with the big fuckin' mouth weren't pregnant, I would have whipped her ass," said Treva, glaring at Brenda, cigarette hanging out of the side of her mouth. "If you don't stop talking like that in front of my family, I'll whoop yore tail myself," said Sissy, kicking her chair back. Treva grabbed a knife and leaned over the table. "Then come and get it, bitch." As Treva started to get up, Early stood in front of Sissy, and Harley quickly disarmed the wild woman, walking her toward the door in a submission hold. "You're hurting my wrist, son," she cried. "Early, get her pocketbook," he said as he escorted her out the door and to her car. He opened the door and threw her in with her purse following. "Now, I wont ye to git out of here, and don't come back!" "But don't you want to hear about my plans?" she cried. "I know all I wont to know about ye. Now git!" he said, pointing to the road. "I'll 'git,' but I'll be back to 'git' what's mine!" she said, mimicking his accent. "You haven't seen the last of me," yelled Treva as she tore out of the yard.

Harley and his family discussed the appearance of Treva, and all agreed that she was probably his birth mother. They also agreed that she was a bona fide nutcase and how blessed they were to have her out of their lives. "I feel sorry fer her, but I'm glad the way life has treated me, and you'uns are a gift," Harley said, voice trembling with anger. "Well, I jest wont to know one thang," said Early. "What's that?" asked Sissy. "Who in tarnation is Scrod?"

Chapter 41

GRAVE SITUATION

One hundred and two souls rested in the hallowed ground of Calgary Cemetery. Their gravestones, some at least a century old, stood guard on the hillsides, gazing protectively down on the lush valley below.

Faded inscriptions on tilted gray markers told the stories of difficult mountaineer life in olden times:

"Rebekah, infant daughter of Robert and Hannah Sharp," and next to that stone another, identifying Hannah's passing with the same death date as her daughter's.

The causes of death were not inscribed on their stones; however, history proves that, due mainly to insufficient medical care, many pioneers met their demise from disease, such as pneumonia, typhoid, and diphtheria. Others succumbed to injuries suffered in mine accidents, farming, and logging.

And there was a special section of hillside devoted to those who gave their lives in wartime. Newer graves, with shiny stones and bare spots where grass had not yet taken hold of the clumped red soil around the edges, bore the names of many folks of whom Harley had sat lovingly at their knees, icons like Benny and Maw Ruggles. These were the ones who exemplified the strength, goodness, and dogged resilience of their ancestors. And there were markers commemorating the ones who had been taken too soon, those with whom he had romped the hills, creeks, and meadows as a child, some who had fallen into disgrace.

Harley shut his mower down and rested by the grave of his brother-in-law. "Roland 'Bucky' Faulkner, 1947-1972" read the inscription on the marble stone. "Sorry son of a bitch," Harley muttered as he studied the stone. He still hadn't forgiven the man who'd beaten his sister to a pulp and attempted to murder Early. But he was thankful for Bucky's descendant, Glory, whom he treasured as his own child. He reached in his hip pocket and took out a can of Skoal, screwed off the lid, placed a pinch of the powder between his lower lip and gums, and replaced the can, which had already formed an impression in the hip pocket of his jeans.

He sighed as the soft spring breezes dried his sweat. As he beheld the long grass, dancing in the breeze at the edge of the cemetery, and the fields of wildflowers carpeting sections of the valley below, he thought that this place was the most beautiful in the world. As he directed his gaze toward the entrance to the cemetery, his heart leaped at the sight of his beloved mother kneeling, tending to Benny's resting place. "I'll always be here for you; I'll always be here for my family," he thought as he returned to his chore and started the lawnmower.

Treva was pissed. After all she had done for the boy—brought him into the world—he had refused her offer of the "good life." "He and that little whore he's married to would rather live in squalor holler for the rest of their lives and raise my grandbaby with a bunch of snot-nosed, inbred, hillbilly brats!" said Treva as she wrestled her few belongings into her suitcase, flung open the door to room seventeen at Flower's Motor Court, and marched defiantly out to her waiting Ford.

It was 1:30 p.m., and she needed a drink. "You can't even find a drink in this damned dump," she shouted to a startled passerby as she made a hard, noisy left on 25W, heading northward. She had one more stop to make before she left the state of Tennessee.

Glory was playing with Spike and Whitey when Treva came plowing into Margaret's yard. "Little Bee, Little Bee, we got company," squealed the tyke, running for the house as fast as her little legs would carry her, the dogs following close behind. Treva almost ran over all of them as she stomped angrily up the stairs and across the porch, where Brenda met her at the door.

Brenda was amazed at Treva's appearance: blonde hair in wild disarray, dark circles beneath her eyes. She looked like a coon wearing a fright wig.

Glory stood warily behind her aunt, clutching the tail of Brenda's sundress tightly. "Where's Bobby Ray? I need to talk to him," Treva said curtly. "His name is Harley," replied Brenda icily.

"I don't give a shit! You call him what you want to call him; I'll call him what I want to call him. Now where is he?" Glory had begun to whimper, and Brenda was even shaken by the woman's fierce demeanor. "I don't know if I want to tell you from the way you're acting…" Treva backed off, gathering all of her will to appear calm and remorseful. "Listen, honey, I'm on my way back to Dayton. I just wanted to tell him that I'm sorry for coming into his life. Will you help me?" said Treva, tears brimming in her eyes. "He and Margaret are cleaning up and mowing the church cemetery. It's about three miles up the road to the right; there's a sign that says Calgary Cemetery," said Brenda reluctantly. "Thanks," said Treva tersely as she turned and raced to her automobile.

Brenda closed and locked the door. "Oh shit, what have I done?" she said and headed for the phone. Glory followed closely, the tail of Brenda's sundress still within her tiny grasp. Brenda called Sheriff Dossett's office to report the bizarre encounter and her suspicions. "He's out in yore neighborhood right now. I'll have him stop by," said the dispatcher. At that moment, Sissy's car pulled into the yard.

Brenda met her on the porch. “Sissy, when Scrap and Early get back from town, have them get up to the cemetery as fast as they can,” she said, as Bob Dossett honked his horn. “What’s wrong?” cried Sissy. “Nothing yet…please, stay here with Glory,” said Brenda as she ran to Dossett’s patrol car.

Margaret sang softly as she trimmed the grass from around the edges of Benny’s grave. “I went down to the river to pray, studyin’ about that good ole way. Who’s goin’ to whar that robe and crown? Oh Lord, show me the way!” “Hey, Margaret!” Margaret flinched at the interruption. “Treva? What ye doin’here? I thought ye was gone home?” said Margaret, standing uneasily. “I just came by on my way. I thought I’d stop and say good-bye to you and Bobby Ray.” Margaret hated that name, but she saw no sense in trying to correct her. “He’s way out yonder at the edge of the graveyard amowin’. He should be finished direckly.” “That’s all right, honey. I’m in a hurry, so I’ll just go out to meet him. I’ll say good-bye to you on my way out.” Treva started toward the sound of the buzzing lawnmower, then turned quickly back to Margaret. “Why don’t we just say good-bye now?” she said, spreading her arms wide for a hug. It was natural for Margaret to reciprocate an act of kindness, no matter who the person was, and she widened her arms to return Treva’s embrace. As they came together, Treva snatched the shears from Margaret’s hands and plunged them deep into her back. “Ye’ve kilt me!” cried Margaret as she fell on Benny’s grave. “I certainly hope so, ‘Mommy’,” said Treva.

The sun had moved westward and behind Treva’s back as she approached Harley. He had his back to her as he was about to finish mowing the last patch of hillside. She admired his broad, shirtless back, which reminded her so much of his father’s, and the strawberry birthmark that reminded her of the short time she had with him when he was a baby. Harley geared the mower to idle speed as he crested the hill, and she spoke to him. “Hey, honey, it’s me!” He squinted and shielded his eyes at the silhouette, then frowned at the recognition of the smoky voice. “What do you want, Treva? I thought ye was goin’ home.”

“I thought I would give you one more chance to come back with me, Lonnie,” said the silhouette in a throaty whisper. She removed Harley’s shirt, which was draped over a headstone and, on tiptoe, slipped it over his head. “There you go. Now listen to me one more time. I can take you away from all of this. I’ve got some money saved up. We don’t have to live in stinky old Dayton. We can go to California—land of milk and honey. You and me can get jobs; Brenda can stay here and tend to the grandbaby. And we’ll all live happily ever after! What do you say?” said Treva,

“Are you crazy?” said Harley incredulously, fearful of the wild woman babbling excitedly before him. “Yes, I’m crazy! Crazy for you, Lonnie,” she half moaned, half screamed, drawing him into a wild embrace and burying her head in his chest. Disgusted, Harley pried her hands off him and shoved her roughly. “Get out of here, Treva! Get yore ass back to Dayton,” he bellowed as he revved up the mower, wrapped a cord around the handle, and pushed the machine toward the hillside.

He couldn’t discern her words over the roar of the lawnmower, but he knew she was screaming. “You’re a dead man, Lonnie. You’ve fucked with me for the last time!” she hollered, pointing the pistol at him with a steady hand. Harley heard the report of two gunshots over the noise of the lawnmower and fell before he could realize what they were. The lawnmower continued on its own down the hill, cutting a swath through the tall grass for a long way before it crashed into a grassy gulch. Treva didn’t hear the screams of Brenda Baird, the thunderous report of Bob Dossett’s pistol, or have time to celebrate her long-awaited, sweet revenge against Lonnie Cavanaugh. She was denied any feeling as the bullet shattered her skull. She was dead before she hit the ground, spared of the misery of the wicked insanity that had overtaken her.

"Baby!" cried Scrap, recognizing his daughter's crumpled frame as he and Early crossed the entrance to the cemetery. The old man knelt stiffly beside Margaret's still form. He scooped her in his arms, his tears spilling on her deathly white face. Screams from the other side of the graveyard brought Early to his shocked senses. "Ye take keer of Momma, Papaw. I'll go see what's happenin'." As Early reached the scene, Brenda, sundress saturated with blood, was sobbing hysterically. "She's killed him and Margaret, Early! She's killed them!" The sheriff approached the two solemnly. "Early, git Scrap's truck and drive it out here."

Chapter 42

THE LAST SANGIN'

Harley was tired but pleasantly so. "Whew, ye've about wore me out, Momma," he said as he set himself down on a lichen-encrusted stump. "We've plum dug ever bit of 'sang off this mountainside, ain't we?" said Margaret as she huffed and puffed up the hill to join him. "Ye have," laughed Harley, noting the distinct difference in her potato sack bulging with ginseng and his slack bag. They sat in silence for a while, catching their breaths, enjoying the panorama before them.

Caryville Mountain was dotted, sprayed, and splotched with a riot of springtime color—pink and white dogwoods, flame azaleas, yellow lady slipper orchids, mountain laurel, and a host of other brilliant flora— bursting forth in an explosion of pastels and brilliant whites. In the branches of a tulip tree, a mockingbird joined in the celebration of rebirth with her outrageously joyful song.

This was one of many scenes that kept Harley going when he sweltered in that Vietnam hellhole. This was the vision that ignited every child of the mountains' desire to return home. This was heaven. "Ye hongry? I brought ye a samwich," said Margaret, magically producing a waxed paper-wrapped parcel from her knapsack. "No thanks, I'm not too hungry right now," said Harley, regretting his refusal at once. He knew that she, like most folks who'd never had much, would be offended if he turned down the offer of food.

Margaret ignored his rejection. "It's yore favert," she said, deftly unwrapping the package with hands worn and gnarled from a lifetime of hard work. She extracted a jar of lemonade from her little knapsack and handed it to Harley along with the sandwich. Harley graciously accepted the drink and sandwich, a thick-cut slice of bologna on white bread, slathered plentifully with a layer of Miracle Whip. Capping off the bologna was a slice of sweet white onion. Normally, after a morning of hiking in the mountains, he would have devoured the sandwich, washing it down with healthy gulps of liquid. Today he nibbled on the sandwich and sipped at the jar.

"That woman hurt ye bad didn't she, honey?" said Margaret, refusing to utter the name of Treva Cavanaugh. "I'm healin' all right, Momma," said Harley, rubbing his shoulder tentatively. "I ain't talking 'bout yore body, honey; I'm talkin' 'bout yore spirit." Harley remained silent as the mockingbird continued its inane chatter. Finally he spoke.

"Momma, you know how much I love ye. I know how much you'uns love me too. Ye've never done nothin' to make me feel like I'm not family. But I've always felt like I was on the outside lookin' in. I figured if I ever found out where I come from, then that feelin' would go away," said Harley sadly. "Now that I've found out where and who I come from—a criminal and a crazy-woman—I feel like I'm not good enough to belong to you'uns. I feel like I don't belong anywhar." Margaret dug her hoe in the soft earth, pulled herself off the stump, and got nose to nose with her boy. "Now ye listen to me, Harley Moses Baird. Nobody belongs like ye do. Ye belong to all of us, not to that cruel woman and man who give ye up; she was jest a vessel to hold an angel. Most of all, ye belong to me. The good Lord picked ye out of all the babies in the world and placed ye in my lap. Actually he placed ye in Benny's arms, and Benny set ye in my lap," she laughed. "And from that vury time, I've loved ye more than any woman who could have borned ye. Yore mine, and ye'll be mine until the end of time, son."

She wrapped her thin arms around his neck, and they held one another for a long while. Then she released her hold on him, sighed, and stepped back. "Well, I've done all that I kin do here. I better be gittin' to the house. Ye comin'?" "No, I thank I'll stay here fer a little while longer," said Harley. "Well, don't' be late fer supper; we're havin' greasy beans, ham, fried taters, cornbread, and that hot chowchow that Little Bee and I canned last year that ye like so much," she said. He watched as she made her way along the sun-dappled forest floor, using her hoe as a walking stick.

As she gained distance, her slight form became diaphanous. The notes of a pennywhistle floated on the air, mingling with the cry of a Red Tailed Hawk, and she disappeared in the moats of dust that danced lazily in the shafts of shimmering sunlight. "Hold your horses; I'm a comin'," echoed Margaret's voice gaily through the woods.

Chapter 43

WAKING MOMENTS

"Arry? Arry?" The voice called from what seemed a far distance. At first, no matter how hard he struggled, Harley couldn't open his eyes. "Oken u ice, Arry. Immee, Benna," the voice, closer now, spoke with great urgency. Harley had an uncommon need to discover the source of the voice. After monumental effort, he managed to open his eyes to slits. With the exception of the strange voice, the place where he rested was quiet and gossamer white. Another voice, deeper than the first, spoke in the same unintelligible tongue.

"Hew me mish bare. I av to sheck hiss vitaws," spoke the second voice. He felt movement and heard rustling near him, the firm pressure of a hand on his wrist as his vision began to clear. "Wake up, Mishure Bare," said the second voice, emanating officiously from the white apparition, which seemed to be leaning over him. He attempted to ask his whereabouts but discovered that he was unable to speak. Suddenly he felt a searing pain in his chest and shoulder, and his eyes flew open in response to the rude wake-up call.

He groaned as the nurse bent over him. "You're at the University of Tennessee Hospital. You are recovering from an operation. You have a tube in your throat to help you breathe, Mr. Baird," yelled the hefty woman as she adjusted something hanging next to his bedside. "I'll get you something for your pain." He heard squeaky shoes fade from earshot. His throat burned like fire, and he attempted to ask for a glass of water as painful reality washed gradually over him. Suddenly the face of an angel appeared in his clearing field of vision.

"Harley? You're all right, honey. You're all right," said Brenda as she tenderly smoothed his hair and bent to kiss his cheek. "You've been shot. Your lung collapsed. But the doctor says if everything goes right, they'll take out the tubes tomorrow." She lightly touched his shoulder, which hung securely in an elevated sling. It was throbbing with pain as clarity reintroduced itself to him. "Your shoulder was damaged too, honey, but they fixed it. You'll…," she was interrupted as the squeaky shoes marched back into the room. "Here you go, Mr. Baird, this will make you feel more comfortable," said Nurse Squeaky as she flicked the syringe with her middle finger, swabbed his forearm, and injected him with a hefty dose of Demerol. As the drug asserted itself, he reached out and touched Brenda's belly. He wondered about the whereabouts of Scrap, Sissy, Margaret, and Early and searched Brenda's face in an attempt to communicate his concerns. Then, as the narcotic took effect, he closed his eyes, and those thoughts eluded him for a blissful while.

Mercifully Harley was spared remembrance of the events leading to his hospitalization. Bob Dossett and Early had gently placed him in the back of the truck, where he lay unconscious with his head in Brenda's lap.

"Git him down to LaFollette Hospital. I git good reception up here on the mountain, and I'll radio to have an ambulance waitin'. Our hospital ain't geared up to take on somethin' like this. We got to transport him and Margaret to Knoxville. I'll take Margaret and Scrap in my car," said Bob as Early backed up and knocked over Bucky's headstone. Dust from the gravel path that circled the graveyard nearly obscured the truck as Early barreled out the gate.

In the commotion Bob failed to hitch a ride back. He ran as fast as a heavy-smoking, out-of-shape sixty-year-old could run, and was huffing and wheezing like a locomotive when he finally reached Scrap and Margaret. The old man was still on the ground, holding his daughter in his arms, the shears hanging morbidly from her back. "I thank she's gone, Bob," said Scrap, his throat hoarse from sobbing.

Dossett placed two fingers on her carotid artery. "Don't thank so. She's got a pulse, but it's mighty weak. Git her in the backseat, and you git in with her, Scrap. Make sure those shears stay put. I'll git a blanket out of the trunk," said the sheriff as he opened the door to the patrol car. "Hang in thar, honey," said Scrap as he gently arranged Margaret's body in the backseat, and Dossett carefully placed a blanket over her.

When the patrol car was well on its way down the mountain, quiet returned to Calgary Cemetery. All that could be heard was the chirp of crickets, the occasional caws of crows, and the buzz of flies, feasting on the shattered remains of Treva Cavanaugh.

Chapter 44

THE FAMILY OF MAN

Scrap sat contentedly, like a large Buddha, on the edge of the porch as children used him for playground apparatus. "Pappy! Pappy!" they squealed as they climbed his frame and gamboled like puppies at his feet. He had suffered a stroke months ago, but nobody would know it. He called it his "stroke of luck," and he was correct. His heart, inexplicably, had gone into atrial fibrillation. Blood had congealed in the upper chamber of his atrium, and when his fluttering heart had kicked back into gear, it passed a blood clot to his cerebellum ("the little brain"), the part of the brain that controls all of the voluntary actions of the body, such as equilibrium, posture, and motor learning. After a bout with severe vomiting, dehydration, and walking like a drunken sailor, Scrap reluctantly went to the hospital where he was diagnosed with having a major stroke. The doctors said that he was lucky the clot wasn't passed to the largest, most developed portion of the brain, or he would have suffered major damage or death. With the help of medications, the big man recovered completely. The only manifestation of the stroke was that, occasionally, he had a tendency to go to his right when the movement wasn't on his agenda. "I cain't blame this ole heart of mine. It was jest tryin' to do its job," he said.

"Git off yore Pappy!" scolded Rhonda who, along with the rest of her sisters, Ruby and Joyce, had made peace with their father and were frequent visitors to his house. "It's OK, honey, thar jest playin'," said Scrap as a rowdy youngster tugged at his hair, which was still thick, especially for a seventy-nine-year-old man. "OK, do what ye wont; it's yore birthday," said Rhonda as she strode to meet a car filled with visitors.

Ruby, her husband, Ralph, and four of their grandchildren piled out of the automobile. As the kids scrambled down the hill to play with the older children, Ruby waved to her father. "Happy birthday, Daddy." Scrap returned her wave as he tousled a grandchild's bushy noggin. He was doing what was expected of him, and he didn't bother to help Ralph unload the folding chairs (compliments of Harper Woodson Funeral Home). Besides, it was his birthday.

"Here, Ralph, let me give ye a hand with that," said Harley, gingerly reaching into the trunk. It had been five months since the "incident," and Harley was healing well physically.

He and Ralph set the chairs up on either side of the long table, under the shade of the huge oak in the front yard. The table consisted of sheets of plywood supported by sawhorses and was covered by white tablecloths that fluttered in the cool October breeze. The cloths were anchored with bowls of every kind of food imaginable, bounties from the recent harvest of well-tended gardens.

Brenda approached the table, carrying a bundle in one arm and a casserole in the other.

"Harley, please take the baby for a minute. This casserole just came out of the oven, and it's hot," said Brenda, placing Harley's namesake in his arms and dropping the casserole on the table like a hot potato. Harley goo-gooed at little Harley Dwane Baird, born two months ago. Early ambled up to the table and gestured for Harley to hand over the baby. The baby whimpered during the exchange. "What's a matter, little feller, you gittin' hongry?" said Early. "By the way, I'm gittin' hongry too—my stomach thanks my throat's cut." "Yore always hungry," said Sissy as Glory asked to hold the baby. "Why don't ye let everybody know that it's time to eat." Instead of going down the hill to relay the message, Early cupped his hands to his mouth and yelled at the top of his lungs, "Hey, you'uns! Dinner's ready! Git up here!"

The response to the announcement was squeals from the little children and young adults, who attacked the hillside like the Mongol horde. Adults followed behind, assisting old folks along the way.

When everyone was seated and some of the younger ones were getting their hands smacked for attempting to dig in, Scrap spoke. "I'm pleased as punch fer havin' you'uns here today for my seventy-ninth birthday. We've all been through a lot lately, but fer you'uns and the Almighty, I don't know if some of us would have made it. Now I'd like to ask ye to bow yore heads. And I'll ask Margaret to say the prayer."

Margaret had come terrifyingly close to losing her battle. The puncturing shears had caused the loss of her spleen and a host of other internal injuries. "It's a miracle that she lived," said all of the surgeons who tended to her. "She's lived her life at the foot of the cross; she's entitled to miracles," said Reverend Bunch, who'd spent hours at her bedside praying for all he was worth. Margaret topped the prayer lists of every congregation in Campbell County too. And her recovery was proof to them that prayer, indeed, is a very powerful thing. It had been four months since she was released from the hospital. Her body was still mending, but her spirit was stronger than ever and an example to anyone who believed in heaven and its angels.

Heads were bowed as Margaret stood slowly, walked to the head of the table, and kissed Scrap on the cheek. "Dear precious Heavenly Father, we are gathered here today fer Daddy's birthday. But we are also here to praise Yore blessed name fer givin' us this sweet life and fer this sweet family. We are here, Lord, but fer Yore healin' and lovin' hand; we are here, Lord, to live as Ye expect us to; in peace and harmony, and to accept ever'one as our brothers and sisters, sons and daughters, and grandbabies, like our new one, little Harley Dwane.

Thank Ye so much. In the name of Jesus Christ, air Lord and Savior." There was a chorus of "amens" at the end of the prayer, and Harley stood to help Margaret back in her seat between him and Brenda. "Pass those taters," commanded Ralph as elbows bent furiously at the table, folks gobbling up the sumptuous repast like there was no tomorrow.

Later that evening, when the guests had returned home, dishes were done, and food put away, Margaret and her family sat on the front porch, discussing and laughing about the events of the day. "I thought Ralph was on a diet. He about cleared ever'thang off his end of the table," laughed Early, who sat on the edge of the porch whittling on a cedar stick. "He probably wont eat fer another couple a days," said Scrap, who'd settled himself comfortably in the biggest of the rockers. "I'd talk," said Margaret. "Daddy, I bet that ye ate almost a whole ham. That ain't good fer ye." "Well, yore probably right," said Scrap as he eased himself out of the chair. "I guess I'd better walk it off on my way to the house," he said, bending to kiss his daughter and the head of Harley Dwane, as the baby slumbered in his mother's arms. "Night, Papaw," said Glory, who stood on tiptoe to receive a big cuddle.

Sissy stood to kiss him also and give him orders. "Night, Pappy. Now don't fergit to take yore medicine." "That rat poison? Little Bee's got all my pills measured out fer me, don't ye, Little Bee?" "That's right, Scrap, all we have to worry about is that you take them when you're supposed to," said Brenda. There was a hail of "good-byes" and "Love you, Pappy" as Scrap made his way down the hill. Harley was glad to see the kitchen light appear in the little house. "He's probably takin' his pills right now. Keeps 'em in the kitchen, right, Brenda?" "Yes, but somebody check later and make sure he took them," said Brenda, swaddling little Harley with a blanket as the night breeze came up. "Speakin' of leavin', we'd better be gittin' up the road; what do ye say, honey?" "I'm ready, Harley," said Brenda as she got up from her rocker. As the baby whimpered, Margaret stood and hobbled over to Brenda. "He's getting cranky. It's been a long day for him already," said Brenda as Margaret reached for the child. "He must be tuckered out. Ye tard, young'un? Mamaw Margaret will rock ye to sleep." The baby stopped fussing and immediately fell to sleep. The family gathered around Margaret, examining the child's angelic face for a moment. "Ye know, Maw said that babies are closer to God than all of us, that we lose that closeness when we git older, and that we spend the rest of air lives searchin' for that holiness babies possess." Harley smiled and gathered as much of his family in his arms as possible. "I don't thank you'uns ever lost it," he said. And the baby, the carbon copy of his father, smiled too.

ACKNOWLEDGMENTS

Many thanks to:

Little Bee
John Caldwell
Sam Chapman
Tommy C. Stiner (Colonel, U.S. Army, retired)

CPSIA information can be obtained at www.ICGtesting.com
Printed in the USA
LVOW10s2321250515

439687LV00001B/30/P